WAR AND PASSION IN A
WOMAN'S WOUNDED HEART

BY
HER
OWN
HAND

A NOVEL

JACK DEVENY

By Her Own Hand

This book is a work of fiction. Any references to historical
events, real people, or real places are used fictitiously. Other
names, characters, places, and events are products of the
author's imagination, and any resemblance to actual events
or places or persons, living or dead, is entirely coincidental.

First Edition: 979-8-9994951-0-5

Book: 979-8-9994951-0-5

eBook: 979-8-9994951-1-2

LCCN: 2025914891

Cover design by: Laura Boyle

Edited by: Terence Clarke

For permissions or questions, please contact:
tangocorazon@yahoo.com

Distributed by: Ingramspark

Published by John Deveny

ACKNOWLEDGMENT

To my editor Terence Clarke, whose skills and dedication made this work possible.

For my wife, Jackie
A single embrace from you, and suddenly
my splintered soul is healed.

CHAPTER I

HORROR

Eliot Lange knew it was only a matter of time until his best friend, Will Madsen, did something deadly. It had to happen, but when would it be?

Will. The boy who had never wanted anything more than to tend to his living plants, but now a threat to all living things. Eliot could still see him as he had thrown back his thick, unkempt hair, securing another flower into the earth. Then, Will would stand back and cross his arms before his slender body, proud to have given grace to ground.

How had it all happened? Eliot had been forced to go and fight in Afghanistan in 2012, by his military father as a punishment. But Will had not needed to go. So, why had he insisted on doing so? What possible difference could two men from Sacramento, in their early twenties, make in a land where war might never end? And why would Will, by far the gentler of the two, take up arms?

As Eliot sat on his bunk in an outpost in Nuristan Province, running his hands through his red hair, streaked with blonde, his green eyes began to tear up. He already knew the answer. *Always together.* That's what Will had always said. And that shared phrase between them was the bond that had sealed their friendship since boyhood.

Eliot remembered that other night, when Will was injured by a wound that, indeed, was worse than any other. Staff Sergeant Eliot Lange was sent out on a fire fight that he already knew would be the worst he would ever face. He had been chosen because, simply put, he was the best leader. He had quickly assigned the unit he would need, purposely passing over Will.

"No!" Will had said, grabbing Eliot's arm. "You can't leave me behind."

"I've got all the men I need, Will."

Will drew close, his voice a whisper. "Together…always. Remember?"

It was more than Eliot could bear. "All right but stay with me."

When they had reached their drop zone and jumped from the helicopter, Eliot saw that things were not as bad as he had been told. The marines had arrived ahead of them and most of the fighting was over.

Still, he kept Will close behind him, watching for any stray Taliban fighter who might have survived. And then the worst happened. From out of the rubble of a destroyed building, a suicide bomber rushed in their direction, quickly detonating his vest, filled with explosives.

Eliot pushed Will to the ground, covering his body with his own as shock waves rumbled the earth. Casualties everywhere. Men's bodies torn, arms and legs strewn across the earth, splattered and soaked with blood.

But none of it seemed worse than the look in Will's eyes. Like a man hypnotized, he wandered among the human wreckage, stunned by what he saw. His psyche had suffered an injury it could not fathom.

As medics tried desperately to tend to those barely alive with serious injuries, Will stood frozen in place.

Days later, Will would hear something or see something that wasn't there. Something as simple as a coffee cup falling from a table, would cause him suddenly to startle. With that, Eliot knew that his dearest friend was in the grips of the wound that would not heal—PTSD. It always chose as its host the most vulnerable, the kindest.

Eliot had tried to get Will classified and sent home, but so far, nothing had been done. Eliot knew Will wouldn't go anyway. *Always together.* Those words haunted Eliot now as he sat on his bunk, as always across from Will, who tossed and turned in another night of tortured sleep.

Eliot wondered how many all-night vigils he would have to go through before something tragic happened. On two previous nights, Will had suddenly awakened from his terrors and grabbed his M4 carbine rifle, his finger on the trigger. Eliot had managed to wrest the weapon from him before Will did any harm to himself or someone else.

On another occasion, Will had jumped up from his bunk and slapped Eliot. The shocked look on Eliot's face had forced Will back to reality. Then Will cried, weeping as Eliot held him.

Weary, needing sleep, Eliot felt his head drifting downward, the lids of his eyes drawing their hoods, anxious for rest. Then he quickly jerked himself back to consciousness, rubbing his hands over his face.

He thought he had only dozed for a few moments. But Will was gone. Eliot looked for Will's rifle. Gone. He got to his feet and rushed towards the doorway. Looking down the hallway he glimpsed Will running out the door.

By the time Eliot reached the exit, Will had already gone 'outside the wire.' Running barefoot, Eliot chased after him. The alarm sounded. Behind him, Eliot could see soldiers coming in his direction.

Eliot ran as fast as he could. Spiked weeds stabbed into his naked feet. Up ahead, he saw Will standing in a forested area, near a village. Will raised his rifle and fired shots into the air, shouting into the darkness. "I'll kill you! I'll kill you all!"

Eliot ran up behind and wrapped his arms around Will. Will slammed his elbow into Eliot's midsection so hard that he fell to the ground. Now, Will fired shots at trees, pieces of bark snapping and splintering as they tore away from their branches and trunks.

As Eliot got to his feet, awakened villagers came out of their earthen homes, shocked by what they saw. They quickly took cover. But one man stood and stared.

Next, Will turned his gun on Eliot, about to fire. Eliot grabbed the rifle's muzzle and turned it away, but as he did so, the gun fired another round. The villager who had stayed behind as an awed witness, was now struck by the stray bullet in the leg. He fell backwards in agony, grasping his wound.

With the rifle now in Eliot's hands, he ran towards the injured man. He dropped the rifle, bent down, and with both hands put pressure on the man's wound. He knew that even if he stopped the bleeding, the leg was destroyed. Flesh and muscle were torn away, exposing shattered bone. The man moaned in pain, pressing his hands over Eliot's. Blood poured and seeped through both men's hands. Eliot knew if the man didn't get help soon, he would certainly bleed to death.

Eliot turned and looked for Will. He had disappeared. Eliot stood and looked about in every direction. Suddenly, the soldiers pursuing Eliot and Will appeared on the scene, turning their Surefire flashlights in every direction. One of the halos of light landed on Eliot's face. The soldiers saw Eliot with blood on his hands, standing over a wounded civilian and close by, a rifle on the ground.

Panic.

Eliot ran away as soldiers shouted at him to halt. The wounded man held up an outstretched hand, covered in blood, as he begged for help. Two of the soldiers were quick to apply a tourniquet, but it was too late. The villager died as they worked to save him.

Running through the forest with soldiers close behind, Eliot could see Will running off to the right, no more than fifty feet away. Still consumed by fear, Eliot dove into a nearby thicket, surrounded by trees. Thorns pierced his skin as he crawled on his belly. Jagged branches clawed at his arms and face, tearing his undershirt to threads. Flashlights swarmed through the thicket as soldiers cursed, trying to push back the layers of barbed spikes.

Eliot saw an opening a few yards away. He dug his hands into the dirt and pushed his way through it. Behind him, one of the soldiers had managed to breech the wall of undergrowth, shouting as he came through. "You son of a bitch! They'll hang you for this!"

Straight ahead, Eliot saw a long, rock embankment that led down to a ravine. He knew if he could slide down the smooth surface and still survive, he might be out of reach. Plunging feet first, he spread out his arms and legs to slow his sudden descent.

As he tumbled to the bottom, he immediately saw a cave carved out of the rock. He looked up and realized it was too concealed to be seen from up above. Breathless, he sheltered in the cave as flashlights shot down at the ravine's bottom and a nearby stream. Then, finally, the long lines of light disappeared.

Throughout the rest of the night, Eliot had only brief moments of sleep. And they were possessed by nightmares. He saw Will firing bullets into the air, but Eliot could not hear the sound they made. He saw the bullet that he had accidentally fired at the Afghan villager, and it made no sound. He saw the villager's mouth open in agony, and still the nightmare was covered in silence. Then, he saw the bullet as it tore through the villager's leg, emerged from his flesh and in slow motion, struck Eliot in the chest with a sound so loud that Eliot jolted from his nightmare.

In delirium, Eliot sat up and touched his chest, as if the bullet he had dreamed had pierced him. He wished it had.

It was early morning when he emerged from his hiding place. He looked above and at the surrounding area. No sign of life. He examined his injuries. Long streaks of dried blood snaked across his chest and arms from all the thorns that had torn through his skin.

He should have been happy to be alive, but guilt rushed through him as he realized all his superficial wounds were pathetic, compared to the grievous wound of the Afghan villager he had not meant to hurt.

Eliot could still see the villager crying in pain, even as Eliot was trying to push back the blood that would not stop streaming from the man. Had the soldiers gotten to him in time? Was he still alive?

But there was more remorse. Eliot looked down at the rocks beneath his bare, bruised feet. Their stone surfaces were imperious to pain. But Eliot knew that what he had done to his best friend would be an agony that would never cease. Why had he run away from Will? Why hadn't he stopped and helped the soldiers find him, whatever the consequences might be for Eliot himself? He knew the answer. Because he was a coward.

Where was Will now? Had they found him? Was he getting help? *Always together.* Those words left a bitter taste in Eliot's mouth, like salt being rubbed into an open wound.

Although his feet were battered and swollen, he could still walk to the stream close by, his legs shaking beneath him. He put his feet into an ice-cold pool at the side of the stream and sat down. After a time, he could see the swelling subsiding.

He stood up and knelt in the water, running it over the cuts on his chest and arms. Then he saw his own reflection, his own face mirroring back to him. Who was this? Whose face?

The answer came to him as a cruel irony. This was the face of Staff Sergeant Eliot Lange, the man who had valiantly led men in battle, again and again, always from the front, inspiring men, causing them to overcome their fears and summon courage.

Eliot stood up and kicked his foot through the watery image, as if to make it disappear. But the water only settled once more, bringing back grim realities. Now, Eliot knew that he would not only be branded as a deserter, but one who had shot an innocent civilian and possibly murdered him.

Dazed, Eliot walked from the stream, not knowing that the international media had already splashed the story of a US serviceman, on the run for killing an unarmed Afghan villager.

A day later an Afghan woman with her two children, found Will kneeling in the bottom of a dried-out riverbed, holding up weeds as he wept. The woman took her children's hands and ran back to her village home. Her husband went to the army fort and told them what his wife had seen. The same soldiers who had pursued Will, then brought him back to the base. Finally, Will was sent home for treatment.

Madeline Crowne knew this could be the last night of her life. She wasn't afraid. It would bring an end to an existence that she saw as a lie.

All the men and women in her fort in Afghanistan, thought she was the best fighter they had ever seen. Although in 2012, the official sanction to allow women into combat was still a year away, Madeline's commanders had turned a blind eye to the restriction in her case. They needed fighters like her more than ever, as the war dragged into yet another hopeless year.

In 2013, she was awarded a Silver Star for bravery and promoted to Sergeant First Class. But in Madeline's mind, that was all a fraud. None of them knew the real reason she had gone to war.

The soldiers on every base where Madeline had been assigned for the last two years, couldn't understand how anyone could place themselves in such conspicuous danger for so long, and still survive. For Madeline, it was simple. She saw the face of every Taliban fighter as the cruel countenance of her stepfather Frank, as he had beaten her younger brother, John.

Sitting on her bunk in the middle of the night, about to go out on the most dangerous engagement she had ever known, she grasped the back of her long, black hair, her dark eyes alive with this ancient anger. Why had she allowed Frank's violence to go on for so long? What had she ever done about it? Nothing.

What could a girl on the eve of adolescence do to a grown man, as he plied his trade on a shy, withdrawn boy of eight? Madeline had uselessly pounded her frail fists on Frank's back, time and time again. Whenever he had been aware of it, he had only laughed at Madeline's feeble attempts at rescue.

And when Frank had tired of his brutality, he had turned to his other distraction—enabling the alcoholism of Madeline's mother. Claire Crowne had been too busy destroying what was left of her liver, to care, or even know what cruelty was being perpetrated in her rundown home.

When Madeline had come of age, she could no longer live in such destruction, and she had joined the military, leaving John behind. She had immediately volunteered to go to Afghanistan, hoping that if she were a world away, engaged in a greater violence, the guilt of forsaking her brother would somehow cease its torment.

But it had followed her, torturing her every night, as she wondered what new hell John was being forced to endure. She knew that if she were killed tonight, she would at least finally be free of the remorse, that, in her case, was relentless.

She did not know that what was about to happen would be worse than any death she could imagine. Death brought about the end. But this wound that she would suffer tonight would become a living death, resurrecting itself in agony each new day.

No soldier wanted to go to a village under Taliban reprisal. Especially one that had cooperated with US forces. In this case, such cooperation had brought about the deaths of Taliban soldiers and a high-ranking Taliban leader.

So, Madeline knew there would be blood. For days US intelligence had intercepted Taliban cell phone messages, speaking of an impending massacre. Many of the soldiers in Madeline's forward base had heard what the Taliban did to collaborators. But Madeline had seen the violence firsthand.

The women always took the worst. In the aftermath of an earlier reprisal, Madeline and her unit had been called out to a village that had been destroyed. The fighting was over, but Madeline had seen the atrocities that had been

9

committed. Among the dead bodies of the Afghan men, Madeline had also seen the women who had been violated, some screaming in agony, others paralyzed in shock. Some had been stoned to death, their bodies mutilated.

Now, Madeline and other soldiers were flown out in two Black Hawk helicopters. An Attack Apache helicopter sent along for support. Before they even landed, they could see the village under full attack. As Madeline's group jumped from the helicopter two of her soldiers were shot and killed. She and the others crawled on their bellies for cover. An instant later the Apache chopper, attempting to lift off, was hit with a rocket propelled grenade and crashed to the ground in a fireball. Madeline radioed for support as bullets flew past her. Two more soldiers were hit.

The village was alive with fire. The straw roofs of the mud brick houses were ablaze in flames and smoke. Pinned down, Madeline could only see dead bodies strewn everywhere. She and her soldiers returned fire, not knowing what they were shooting at through all the dense smoke.

Then, through the thick haze, a figure emerged. Madeline was about to take a shot when she realized it was a child, no more than ten years old. Madeline shouted at her soldiers to cease fire as the child ran towards her.

Madeline jumped up from her position, wrapped her arm around the girl's waist and pulled her to cover. As tears streamed through all the soot that had blackened the girl's face, Madeline saw that she had black hair and eyes, like her own. She could have been Madeline's sister, or even her own child. Trembling and with a grief-stricken face, the girl clasped Madeline's body with strength Madeline didn't think possible in one so young.

The moment of tenderness was soon torn away. Taliban fighters ran from the smoke, firing their weapons. Another

US soldier was hit. Others fired back, taking down several of the Taliban. But then, another figure appeared through the gray fog, appearing to be holding up a rifle. Madeline pulled away from the girl, grabbed her rifle and fired.

The figure fell downward, tumbling towards Madeline. The body came to rest at Madeline's feet. The rifle that Madeline thought she had seen the figure brandishing, was nothing more than a long staff, now broken on the earth. The child that a moment before was clutching Madeline's body, now pulled away and fell upon the figure on the ground.

Screaming, the little girl repeated a singular word, over and over again. With all her time in Afghanistan, Madeline had learned enough Pashto to know what the word meant. Mother.

The bullet Madeline had fired had struck the woman in the chest, tearing open her cloak. Madeline stared in horror as she saw the grievous wound she had caused. Blood gushed from the deep gash, pumping and pouring downward until it spread out of the woman's enlarged stomach. She was pregnant.

Madeline froze as the girl wailed, rubbing her tiny hands over her mother's stomach, as if pushing the blood away would somehow save the unborn. In torment, screaming, the woman pressed her hand to her stomach and grasped the head of her daughter with the other.

Madeline wished to scream, but the guttural sounds choked in her throat. She fell to her knees, desperately trying to put pressure on the wound with her hands. But the blood swept through her fingers, in free flow toward the pool of blood below.

The woman looked up at Madeline, who realized she was in shock. Then, the woman's eyes rolled back, and Madeline knew she was dead.

The child rose up and, with bloodied hands, slapped Madeline's face. Madeline felt the warm blood as it slithered down her cheek, mixing with her tears. Then, in a shock of her own, Madeline saw herself hovering over the entire tragedy. She saw the girl fall over her mother's body. She saw the woman's stomach slowly sagging to one side.

Next, she saw herself running fast towards a forest, even as she witnessed it all from up above. Her illusion was soon shattered when her shoulder smacked into a tree. She pushed herself away and saw her bloody handprint, impressed on the tree's bark.

Run! The only thought rushing through her mind now. *Run Madeline!* She shouted into her reeling brain. *Run and it will all go away. It'll be gone. It was a dream, a nightmare that didn't happen. How could it? It's impossible, all impossible!*

Sprinting between trees, she tore off her helmet, night goggles, and flack vest, thinking that if she abandoned the accoutrements of war, she would somehow be free of the guilt that was engulfing her. It was everywhere, matching her every stride. She could feel its black breath on her neck, its voice pounding into her ears. *You did it! It was real. You are dammed!*

Up ahead she saw a river. She threw herself into it, opened her mouth and gulped down all the water she could. *If I drown, I'll be free. It'll be over!*

But the tools of war were not done with her. Her camo pants ballooned, floating her back to the surface as her body listed in the water.

In the morning, she woke up face down on the shore of the river. The riverbed rocks pushed into her face. She crawled further up the shore and sat down. She wrapped her arms about her legs and pressed her face into her knees.

Rocking back and forth, the events from the previous night rose up like a black cloud that enveloped her mind and heart.

Beneath her closed eyes, she saw the child she had saved, only to murder her mother and the child's unborn sibling. She saw the child weeping, her hands covered in blood. Where was that child now? The child Madeline had orphaned. She saw the face of the mother, the last look of shock in her eyes, before death itself smothered her.

Madeline covered her face with her hands. She could not stand to see more. Wiping tears from her cheeks, she looked out on the landscape of river and mountains. The cruelest, longest war of all. But of all the many atrocities that had been committed on that torn soil, despite all she had witnessed, she felt that what she herself had done was worse than any horror the land had ever seen.

Afghanistan.

CHAPTER 2

ENCOUNTER

Tenderness had never touched me. No man's hand had ever wanted to give me that. It didn't matter. Not then. Then, all I ever wanted from any of them were the sensations, the seconds, the instant of entrance, so I could disappear for a while into a place where the person I had known as a young girl as Madeline, no longer existed. But then, afterwards, she always came back to me, each time more shattered than before.

That was then. Now, everything is different. Now, at this moment, I know I could never walk down 3rd Street, or any other street in Sacramento, without Eliot holding my hand as he is now.

It's all in his hands. Even in the pitiless heat of July, his fingers are still cool and smooth. How had he kept them so soft after everything our hands had done in war? It doesn't matter now. His hands make us safe, moving away from memory.

He doesn't grasp my hand, lace our fingers, press our palms together, the way most lovers do, I guess. I've never known what real lovers do. No, with Eliot, it's like he's making a sculpture of our hands, his fingertips, the crevices, the joints, sliding, silently touching, stroking each surface, each line and wrinkle like an artist working with moist clay. Our hands were meant to be molded together like this.

Now, as we are on our way to my dingy little room, to make love for the first time, I smile inside myself. He'd wanted to wait so long before we made love. Wanted to be my friend, first. He didn't know he was already inside me, in a place warmer than womb.

He's so pretty. His full head of blonde hair, mixed with red, like the lines of the horizon on a setting sun. Tall, slender, gangly almost, but graceful when he touches me and gives me those green eyes swirled with gray.

He doesn't like it when I called him pretty. Makes him blush. Now I smile so he can see me, and he smiles back in that way of his, with one corner of his mouth curling up. Somehow, that makes me sad. Friends. He wanted to be friends, first. Aren't friends supposed to tell each other everything? I know I hadn't, even though I wanted to. Would he still want me after that? They call that a lie by omission, I think. Holding something back you shouldn't.

I can't think about that now, because we're almost there. Strange. Here we are at 2AM on South Side, Sacramento's most dangerous neighborhood, and we're not afraid. Sure, we could use what the army taught us to defend ourselves, but we didn't need that now. Our hands make us safe.

In the 13th year of the new century, we're both 24, but we've been through more than most people experience in a lifetime. Even with all that, we're grinning at each other like we're kids, and on our way to share intimacy for the first time.

The way she's looking at me now. Those black, deep-set eyes of hers, go straight through me. I didn't think I'd ever find the bottom of those eyes and that was OK. I just wanted to feel myself inside them.

I love her long, black hair, the way the thick strands, falling and parting over her shoulders sway as she walks along. I couldn't take it anymore. I had to let go of her hand for a moment, so I could slide my fingers through all that lovely blackness. She looked at me as if I'd released her from gravity and she was alone and untethered. So, then I smiled and caressed her cheek. She smiled back. Back on earth again. With me again.

She was so small and thin. How could such a small body hold so much strength, and still hold back so much pain? She stopped us and glared. She saw that look on my face. The way veterans look at each other sometimes, without saying a word. Wondering. What have *you* been through? What did *you* have to see?

There was something she was holding back, worse than all of it, and I wouldn't ask. How could I, after what I'd done? No. We had to earn each other's trust first. I took her hand again. It was so easy to hold those tiny fingers, as they climbed through mine. Now, I had to change the silent subject. I knew this would make her happy.

"Hey, what do you say we stay up all night and then go to that ice cream place, the one you love so much, on Franklin Boulevard?"

That got a smile.

"I think you're the nicest nut I ever met!"

We finally got to her place. God, what a dump! We'd always gone to my place before, which was no palace, but this? One stiff breeze could bring the whole place crashing down. I would have loved to have seen the place when it was a valiant Victorian. Right now, the second floor was begging the first to bear its burden, and the first floor had no such ability. I smiled and shook my head. She couldn't help but laugh while she talked.

"What? What's so bad about it?"

I put my arm around her.

"It's OK, Maddy. Tonight, we'll resurrect the place to its former glory!"

"We'd better!"

Going up the inside staircase, I didn't dare put my hand on that dangling banister, or it would take my hand with it. Going up ahead of me, she looked back and made the obvious understatement.

"Oh, look out for that railing, it's a little loose."

"No, really? You're kidding."

That earned me a swat on the shoulder.

When we got up to the landing, the first thing he had to see, naturally, was the bathroom I had to share with the other two tenants across from me. Even though I'd closed the door tight before I went to meet him, they had as usual flung it wide open and left the light on. That naked light bulb that never stopped dangling from the ceiling. I can't really blame them. With the door shut, the smell in there would only get worse. But now, he could brightly see all the decayed plumbing, and he acted like he didn't see any of it. Just kept giving me that Eliot smile, pretending like we were checking in to some fancy hotel.

I didn't know what the other tenants did for a living, but I had some strong suspicions. The woman across from me, ushered in so many male guests, she might as well have had a revolving door. I think the other tenant, the man, had a habit. I'd seen those same dead eyes in my brother, John. The eyes that see without seeing. Thank God, nobody asked questions on South Side. That's why Eliot and I were hiding out there.

When I unlocked my door, I held my breath. I had tried to clean the place up for him. Make it look nice, especially for our first time. I'd stolen some roses from Capitol Park the day before and put them in a big tomato can that I'd carefully peeled the label away from and then polished the tin until it shined. I placed it on the lone end table next to the couch. I was afraid that end table might collapse any minute from the weight. Any time I put anything on it, its chipped, peeling wood swayed a little, like it had held too many burdens for too long.

Tried to get some of the stains out of the couch and I'd done pretty good, but the yellowed stuffing that stuck out of the cushions didn't help much. I put a clean sheet on the bed that was part of the couch. That much was clean. When I'd put the sheet on that afternoon, I'd imagined the two of us lying there, holding each other, naked. Tried to imagine his uncovered body, fully warm around me. I'd giggled to myself because I couldn't help wondering if that strawberry blonde hair of his was all over his form, even in the most secret places.

The peeling wallpaper with its faded floral design, circa 1950, was hopeless. I couldn't do anything about that. The old wooden clock that barely clung to the wallpaper still ticked, even though its crusty wood was itself running out of time.

I didn't worry about my closet, off to the right. He wouldn't want to go in there anyway, but to be sure, I'd jammed the door at the bottom with some waded-up paper. The closet held something I could only share with my own reflection.

When we walked in, I didn't turn on the overhead light. The yellowed dome, at one time white, that covered the light bulb, would only show how shabby the place was, especially the weathered brown carpet, its frayed fibers like so many random weeds. Oh, hell! This was no place to bring him to, for what we were about to do. I couldn't help it. I started crying.

I held her as tightly as I could, feeling her body quiver. The bones inside seemed to tremble against her flesh, as though straining to find some strange comfort. I had to hold back my own tears, feeling almost as sorry for myself as I did for her. Wasn't I at least somehow responsible for what she'd come to, after the way I had let her down, all those years ago? Too much time and too much terror had wiped my face from her memory, thank God. I didn't know how I was going to tell her about it, but I knew I had to, eventually. Whenever "eventually" came.

Oh Maddy, why can't they all just leave us alone, stop chasing us, wanting to put us in prison for things we didn't do? Didn't mean to do.

She slowly released herself from my embrace and took a step back. With the heels of her hands, she wiped away the few threads of tears. She took in a deep breath as the corners of her mouth strained to smile, before she spoke.

"Sorry about that, honey."

I took her hand, slowly squeezing it.

"It's all right, Maddy. We're together now."

I rubbed the tears from my hands, harder than I needed to, on my jeans. My one and only pair of blue jeans, left over from Afghanistan. He still had his too, faded, with the knees starting to bust out.

At least I had the wine, his favorite, Merlot. Bought it with some of the last money I had. Where was the money going to come from, especially for John, now that he needed my help more than ever? But I couldn't think about that now. Tonight, I was going to be selfish and think only about Eliot and me.

The wine was going to be my big surprise. My big reveal, so to speak, to make up for all the soiled stuff around us. I'd put the bottle on the table in the tiny alcove, recessed in the far wall. That little cave carved out in the wall was just big enough to hold the creaky card table, my only semblance of dining area, and a rusty sink where I could at least brush my teeth all alone and not have to worry about someone bursting in on my normal functions, the way they often did in the communal bathroom.

The alcove's other advantage was that it was shadowed, and you didn't notice it right away. So, I turned my back to it and took a few steps backwards, my arms fanning out and a smile on my face.

"Got a surprise for you."

He grinned and put his hands on his hips.

"What are you hiding back there?"

I stepped aside with a little bow, flung my arm out and pointed to the wine.

He laughed and blushed at the same time.

"Well, you little shit. Where did you get that?"

I did my best impish grin.

"At Shorty's Bottle Shop. The only liquor store on South Side where you have to wait in line with the holdup guys!"

He wrapped me up in a bear hug, as we both laughed out loud.

"Well, handsome, you going to open that bottle, or not?"

He smirked, grabbed the bottle in one hand and the corkscrew in the other. The cheapest corkscrew Shorty's had to sell. I watched as he grasped the body of the bottle and plunged the corkscrew within. He had such powerful hands. I stared at the green veins in his arm as they strained, the thick, red hair on his forearm rising, the spangle of almost orange freckles, spread out against his skin.

I had a strange fantasy. One I had a hard time admitting, even to myself. As he slowly brought the cork from the bottle, turning it, revolving it, the cork's skin shined with red wine, the moisture oozing from every tiny crevice, and I wondered what it would be like when he was finally inside of me. Later, I was so grateful that I hadn't felt my cheeks redden with a blush. Otherwise, I'd have had to explain it to him, and that would have been too weird. He looked over at the table.

"What, only one wine glass?"

I'd only bought one of those cheap plastic wine glasses. I could have bought two, but I wanted to share the same glass with him, taste his taste on the rim, be in the place where his lips had been.

I'd have to make a joke of this. Otherwise, I was afraid he'd know my crazy fantasies, even though I *knew* he couldn't possibly know them!

"What makes you think you deserve your own glass?"

He put one fist on his hip.

"Hmm. The service in this hotel is lousy!"

He poured some wine, and we shared sips. Then we kissed with closed lips. Sounds kind of funny. Now, everyone kisses with open mouths, but we both knew we wanted to start slow. I loved the way we could talk to each other without words.

We sat down on the couch and passed her funky little wine glass back and forth. I teased her about it, but as far as I was concerned, that glass was made of solid crystal. I reached into my T-shirt pocket and pulled out the Marlboros. We both knew smoking was bad for us, but when you're over there, you grab onto anything you can lay your hands on to relieve the tension and the terror. Waiting to go out on missions. Endlessly searching for T-Man, the Taliban fighters, who knew the turf a whole lot better than we did. Wondering, as you take off and hear the bird's blades whipping on and on above you, will I freeze up this time? Will I do something that hurts another soldier?

Enough of that. I took a smoke out of the pack and reached into my pocket for the old, dependable Zippo lighter. Those things would go on lighting long after all the wars ended, if they ever did.

I noticed she had an ashtray over there on the table. Got up and put it down between us, as I sat back down again. The ashtray had had it. Green glass with four corners on which to rest cigarettes, and it had only one slot left! All the others looked like so much chipped teeth. I had to say something.

"Where did you get this thing?"

I got the raised eyebrow.

"Who says *I* got it? You think I decorated this place or something?"

"No, just wondering if anybody was hurt in the accident."

She hauled back her hand like she was going to give me a hard slap, then slowed down when she got to my face, and gave my cheek a hard pinch instead. I think I would have preferred the slap.

I lit up the smoke and we shared it, feeling each other's warm lips on the slim, white cylinder, as it passed from our fingers and onto our mouths. Finally, I set the cigarette down on the ashtray's lonely perch, and watched it burn. I wanted to be inside her so bad, I couldn't stand it. Wanted to be joined so we'd never come apart.

She was so beautiful, the way she was looking at me now, I was afraid I would lose her, the way I'd lost the others that I'd loved in my life. Will. What were they doing to him now? Damn VA hospitals! They didn't have a clue about PTSD, and there was no way I could go and see him. It was as hopeless as her trying to find her brother down here.

I knew that look Eliot got, when he was thinking about his friend. He'd look away, bowing his head, the skin of his eyelids slowly falling and closing, like smooth curtains. I didn't feel hurt, as though he'd let his mind wander or something, when he should be feeling there was nobody in the world but us. But I knew what he was feeling inside. It always attacks you when happiness is too near.

He got up and paced the room. Rubbed the stubble on his face over and over again, as if he could wipe it away. I set the glass and the ashtray on the end table. Reality was back.

"I'm sorry, Maddy. I was thinking…".

"I know."

He suddenly stopped pacing and looked straight at me.

"You've gotten to know me too fast."

"Your eyes make it too easy. I know your eyes now, Eliot."

He sat down next to me, hunched over, head down, squeezing his hands together into a single fist.

"Yeah, but why now, when everything is so perfect?"

"*Because* it's perfect."

I knew how he felt. It always came to me in the middle of the night. Always the same nightmare. John pointing his finger at me. I was the one who had abandoned *him*. Betrayed him. While he addicted himself to opioids, I addicted myself to adrenalin. The adrenalin of battle. The only thing that kept PTSD away, at least until that day. The one day I couldn't forget.

I put my hand over Eliot's fingers, trying to stretch my palm wide enough, squeeze hard enough, to make his pain disappear.

I looked down at those slim, white fingers, still so delicate, and felt even worse. Here I was thinking only of myself, and she was giving me all she had, from what she had left.

Got up and started pacing again, digging in my pockets for something that wasn't there.

"You know what's so crazy about it all, Maddy? They don't even go after war crimes anymore, let alone deserters."

She smirked with a small laugh.

"Yeah, but they want us."

I stopped and looked straight at her.

"And we know why."

She looked down.

"We sure do."

I looked up at the ceiling, like there was an answer up there.

"And I guess it doesn't matter that you got a Silver Star, and me a Bronze."

She clasped her hands together, grasping them, like she could bring forth an answer to it all, but could only say what we both already knew.

"Those medals have been revoked. You know that."

I leaned down and let one of my hands fall over hers, softly as I could, like a breath you can barely feel. Pulled back a little, letting my hand hover for a moment, like I was releasing her pain, and then holding again, stronger this time, to let her know I was really there.

I took hold of her shoulders. They were like a narrow cross that presented her slim statue. I drew her up to me, tightening my fingers on their firm, rounded corners. They were the strong bearings I could cleave to. I beheld her now as if the first time.

She lifted her arms straight up, my hands falling away, as her breasts invited me to slide away her shirt. From her waist, I raised the threadbare garment which struggled through the bundles of black hair, so we both laughed a little as the shirt fell to the floor.

Her breasts were like softened globes, shaped to her body. The centers were the color of Merlot. I wished I could make silk brushes of my fingertips.

My cheek fell to her right breast. I heard her heart summoning itself from its depths, the beat at first irregular, sporadic, then stronger, full of itself, proud. Alive!

She grabbed the back of my head as if it were her sole support. I could feel her fingers pulling at the strands of my hair to the point of actual pain. Gratefully, she let go. As I raised my head, she stepped back with a silent, apologetic smile.

She slid off her jeans and underwear as smoothly as if she were wiping away water. She tossed my T-shirt aside like she was tossing away an old rag, which it was. Then she slowed down as she carefully knelt in front of me, looking up at me as if my face possessed some magnificence that I didn't feel it deserved.

Without taking her eyes away, she opened my jeans and let them fall to the floor. She was surprised to see that I wasn't wearing underwear. I didn't have any good enough for her, so I'd decided to go without. Felt my face blanch, as she gave me one of her mischievous grins.

I knew he wanted everything to go slowly, so that we could discover each other from moment to moment. I slowly stood up and took the cushions off the couch, setting them to one side. From the other side, he pulled out the bed and unfolded it onto the floor. We looked down at the pristine sheet, and then at each other, and we both knew. This was ours. No matter what they'd taken from us, here, now, in this moment, nothing could take it away. Our eyes glistened as we gave each other quivering smiles.

I thought of all the other lovers that must have laid on this bed. Those that had sought sex for its own sake, over with quickly, and abandoning each other even more quickly. I'd never abandon Eliot. He was not one of those that gives love, only to be betrayed. I'd never betray him. Those others maybe had lain here weeping and alone, lost in faithless dreams, and I knew that I would never leave Eliot to loneliness.

He reached across the bed and took my hand, giving it a slight tug. Our knees went down to the bed at the same time, forcing the old mattress to groan underneath us. Its complaint only made us smile.

As we knelt in front of each other, she ran her hands through my chest hair. Her eyes seemed fascinated by its thickness, the curls and tangles, almost as if the rest of me wasn't there. It didn't matter. It felt too good to question it. Her fingers slid through hair, twisting, heaping one thicket on top of another. I was lightheaded already. How was I going to make it through this?

I placed my hand on her stomach as softly as I could, letting my fingers find the well-toned muscles, each in its own firm row. I was creating a small tremor in every fiber of her, every one of them warming to my touch. A strong breath rose in her chest and flowed over my neck.

Together, we fell back on the bed. As the mattress creaked again, we both laughed.

Then he was within me. It wasn't like any other time I'd known, when it felt more like a knife, penetrating me at the most vulnerable point. This was a sheath of skin, folding, caressing, making itself one with me, as if returning to an embrace it had already known.

Moistures, scents, flowed between us, escaping in fluids that streamed back on themselves, as he withdrew and re-entered, again and again. When the moment came, I could feel startle and wonder bursting on my face, even though I couldn't see it. The look of astonishment in his eyes mixed with wonder. Now he was fully vulnerable. Safe. Mine.

Then a police helicopter came, and we discovered our scars. The cops were always looking for somebody on South Side, especially in the middle of a hot, Saturday night. I'd seen it so many times before…the intense search light that swooped over houses and penetrated windows, that now, threw down blinding beams on the one place we'd made sacred.

Circles and ovals of opaque light swarmed about the room, then flashed into strange abstracts on the bed. I looked at my wrists. My woven bracelets had come loose as we'd made love. Fast as I could, I tried to fasten them back together, but he'd already seen the scars.

He knew what they were. Escape scars. *Get it over with, Maddy,* I thought. *End it.* I crossed my wrists and put my arms over my chest. The body that moments ago I was so proud to expose, was now ashamed of itself.

Rolling away from him, I curled into a fetal position. As quickly as it had come, the helicopter disappeared, leaving us again in darkness. The only sound in the room was the wall clock, reminding me again that with each tick, each second, blackened memories would always return.

I let her lie quietly for a while. I had known a guy over there who had tried to check out that way and failed. Later, he got a hold of a Beretta M9, put the pistol in his mouth, and pulled the trigger.

I rolled over to her, assuming the same position she was in, forming myself to her body, as if the two of us were together in a single womb. Carefully as I could, I took hold of one of her forearms and kissed the jagged scar on her wrist. Then I gently wove the fibers of her bracelet, molding the strands back into position.

With tears in her eyes, she turned towards me, offering me her other wrist, and I repeated what I had done. Weeping, she held me in an embrace so tightly, I could feel her pain passing through me. I held her until I could feel the sobs that came one on top of the other, silently subside, and her quaking body finally came to rest.

I had to do more. Had to show her more. Show her that she hadn't been alone in wanting to die. Cautiously, I untangled our clasped bodies, and she gave me a curious look, as though wondering: "Why is he letting me go?"

Taking hold of her hand, I put it on my lower back and pushed one of her fingers onto the opening where the bullet had penetrated.

Vets can speak to each other in single words. Pain can be expressed in a sole syllable. With a fresh tear in her eye, she uttered just one word.

"How?"

"Trying to get myself killed."

Then *he* was crying. Not like me, all over the place, but in deep moans, like he was trying to push sorrow down into himself, deep enough so it would disappear. I ran my fingers over his wound, wishing my hand was a wand or at least something, that I could use to wave his pain away.

Finally, as dawn arrived, we both came to rest. Through the cracked venetian blinds that hung haphazard over my lone window, the jagged shades of deep red and watery yellow, fell across the bed.

He tried to get up without making the bed squeak, lifting himself carefully, a hand, a leg, each limb one at a time. It made him look silly. Then he slid into his clothes as though they were made of wrinkled paper that would tear at any moment. I sat up on the bed, my legs underneath me. I wasn't anxious to get dressed. He'd made me proud of my body.

Now, he was tiptoeing around the room, looking for his shoes. I had to tease him about this.

"Eliot, what are you going to do next? Slither out of here like you're afraid you're going to shock the neighbors. Believe me, you could walk out of here stark naked and none of them would even notice!"

He blushed as I got up and hugged him. Then he finally found his shoes and put them on.

"I guess you're right. I just wanted to be respectful."

Amazing. How could naivete still exist in a world on fire? I touched his face.

"You wouldn't know how to be anything else."

He put his hand over mine, pressing my fingertips to his parted lips. Then our hands fell away as he turned to the door. Gripping the knob, he turned back to me.

"Same place tonight?"

"No, not near the church. Across the street, in the park, next to the pool. And make it 3AM, not two. Even the FBI doesn't want to be on South Side at that time."

He shook his head. "You've seen them, too."

I cocked my head to one side. "Who else goes around South Side in black polo shirts and khaki pants?"

He grinned and sniffed. "Saw a guy the other day, I wasn't sure. He had a dirty gray T-shirt and baggy khakis."

I cocked my head to the other side. "Did the pants have cargo pockets?"

Despite himself, he had to smile. But fast as it had come, the smile faded away. His hand still on the door-knob, he turned it repeatedly, in a motion I don't think he was aware of.

"They'll never stop, Maddy."

I looked away, as if doing so, I could avoid the truth.

"I know."

Then he was gone.

I got dressed, tugging on my worn clothes like they were layers of old skin, I wanted to discard. He'd made my flesh new. New and free.

I started to fold the bed into the couch, and on an impulse of its own, my arm let the bed thud back to the floor. I had to be where we'd been. Took my clothes off again, like a crazy woman, and laid back down in the place we'd made.

I wanted to find what was left of him in the sheet. I ran my arms and legs over the folds, hoping to find a place that was still warm with his body. Nothing left. He was gone. Wait a minute! The smell of him. It still had to be there.

I smothered my face through the long lines, left from our forms. It *was* there! It was him. The smell of old wood and dust still hovered in the creases and wrinkles. I felt the soft scent flow through my nose. I inhaled all of it that I could, until it was gone. Then I sat up and touched my lips, remembering where he'd placed his fingers, before he left.

I caressed my lower lip repeatedly, thinking I could taste his skin... that it was still there. Of course not, Madeline! He's long gone. But I knew that he'd be back, and that thought was enough to make me get up and get dressed *again and* put the bed away.

My rundown-one room apartment didn't seem so bad now. In fact, it was almost perfect, or it would be, when he returned.

And because everything seemed so perfect, I had to think of Mira. The thought of her was always nearby, right next to me, anxiously waiting to shatter anything that might bring tenderness or redemption.

Eliot didn't know anything about her. Another lie by omission. The FBI would go on searching for Sergeant First Class Madeline Kaye Crowne, and Staff Sergeant Eliot Simpson Lange, for war crimes they didn't commit.

They might go for months, get bogged down in mountains of paperwork and useless regulations, that changed by the day, any maybe even give up. But not Mira. Not her. She had other crimes she wanted to prosecute against me, and her retribution would be worse than anything the government could ever conceive.

Mira had Interpol after her, thanks to me. I was the one who played whistleblower, and she wanted me. Revenge fueled by rejected passion makes a hell no one can imagine.

Going down the front porch steps, I knew my feet were falling on dilapidated boards, but I never heard a sound. I only heard echoes from every sound she and I had made together. Every breath, every touch, kiss, and caress, however silent, came back to me in remembered whispers.

It was all so wonderful, I could almost forget how I'd betrayed her back then, when we were little kids. How could that be important now, after everything we'd shared, every-thing we could hope to share again? But it was.

I was the kid who stood up for the rag-tag girl, back then, that everyone wanted to see expelled. I'd felt like such a hero that day. Then, when all the right threats were used against me, I had to turn coward. What would I have done to someone who turned on me like that? I think I'd kill them.

To erase that memory, I placed my hand over my face and inhaled the memory of her. Her scent. Her moisture. I would have looked funny to anyone spotting me, a guy standing out on the street, sniffing his own hand. Thank God, nobody was watching.

But someone was. Without looking around, I knew I was being watched. It's an instinct you get from combat. Across the street, a woman was staring at me. Even with a black hoodie over her head, I could see her dark eyes locked on me, like someone sighting a weapon. Out of another instinct, I looked down and felt for the folded knife in my pocket. When I looked up again, she was gone.

CHAPTER 3

BLOOD

Trapped between the ecstasy of Eliot and the terror of Mira, Madeline went to her sacred place. The place no one knew about. The place that brought comfort and resolution, if only in reflective fantasies. The vanity.

Going to the closet, she bent down and pulled out the wadded paper she'd used to jam the closet door, yesterday. No one, not even Eliot, could see the closet's contents.

Then she stood up straight, standing still in time for a few moments, before opening the closet door. It was all a part of a carefully performed ritual, allowing herself a reverence the world had robbed her of. In the world of the vanity, she could even accept, if only for a while, her own striking image, though she had always turned away from it in the past.

Slowly placing her hand on the closet doorknob, she closed her eyes and held her breath, always fearful that somehow, the precious vanity would have disappeared in her absence. Opening her eyes, she was amazed that it was still there, waiting, patiently in silence and darkness, to receive her image in the emptiness of its mirror.

With eyes half closed, she smirked to herself. Who would want a piece of relic furniture, made after the last World War? How would it have disappeared? Who would take it?

She looked up at her reflection, shaking her head at a sad irony. The only thing that could never hurt her, was this inanimate object.

She continued her ritual. First, take in all the vanity's details. Look at the old wooden drawers on either side, battered and scarred by many predecessors, but still proudly holding their crystal knobs intact. Then, see the long wooden tray between the drawers that had been joined and lowered with deliberate care, so as not to obstruct a full view, and to allow the sitter to easily reach down for each appliance.

Look at the thousand smears of makeup; reds, greens, blues, blacks, swirled into ancient abstracts on the widened tray. And next, carefully pull out the padded stool from beneath the superstructure and set it neatly before the mirror.

Then, sit cross legged before it all, for a final act. Stare into the oval mirror and ask the question her image could never answer. Who is this? Whose face? Could this be the killer of the world's most vulnerable? How? How had it happened?

And because there was no answer, she dressed herself in mourning. She got up and changed into a pair of black Levi's and her one black cotton blouse. She slipped her feet into her black Keds. Seated again, she reached for the drawer on her left and carefully withdrew the black veil from Libya. She held it up to the mirror, presenting the veil's handmade weavings, their design still alive after a millennium.

At the top, a firmly knitted skull cap with crisscrossing bands was strong enough to escape the indifferent damage of time, but the long strands that ran through and reinforced the veil's larger patterns, had begun to show signs of age. Here and there they had twisted and frayed, fragments, finer than the legs of spiders, coming loose from their moorings.

Mira had bought it for her at a street bazaar in Tripoli. Madeline remembered that day so well now. They had wandered for hours on the narrow sidewalk, its thick, white bricks speckled with gray. Up on the high left walls, scarves of every color and texture hung down long and loose, mixing their colors together, as soft breezes found their way through the crowded stalls, bustling with people.

Down on the ground, table after table of leather sandals, copper pots and bowls of all sizes- shined in the sunlight that somehow managed to seep through the menagerie. Further on, lighted kiosks in which gold bracelets and necklaces were displayed row after row. On their right, more tables with packaged shawls and T-shirts, some even bearing the images of Bob Marley or Che Guevara.

And all of it was anxiously being hawked by the animated vendors. Mira knew how to wave them all off in a few words, as she casually clasped Madeline's hand. Mira's hand had felt so good to Madeline that day. The hand that had twice saved her.

And Mira knew how to find a prized gift. With her free hand, she dug through piles of what seemed to be nothing more than discarded veils, until she found the black one. Letting go of Madeline for a moment, she held the veil up. *This* was the one.

Madeline smiled in astonishment. Mira was so proud of her accomplishment that she didn't even bother to haggle. Any price would have been worth it.

Afterwards, they celebrated their sales victory at a sidewalk café, feasting on Asida, the rich-flour pudding, and rinsing it down with sweet tea, served thick in small glasses, along with mint and peanuts.

Now, Madeline held the veil up to the mirror, its decayed reflection reminding her of the slow descent of her relationship with Mira. Madeline had thought Mira wanted only friendship, and not something more. But as all of that had crumbled, few of the other things that came with Mira had been destroyed. All the deception. All the death.

As Madeline secured the veil to her head, it crested on her shoulders with still enough power to triangulate her form and fall to her breasts. To rescue herself from a dark reverie, she thought of the *white* veil, and the way it had brought her and Eliot together.

It was 3AM that morning on South Side, and since all her efforts to find John had once again failed, she had decided to walk up to 12th Street, where only the homeless slept in vacant storefronts. She came upon a small store that had somehow escaped the randomness of urban renewal, sandwiched in between a coffee house and some new condominiums.

The store's single display window showed many items of Hispanic origin, laid out on top of a silk scarf that depicted folk dancers. Men in white peasant's clothes danced gayly with women in full skirts, their bright colors held in a spinning motion. In the folds of the scarf, carefully laid jewelry, bracelets in copper and silver glistened in the darkness. Long, dangling earrings with tiny gold crosses and rhinestones languished in a lush display.

Then she saw what was set back from all the rest. A single white veil, splendid in its meticulous patterns, mounted on a mannequin's head, which was turned to the side. It struck Madeline as odd that the veil was not presented front and center in its true glory. Then she smiled as she realized the placement was deliberate. All the rest was simply meant to catch your eye and draw you in. The next step was for the viewer to step inside the turned away beauty of the veil. Very clever.

The veil would make any woman appear magnificent. It's tiny stitching seemed to dance fluidly through the garment, mimicking the movements of the dancers in the scarf below. She saw the little droplets of lace as they cascaded downward. She lost herself in whimsy, wanting to smile again, but the sudden thought of the joyful tears of her black veil came back to her. The white veil could not possess that much happiness. There wasn't enough for two smiles.

As she stood in place, as though hypnotized, her combat instincts kicked in. She was being watched. She knew better than to turn suddenly. Experience had taught her that. In the reflection of the glass, she sought to see who it was that was eyeing her.

Some guy looking at her as if he already knew her. He stood at a respectful distance across the street, his hands crossed in front of him. For what seemed like a lifetime, neither one moved. Then, in a slow, roundabout fashion, being careful to keep his hands in plain view, he approached her. From his own days as a soldier, he knew how to come upon another in a non-threatening way.

Within a few feet of her, he spoke to her reflection in the glass. "It's beautiful, isn't it? The veil?"

She looked away from the mirror of his face. "Yes. Yes, it is."

Another lifetime passed.

Take a chance, Eliot, he thought to himself. *Say something. You can't keep standing here like this.*

He decided to try dispelling the silence with small talk, coupled with a big risk.

"I've seen it lots of times when I've passed by here. It would be beautiful on you."

She raised her head, slowly turning with her arms crossed and looked him in the eyes. "How would you know what would be beautiful on me? Is that your idea of some pickup line?"

He stepped away, his face down, fresh from scolding.

"I'm sorry. I didn't mean to intrude, but that veil reminds me of a friend of mine. A guy I knew in the war. He always liked beautiful things."

Now it was her turn to feel humiliated, as her voice softened into sympathy. "Did he make it back?"

He lowered his head, stuffing his hands into his pockets. "I almost wish he hadn't. The way he is now."

Out of respect, she let a moment pass before she spoke again. "Is he getting help?"

His words came in whispers so faint; she almost didn't hear him. "They can't help what he has."

And she knew. Instantly, from her own torment with PTSD, she understood. And as war reduces all to children, her tone came forth nearly childlike.

"I know. I was there, too. My name is Madeline."

He looked at her with a smile tainted with sorrow.

"I'm Eliot."

She took his hand, and they walked away together. And as if all the rest hadn't made her fall for him, the feel of his hand certainly did.

But from across the street, there was someone else watching. One who knew how to shadow anyone, without being seen.

Lost in the remembrance of their first meeting, Madeline never heard the door open. She wouldn't have anyway. The intruder could enter on spider's legs. The woman who never wore anything but black. The black turtleneck, taut on her slim torso. The fitted black pants formed to her slender legs, and rising above it all, the crush of thick, black curls mounted like a crown on her head. Except for her hair, the two women could almost pass as sisters. The same skin, darkened by deserts. The aquiline nose that pierced its way forward, presenting the sharp features, and the black eyes that never stopped their searching.

Madeline arrested the shock that came to her shoulders when she heard Mira's voice.

"You shouldn't hold on to mementos, Madeline. They're dangerous, you know."

Madeline stayed steadfast, holding her stare in the mirror. Mira slowly came up behind her. Using two pinched fingers, she carefully lifted the black veil from Madeline's head and held the veil up to the mirror. For a moment, she looked at it in sadness, but then quickly returned to sarcasm.

"I would have thought you'd gotten rid of this old relic by now."

Madeline looked up at Mira's reflection.

"You're the one that got it for me," she said.

Mira dropped the veil and turned away. "The beginning of a long line of mistakes with you."

Madeline turned on the stool and picked up the veil. She placed it on her lap, stroking it as if it were a living thing.

"It was all a mistake, Mira."

Mira smirked as she turned back to her. "You didn't think so that day. Remember that? You'd have slept with that veil if I'd let you. Silly girl. You didn't know you were being courted, did you?"

Madeline looked down at the veil. "No. I thought I'd finally found a friend."

Mira snatched the veil from Madeline, tossing into the air.

"Yes! A friend you needed!" Mira said. "The one who picked you up on the road when you were on the run."

Madeline stood up, face to face with Mira. "And showed me how to make money from death!"

Mira took a step back. "And what would have happened to your precious brother if I hadn't?"

Madeline walked to the window and looked out on the nearby freeway. All the cars speeding by to nowhere. Nobody in those vehicles knew about any of this, and Madeline felt that few who could know of it would care.

"He would have been better off if I'd never met you."

Mira began to stroll about the room. "Oh, did I fail to mention it?" she said. "I *found* John."

Madeline spun around and grabbed Mira by the shoulders. "Where is he? What did you do to him?"

Mira shook herself free. "I gave him what he needed, sweetie. He was very grateful."

"Damn you! Where is he? Where did you find him?"

"It wasn't hard. You kept looking for junkies. I found the dealers. They'll tell you anything, for a price."

Madeline resisted the temptation to take hold of Mira again. "Does he know I'm here? Know I'm looking for him?"

Mira slowly paced the room, preening, proud of herself. "Yes, well. Once he had his medicine and I told him all about us, he wanted to know all about you. He heard you were a hero. I guess he hadn't heard the other news."

"Just tell me where he is, Mira. I'll do anything you ask."

Mira wanted a moment before she replied. "Even give up your new boyfriend? Yeah, I saw him leave. Saw that look of rapture on his face, the bastard."

Madeline felt her hands gripping into fists. "Leave him out of this!"

Mira's lips curled into a sly grin. "Eliot. Eliot Lange. The son of a bitch saved my life once."

Madeline froze, shocked by what she'd just heard. "How do you know him? He's not part of your dirty business."

"Maybe not Maddy, but the guy paying for the mercenaries that Eliot was with? That guy surely was."

Madeline looked back to the window. "Eliot *had* to join up with them. He didn't have a choice, any more than I did with you."

Then Mira used what she had been saving. The one thing she was nearly certain would strike a nerve. "By the way, honey. How long have you known Mr. Lange?"

Madeline gave Mira a wary look. She knew that Mira never asked a question without already knowing the answer.

"Why should you care?"

Mira answered offhandedly. "Just curious. Would you say a few weeks, a month?"

There was a motive in everything Mira did. Madeline weighed her words before responding. She decided it was safe to tell the truth.

"A little more than a month, I think."

Mira glared into Madeline's eyes. "You may have known him longer than that."

Madeline narrowed her eyes on Mira.

"What are you talking about?"

With a leer, Mira replied. "Maybe you should ask *him*."

Feeling confused...outflanked...Madeline counter-attacked. "Have you been watching the news, Mira? Once Interpol put out that Red Notice on you, they found out you were here, and it won't be long before they partner with the ATF. They're interested in anything that involves illegal arms dealing."

Seemingly unfazed, Mira mounted her own counterattack.

"Then I'm not alone. You don't think the FBI won't get chummy with the CIA, after what you did over there? What nobody else *ever* did over there?"

Madeline jammed her elbow into Mira's mid-section, and Mira slammed against the wall. A guttural sound shot out of her mouth. Quickly recovering, Mira grabbed Madeline's wrist, bending it downward and twisting it counterclockwise. Mira applied more pressure as Madeline screamed. She was frozen in pain. In another second her wrist would snap. She somehow summoned enough strength to bash her free fist into Mira's eye.

Mira shrieked as she grabbed at her eye. A slim trail of blood seeped between her fingers. "I'll kill you for this!" She grabbed the vanity stool and threw it at Madeline, who ducked as the stool smashed into the vanity's mirror, broken pieces of it collapsing to the floor.

One broken leg from the vanity stool had fallen at Mira's feet. She took it up like a club, swinging it wildly. Madeline dodged most of the blows, but one caught her shoulder, sending her to the floor. Mira rushed over to her; the club held high in the air.

"Now, you bitch!"

In a split-second Madeline rolled away and seized a shard of broken glass, as the club pounded on the floor. In another second she was on her feet- behind Mira, who was still bent over. She wrapped her arm around Mira's throat, putting the glass's sharpened point to her neck.

For a moment the two were frozen in place. Their breathing surged, their lungs panting for oxygen. They stared at each other in the mostly shattered reflections from the mirror.

"What are you waiting for, Maddy? Do it!"

Madeline released her grip and let the shard fall to the floor.

Mira sneered. "I knew you didn't have the guts. Now that you're in *love*!"

She grabbed a handkerchief from her pocket and pressed it to her eye. As she turned to go, she looked back at Madeline. "It would be a shame if something happened to your boy-friend. He's so lost in love; he'd never see it coming."

Madeline fell to the couch sobbing as Mira's footsteps receded down the stairs. She wept until there was nothing left but sleep.

She slept the whole of the following day. In the middle of the next night, a knock at the door woke her up. She tried to summon her senses as fast as she could. Images flashed through her mind, smashing into each other: Eliot opening a wine bottle, Mira looking at her in the vanity mirror, Eliot inside of her, Mira threatening to hurt Eliot! Was Mira back? Was this her?

In delirium, Madeline grabbed the shard of glass from the rug, bounded to the door, and flung it open. It was Eliot.

He looked at her as if she were an apparition. This couldn't be the same woman he'd made love to, only hours ago. *This* woman's hair was tangled in knots, her eyes crazed, and what was that she had in her hand?

Still in a haze, Madeline wondered what was the matter with *him*. Why does he look so shocked? One look at what was left of the vanity mirror- answered her questions. She realized how she must look: a disheveled woman, holding on to a lethal weapon. *What must he think?*

She let the shard fall to the floor, and Eliot put his arms around her. When she tried pulling away, he grasped her shoulders.

"Maddy, are you all, right? My God, what happened here?"

Now she did turn away.

"The past, Eliot."

He looked about at the wreckage, still stunned. "Did someone break in? Assault you?"

"A woman I worked for when I was selling arms. She was here. She wants to get even with me."

His incredulity, or perhaps it was his fear for her, caused him to take her hand and bring her close again.

"Get even with you! For what?"

Madeline turned her back to Eliot, and crossed her arms, running her hands up and down. She spoke in stutters. Her voice faltered.

"I…I did some bad things when I was with her."

Eliot turned her around. "So did I when I fell in with those mercenaries. It's what we *had* to do when they were after us."

Madeline looked down and shook her head. "No. It was worse than that."

Eliot lifted her head, stroking her cheek. "Couldn't be any worse than what I did to Will. The way I deserted him."

Now it was her turn to offer consolation. She caressed Eliot's hair. "You didn't have a choice," Madeline said. "All those witnesses. The judge never would have understood."

A sad, half smile came across his lips. "Just like you in that village."

Eliot knew she had killed a civilian, the same way he had killed an innocent Afghan, while trying to stop Will, in the middle of a full-blown PTSD event.

Eliot even knew the special innocence of Madeline's victim and what war can do, to people who would never otherwise be capable of such violence.

They collected themselves. Madeline's senses returned, and she had questions for him.

"The woman who's out to get me is named Mira. She said she knows you."

He looked at her as though amazed. Turning his back to her, he paced the room. *How is it possible?* he thought. *After all this time? It can't be!*

Madeline approached and put herself in front of him. "Eliot, look at me. Mira said she knows you from an arms deal."

Shaking his head, he tried turning away. She followed him.

"It was a long time ago," he said, "when I was with those rogue mercenaries, British, Australians, all the rest of them."

"OK, I understand that. But she said I've known you longer than I have. What did she mean by that?"

Lies did not come easily for Eliot. But he had to lie now, or he might lose her. He could not tell her how, in a drunken haze one night, he'd confessed to Mira, what he failed to do for Madeline, when they were children.

"I don't know what she's talking about," he said. "You know what a liar she herself is. She's probably trying to find a way to turn us against each other."

Knowing of Mira's deep desire for her, and what by now could be Eliot's jealousy, Madeline nonetheless believed him. This was Eliot. He wouldn't lie to her.

"Did you save her life?" Madeline said.

He looked around at the destroyed vanity and the glass. "Right now, I wish I hadn't."

"So how did it happen?"

He smirked to himself. "It was a sniper. I saw him just in time. Guess I was in the wrong place at...you know, the wrong time."

"Or you were too good a shot." They shared ironic smiles. But Madeline had more to share. "She says she found my brother John".

He drew close to her.

"What did she do?"

"Gave him drugs, what else? Gives her a good head start on revenge."

He caressed Madeline's arm. "We'll find John before she can do anymore damage."

She placed her hand over his.

"You don't understand," she said. Mira can be everywhere, all at once."

It was then that she noticed what lay crumpled in the doorway… the thing he had had behind his back and had dropped in shock-when he'd seen all the rubble.

The white veil.

She picked it up- as if it were a living thing that had been abandoned. She stared wistfully at the delicate patterns, almost oblivious, even to his presence.

Eliot stood back and smiled, proud simply to be a witness.

A single tear shimmered in Madeline's eye. "I could say you shouldn't have, but I won't."

He looked at her, his own eyes glimmering. "I'd never want you too, Maddy."

They held each other, the veil pressed between them. Then he pulled away, and she pressed the veil to her breast.

"Aren't you going to try it on?" he said.

She handed the veil to him. "I want you to put it on me."

He took the veil from her, lifting it high above her head, and let its long lines slowly descend about her. Her dark features glowed through the pristine shroud. It seemed to Eliot that her black eyes made it glorious.

He stared at her in awe. She had to see what he was seeing. She had to see herself. Without thinking, she turned to the broken vanity and saw an otherwise elegant woman, in fractured images.

But the moment was quickly lost.

She slid the veil from her head and sat down on the couch, staring at the veil as if it were a betrayed illusion. Eliot sat down next to her and put his arm around her.

"I'll get you a new vanity, Maddy."

She responded with a wizened look. "With what? I didn't think you could afford the veil."

He shook his head. "I couldn't. I gave blood to get the money for it today."

She let out a sigh. "Not the blood bank on 12th Street, where all the winos go."

He leaned back and looked up at the ceiling. "Stood in line for two hours."

"Eliot!"

He let a moment pass before he spoke again. "So, what did you do that's got Mira after you like this?

She had to lie to him. She had to hide her fear. She had learned how to do that when she had captured Taliban fighters. She knew that they would mutilate any Afghan woman who joined the national army. So, what would these fighters do to her- if they managed to get free before she got them to the Parwan Detention Facility? Some American Christian whore, without a veil.

"I blew the whistle on her. To Interpol on a terrible deal, she made in Syria." Madeline knew this was a half-truth, a lie by omission.

47

Eliot embraced her. "So, you, see? You did a good thing! Who knows how many lives you saved?"

She did not tell him how many lives had actually been lost simply because of the fact that she had not been heroic soon enough. All the aftermath. Especially all the innocents who died. She could never tell Eliot about all that.

Madeline suggested they go for a walk. Out on the street, he talked in rapid sentences.

"OK," Eliot said. "The first thing we must do is get you to my place. Get your things and--"

"I'm sure she knows where you live."

Eliot stopped and rubbed his chin. "Yeah, you're right. We'll get your things, put them in my place for the moment, and find someplace else."

Madeline shook her head at Eliot's innocence. He still did not understand who he was dealing with.

"Mira will find us again," she said.

Mira did find them, even sooner than either one of them would have thought possible.

CHAPTER 4

COLLISION

Eliot helped Madeline gather her few possessions. She put the black and white veils into a clean pillowcase, carefully folding them into place.

When they were about to leave, she took one last look at the destroyed vanity, fearful of the destruction yet to come.

As they were crossing the street outside, a black Mercedes was parked nearby and pulled out suddenly. If Mira had not had a white patch over her eye, Madeline would have never seen her through the car's tinted windshield.

Mira slammed on the throttle, the car roaring straight at Eliot. Madeline shoved him out of the way, and he tumbled to the asphalt. Madeline was caught before the speeding vehicle, which was now just a few feet from sudden impact. Mira smashed her foot on the brakes. The car spun in circles, brakes screeching. Smoke rose from the concrete.

As the car turned in crazed circles, one fender struck Madeline's thigh, sending her to the pavement. Eliot quickly got to his feet and covered her body.

Mira regained control of her car and sped away. Nervously scanning her rearview mirror and cursing herself, she was at least glad to see Madeline getting to her feet, with Eliot's help.

Eliot held her. "Can you walk?"

With his help, Madeline took a few precarious steps. So far, so good. Then Eliot saw a large oval of blood seeping through her jeans, on her right thigh. Not good.

Nearby, a car had stopped, the driver having witnessed the scene. He was on his cell phone and called out to Eliot. "I'm calling an ambulance!"

Dammit! Eliot thought. *We can't take her to a hospital. Everybody's looking for us!*

Taking her into his arms, he carried her back to his place, two blocks away. He had carried wounded soldiers a lot farther, but in this case, his knees weakened every time he looked down, to see if her blood stain had increased. It did not look like it had.

Eliot's place was somewhat better than Madeline's. It was a three-story building with single apartments, and the long cracks that ran through its plastered exterior, displayed its age. His apartment was on the third floor.

As he rushed them up the stairs, taking them two at a time, he looked down to be sure Madeline was all right. She looked at up at him in awe, seeming oblivious to the pain.

He kicked open his apartment door and laid Madeline on the bed. He had to check the femur, to make sure it wasn't fractured. *Thank God,* he thought, *for the trauma training I got from the mercenaries I was with.* They had had no hospitals to go to.

Carefully, he unzipped her jeans and slowly slid them down. The blood was coagulating. Good.

"Maddy, I've got to check the bone. This might hurt."

"Couldn't hurt me anymore than the look on your face. It's all right, Eliot."

He gently rubbed her thigh bone, increasing the pressure by degrees. No reaction. He breathed a sigh of relief and got to his feet.

"OK, let me dress that wound."

"Take your time, handsome. This is the first decent bed I've laid on in months."

He grinned. "You call this decent?"

While he boiled water to disinfect her wound, Madeline looked out the window, fearing what Mira would do next. They'd been lucky so far, but that kind of luck did not last. Not with Mira.

She looked over at Eliot, as she sadly mused to herself. *That man over there, shaking a saucepan to try to get it to boil faster, was the one Mira wanted dead.*

A darker thought crept through Madeline's mind. *If only it could be me, instead of Eliot. Then I wouldn't have to live without him.*

Unaware of her reverie, Eliot turned to her with a smile. "It's boiling now. We're all set." He went to a bureau drawer, pulled out a T-Shirt, and held it up. "My last good one." He glanced down at it. "Well, old friend, time for us to part ways, so to speak. Bet you never thought you'd do anything this noble."

She smiled to herself, loving the way he could still kid, after a brush with death. *Was anyone really this naïve?*

He ripped the shirt in half and set one part on the bed. Then he dipped the other half in the boiling water, shaking away excess moisture, as he leaned over her. Still trying to lighten the mood, he continued joking. "This is going to sting, beautiful. Do you think you can take it?"

She smiled at him. "Go easy on me, doc. I've never been hurt before."

As he wiped blood away, he could clearly see the wound. It was about five inches long, but not very deep. Once he had cleaned it, he wrapped the other half of the shirt firmly on her leg, tying the cotton tightly into place.

"That should hold you for now," he said. "But I'll get some Neosporin and some bandages from the drug store on 5th Street."

She looked at him ruefully. "But Eliot, we can't stay here. Not for another minute."

Realizing she was right, he leaned back and let out a long sigh. Then inspiration struck. Madeline could see it on his face, as his eyes suddenly brightened. "Do you think you could make it over to the levee? It's about a mile."

She was happy to hear any idea that would put space between them and Mira. "You might have to carry me part of the way. But yeah, I think I could. What do you have in mind?"

He stroked his chin. "My folks had a bungalow out there, near the river. We'd go there sometimes in the summer. Dad always had the crazy idea that he'd leave it to the Army Corps of Engineers, because they patched the levee so many times, whenever we got heavy rains. I don't think anybody lives in the old place now. Last time I saw it, it was falling apart. We could go there!"

Madeline looked away, involved in her own thought. *Was anything out of Mira's reach?*

Puzzled by her hesitation, he grasped her arm. "She'd *never* find us out there!"

She had to tell him what he was up against.

"It's not just revenge Mira wants, Eliot. She wants *me*. Understand?"

He released her arm, his eyes shifting with slow comprehension. "Now I *know* that she won't give up."

She let that sink in, before speaking again. "How far out the levee is this place?"

"Miles down the road, but I know we could hitch a ride. The farmers out there are friendly."

With difficulty, they made it to the levee and twenty minutes later, found themselves bumping along in a beat-up truck, with a grizzled farmer who wore a big smile and liked to talk.

"What you folks doing way out here, if you don't mind my asking?"

Eliot did the talking.

"Going out to my parents old place in Freeport."

Now they had the farmer's full attention.

"Which one? I know them all!"

"It's the white bungalow, right between Freeport and Hood."

The farmer looked at Eliot as though he'd just said something amazing.

"The old Lange place?"

"That's the one."

The farmer shook his head. "Ain't nobody lived there in years. I wasn't aiming on going out that far, but you look like such nice folks, you and your wife, I don't mind going a little further."

With softened eyes, Madeline and Eliot looked at each other. *Your wife.*

Travelling down the levee road, the couple felt as if they'd been transported to another world. Mounted as they were atop a twenty-foot levee, the horizon stretched out before them and seemed to never end. On the right, Eliot looked down at the Sacramento River, shining in the late morning sun. The river rolled forward, seeking other tributaries that would all eventually flow into the Pacific Ocean. It struck Eliot now that minutes away and only a few hours ago, someone had tried to kill him. Madeline had saved him, placing herself in harm's way. He looked over at her, wishing that she could somehow share the same realization. But she was lost in her own world.

Madeline looked left at the farmlands that stretched out below. She gazed at the well-marked acres of corn, wheat, and green vegetables. Here, she thought to herself, everything was growing naturally and meant to nourish the body. On South Side, everything was in decay, with drugs and deception, and all of it by a dark and unnatural design.

Seeing the faraway looks in his rider's eyes, the farmer had to say something. "You two look like you ain't never seen farmland before, especially you, young lady."

Madeline wakened from her reverie. "I didn't think people lived like this anymore."

The farmer laughed. "Why sure they do! Shoot, my family's been out here for three generations."

Eliot was stunned by the farmer's innocence. He had picked up two strangers and trusted them. On South Side, a stranger was someone to be used. Kindness was a weakness, meant to be taken advantage of.

As they neared their destination, Eliot knew that once they had shelter, they would need food. That meant taking the risk of exposure. From the slum they had escaped, no one cared who he and Madeline were. Many people on South Side were too busy evading the law themselves to be concerned about others, but Eliot doubted that any of those were being pursued by federal authority.

They had to take a chance hitchhiking, Eliot thought to himself. Though Madeline's injury was not serious, she would never have made it all the way to Freeport. But how many chances could they take?

The farmer seemed like someone who probably had no time for media, although even this far out in the country, many people had CNN. With stories as gruesome as his and Madeline's, two natives from the Sacramento Valley, any local channel surfer would stop his searching.

Then Eliot thought of Tom Obregon. He might be able to help. Eliot remembered that Tom and his father Luis, ran the Freeport Market. Eliot had heard that Tom served in Iraq. Maybe Tom would understand, or Eliot could try to make him understand.

Eliot recalled how he and Tom had hung out together, when Eliot and his parents spent the summers near the river. A painful memory surfaced in Eliot's mind.

During one summer, as Eliot and his father had been shopping in the Obregon store, Eliot had accidentally dropped a soft drink onto the floor. Glass and liquid had splattered in every direction.

Tom had been quick to grab a broom. "It's OK, Eliot. I'll take care of it."

Colonel Lange had not been so understanding. "Damn you, Eliot! Look at the mess you made." Eliot's father had then snatched the broom away from Tom. "You're too stupid to be my son...*anybody's* son! *You* clean it up."

Tom had yanked the broom away from the Colonel. "It was an accident! He didn't mean to do it."

As the other customers had stood in shock, Luis Obregon had been quick to intervene. Coming from behind the grocery counter, he then set himself directly in front of Eliot's father. "You don't need to talk to the boy that way. He meant no harm."

"I'll talk to him anyway I want!" the Colonel had shouted.

Hands on his hips, Luis had glared back. "Leave. Now. We don't want your business."

Grabbing Eliot by the shoulder, the Colonel had then headed for the door. With a scowl, he had looked back at Luis, and then shoved Eliot through the opening, nearly sending him to the ground.

Tom was about to react when Luis softly restrained him. "That's enough Tomás. Pity the boy with such a father."

Eliot remembered now, that despite his father's admonitions to never go into the Obregon store again, he and Tom, still found ways to bump into each other. Eliot prayed that he and Tom still had a connection.

When the farmer dropped Madeline and Eliot off, and they walked down the levee, they could barely see the house. The row of bushes out front had grown so high and entangled with weeds, that only the bungalow's small attic roof was still visible.

The stones from the gravel pathway that led up to the front door were randomly dispersed over the browned-out lawn. The front porch steps were warped, their paint cracked and peeling away. The screen door hung by a single hinge.

When Eliot opened the front door, a gust of air rushed back at them, as if the old house had been holding its breath, waiting again for human habitation.

The first thing that struck them was the smell. The spoors of mold and mildew assaulted their nostrils, reminding them both too keenly of the odors of South Side. Had they escaped one form of decay for another?

As they looked about the living room, they slowly comprehended the differences. Here, although left to neglect, the couch, end tables and lamps still bore the signs of quality furniture. The wood of the furniture was solid oak, still intact. The glint of gold leaf on the lamps, though tarnished, still shined. Even beneath the thick layer of dust that clung to the coffee table, mahogany managed to emerge.

On South Side, they knew every scrap of furniture was beyond resurrection. If you tried to clean it, it fell apart in your hands. The smell of dirt that hung in the hallways was impenetrable.

Madeline bent down and ran her index finger over the dust on the coffee table. She rubbed the dust between her finger and thumb, as a thoughtful expression appeared on her face. She smiled at Eliot.

"It's not clean, but at least it's not South Side."

He embraced her. "We'll get it fixed up."

Holding each other tightly, they felt a chance for some kind of future, however brief and fragile.

They then began to inspect the dining room, walking across its still firm hardwood floors. In the dust beneath their feet, tiny creatures scurried for cover. While Madeline sensed the room's possibilities, Eliot suddenly remembered a more urgent need.

"We're going to need some rations."

Distracted from her thoughts of renewing the house, Madeline turned to him. "You must know a store out here somewhere."

"Yeah, but I'm a little nervous about going."

She narrowed her eyes. "Why? I thought you said they'd never find us way out here."

He rubbed his chin. "It's not the FBI I'm worried about, not even Mira. It's the news. I'd forgotten about that. We can't be recognized."

Madeline looked down. "So, what do we do?"

"There's a grocery store about a mile down the road. I used to be friends with the owner's son, Tom. He might help us."

Madeline gave him a wary look. "Are you sure can trust him?"

"I hope so. We'll have to risk it."

When Eliot got to the Obregon store, he pulled up the hood of his sweatshirt. Peering through the store's front window, the only person he saw inside was Tom, wiping down the well-worn wooden counter.

Eliot was surprised to see him, fully grown into a man. The last time Eliot had seen Tom, the two of them were no more sixteen. Then, Tom's jet-black hair was slicked back and lifted into a pompadour. Now, it seemed to shine even brighter, cut short in bristled rows. The only thing that hadn't changed were Tom's eyes. They were just like his father's, warm and dark.

When Eliot opened the store's front door, he was momentarily surprised by a jingling sound over his head. Then he realized it was only the little bell that hung over the door, announcing a customer's entry. He smiled to himself. Some things never change.

Barely glancing up to look at Eliot, Tom spoke.

"Help you, sir?"

Eliot pulled back the hood of his sweatshirt. "How you doing, Tom?"

Stunned, Tom stared at him. "Jesus! Eliot?"

"Yeah. Been a long time, huh?"

Tom tossed aside his cleaning rag. "It sure has. How *you* doing?"

Eliot looked back to the store's office. "I'm OK, I guess. Hey, where's your dad? Doing the books?"

Tom retrieved his cleaning rag, wiping the counter in a slow, circular motion. "Lost him last spring."

"Oh God, Tom, I'm sorry. He was a good man."

Tom wiped his hands with the rag. "He was the best." A moment of reverence passed, before reality returned. "I heard you were in trouble."

Eliot looked around at the shelves of the store. All the things he had known as a child were still there. The loaves of bread were still firmly placed together into neat rows. The bottles of mustard and ketchup still stood next to the pickles and olives, and up on top, almost out of reach, the one-pound tins of coffee. *I guess Starbucks hasn't invaded this far out,* Eliot thought to himself. *Not yet anyway.*

The sense of sameness that he'd allowed himself, soon disappeared. Everything was different now.

"Yeah, Tom. Big trouble. But it's not what you think."

Tom spread out his arms and gripped the counter. "It never is the way the news blows everything out of proportion."

"I heard you were in Iraq."

Tom nodded. "Two tours. Nobody over here knows what's going on over there. Nobody wants to know."

Eliot gripped his arm, as if it had suffered some injury. "Especially about PTSD."

Tom leaned back from the counter. "Friend of mine committed suicide, a week after he came home. Nobody saw it coming."

Eliot dug his hands into his pockets. "That's how it was with my buddy, only he snapped one night, went outside the wire, and stared firing his weapon. I tried to stop him but only made things worse for both of us."

Tom stroked his cheek. "One of the guys I served with got accused of a war crime I know he didn't commit. I was there. He got cleared, thank God."

Eliot looked down at the counter. "I wish I could say the same for her and me."

Tom seemed puzzled. "Her? What do you mean?"

"You've probably been reading about Madeline Crowne, too."

Now, Tom seemed amazed. "I have. You two are together?"

"Yeah, down at my parents' old place. Trying to lay low for a while. Figure out our next move."

Tom's eyes narrowed. "So how did you end up with *her*?"

"We knew each other from grammar school. We both had it bad at home, back then. You remember…my dad."

Tom let out a long breath. "I sure do. I don't know how you took it so long."

"She had it worse than me. We're just trying to help each other now."

Tom let a moment pass before speaking again. "The papers said she was in some kind of firefight and…"

Eliot interrupted him. "It was a big Taliban reprisal. They wanted to get even with a village that had cooperated with us. They were even shooting kids. She tried to stop it all, and then…oh hell, you don't want to know the rest, Tom. She didn't mean to do anything wrong."

A silence that could only be shared by the survivors of war, passed between them. Then Tom spoke, softly.

"It's OK, Eliot. You say it's all right; I believe you."

Eliot pulled himself together. "We're going to need some food, and we don't have much money."

"Your credit is good with me. You know that. What are you doing for transport?"

"Nothing. We sure could use some."

Tom smiled. "Dad's old pickup is still out back. It won't go much over forty, but it still runs."

"Jesus, thanks, Tom."

Eliot gathered up provisions, while Tom bagged them. After they loaded them up in the truck, Eliot turned to him. "Tom, I don't know how to say…"

"Don't have to say anything. Anything I can do. Just let me know."

While Eliot was gone, Madeline roamed the house. She wasn't surprised to discover they had no electricity, but they still had running water, cold as it was. The furniture left in the downstairs rooms was covered in dirt, while tiny particles of dust floated in the air above couches and armchairs, sparkling in the sunlight that seeped through the decayed curtains.

Climbing up the stairs to the bedrooms, she sensed that something bad had happened up there. It was a defense she had developed in combat, when she was sent out on missions to villages, that were under heavy attack. To steel herself in those situations, she imagined the faces of the dead that she would have to behold. It had always amazed her how accurate her images had been. Some of the psychologists on base called it precognition, although few believed in it.

But now, as she reached the upstairs landing, she knew that violence had preceded her. Slowly going from one bedroom to the other, she found only the mundane. One bedroom with peeling posters of rock stars. It must have been Eliot's. The second bedroom, only a bed and nightstands. This one must have been the guest room.

Entering the master bedroom, she saw only a well-made bed, its white spread tucked neatly into place at the corners. Covered with dust. Then, walking around the bed, she saw it. There, on the floor, next to the bed, lay a large ancient stain of blood. Its redness had decayed into blackened swirls, the uneven edges crusted in purple.

Suddenly, Eliot was behind her, his arms loaded with groceries. "Oh, you found it. I didn't want you to see that."

She looked at him, stunned. "What happened here?"

He set the groceries down on the floor and put his arm around her.

"Something you don't want to know about, Maddy."

She stepped back from him. "I want to know everything about you, no matter what it is."

He looked down at the blood stain. "My father committed suicide in this room."

She looked again at the stain, and then at her wrists. "Sounds like somebody I know."

He grasped her in a sudden embrace. "No! You're not anything like him. He liked to torture people with words. For him, words were weapons."

She looked once again at the gruesome stain. "Sounds like my stepfather, Frank. Only he used the back of his hand, especially when I tried to protect my brother John, who had to take the worst of it."

Eliot gave her a moment before speaking again. He wished to respect her pain.

"What about your mother?"

She turned away. "She was always too drunk to help anyone. The rare times she was sober, she'd swear she was going to leave Frank, but then she'd reached for another bottle of bourbon."

Seeing the look on Eliot's face was more painful than her recalled memory. It was time to "drive on," as they said in the army whenever the soldiers had to witness something too painful to express. It was a piece of jargon used to alleviate anguish. She had to be finished with Eliot's story now, and "soldier on".

"So how did your father take his life?"

Roused from her pain, he spoke to his own.

"He did it the military way, a bullet to the head. He was a colonel in the army and a harsh disciplinarian. All the men under him were terrified, but none more terrified than his own son. He was harder on me than any of them."

"And what about *your* mother?"

"Almost as hard on her, and I couldn't do anything about it. When he retired and my mom passed away, he didn't have anybody left to torture. He knew *I* was never coming back."

Madeline put her arms around Eliot. "Tell me the rest. I know there's more. There's always more."

It was time to tell her what he had dreaded confessing. It was the only way they could be free. The only way they could stay together. "One day I saw someone who looked like she'd taken a lot worse than me, and I wanted to help her."

She pulled away, wondering at what he had just said. "So, who was she?"

He straightened himself. "You."

Her eyes shifted, trying to comprehend. What was this? "Eliot, what are you talking about?"

He began pacing the room, talking without looking at her.

"Remember when you were at Saint John's Catholic school, in the 8th grade?"

Madeline smirked. "How could I forget? I wasn't there long, but I haven't forgotten it."

He stopped and fixed his eyes on her. "I was there, too."

She looked at him with dull seeming surprise. "You're kidding. Why didn't you ever tell me about that?"

He held his stare. "Because I was ashamed."

"For what?"

He went back to pacing.

"Remember Sister Margaret, Maddy? What she did to you?"

She felt an old anger rise and take hold.

"That bitch. By now, I hope she's burning in hell."

Eliot nodded in agreement. "She made your life a hell that day. Introduced you to the class of us rich kids as the poor girl the school had taken in as a charity case, and how magnanimous the church was for doing so."

Anger began to sear Madeline's heart. "Yeah, and then she proceeded to lay out all the sordid details of my family, saying it would be good for my soul. The only thing it was good for was her sadism. She loved every minute of it."

Eliot bowed his head. "You couldn't stop crying. That's the thing I remember most. You wanted to fight back, but the tears wouldn't let you. So, I tried."

She took hold of him. "That was you? The kid in the back of the class who stood up for me?"

He looked away. "But not for long. Not long enough."

Now, Madeline walked the room, wide-eyed, reliving the incident, as if to herself alone. "You shot up out of your seat, shouting back at her for what she did to me. The other kids couldn't believe it."

He stood before her. "Yeah, but then what happened?"

She looked at him with a saddened smile. "She made you take it all back. Said if you didn't apologize, she'd tell your father about the whole thing, and you'd be expelled."

He dug his hands into his pockets. "I wouldn't have minded being expelled. Those kids were all such snobs. I didn't want to be friends with any of them. Will was the only friend I had, the only one I needed, until you."

Madeline took Eliot's hand, trying to hold it as tenderly as he always held hers. "Then Sister Margaret didn't waste any time telling the whole class how badly your father came down on you. She knew everything about everybody."

He put his hands on her shoulders. "Yeah, but didn't you hate me for going back on you like that?"

She grinned. "At first, I did, yeah. I wanted to kill you. Then I thought of Frank, and the way he always treated John. And then I thought of something else."

His hands slid down her arms. "What was it?"

Her eyes began to water, the fluids hovering in their hosts, as her voice hesitated.

"You were the only one who ever stood up for me."

They took each other in a deep embrace.

"Oh Maddy, if you only knew how long I've been beating myself up for that day."

She molded her cheek to his chest. "You didn't have to. I never forgot how brave you were."

He loosened their embrace, looking into her eyes. "And I never forgot you. When I managed to sneak back into the country, so I could see Will, I was in a near empty bar one night, and I saw your face flashed on CNN. 'Madeline Crowne, wanted for war crimes, believed to be in Sacramento.' I couldn't believe it. I had to find you."

She crossed her arms. "It was a good thing you did, before they found *us*."

Absently, he rubbed his forehead. "Your headlines were bigger than mine."

She ran her hands up and down her arms. "I did something a lot worse."

He took her in his arms again.

"Maddy, anybody can do anything when they've got PTSD. Will did, and now they've got him...".

She broke away. "He didn't do what I did!"

He took a few feet back. He needed to give her some space. A moment passed before she spoke again.

"I see you got the groceries. Did you have any trouble?"

Thank God, Eliot thought to himself. *I've got some good news to deliver.*

"No, I made sure there was no one in the store before I went inside."

"And what about your friend, Tom?"

"Oh Maddy, that's the best part. He knows all about us and he wants to help. He even let me buy these groceries on credit. There's more down in the truck."

Incredulous, Madeline stared at him. "The truck? What truck?"

"It's right outside. Take a look for yourself. Tom loaned it to me."

Madeline went to the window, pulled back the decayed curtain and looked down. So, it was.

"Not pretty, Eliot, but I assume it's serviceable."

He laughed. "Know what's funny about you?"

She shook her head and grinned. "No, what's so funny?"

"Whenever you get sarcastic, I know you're all right."

Then they went to his old bedroom and made love.

Days passed and they allowed themselves the fantasy that all was normal. They went about the house straightening things up and dusting everything off. They swept the floors. They cleaned the kitchen and bedroom. Eliot figured a way to pirate electricity, by feeding into a power pole.

But the lover's sweet respite nonetheless gave their memories time to catch up to them. They had been running for so long, the darkened past had had to wait for its moment, standing still in its blackened robes, waiting to shroud them in sadness.

But it did catch up, as it usually did for both of them in the evenings, when the sun slipped below the levee, leaving the land on the other side covered in a premature darkness.

Separately, they would wander the house, seemingly unaware of the other's presence. Then Madeline would go to an upstairs window and watch the sun's reflection as it melted into the river. Eliot would stand on the front porch, leaning against one of its massive supports, and look down on the brown earth, as it turned to black.

Madeline would remember joining the army, suddenly free of all her family's afflictions. But faster still came the memory of John's eyes as he begged her not to go. She was nineteen then, and he sixteen. He was small for his age. *Why did he have to be so frail?* she thought. His hair was white, blonde, his eyes the shade of blue that sleeps in frozen ice. With their appearances in stark contrast, they were never seen as siblings. Each had a different father whom their mother could not remember. Frank had stepped in later, to keep alive the alcoholism of Madeline's mother, and to brutalize John.

Eliot would remember the curse Sister Margaret put on him. In a final act of cruelty, she informed Eliot's father of everything that had happened that day in school, even though Eliot had apologized to the nun.

Colonel Samuel Lange did not berate his son. Eliot thought that for once, his father's words would not rain down on him like so many sharpened knives, but he knew there would be more. There was always more.

In blunt terms, his father informed him that once Eliot graduated high school, he would be forced into the army, the last place he wanted to go. Besides, his father had ruthlessly reasoned, it was time to toughen him up. His friendship with Will was unnatural. Eliot spent too much time with that weakling, his father even intimating that their relationship hovered on homosexuality.

And it was during these memories of Will that Eliot would always step down from the porch and stand on the darkened soil. It reminded him of Will, who loved planting things and watching them grow, amazed by creation. Whenever one of his plants emerged from the ground, Will would rejoice. He would jump up and down, his shaggy hair flying in his face, as his gangly arms and legs swung about in awkward motions of which he was blissfully unaware.

And Will had been the earth that kept Eliot grounded. In gentle conversation, he would always remind Eliot that he was better than the brutality he had to suffer from his father. Then, in one of his spontaneous embraces, which always came with a warm squeeze, he would remind Eliot that he was meant for great things. Caught up by the naivete in Will's eyes, Eliot would almost believe him.

But then, when Eliot entered the army, Will was determined to go with him.

"We'll never be separated Eliot," he had said. "We'll always be together."

"No, Will!" Eliot had replied. "This isn't for you. You love *living* things. War is all about death."

No amount of reasoning could change Will's mind, and when Eliot was sent to Afghanistan, Will made sure he was on the same C-17 aircraft when they landed there.

Then, when darkness came, and the only thing Madeline and Eliot could see was the blackened outline of the levee standing like a wall that locked them both in dark memories, they would retreat to the bedroom.

Holding each other all night, they never said a word about their silences. They both knew where they had to go, despite all the terror that awaited them.

I got up in the middle of the night, so he wouldn't see me go. It was still the best chance I had to find John, without the government or Mira catching up to me. It wasn't easy to untangle myself from Eliot's arms. If I hadn't learned in Afghanistan how to move about so quietly, I never would have pulled it off.

But when I slid into my clothes and tiptoed to the door, I made a big mistake. I looked back at him. I couldn't help it. He was so beautiful in slumber, and I could still feel his warm body against me. But I had to get away from there.

I was out the front door and had my hand on the truck's door handle before I heard his voice behind me.

"You're not the only one who can sleep with one eye open."

I felt my shoulders slump. I turned around.

"Was it when I stopped to look back at you?"

He gave me a big grin. "Yup. If you're going to retreat, don't make a big production out of it."

I shook my head. "I should have never fallen in love with a veteran."

We stood there for a moment, before he spoke in a soft voice.

"Maddy, I know how bad you want to find John, how bad you want to help him, as bad as I want to see Will. But you *can't* go down there alone!"

I always hated the *can't* word, and I let him know it. "For a guy that's so smart, you still don't get it. Mira's after *you*, more than me. She knows that getting rid of you would hurt me more than anything!"

He set himself into a kind of combat stance. "I'll stop you, if I have to."

I jerked the car door open. "The hell you will, mister. I've taken out bigger guys than you. Don't think I won't do it!"

He glared back at me. "And I could do the same to *you*!"

I gave him a sidelong look. "Like you would. Don't be ridiculous."

He took a step back. "OK, we'll make a deal. If we leave together now, I'll try to sneak into the VA hospital where Will is. It's early enough in the morning that they might not see me. I know they're looking for anybody that fits my description, but it's worth a chance."

I nodded. "So far, your idea sounds good."

Then he was quick to come back at me. "*But* you drop me off there first and then wait for me on the corner of 5th and T Street. Wait until I get there. I won't be long. I can't stay there for long. Then we'll try to find John together."

A few minutes later, we were on the road.

She'd agreed to the deal, but I knew the danger that was waiting for us down there. Mira had to be prowling around, waiting for Maddy to come back for her brother. For Mira, John was the bait that would reel Maddy in.

I knew the VA had security guards, but I was hoping that at this hour they'd be a little sleepy, and maybe I could slip past them.

It was a shame that that old pickup couldn't do more than forty miles an hour. At this rate, it was going to take us more than forty minutes to get into town, and at a time like this, the memories can move a lot faster than that.

I looked over at her as we bumped along the old levee road and knew she was lost in her own dark thoughts, staring out the window at nothing. Trying to distract myself from the past, I gazed down at the river below us, watching its wide arms as they shaped themselves to the levee, turning again and again, until they disappeared into the horizon. I could see the first light of dawn, almost as if it were emerging from the river, like a resurrection.

But then I saw the waves below as they dug into the levee's earth, slowly tearing away at the embankment. Here and there on the river's waves, fragments of tree limbs and overturned roots, were helplessly carried along by strong currents and undertows. How long ago had these wooden splinters once stood as strong trees, before they became the river's orphans?

And that made me think of Will. He'd want to rescue every one of them and plant them all over again.

I didn't look over at Eliot because I already knew what he was thinking. It's easy to do that, when you've got your own ghosts to worry about. I gazed down at all the farms below as we passed them one by one. Year end, year out, they planted seeds and reaped another harvest, in an endless cycle of renewal.

None of it was ever shattered by violence and death. None of them could ever know what Eliot and I had to see and had to do. Did any of them care, or did they only pretend to, especially after the war dragged on for years, going nowhere?

In my first tour in Afghanistan, I came home on leave with a Silver Star, but I wasn't wearing it. It should have gone to one far more courageous than me.

It all started in the predawn hours of a cold day. We were out on foot patrol in an area of Kandahar, known for Taliban ambushes. For a while, everything seemed routine, but the thought is always there in the back of your mind. *What's out there? What's out there that I can't, see?*

The worst was worrying about an IED, the improvised explosive device, buried in the dirt. The Taliban made them out of anything they could lay their hands on. Some had as much as 25 pounds of explosives, spiked with motorcycle parts, rusty spark plugs and jagged chunks of steel, all of it hooked up to detonators. All you had to do was step on it.

The explosion from one IED can instantly kill several soldiers, and we'd already lost seven that way. Worse still, once the explosion is over, and before the dust and dirt can clear, the enemy can launch a firefight, which they usually did.

As we plodded along that morning, my mind drifted into thoughts about John. I didn't like the letters I was getting from him. Our stepfather Frank kicked John out of the house after our mother died of the alcohol.

Then John starting writing about some friends he was staying with, which gave me hope, until he mentioned their names. I knew them all and they were all druggies.

I never saw what my right leg stepped on that chilly morning in Kandahar. A second before, my foot was stirring up dirt. In the next instant I heard a click and knew that I had triggered a pressure-plate, rigged to an IED, buried in the soil.

I heard a popping sound as small stones tossed into the air. The bomb had failed to ignite.

The first one to rush over to me was Private Benson. "You were damn lucky, Sergeant!" he said, letting out a long sigh of relief, shared by the whole platoon.

"We *all* were!" Lance Corporal Anne Simonsen said, as she gave me a big hug. Even though we were dressed in full "battle rattle", flak vest, Kevlar helmet, ammunition, and whatever else they could load on us, I could still feel her hands holding me tight. "Are you all right, Maddy?"

I think the biggest comfort came when I heard her say my first name. That, and seeing her freckled face and all that red hair, bunched up in her helmet. Women in combat had a special bond then.

Anne and I had a bond of our own. More than any-thing, we wanted to protect the most vulnerable, the women and children. We'd talk about that, between ourselves, sometimes late at night. She knew the background I'd come from, and even though she'd been raised in a warm family, she understood the pain of one who had not. She had a compassion that could comprehend anything.

She released me from her big bear hug and gave my shoulders a shake.

"I'm going to buy you a beer tonight, Madeline Crowne!"

"Make that two!" one of the soldiers cried out. "No, make it a six pack!" another one said.

Then we got hit. Fire came at us from everywhere. We all scrambled for cover against nearby boulders. I poked my head up just long enough to see where it was all coming from. The Taliban were in concealed positions in the hills above us. We were pinned down. I barked out orders, getting everyone organized, but firing back was useless. The bullets rained down us in continuous fire. The sound of tat-tat-tat kept coming, ricocheting over the boulders.

Then the Taliban launched an RPG, a rocket propelled grenade. The first one killed was Private Benson, the man who moments before was praising my good luck. He now laid bloodied and motionless. Two others had died with him and a third was badly wounded.

With no care for her own life, Anne ran over to the wounded man. She was good with battle trauma and im-mediately went to work on him. Then, to get a better look at the wounded soldier's injury, she took off her helmet and was instantly shot in the head.

I froze. I watched the dark red blood flow from her fatal wound, as it poured into her light red hair.

I rose up from the rock I'd been hiding behind and fired back. I used every cuss word I'd ever heard to throw at them, along with every bullet I had. I rallied the men. Seeing me half exposed and half-crazy they fired back. Together, we laid down a lot of fire, but two soldiers were wounded and exposed. I pulled them both to cover, bullets zinging and popping all around me. What I did infused our soldiers further, and the enemy decided it had had enough, and re-treated to higher ground.

When we got back to base, torn and wounded, I couldn't look at Anne's body. I'd seen a lot of fallen soldiers, but I couldn't bear to look at her. Why did it have to be Anne? Why couldn't it have been me? Then I never would have done what I did a month later, that night in that village.

For the first time since we started into the city, Maddy and I looked at each other fully and we both knew. If I *did* get to see Will, what were the chances I'd get caught, and she and I might never see each other again?

He grasped my hand tightly, as if it might be the last time. What Mira had done before was out of jealous rage. Now, she'd had plenty of time to think and plan. She knew well how to scour any city and find human beings violent enough to do anything, for the right price. Even with the ATF after her, she'd never stop coming. Somehow, I had to protect Eliot, even if it meant my life.

CHAPTER 5

AMBUSH

Two blocks from the VA hospital, Eliot pulled the truck to the curb, leaving the engine running. They knew they had to leave each other quickly. Lingering, however brief, leads to longer hesitation, and war had taught them that that could lead to disaster.

Seconds from separation, they each grasped for the most precious memory they could suddenly summon of each other. Eliot thought of holding Madeline at night, her sleeping breaths coming like whispers against his face. She thought of his cool hands as they slid along her skin, seeking warm crevices.

"Remember," he said. "Wait."

She nodded, and then Eliot was gone. She slid over to the driver's seat and headed to the meeting place on which they had agreed. It was not far away. Just enough distance to bring back the past.

When she came home on leave that first time, she found that John's friends had turned him into a full-blown opiate addict. She had got him into treatment, but the hospital was overwhelmed by the new drug epidemic. There were too many patients to tend to, and like so many others, John's case fell through the cracks, receiving little or no attention. It was not long before he was out on the street, scoring again.

He wrote Madeline letters, begging for help. She sent him all the money she had, but it was never enough for the kind of private care he truly needed. Then Madeline met Mira and made enough money with her to get John the best care available. Only now, it all had to be sent secretly. Madeline was a fugitive of military justice and an illegal gun dealer, even though she didn't yet know the full implications of that.

Through Mira's underworld contacts, Madeline was able to send John money via a nebulous network, using illicit lines of transfer. Mira had sworn she hated using these methods, but she said she would risk anything to help Madeline's brother. It had all seemed so noble.

But then the ease with which Mira implemented illegal acts aroused Madeline's suspicions. To make the transfers, Mira needed only to make a few phone calls. And though Mira spoke only in Arabic to her contacts, Madeline could not help but notice how brief and offhanded the conversations seemed to be.

And when Mira would hang up the phone, assuring Madeline it had all been arranged, Madeline would feel Mira's hand softly stroking her arm, for a length of time longer than needed for mere assurance.

By degrees, Mira's intimacies escalated. One night, as the pair shared a glass of wine, gazing out the elegantly beveled and encased windows of Mira's refined apartment, Mira turned to kiss Madeline. Madeline proffered her cheek, but the kiss found her lips… brief, but intimate.

As Madeline turned away and the moment passed, Mira smiled. She would wait.

Then a day of dreaded discovery came. Rushing home from a business deal that had taken her to a dirty desert location, Mira was anxious to get into the shower. As she threw her purse down on the bed, quickly got out of her clothes, and went into the bathroom, Madeline saw the tiny paper packet that had fallen from Mira's purse.

She picked it up and was about to replace it, when she felt small, jagged edges in the envelope's interior. Curious, she opened the envelope and saw its contents.

Raw diamonds.

Mira had assured Madeline that all her arms deals were legitimate, with the proper "End User Certificates" for shipping. But who deals in diamonds, especially *raw* ones, if not an illegal arms dealer? And how many times were diamonds used in money laundering? Madeline had heard of many such stories while in Afghanistan.

She tried banishing the thoughts from her mind, reminding herself that all this was intended to help John. And after all, Mira was the woman who had rescued Madeline on the road, when so many were after her.

Even though Madeline had kept her suspicions to herself, it amazed her now, as she neared the meeting place on South Side, how clever Mira had been at perceiving tension in Madeline's eyes. They would be having a finely prepared dinner under the vaulted ceiling of the dining room, elegant place settings in front of them, and Mira would suddenly look up, fixing her eyes on Madeline.

By looking away and attempting to make small talk, Madeline would only betray herself. She violated her first commandment. Never look away. Always look an adversary in the eyes.

Then, with the passing days, the encrypted emails through which Madeline and John had stayed in contact, slowly began to fail. Madeline immediately informed Mira, who said the problem would be quickly solved.

Tech experts came to the apartment, and for a time, the sister and brother were once again in contact, desperately trying to catch up on their messaging. But then the lines would fail again, and the technicians could only shake their heads.

A few days later, Mira told Madeline the money transfers had stopped. Mira's contacts had betrayed her and there was no one else she could turn to. Madeline knew that without the money to support John's care, he would soon be on the street.

It didn't take long for Madeline to see through Mira's plan, especially when Mira became evasive, alluding to possible solutions as she stroked Madeline's hair. Madeline felt her skin quiver as her anger arose. Mira was using this kind of suggestive, toying torture as a means to fulfill her desires. It was time for desperate measures.

Now, as she parked the truck at 5th and T Street, Madeline knew that, if Mira should appear, however well-armed, *Madeline's* desire for revenge would be stronger.

Eliot crept to a side window of the VA hospital. He hoped Will was still in the same room, but he had to be sure before trying to slip past the reception desk and the guards nearby.

Eliot had seen Will once before and later wished he had not. The pain of that incident struck Eliot now as he peered through the window. He couldn't bear to see Will that way again.

On that occasion, Eliot had purposely chosen visiting hour, the hospital's most hectic time. Wearing a hooded sweatshirt, he sat in the waiting area, pretending to read a magazine as security guards directed visitors to rooms, or helped nurses push empty gurneys down the long halls.

He constantly scanned the reception desk. The nurse at the desk was sometimes called away by visitors or physicians with questions. He needed her to be gone just long enough for him to quickly scan the hospital registry, for Will's name and room number.

Eliot was certain that the hospital staff had been made aware by military authority that he might attempt to see PFC William Madsen, the soldier implicated with him in a war crime.

As Eliot waited in what seemed like endless minutes of fear and tedium, the nurse was finally called away by a lost visitor, far down the hall. He had to take a chance. He sprung to his feet and found the register behind the reception desk. Scanning through the names as fast as possible, he found it – Madsen, room 164.

He had to move fast.

As he turned to go, he saw his own likeness. A photograph of him at his military graduation was propped up under the reception desk counter. It struck him how much younger he looked then, but there was no time for that.

He rushed down the hall and tried opening the door to Will's room as noiselessly as possible. When he first saw Will, he appeared to be sleeping, but as Eliot drew nearer, he saw what he most feared. With eyes half hooded, Will was staring at nothing. The vacant look in Will's eyes crushed Eliot's heart. PTSD had taken his best friend's life. Will was alive, but he was dead.

Leaning over Will, Eliot tried to find some sign of life, a blink, a flicker, anything Eliot could cleave to. Then Will's eyes began to move, slowly at first, from side to side. Eliot held his breath. Will's right eye looked up and fixed on Eliot.

Seeing a sign of recognition, however faint, Eliot drew closer. Then Will's right hand suddenly grasped Eliot's arm with a strength so desperate, Eliot felt himself wince.

Will's lips, straining to open, spoke in a whisper, barely audible. "Always together."

Eliot pulled down the hood of his sweatshirt, and with tears in his eyes, repeated Will's phrase, as he embraced him.

Then there came a bang at the door. Turning suddenly, Eliot saw a nurse pushing a food cart into the room. At first, the nurse's face showed surprise; but then came a look of slow recognition. She quickly pushed back the door and called out down the hall.

"Guard! Down here. The one you're looking for!"

Eliot pulled away from Will, turned to the window, threw it open and climbed out. He looked back for one last look at Will. His arms, suddenly torn from Eliot's body, shook in suspension, trying uselessly to reform a lost embrace.

The nurse had run from the room.

Now, as Eliot looked in again through the same window, he could see enough of Will's face to be certain it was him. Will appeared to be sleeping, but then he began to turn from side to side. It was then that Eliot saw them. Wrist restraints could mean just one thing. Will's condition had indeed deteriorated.

Eliot turned to go. The sight of his friend in this state was too painful to bear. But Eliot thought, *I can't leave him. Not yet.* If only Eliot could see him long enough, if only Will could be conscious enough so that Eliot could say how sorry he was for abandoning him that previous night, this would all be worth it. He had to take the chance, for a chance at forgiveness.

Eliot eased the window open and slid into the room. But before he could get to his feet, Will was shouting out his name.

"Eliot! Eliot!"

Eliot tried calming him, but it was already too late. Once Eliot had been discovered, the hospital had gone on high alert, and a guard had been posted outside Will's door.

The door burst open.

As the guard reached for his nightstick, Eliot grabbed his arm, twisted it behind him into a hammerlock and forced him to his knees.

The guard called out for help. "Sam! Down here!"

Then Will cried out as he yanked at his restraints. "Leave him alone! He's, my friend!"

Hearing the second guard running down the hall, Eliot yanked the first one to his feet. The second guard pushed through the door. Eliot shoved the first man at the second, sending him stumbling against the wall.

Eliot made for the window. Dazed, but conscious, the guard brandished his gun as he shouted.

"Stop! I'll shoot!"

Eliot raised his hands in surrender, but as the guard drew near, Eliot shocked him with a powerful headbutt. He vaulted through the window and ran down the street. He was almost to his meeting place with Madeline, when he stopped to catch his breath.

Defeat. Rage. There had been no time for Will.

Madeline sat in the truck, gripping the steering wheel so hard, that her knuckles ached. She sat back and took a deep breath.

She ran her hands over the wheel, in a circular motion of which she was unaware. She looked over at a wall clock hanging in the window of a pawn shop across the street. She cursed herself. The clock's black hands had moved too fast. It had already been thirty minutes, and where was Eliot?

Would he be here soon? Had he been caught, trying to see Will? Desperate to distract herself, she scanned the street, which only made matters worse. Was Mira out there somewhere, and who might she have with her? Was she with John, giving him drugs again? Madeline banged the heel of her hand against the steering wheel. It was all so crazy! Why were she and Eliot taking such chances to help people who seemed to be beyond help?

Then she saw John.

He was there at the corner, no more than thirty feet away. She bolted from the truck and ran straight to him. Startled by what he thought was a stranger, John made a faint attempt at self-defense, pulling back his arm in a fist.

But he realized it was Madeline and dropped his hand to his side. His whole body seemed to go limp. For a moment, the two stared at each other in amazement. And then Madeline threw her arms around him. He grasped her close.

As the shock of seeing each other subsided, they slowly came out of their embrace. Madeline ran her hand through John's white, blonde hair. It felt thinner. He was thinner too, and his eyes were tired. Older. She spoke their first words.

"I've been looking for you for so long, Johnny."

He clung to her hand. "I didn't know what happened to you, Maddy. I didn't even know you were back, until the news said you might be in Sacramento."

She looked away. "I had to get away as fast as I could. I had to get home and try to help you, try to explain why I couldn't send the money anymore, try…"

"It's all right," he said, as he released her hand. "I knew it had to be something that went wrong. Something that wasn't your fault. But when the emails didn't work anymore and the transfers stopped, they wanted to send me back to the county facility. I *couldn't* go back there. It's worse there!"

Madeline shook her head. "And then my friend Mira found you."

He put hands in his pockets, his eyes downcast. "Yeah. She said she knew you. Said you worked for her, and that's where the money was coming from to pay for the Rehab Center."

"That much is true, John. But there's a lot more."

John drew closer as he looked her in the eyes. "She said she picked you up on the road, after you ran away from the army. Said she wanted to help you."

Madeline smirked. "That's a half truth."

"You know, I never believed what they said about you on TV, Maddy. What they said you did to that woman. I knew you'd never do a thing like that."

Madeline turned away. Crossing her arms, she looked down at the pavement. The guilt she felt for what had happened in that village in Afghanistan that night was splintered, hard, and jagged. Pulling herself together, she turned back to John.

"What else did Mira tell you?"

"She said she was an arms dealer, and it was all legal until you sold some guns illegally to Syria. Then when the government found out you tried to blame it on her and ran away."

Madeline stroked his arm. "You didn't believe that did you, John?"

As his eyes shifted, she saw them twitching. She'd seen the same nervous reaction from a soldier she knew in Afghanistan, who got hooked on heroin.

John rubbed his eyes. "Of course, I didn't. But she saw how strung out I was then, and she gave me some money."

"And a few days later, she conveniently ran into you again and gave you some drugs."

He turned away. "You don't know what it's like, every day, trying not to want it, trying not to need it, but giving into it every time! I'm sorry. I couldn't help it."

Madeline took him by the shoulders and turned him back to her. "I know, John. Mira knows how to take advantage of people who are in trouble."

A silver Range Rover pulled up to the corner, opposite Madeline and John. The car sat, the engine revving. The driver's window inched down just enough for Madeline to see Mira's face. Mira's thick, black hair was slicked back and pulled up into a tight bun atop her head.

One of the back doors opened and a man got out. He wore jeans and a black T-shirt and weighed easily two hundred pounds. His shaved head emphasized the grim look on his face. The front passenger door opened, and another man emerged, lighter in weight, but more muscular. His hair was cropped short, and he wore black khakis and a gray turtleneck. Both men wore side arms.

Mira turned off the engine and got out of the car. She and the two men stood across the street, staring at Madeline and John.

"You'd better get out here John," Madeline said. "There's going to be trouble."

Mira and her men began to stroll across the street.

"No!" John said. "If there's trouble, I want to help you."

Then Madeline saw Eliot, who was standing in the shadows beyond the Range Rover.

Madeline whispered to John. "There's a man over there by the SUV. Don't look at him. He's, my friend. He knows how to help me."

"But when will I see you again, Maddy?"

"I'll find you. But you must leave. Now!"

John quickly walked away, looking over his shoulder again and again as he disappeared down an alley.

Now, a few feet from Madeline, Mira stopped.

"Good morning, Madeline. Nice day to do some

damage, don't you think? I see little brother didn't hang around to watch the carnage. Smart move."

Madeline glared at Mira. "Haven't you done enough to him?"

Mira smirked. "I've just been giving him what he needs, sweetie. *You* can't help him anymore."

Madeline withheld her anger. She knew how Mira used that emotion for manipulation.

"It's never enough for you, is it Mira? Anyone whose down and out is someone *you* want to use. I'd say that's a pretty good definition of cowardice, don't you think?"

Mira grinned. "Always good with a comeback. By the way, where have you been hiding out all this time? Even my best resources couldn't find you."

Madeline got closer to Mira. "Somewhere where the stink of you couldn't sniff us out."

Mira backed away, controlling her own anger. "And what have you and your lover been up to?"

Madeline smiled. "If you're asking if we've been intimate, the answer is yes. We do it all the time."

Mira's anger simmered in her eyes. "And where *is* Mr. Lange at the moment?"

Madeline nodded in Eliot's direction. "He's right behind you."

Surprised, Mira spun around. The two men turned with her.

"Perfect!" Mira said. "Just who I wanted to see."

"There are two of us, Mira, and three of you," Madeline said. "That gives Eliot and me a distinct advantage."

Mira glowered. "Ah, but my guys are armed. I don't see you and lover boy here flashing any weapons."

Madeline folded her arms. "Like I said. A distinct advantage."

Madeline and Eliot looked at each other. They knew they had to move, before Mira's men had a chance to un-sheathe their guns.

"Joe," Mira said to the shaved-headed man. "Put him in the car." She then turned to the second man. "Luke, take her with them. We're going to take you two lovers for a ride. I can't wait to see your love nest, wretched as it may be."

As Mira's men reached for their guns, Eliot grabbed Joe's wrist, yanking his arm backwards and twisting the wrist until Joe cried out in pain. Madeline grabbed Mira's shoulder and spun her around. With her other hand, Madeline got a firm grip on the waistband of Mira's black jeans and heaved her into Luke. Mira and Luke fell to the ground. Luke's gun spilled out of its holster.

Joe broke loose from Eliot and punched him. Eliot took the blow and attacked Joe with a kick in the groin. As Joe fell to the ground, Eliot tried grabbing for his gun. It was pinned beneath Joe's immense body.

Scrambling on the ground, Mira got Luke's gun. Getting to her feet, she pointed it at Madeline.

Eliot, finally wresting Joe's gun from beneath his body, pointed it at Mira.

"Drop it!"

"But now, *I* have the distinct advantage. You drop the gun, Lange. You're not going to shoot me while I have a gun on her."

The sudden seconds of assault now turned into slow, ag-onized moments. The only sound was the heavy breathing of all the combatants. With a helpless look at Madeline, Eliot lowered his arm.

Joe got to his feet and grabbed the gun from Eliot. He slammed it against Eliot's face. Blood burst from Eliot's cheek, and Joe moved to repeat what he'd done.

Madeline cried out. "That's enough! Leave him alone!"

"Obey her, Joseph," Mira said.

Joe wished to strike again. But Luke came up behind him and carefully took the gun from Joe's hand. In that instant Eliot knocked the gun from Luke's hand. It flew into the air, landing several feet away. Mira looked away just long enough for Madeline to grasp her arm and the gun from her hand.

She stepped away and turned the gun on Mira's men, back and forth between them and Mira herself.

"Everybody back off!"

But as Eliot went to retrieve the fallen gun, Luke jumped him. They fell to the concrete, each trying to gain the upper hand as they rolled about. Madeline knew she had no shot. Misdirection could kill Eliot.

Joe pulled out a knife and came at Madeline, who pointed the gun at him.

"Drop the knife. Now!"

The command had no effect. Madeline's mind flashed to the memory of the last time she had shot and killed someone. A man who had tried to help her. Her hands shook.

"Shoot him!" Mira cried out. "Like you shot Ahmed! Go ahead. Shoot!" Madeline's arms fell to her side, the gun clanking onto the concrete.

"I knew you couldn't do it," Mira said. "I was counting on that."

Joe picked up the gun and pointed it at Eliot's head. "Get up, you son of a bitch!" Eliot and Luke got to their feet. Luke went to recover the other gun.

"I'd like to finish this one right now, boss," he said to Mira.

"Easy, Joe." Mira glanced at Madeline. "That's a privilege I've been saving for myself. A long, slow, enjoyable one."

From the opposite direction, two black SUVS came speeding up the street. The cars stopped suddenly at the corner. Six men threw open the doors and jumped out with drawn guns. They wore black flack vests, with ATF emblazoned in bold yellow letters on the front. They were no more than a block away.

"ATF!" Mira shouted. "We've got to get out of here."

"I'm not running!" Joe cried, as he fired at the oncoming agents, who quickly took cover behind nearby trees.

Luke ran and was shot in the back. Joe ran towards the agents, firing his gun. He too fell. The agents advanced.

Mira threw herself to the ground. Madeline and Eliot did the same and crawled as fast as they could in the direction of the Range Rover. They hurried to their feet, keeping low as they got to the car. Bullets flew past them as they flung open the car doors and jumped in. Eliot started the car and revved the engine. He slammed his foot on the throttle and made a U turn up a one-way street in the wrong direction.

As they roared up the street, two cars were coming straight at them. With horns blaring, the first one swerved to the left and struck the curb. The second spun into a turn, directly in Eliot's path. Grasping the wheel, Eliot threw the SUV into a hard turn. It slid into a circle and the engine stalled.

Eliot got it started again and turned to Madeline. "If we can get to the levee, we can lose them. I know a place where the levee drops down. They'd never see us."

Madeline looked out the back window. "How far?"

Eliot gunned the engine. "Five minutes."

Madeline let out a breath. "Make it three."

Eliot grinned. "I'll try."

As they sped towards the levee, Eliot watched the rear-view mirror. Madeline never took her eyes off the rear window. No sign of any SUV. As they roared up the ramp that led to the levee, their car smashed onto the dirt road, jolting them in their seats.

They neared the hiding place. Eliot could just make out the narrow footpath that led down the levee, barely visible from the road. They heard a siren, and both looked out the back.

"I can't see them," Madeline said. "Can you?"

"No. They must be coming up the ramp. But we're almost there."

As they got to the path, Eliot had to slow down. The path was too narrow for an ordinary car, but Eliot knew the Rover could handle it. As they drove down the path, the SUV lurched forward, rocking side to side.

At the bottom of the trail, a cove was carved out in the levee, big enough to conceal a car. Eliot swung the SUV into the enclosure and turned off the engine. Moments later, they heard the siren screeching past them up above.

Would the ATF return? Having found nothing, would they retrace their steps? Would they come back and slowly examine the levee, and worse, would they see the Rover's tire tracks, dug into the footpath?

After several minutes, Eliot opened the SUV door. "I'm going to crawl up there and see if I can see anything."

Madeline grasped his arm. "OK, but be careful."

He smiled as he touched her cheek. "What? You're worried about an old veteran like me? You know how many times I had to crawl through dirt in Kandahar?"

"Me too," she said. "But we had an army behind us then."

Eliot ascended the embankment. At the top, he raised his head just enough to see the road. The black SUV was coming back. Eliot ducked his head as the car passed by.

They waited several minutes before going back up onto the levee.

Back at their house, Madeline sat down at the kitchen table. She hung her head. "They'll be back, you know."

Eliot rubbed the back of his neck. "I know."

Madeline looked out the front window, staring at the levee. "And they'll probably bring the FBI with them. Then we'll have all of them after us."

Eliot took Madeline into his arms. They were desperate to somehow make themselves safe.

She pulled away. "But there's something even worse than all those agents."

He took her hand. "What do you mean?"

She looked away. "Her."

Eliot shrugged. "No. She was either arrested or killed with the others."

Madeline shook her head. "You don't know her. With Mira, anything is possible. She knows how to survive, and she always told me that she had a *long arm*."

Eliot stared at her. "What's that supposed to mean?"

Madeline folded her arms and walked around the room. "She always said that wherever she was in the world, she knew some crooked official she could reach out to. That was her big advantage. One that's built into every government, and she knew it. If she couldn't buy them, she'd blackmail them. She knew of so many dirty deals she could uncover that would make any government nervous." Madeline turned to Eliot. "We've got to get out of this country."

CHAPTER 6

MIRA'S POWER

I won't be here for long. Not after that phone call they let me make. I won't even make the news. Some people would be too uncomfortable to see my name splashed in the headlines.

Eliot might think I'm dead or locked up for life. But not Madeline. That's all right. They'll be time for her. Time for both.

Such amateurs! They may know a lot about war, but they don't know the world. What *really* makes it turn.

All these Americans are naïve, growing up in their cozy little country under the rule of law. What a luxury! In Lebanon, for centuries, law has belonged to those most capable of cruelty, or better yet, corruption.

Take this cell for example. The walls are clean and unmarked. The bed is comfortable enough and the toilet works. There's even decent ventilation and what's more, a window!

In the jails I've seen or been in, the walls were either covered in decayed filth, or smeared with scratched out messages, all of them pleading for help that would never come. The beds were broken and covered with lice. The toilets were backed up to overflowing, human waste seeping onto the floors. Often enough, men and women were packed in together, all of them going insane.

Now, as I look about my pristine surroundings, I can't help feeling that what these Americans need is a good invasion.

I don't care what pathetic family backgrounds Madeline, and her lover had to grow up with. They never had their front door kicked down in the middle of the night. They never saw people dragged out of the house, never to be seen again.

Madeline. She always came sniveling to me about her precious little brother. When I was born, Israel was invading Lebanon for the *second* time! When I was a child, much younger than Madeline's brother, I saw the aftermath of the Israeli withdrawal. Dead bodies strewn in the streets, hauled away in makeshift carts.

Always it has been the same. When my grandmother was born, French colonization finally ended. Colonization? Imperialism is the proper word! And *then* what happened? Civil war. The vacuum that inevitably falls on a country once the conquerors have left.

That was nothing. My mother told me the stories of *her* childhood when she had to witness the Palestinians using Lebanon as a base to attack Israel. And after that? More civil war.

By the time I was fourteen all my family were dead, and I was alone on the street. I had to survive any way I could. First with petty theft, then later learning how to steal and sell on the black market. Little by little I got better at it, selling the small arms left behind by the Israelis and Hezbollah. I even had a crew working for me.

Then the big boon came. The fall of Gaddafi. Another vacuum. Only *this* time I would use that vacuum to my advantage. My crew and I rushed to Libya. There were tons of weapons left unguarded in warehouses, many in their original packaging. The locals rampaged through the stores, gathering up whatever they could carry, but they didn't know what they were doing.

My crew and I were quick to organize, crate and move the best arms outside the city. We set up storage places in abandoned earthen homes, spaced far enough apart to not arouse suspicion.

Of course, we always had to worry about rebels, armed militias, and assorted crazies, anxious to steal our wares. But I soon developed relationships with corrupt politicians, one of whom had far-reaching contacts. Before long I was shipping guns to Sierra Leone, Mogadishu, and Liberia.

I never went back to Lebanon. The smell of death will never leave its air. *But*, Ms. Madeline, I am still Lebanese, and we have long memories. We know how to extract revenge from rubble.

Why did I have to pick you up on the road that day? If I had known the agony you were going to cause me, the *longing*, I would have let Rami shoot you, even though I know Ahmed would have stopped him.

I wouldn't have even been in Afghanistan, if it weren't for that deal. That warlord was willing to pay three times what those AK-47s were worth. I accuse myself of greed.

All my other deals were either done in my warehouses in Tripoli, or best yet, over the phone. So much more convenient and a lot less dangerous. But the warlord was old school. He wanted to see the face of the person he was dealing with. That son of a bitch recruited from locals, Afghan army deserters, and illegal mercenaries, of which your lovely Eliot was a part, I might add. The warlord didn't care about Americans or Taliban. He only wanted to protect his turf, and I was the idiot that went over there to help him.

Ahmed was the first one who saw you that day on the road. It would be Ahmed. Like you, he was always looking out for the lost, the fool. We were rumbling along in our Land Cruiser over a bombed-out highway. I was in the back with a few of the empty green crates left over from the deal. Rami was smoking and singing some crazy song to himself as Ahmed did the driving.

When Ahmed saw you in the ditch below us dragging yourself along in torn fatigues and a battered cap, he brought the car to an uncomfortable halt.

Ahmed turned to Rami. "Who is that down there? Is that a man or a woman?"

Rami and I looked out and immediately recognized the US army fatigues, bedraggled as they were.

Rami sneered. "American. Probably deserter. Let the Americans deal with it. C'mon, let's go."

And that may very well have been the end of it if you hadn't looked up at me with those black oval eyes. Your legs had gone as far as they could go. Your whole body teetered, about to collapse. And even with the dazed and disoriented expression on your face, those obsidian eyes had survived.

What was I doing being spellbound by a dirty deserter with mud caked on her face? It was those eyes. Those eyes could survive death.

Then, as your head fell forward from exhaustion, your cap fell to the ground and your long black hair cascaded onto your shoulders.

Ahmed cried out. "It's a woman! See?"

Rami shook his head. "So, what? The Americans are probably after her right now. Let's get out of here!"

Ahmed appeared hypnotized. "She looks so alone. So desperate."

And so beautiful, I thought to myself. *Damn her!*

I turned to Ahmed. "Help me get her into the car."

Rami slapped his forehead. "Boss, are you crazy? She'll get us all in trouble."

As Ahmed and I descended into the ditch and Rami paced the road, you fell face forward into the dirt. When Ahmed picked you up you collapsed into my arms. Your body. Your body so weak and barely alive still possessed a power I had never known. Even in its trembling and tiny tremors, your limbs clung to me as if they'd been waiting to unite with my soul.

Why did you have to be a woman? I never wanted one before. Why couldn't you have been a man? Men are so much easier to control. I'd had plenty of pretty boys that I could use and dispense with on a whim.

You were the only human being that I ever allowed myself to love, after I'd lost all my loved ones. And what did you ever give me in return? Nothing but a yearning that only led to desperation. Even after I saved your life twice you turned away from my touch.

Shouldn't you be sent to the hell of the ungrateful after all that? Not if you could continue to torture me.

"Let me take her," Ahmed said to me.

It was a good thing he did. Another minute holding your body would have been too much for me.

Ahmed lifted you up with his powerful arms. He cradled you like a child being carried off to bed. I was glad now that he kept his black hair and beard cut short. Otherwise, those soft eyes of his would shine through. He had too much heart. A dangerous thing in my business, especially in negotiations.

If Rami had a heart, he wasn't interested in using it. The only problem was keeping him under control.

When we got back up on the road, Rami was standing there with his fists on his hips. "This is the stupidest thing...".

"Shut up!" I yelled at him. "Help Ahmed lay her down in the back."

Reluctantly, Rami helped to push your legs inside. Your body was so limp I was afraid you were already dead.

Rami stood back and pulled the pistol from the holster on his waist. "Why don't you just let me finish her off boss? She'll be dead before we get out of here."

"Put that piece back where it belongs," I shouted at him. "Or I'll use mine on you!"

Grumbling to himself, Rami got in the car. While Ahmed drove us down the road, I got all the water, and Gatorade I could find. We always carried plenty. You tried to drink all of it.

As you laid on the floor of the truck, your body trembling, I kneeled next to you. I lifted the back of your head, careful to give you only one sip of liquid at a time. That method didn't last long.

From a strength I didn't think possible from one nearly dead, you grabbed my wrist and forced the bottle to your mouth, taking in gulps so massive, the liquid flowed over your face and neck. It took all the strength *I* had to restrain you.

An hour later you were doing well enough for me to give you a Powerbar. You were even able to sit up. Taking in a deep breath and letting it out, you drew in your legs and wrapped your arms around them.

Ahmed looked back at you. "How are you feeling... better now?"

You lowered your head to your knees. "Yes, much better. Thank you."

I let some time pass before I asked you the inevitable question.

"What are you doing out here?"

Rami looked back. "I told you, she's…".

I glared back at him. "Keep your eyes on the road, idiot. We don't know whose out there."

Despite the interruption, my question still dangled in the air. You shook your head and wiped away some moisture from the corner of your eye. *Good,* I thought to myself. *We've got water in her. But were those tears I saw?*

Then, you had to see the empty gun crates next to me. The ones left over from the deal.

You looked back to me. "Aren't those for AK-47s?"

There was no point in lying.

"Yes," I said. "Yes, they are."

Your eyes narrowed. "You're selling guns out here? To who?"

Time to try a little subterfuge. "There's a man out here who's trying to protect some of the surrounding villages. He gets help from some of the locals, a few Afghan army deserters…"

You stopped me in mid-sentence. "So, he's a warlord, right?"

Rami looked back at me. "You forgot to tell her about the mercenaries the warlord hired."

Ahmed gave Rami a sharp punch to the shoulder. "Let them talk. Watch the road!"

"Yes!" I barked at Rami. "Keep your eyes on the windshield. They warned us about random checkpoints, remember?"

I came up with a rationalization that I thought just might work on you, hoping it wouldn't backfire on me. "You've seen how bad it is out here for these people. The warlord isn't Taliban. He just wants to protect his own. Isn't that what the United States is doing here? Trying to protect the most vulnerable?"

My words had a greater impact than I thought they would. That moisture came back to the corner of your eye, only this time, it managed to trickle down your cheek before you wiped it away.

Now that I had you in a softened state, I decided to strengthen my position with a recent event that I never thought would come in handy, until now.

I leaned in a little closer to you. "Rami was talking about mercenaries. Yes, the warlord has hired quite a few and they're not like the legal contractors I'm sure you've seen over here. You may think the so-called soldiers of fortune are the wreckage of the world, but don't think too harshly of the renegade. One of them saved my life last night. A sniper had me in his sights and this one mercenary shot him dead before I was the one face down on the ground."

You shook your head. "I didn't think those guys wanted to protect anything but the money they made off war."

I leaned back in my seat. "Sometimes war can make strange heroes."

That had an even greater impact on you. You stared out the window at the desert going past us, lost in some dark memory. I let you linger there for a while before I spoke again.

"What's your name?"

That seemed to bring you out of your self-imposed spell. You looked up at me.

"Madeline."

I smiled. "Pretty. Mine's Mira. I think you know our friends in the front seat. Our driver today is Ahmed. He works for me to take care of his little brother. That other one, Rami, works for me to prove how crazy he is to the rest of the world."

Ahmed gave Rami a playful shove. "You see how well the boss knows you?"

Rami laughed and went back to singing one of his crazy songs. Then, for the first time that day, I saw your smile. It was glorious. You went forward, putting your hand on the back of Ahmed's seat.

"What's your brother's name?" you asked him.

Ahmed grinned, happy to hear you were interested. "Muhammad. It means praised one."

I'd barely had time to breath in the beauty of your smile when Rami suddenly jumped forward in his seat. "Hey, who are those guys up there?"

Ahmed quickly scanned the windshield. "Where? I don't see them."

Rami pointed to the left. "Right there!"

Two men stood on the side of the road, glaring at us. They were about twenty meters away. The nearest one was thickset, wearing a black turban and a camo jacket. His long black beard was thick and unkempt. The second man was tall and lean, wearing a gray cloak that covered his head and most of his body. His full beard was barely visible.

Both men walked towards us, their pace quickening as they drew nearer.

"Slow down," I said to Ahmed. "They might be…"

"They're Taliban!" you shouted.

The thickset man reached into his jacket. The slim one put his hand under his cloak.

"Turn around!" I yelled at Ahmed.

"No!" you screamed at me.

As Ahmed quickly turned the car you lurched forward, grabbed Rami's pistol out of its holster, threw open the side door and jumped out, all with the car still moving. You fired a shot into the air and another at the feet of the oncoming Taliban. They froze in their places. You shouted something at them which I assumed was Pashto, the local language. Whatever it was, they withdrew their handguns from their clothing and laid them on the ground.

Then you motioned to them to go back down the road. As they retreated, the thickset one looked back at you, mumbling something that I could only assume was a harsh obscenity. You fired a round over his head and both men took off running.

When you got back in the car Ahmed stared at you in awestruck admiration. "You are a brave fighter. Never have I seen such courage."

Rami was not so complimentary. "Not bad for a deserter. Now give me back my gun!"

You grinned and politely handed it over. That's what impressed me the most. As fast as all of it had happened, you were able to quickly summon self-control. I knew then that I could certainly use someone like you.

CHAPTER 7

ESCAPE

They had to get the Range Rover out of sight. Eliot put it in the garage and locked the door. Then he went to the side of the house and disconnected the power line they'd been using to pilfer electricity. When he joined Madeline in the house, she'd already closed all the windows and drawn the curtains.

Eliot looked around at the darkened room. "So much for the easy part. There's something else we've got to take care of soon. We need food. I'll go down there tonight, just before Tom closes the store."

Madeline rubbed her forehead. "And in the meantime, we'll have to live here like a couple of church mice."

He put his arms around her. "This is a good way to keep quiet."

She held him more closely.

That night, as Eliot walked down to the store, he was glad it was August now with the sun fading faster below the levee. The weeds next to him still held the heat of the day, mixing with the cool moisture of the earth below. The aroma filled his nostrils, reminding him of a landscape he'd desperately tried to suppress.

But then the stones beneath his feet stirred with the dry dirt, creating plumes of dust large enough to make memory reappear.

Eliot remembered now the morning he had awakened, after he had abandoned Will and shot an innocent Afghan villager. The guilt he felt in this very moment was as real, as grave, as if it was happening now. He could see it all. *Feel it all.*

He could see Will wildly firing his rifle in every direction, shouting the word "Kill" repeatedly. He saw himself trying to tear the gun away from Will, and in so doing, he had shot an unarmed man who had meant him no harm.

Eliot had wondered and worried as he had stood near the stream where he had cleaned his wounds, next to the cave where he had hidden himself from the soldiers pursuing him. Who was the man he had shot? What was his name? Did he have a family? Was he *alive*!

Now, as Eliot kicked beneath his feet the stones that had fallen from the levee road, he knew the answer. He was dead. And Eliot was the man who had killed him. What would that villager's life had been like if Eliot had not tried uselessly to save Will?

Strange, Eliot thought to himself. *Everything else in human memory can fade away, but guilt can survive anything.* He felt that guilt now like an icepick, being pushed and twisted into his flesh. He felt the instrument's sharpened point insidiously seeking new caverns of muscle, veins, any untouched part in which to create new agony.

Eliot looked down at his feet and vividly recalled that day by the stream. In his rush to save Will, he had run barefoot from the barracks. What good was a soldier without boots? What good was he to anyone now?

With his dirty athletic shoe, Eliot pushed aside a rock and dug into the soil. From beneath, an insect scrambled from the hole, seeking a new place in which to shelter.

Shelter. There had been none that day, as he stood barefoot, in a torn T-shirt. His camo pants had survived. They could survive anything, but his naked feet could not. Summoning his senses, he had recalled his survival training. He had quickly fashioned shoes from leaves and brush, binding it all together with soft branches.

Two days later, weakened by hunger and remorse, Eliot came to a mercenary encampment at the base of a mountain. Forty or so men were milling around, some of them hovered over a dice game being played in the dirt. Eliot had fought alongside private military contractors in the past. They comprised almost a quarter of all US fighting forces. They had significant military experience, many in America's Special Forces. Some were even former officers.

That was one kind of mercenary. Concealed behind a group of trees, Eliot immediately knew he had stumbled upon the other kind. He had heard about them and sometimes seen them. They worked for warlords who wanted only to protect their turf, whether it be against US forces or the Taliban. The warlord paid for his hired soldiers with money earned from the highly lucrative opium trade.

When word got out around the world that that kind of money was readily available, it immediately summoned the dredges of the mercenary world. Men who had been expelled from their own country's armies for insubordination and ruthless actions, immediately appeared, willing to fight anybody's war for a high price.

Eliot scanned the menagerie of men before him. Unlike the private military contractors, he had known in their clean black T-shirts, khaki pants and flak vests, these men had bandoliers that hung over their shoulders or crisscrossed on their bodies, filled with ammunition. They all had AK47's held loosely at their sides.

The British and Australian fighters wore military style shirts, the chest pockets and shoulder epaulets worn thin. Colombians had camo bandanas tied tightly around their heads, black sunglasses covering their eyes. Local Afghans dressed in the traditional long flowing vests and pants, their cloth tattered and patched.

Eliot knew it was his only chance. Without food and water, he would die. Then a fight broke out. Two of the dice players in the dirt lunged at each other. One reached for his pistol, the other pulled out a knife. The throng around them jumped on both men. Bodies collided and scrambled on the ground.

A thin Australian with a long red beard fired a shot into the earth. All the combatants froze. Muttering obscenities in several languages, they pulled themselves apart.

As the Australian watched them drift away, careful to be sure hostilities were over, his keen eye caught sight of Eliot. "Hello, who's this then?"

Eliot had no choice but to emerge from hiding.

The Australian looked him over. "What happened to you, mate? Looks like you been in the outback!"

A stocky Englishman with a clean-shaven face spoke up next. "Judging by what's left of his uniform, I'd say he's lost his way."

The Australian grinned. "Deserter, more like."

The men who moments before were at each other's throats, laughed at Eliot's shredded undershirt and ripped camo pants.

Someone speaking Spanish snickered at Eliot's sandals. "Mira sus zapatos." Look at his shoes.

The Afghans shook their heads and laughed along with the rest.

The Australian put his hand on Eliot's shoulder. "You came along at just the right time. The boys needed a good laugh after mixing it up a bit."

Then all the laughter instantly stopped. The crowd of men began to part as a large man emerged through their ranks. He wore a black turban, scuffed with dirt. A long gray scarf over his face revealed only his black eyes. Deep set, they narrowed on Eliot, looking him up and down. The man slid his scarf down, showing a stubbled beard. On his right cheek he bore a scar. He raised his hand, motioning to someone behind him.

A skinny Afghan rushed to his side. The two men spoke to each other in Pashto. The only word Eliot could discern was "American".

The thin Afghan turned to Eliot. "This is Awalmir. He is the warlord here. Even his name speaks of his power. It means one capable of being a great leader. He has what we call *Nafuz*, that means he has high tribal rank and command of many followers. He wants to know what you want here."

Eliot looked at Awalmir. "I need food and water…I can fight."

The Afghan translated Eliot's words. Awalmir paused for a moment, a grim look on his face. Then he called out to a short, stocky Afghan who was lounging on the ground. This Afghan shook his head in disgust. Awalmir called out again, this time his deep voice booming so loudly that the others seemed to freeze in place.

The stocky man jumped to his feet, fetched food and water and brought them forward. Awalmir gave him a hard punch to the jaw, and the man fell to the ground, the food and water falling from his arms. Awalmir stood over him and kicked him again and again. The man cowered and crawled away.

Awalmir looked at Eliot. The warlord's black eyes seemed to the American twice as sinister when enraged.

The skinny Afghan turned to Eliot. "Awalmir wants you to know that this is what happens to those who disobey." He gathered up the fallen food and water and gave them to Eliot.

After Eliot had gulped down all he was given, he sat down on a boulder. The Australian and Englishman sat down near him. The Australian spoke first.

"I'm Nick and this here is James. How long you been in this country?"

Eliot wiped food away from his mouth. "Two tours."

James spoke up next. "So, you been in a lot of engagements?"

Eliot looked away. "Yeah, a lot. I didn't mean to go AWOL. I was trying to..."

Nick held up his hand. "The boss doesn't want to know what you did. He only wants to know if you can fight and fight hard. We don't ask each other questions around here. Right, James?"

James nodded. "You've seen how Awalmir is. He's all right as long as you do your job, but he's got one rule that nobody wants to break. The rule we all must live by. You either finish the mission and get paid, or you end up dead. Nobody deserts. Understand?"

Eliot looked at both men. "Understood."

In the following weeks, Eliot fought in skirmishes against other warlords who were seeking to increase their territory. He never stopped thinking about Will. Had anyone found him? Was he alive? He wanted to call the base, but even with all the burner phones in camp it was too dangerous. The army wouldn't give out any information anyway. He still remembered Will's family's phone in the U.S. Maybe if he called them…

The next morning, disguising his voice, he was able to call the Madsen home. Mr. Madsen picked up the phone.

"Hello," Eliot said. "I'm trying to reach Will."

There was a pause on the other end of the phone before Mr. Madsen spoke.

"Who's calling, please?"

Eliot heard Will's mother in the background. "Who is it, honey?"

"Somebody asking for Will."

"Don't they know he's in the VA hospital?"

Eliot hung up.

Thank God! Eliot thought to himself. *He's alive. They finally sent him home. I've got to get home.*

He would need a passport. That would mean dealing in a grim business, but it was the only way. A Russian in camp dealt in dead men's passports. Every time someone got killed, Anatoly was the first man on the spot, rifling through pockets until he found what he wanted.

Even the other mercenaries were disgusted by Anatoly's practices, although they always looked the other way, knowing that one day they might need his services.

One night, Eliot took Anatoly aside. "I need a passport. I can pay."

Anatoly stroked his full brown beard. "How much you can pay?"

"If what you've got is good enough, I can give you a thousand."

Anatoly laughed. "Come on, American! I know you earn more than that already. You give me three thousand!"

Eliot shook his head. "Show me what you've got and then we'll talk about price."

They went to Anatoly's tent. From a backpack, Anatoly pulled out a dirty cloth sack. He opened the drawstrings and dumped dozens of passports onto his sleeping bag.

The Russian pushed back his long hair. "Let me find one looks like you."

Eliot stood back in horror. He'd seen much of it in war, but this was picking at the bones of the dead. Vultures did it to survive. This was done out of the worst kind of scavenging.

As Anatoly quickly flapped open and closed passport after passport, Eliot tried to concentrate on Will. *This is all for Will,* he thought to himself, as his hands gripped into fists.

"Ah!" Anatoly suddenly cried out. "Here is! Canadian. Except for glasses, look just like you!"

He handed the passport to Eliot. Anatoly was right. The resemblance was good. Even the height and weight were close. The man's name was Robert Campbell. Despite himself, Eliot couldn't help thinking about Robert's life. What had happened to him? What were his plans? Who were his people?

"I'll give you fifteen hundred, Anatoly. No more."

Anatoly grinned. "You give me two thousand. No less."

Eliot paused. It wasn't the money; it was the risk. Anatoly's gregarious nature, not to mention his natural deviousness, was well known in the camp. If anyone got wind of this transaction, Eliot knew he'd be dead. He had to take the chance. There was no other way.

"All right, two thousand. But you've got to keep your mouth shut about this."

Anatoly smiled. "Of course. Just between you and me."

Eliot grabbed Anatoly's shoulder. "That's right! No one else!"

A few nights later, Eliot warmed his hands at a campfire. Nick and James sat nearby. They were uncommonly quiet, looking to each other and then at Eliot.

Nick narrowed his eyes on Eliot. "You're not thinking of leaving us, are you, mate?"

Damn Anatoly! Eliot thought to himself. "What makes you think that?"

James smirked. "We've been hearing some things."

Eliot turned a log in the fire. "Just thinking about the future, when the mission's over."

Nick leaned in closer. "Right. When it's over and we're paid or dead."

Eliot had to move fast. He knew the mercenary camp was roughly thirty miles north of Kabul International Airport. He also knew he could run into Taliban patrols anywhere along the way. If he made it to Kabul, he still had to worry about the large US military presence at the airport, military that were actively looking for him.

The next night it was Eliot's turn to stand watch. Before he went out, he ran a quick checklist through his mind. He'd put enough food and water in his backpack to make the trek. He'd picked up a pair of wire-rimmed glasses from an Afghan in camp. He'd need those if he was going to look like Robert Campbell's photo in the passport. He put the glasses, passport and his money into a waistband pack.

He had his AK47 over his shoulder and his Belgian Hi-Power pistol in his shoulder holster. As he patrolled the camp, he could see the men were all asleep. Nick and James snored along with the rest.

Trying not to make a sound, Eliot slipped away. Then a bullet flew past his head so near, he felt the wind rush behind it. He ran. Nick and James ran behind him, shouting obscenities. James tripped on a rock and fell against a boulder. Nick turned back to help him. Eliot had just enough time to disappear into the darkness.

He ran as fast as he could through a thickly forested area. A large branch he couldn't see smacked his face and threw him to the ground. He got to his feet and wiped blood away from his cheek.

Ahead, the forest opened to a vast field of broken-up boulders, piled high on top of each other. He'd have to scale them. Then the beams of high-powered flashlights scanned over the rocks. He heard a loud, angry voice shouting out in the darkness. Awalmir.

The warlord's voice continued to roar as Eliot leapt over the rocks and bullets ricocheted on the sandstone. He neared the summit... almost there. A sharpened edge pierced his left hand. He lost his balance and smashed against a boulder. His pursuers were only yards away. He sprung to his feet and reached the top. On the other side the sandstone was a smooth face that led almost straight down to a ravine that was covered in brush.

Turning sidewise to slow himself down, he felt his backpack tearing loose from his shoulder and tumbling away. He crashed into the brush. Broken branches ripped at his arms and legs. He saw a stream thirty feet away. As he jumped in, bullets from above pierced the water around him.

He swam underwater, as the AK47, crisscrossed on his body, tugged and pulled him back. That and his pistol were his only defense. He couldn't abandon it.

After several minutes, he swam into a cove that was sheltered by overhanging rocks. He looked up at the cliffs above him. No sign of the mercenaries. He swam up to shore, got to his feet, and accessed his injuries. A deep gash crossed the palm of his hand. He realized the sand beneath his feet could act as a healing agent. He rubbed his palm in the sand, tore off part of his T-shirt and wrapped it tightly around his hand.

He felt his cheek, which had collided with a tree branch. The bleeding had stopped. His arms were covered with long scratches and bruises, but none of them serious.

He pulled off his waistband pack and checked the contents. Passport damp, but not wet. Money OK. Wire rimmed glasses bent but could be straightened. But he had lost the backpack and recalled now how it had flown from him as he had slid down the rock face. If he was going to trek thirty miles to the airport, he would need food and water.

He knew there were villages in the area, but he had no idea which ones were Taliban controlled. Would *any* village be friendly to an armed American? He had to try. Over scrub and petrified chunks of timber, he climbed up to a dirt road.

A few miles later, he saw a small village spread out in a valley. In the moonlight, he could clearly see the dozen or so mud brick homes, their flat rooves of mud and straw compressed on top. There was not a single candle burning in a window.

The he heard voices in the forest above him. Six heavily armed men emerged from the trees. Taliban. Eliot climbed back down the embankment and laid flat against it. He could see the Taliban surveying the surrounding area, one of them pointing to the village. The others descended to the road. If they looked down to the stream, Eliot knew he'd be spotted. He slid the pistol out of its holster.

One of the Taliban seemed to be arguing with another. Their voices grew louder as they stomped back and forth, gesturing at each other with clear anger. They were only a few feet away.

The argument continued as Eliot clung to the embankment, pistol in hand. He looked up, but could only see the Taliban's legs, scuffling on the dirt road. Then a louder voice arose. All grew silent, and the silence persisted. Eliot grimaced. *How long can this go on?*

Finally, the Taliban shuffled away, and Eliot crawled up to the road. They were going back up into the forest, walking away from the village. Seeing his opportunity, Eliot got to his feet and walked down toward the village. He kept down and crept around the low wall that surrounded the compound. He saw the village's water well ahead of him. If he could pull the pail up, he'd have water. But what about food?

He crept up to the well and slowly lifted the pail. A small group of goats nearby, roused by his presence, began bleating, the bells around their necks clanking in the darkness.

The timbered door of a house opened. A tall Afghan man with a black beard, speckled with gray, stood in the doorway. He wore a long flowing Khet partug tunic with his flat Kufi cap slanted to the side. He pointed an M14 rifle straight at Eliot.

Eliot knew that surrender was his only choice. He held up his hands. Using the muzzle of his rifle, the Afghan pointed to Eliot's rifle and pistol. Carefully, Eliot removed the rifle and laid it on the ground. Using only his thumb and index finger, he slowly did the same with the pistol. Then he rose and held up his hands again.

The Afghan looked Eliot up and down. He saw Eliot's left hand, wrapped in its improvised bandage. He scanned the numerous cuts and bruises on Eliot's arms, the dried blood on his cheek. The Afghan lowered his rifle, an actual look of pity in his eyes.

He waved at Eliot to lower his arms. Then he pointed to the open door. As Eliot was about to cross over the threshold, he saw two burnt out houses farther away. He hadn't noticed them before. He looked to the Afghan, who spoke his first word.

"Taliban."

Eliot lowered his head in reverence, a gesture that did not go unnoticed by the Afghan. As Eliot went inside the house, the Afghan retrieved the weapons from the ground and followed him in. He took the guns to another room and came back holding a clean white cloth and water in a clay bowel. He motioned for Eliot to sit down on a low couch in the corner of the room. The Afghan knelt, dipped the cloth in water and gently cleaned Eliot's wounds. Then he rose, went to another room and came back with food and water.

Eliot quickly consumed the rice and curry. Then he ate three pieces of naan, the baked flat bread. When he was done eating, the Afghan handed him a cup of tea.

If only I could speak his language, Eliot thought. *Even if it was only to say thank you.*

Desperate, Eliot pointed to himself. "Eliot."

The Afghan smiled and did the same. "Aakrama." Then he placed his hand over his heart and said: "As-Salaam Alaikum." Peace be upon you.

Eliot breathed a sigh of relief. From two tours in Afghanistan, he had at least learned the correct response. He put his hand to his heart. "Wa-Alaikum Salaam." Unto you be peace.

Aakrama eased Eliot down onto the couch and propped a pillow under his head. Before Eliot fell asleep, he looked around the room. He wanted to remember it. There were faded tapestries on the walls, their yarn beginning to unravel. On the floor, small rugs crisscrossed each other, their once intricate patterns of blue, red, and gold, worn away by years of foot traffic. This was the place where a man who had every reason to harm him, had instead given him shelter.

When dawn came Eliot was awakened by Aakrama's quick movements in the house. He brought Eliot's weapons into the room along with a waterskin and a pouch. Eliot knew what this meant. The village would soon awaken, and its other inhabitants may not be so welcoming.

Eliot got to his feet, took the guns and provisions from Aakrama, and they headed for the door. Then they heard water being drawn from the well. They went to a window and saw a woman covered from head to foot in a black burqa, yanking on the rope that brought up the pail. They hadn't moved fast enough.

The woman poured the water from the pail into an orange plastic container, normally used for gasoline. She walked away, tugging on her heavy burden.

They had to move now. They looked at each other, their eyes saying the words that could not be spoken. Gratitude. Kindness.

Aakrama threw open the door and they rushed out. Out of nowhere, another villager appeared. He looked like a village elder with his snow-white beard and heavily creased forehead. Seeing Eliot, he cried out to the other houses.

Aakrama pushed Eliot to go. Village men bolted from their houses and ran to the scene. Eliot's mind reeled. *How can I leave him like this? What will happen to him?"*

Aakrama gave Eliot a hard shove. Eliot ran to the forest. Looking over his shoulder, he saw the village men surround Aakrama in a tight circle. In the center, the village elder and Aakrama shouted at each other.

Eliot ran through the trees until he was nearly a mile away. He looked back to see if anyone had pursued him.

No sign. He sat down on a rock to catch his breath. He thought of the other friend he had abandoned...Will. Eliot knew then that of all the wounds of war, remorse was the worst.

To clear his mind, he drank from the waterskin. He opened the pouch Aakrama had given him. Inside he found Dhal, the dried lentils, as well as dried beans. Buried deep in the pouch, he pulled out a white tunic shirt with long sleeves. Tears formed in Eliot's eyes as he looked at his shredded T-shirt. Aakrama had thought of everything.

Eliot kept to the woods. He knew if he ran into any Taliban, he could hide among trees or brush. He walked quickly, keeping up a steady pace. He guessed that at the rate he was going he should be able to make the airport by late afternoon. He ate and drank as he walked, not wanting to lose any time.

Hours later, he saw Kabul International Airport, spread out on a wide plain, surrounded by mountains, capped with snow. There was a block long two-story departure lounge connected to a five-story control tower. At the tower's top the command center was circled by tall, slanted windows with intricate antenna systems on its roof.

All of it was overshadowed by the existence of ISAF, The International Security Assistance Force, of which the US Army was a large part. The Joint Command consisted of many nations, Canada, the UK, France, Germany, all their flags flying in front of the Joint Command Headquarters building.

The sprawling camp was encircled by row after row of hemisphere shaped barracks, their exterior walls nearly obscured by stacks of sandbags, piled almost to roof level.

Out on the numerous military runways, DC-3 cargo planes and C-17 troop carriers stood ready. Half a dozen helipads serviced Chinook and Black Hawk helicopters from the United States.

Soldiers and officers of every sort, dressed in camo uniforms, were everywhere, servicing aircraft and going in and out of the barracks. Others jogged together in groups or worked out with weights.

Eliot knew he had to stay as far away as possible from all that. First, he had to get rid of his weapons. He laid them on the ground and covered them with brush and leaves.

When he got inside the airport, he headed straight to the restroom to clean up. Then he went to one of the airport shops and bought a pair of khakis, tennis shoes, and a black baseball cap. He could have bought a shirt, but he couldn't part with the shirt Aakrama had given him. Even though he didn't have much else, he bought a carry-on bag to appear less conspicuous.

He went to the ticket counter and asked for the next flight to the United States. There wasn't one leaving for another three hours. He began noticing US servicemen in the area. Would any of them be booked on the same flight? Three hours was a long time to worry.

When he bought his ticket, the agent glanced at his passport and then handed it back. He'd overcome one hurdle, but he'd still have to go through customs before he boarded. They wouldn't be so nonchalant.

With his full beard, cap, and wire-rimmed glasses, he didn't look at all like any service photo customs might have had of him.

But as the customs agent looked over Eliot's passport, he paused and looked back up at Eliot. The agent was a small man with dark, penetrating eyes. He looked again at the passport photo and then back to Eliot. "Would you mind removing your cap and glasses, sir?"

Eliot tried to remain calm. "Of course not." He took off his cap and glasses and laid them on the counter.

The customs agent beckoned to a man behind him, a large man in an airport security uniform. The agent and security guard talked in soft voices to each other, glimpsing Eliot occasionally.

Have I come this far only to be captured now? Eliot thought to himself. He looked out on the runways and saw a plane taking off. *I only need one to take me back to Will. If I could see him one last time, know he was being taken care of, they could put me anywhere they want.*

The security guard shook his head and stepped away. The agent handed Eliot's passport back to him. "Have a pleasant flight, sir."

When Eliot walked into the departure lounge, he wanted a drink, a cigarette and a cup of coffee, all at the same time. But he knew he couldn't do it. He had to keep his head clear if he was going to get on a plane, and there were still army soldiers milling around in their combat uniforms.

In the lounge's long rows of black leather seats, he chose the aisle that faced the runways to remain less noticeable. He opened his carry-on, took out his cloth pouch and opened it. There were still a few dried lentils left. He chewed on them slowly, thinking of Aakrama…and Will.

A few hours later they called his flight. He went to the gate and passed the final ticket check without a problem. As he was about to enter the sky bridge that connected to his plane, he saw two soldiers off to one side. He recognized them. It was Johnson and Clayton, two men he'd served with in his first tour. Johnson narrowed his eyes on Eliot and nudged Clayton. Eliot knew it had been years since all three had served together, but you never forget a comrade, especially those with whom you've faced death.

Eliot walked fast through the sky bridge. Would they turn him in? Everybody knew what he'd done.

All the way back home, through every stop and long layover, Dubai, Boston, San Francisco, Eliot kept watching for military police. When he got off the plane in San Francisco and out of the terminal, he knew he'd made it. He grabbed the first cab he saw, got to the bus station and arrived in Sacramento.

Now, as he got to the Freeport Market, the "Closed" sign was hanging on the front door. Tom was at the register, counting out change. Eliot tapped on the window, and Tom rushed over to throw the door open.

"Jesus, Eliot! You're all over the news. What happened?"

"Tom, has anybody been by asking questions?"

"Yeah, a couple of guys this afternoon."

"ATF?"

"No, FBI. I didn't tell them anything, but I didn't like the looks on their faces."

"What did the news say?"

"All about a big joint-law enforcement effort to capture some illegal gun dealers and two army deserters. Two suspects were killed and two got away. A man and a woman."

"Did they say anything about another woman?"

"No. Nothing."

"I can't explain it all to you, Tom. The woman I'm with and I have got to get out of the country."

Tom shook his head. "That won't be easy."

Eliot ran his hand through his hair. "I know. We've got papers good enough, but no money."

Tom rubbed his cheek. "Have you got anything you could sell? I might be able to help you."

"All we've got is the Range Rover we took to get away. I've got it locked up in the garage."

"Wow! Those things are worth like a hundred grand."

Eliot gripped the counter. "A lot of good it's doing us."

Tom scratched his chin. "Wait a minute. There's a guy out here who's dealing in stolen cars. He tries to make it look like he's farming, but I know what he's up to. I think he'd jump at the chance to get his hands on that Rover."

Eliot leaned over the counter. "Yeah, but it's a big risk for you, getting mixed up with us like that. I don't want to see you get in trouble. You've done so much already for Madeline and I."

Tom grinned. "It was the least I could do."

Eliot blushed. "Tom, there's no way I can ever thank you, repay you…".

Tom gripped Eliot's arm. "We've known each other since we were ten. I know you'd do the same for me. Bring the car around back late tomorrow night."

Eliot got the groceries he and Madeline needed and headed back to the house.

Standing alone in the middle of a darkened living room, Madeline rubbed her hands up and down her folded arms. The evenings were getting cooler, sending a chill through her body as equally cold realities penetrated her brain.

How could they escape? Where would they go? What about John?

Eliot's entrance interrupted her dark reveries. "I've got some good news. Tom thinks he can sell the Range Rover for us."

"You're kidding!" Madeline helped Eliot with the groceries into the kitchen. "How much does he think we can get?"

"At least enough to get us out of the country, if they don't find us first."

Madeline set a grocery bag on the table. "What's Tom heard?"

Eliot looked at her. "It's all over the news. All about us and the guys that got killed and…".

"And nothing about Mira."

Eliot surveyed the groceries. The ordinary things of life; canned goods, vegetables, fruit. *Why can't our lives be as ordinary as that?* "No. Nothing about her."

They had dinner and went up to the bedroom. As they lay in bed, Madeline rolled over and wrapped her arm around his chest. She placed her cheek on his chest. She felt the slow steady murmurs of Eliot's heart coming one after the other. So deep and powerful, it seemed they could go on forever.

She sat up, rubbing her forehead as tears appeared in her eyes. "It's no good, Eliot. There are too many of them after us, even if we do get away. It's the end of the world."

He came forward and grasped her arms. "No. That could only happen if I could never hold you again."

She put her arms around him, her tears flowing onto his cheek. They laid back down on the bed. He turned and slid his arm around her shoulder. With his other hand, he cupped her cheek and brushed away her tears. His kiss came to her lips on a breath so soft, she barely felt the breeze behind it.

Then his fingers began to trace the landscape of her body. First, slipping down the length of her arm and then inward, shaping to the curve of her torso. Then over her breasts and going downward to her stomach, feeling the pulses of her firm muscles as they began to awaken. His hand curved towards her hip then rolled over her thigh before coming to rest on her pelvis. His fingertips touched her pubic hair and then rose back up the length of her body until they stroked her lips.

He placed himself over her and as they joined, she felt a union so complete that nothing from the past could ever overcome it.

Later, as she fell off to sleep, feeling she possessed a power stronger than any nightmare, the real nightmare… *that* nightmare…returned, vivid and alive. She saw it all as a helpless bystander would, forced to witness her agony and guilt once more.

She saw again the pregnant woman she had shot. She saw her lying on the ground, blood flowing from the chest wound Madeline had inflicted. She saw the woman's enlarged stomach tilting to one side, knowing that the embryo within her would certainly die with her mother. She couldn't see anymore!

Screaming, Madeline jolted up in bed, awakened from the nightmare. Suddenly awakened himself, Eliot was quick to put his arms around her. "What is it? What happened?"

Madeline covered her face with her hands as tears poured from her eyes. "I was there again…*that* night!"

He held her closer. "That wasn't your fault! You didn't mean to do it that!"

She pulled away from him, turning her face to the wall. "A mother…a child that never had a chance to live."

Eliot gripped her shoulders. "Anyone could have done it. Anything can happen in war. You know that."

He eased back down to the bed, holding Madeline until he fell asleep. She might have slept through the rest of the night with him, if it weren't for the memory of another she had killed. The man who had only wanted to be her friend…Ahmed.

The next night Eliot took the Range Rover down to Tom. A few days later, Eliot saw Tom pull up in the driveway and met him out front. When Eliot came back inside, Madeline was coming out of the kitchen.

"How'd we do?"

Eliot smiled. "A lot better than I thought. Enough to get away and more. Now the only question is, where do we go?"

Madeline rubbed her chin. "I've been thinking a lot about that. Let's go to Beirut."

Eliot seemed surprised. "What made you come up with that?"

Madeline went to the window and looked out on the levee, lost in a reverie. "When I was in Tripoli, I used to scan pictures of Beirut on the Internet. It was all so beautiful. They have a seaside promenade called the Corniche. It's lined with palm trees and views of the sea. In the city, there's lots of elegant cafes with fancy people playing backgammon."

Eliot shook his head. "Sounds like a dream."

Madeline turned away from the window and crossed her arms. "It took my mind off dirty gun dealing, but there's another good reason to go there. One that's even better. Mira."

Eliot put his hands on his hips. "What's she got to do with it?"

"Every time she'd see me looking at pictures of Beirut, she'd slam my laptop down and I know why. Lebanon has too many bad memories for her."

Eliot sat down in a chair. "OK, that sounds good, but we've got another problem. What about John?"

Madeline put her arm around him. "*And* Will."

Eliot leaned forward and rubbed his hands together.

"There's no way I could see him now. Especially now."

Madeline knelt next to him and placed her hand over his. "What happened to him wasn't *your* fault, either."

Eliot stood up and rubbed the back of his neck. "Yeah, but at least Will is getting care. John isn't."

Madeline got up and paced the room. "On my first tour in Afghanistan I sent letters to John in care of General Delivery. He was moving around a lot then and it was our only way to stay in contact with each other. He just might be checking with the post office now."

"Try it. Write him a letter tonight. It's worth a chance."

"Do you think we could send him some money too, Eliot? At least enough to get him started back at the Rehab Center?"

"Of course, we can. I'll mail the letter tomorrow in Freeport. Then I'll book a flight for us to Beirut. I'm sure Tom will let me use his phone. I'll have to reserve a cab to take us to the airport, too."

"Good. I don't want to stay here any longer. I'm more afraid of Mira finding us than the ATF or the FBI."

That night, on some of the yellowed stationary left behind by Eliot's parents, Madeline wrote the letter.

Dear Johnny,

I'm sorry I haven't reached you sooner, but this is the only way I can reach you now. You've probably read in the newspapers or seen on TV, what happened after that morning I saw you on South Side. Please believe me, Eliot and I, that's the man I'm with…wanted no violence. I only wanted to find you, to help you.

I'm sure the media has said terrible things about Eliot and me, but like me, Eliot is accused of something in the war in Afghanistan that he didn't do. Eliot is a good man, and we try to help each other, the same way you and I did when we were kids, remember? I'm sorry I couldn't stop Frank from hitting you, hurting you all the time. I just wasn't big enough, strong enough. I let you down, John. I could have grabbed a kitchen knife and stabbed Frank in the back. He had me too scared of him. I know I tried to help you later, but by then it was too late. I don't blame you for turning to drugs. My drug was war.

Eliot and I have got to get out of the country now. I've enclosed some money. Please, John, go back to the Rehab Center. I'll try to send more money later and always remember that I'll always be with you.

I love you,
Madeline

Two days later, when the cab arrived at the house in the early morning hours, Madeline and Eliot were ready.

They'd packed the few belongings they had into two suitcases they found in the attic. Madeline had stuffed her long black hair into the short brown wig she'd used to disguise her identity in her passport photo. Eliot had let his beard grow longer to match his picture, and he wore the same wire rimmed glasses that obscured his looks.

As the cab drove them away, Madeline caught a glimpse of herself and Eliot in the car's rearview mirror. *Will it work this time?* she thought. *We were lucky to get back into the country. Now that the whole world is after us, can we get away?*

Later that morning, Madeline's brother John went to the General Delivery window, the same way he had for days since seeing her. Every day it had been the same. The stout woman with horn rimmed glasses had always given him the same answer.

"Nothing today."

She pitied the boy with the hollowed eyes and trembling hands, wondering to herself how one so young had come to this. Today she had good news.

Smiling, she handed over the letter. "Looks like this is your lucky day." Her eyes followed him as John rushed out the door. She'd never seen him move that fast.

John sat down on the post office steps and ripped the envelope open. The money in large denominations caught his eyes first. Gripping them in one hand, he opened the letter with the other. As he read his sister's words, tears flowed from his eyes. He crushed the letter in his hand and let it fall to the steps, watching the wadded-up ball bounce down to the pavement. He looked at the bills in their large denominations, knowing that his dealer would love them.

He stuffed the money in his pocket. As he turned to go, he picked up the letter. He uncurled it from its crushed folds. He laid it on a step, smoothed out its wrinkles, and read it again.

CHAPTER 8

MIRA'S LAMENT

This will do for now. The parties desperate to keep me silent have set me up quite well. All they want me to do is stay low and out of sight. Of course, they want me on a plane to Tripoli as fast as possible, but I can blackmail my presence here a while longer until I find her. Madeline and her wonderful lover.

I suppose for a place like Sacramento, this is considered the best hotel in town. I've been in better *and* worse. Isn't it funny that when it comes to keeping someone quiet, suddenly the doors to the best accommodations are flung wide open?

I've got everything a gun runner could hope for. I possess a panoramic view of a park, a large flat screen TV, twenty-four-hour room service, and oh yes, Internet. Now that all my shady human forces have failed to find you Madeline, I have tracked you electronically. You and your boyfriend have made the news. *Your* family were a band of misbegotten nobodies whose existence no one would bother to record, but *his* family was military royalty. They have lots of documentation that I've carefully gone through and even though your boyfriend's parents are both dead, they've left behind a lovely paper trail. I've gleaned a great deal from it.

Eliot's family was prosperous enough to possess *two* residences, one in the city and a cottage in the country. Both houses seem to be lost in probate, waiting for a single heir to return. What a pity that your precious lover is too notorious to properly claim his legacy.

You wouldn't go to the downtown residence. Too obvious. But what about the home in the country?

I found a picture of it on one of those globe tracker applications on the Internet that allow you to investigate everybody's business, whether they like it or not. Don't these fools realize that that allows people like me to hunt them down whenever I want?

By the looks of the country estate, *nobody* would want to live there, although it *would* be a handsome hideout. Yes. You just might be there.

Madeline. Madeline mine. You almost were, at least for a moment. That one moment. The only thing that I ever found in this world without a blemish, without pain, were your perfect eyes.

You and your insane scruples. So, what if I made a gun deal more unsavory than all the others? The allegiances your country has made with the sinister forces everywhere, to keep the wheels rotating, are worse than anything I could ever conceive.

All the western countries made the same mistake. The friend of today is the enemy of tomorrow. The *worst* mistake they made was selling too many guns to too many countries. They may have tried to control the flow, but once those arms are sent loose on the world, they can oh-so-easily fall into the hands of someone like me. In the end, the world powers have no one to blame but themselves.

Precious Madeline. Your naïve patriotism. Don't you realize that all of it is too insane to be real?

That night in my apartment as I held you when you were so near death. *That* was real. The way you held me then, the warmth of your body against me as you wept out your guilt, was *my* first encounter with compassion. What a pathetic irony that the only way I could ever hold you without being turned away was through your sorrow.

The only sanity I have ever known in a world gone mad was the feel of your skin against mine. And you threw it all away.

I still remember the day we drove into Tripoli, after I made the mistake of rescuing you on the road in Afghanistan. My one act of charity. I hereby vow not to repeat the same error.

And my second mistake has come back to haunt me. I should never have told you, back in Afghanistan, that Ahmed was working for me to take care of his little brother Muhammad, the same way you wanted to help John. As far as you were concerned from that moment on, you and Ahmed were part of some crazy international family.

You managed to talk Rami into trading places, so you could sit in the front seat next to Ahmed. Rami wasn't happy about the rearrangement, muttering obscenities as he joined me in the back. You ignored it all, much more concerned in getting cozy with Ahmed. What did *I* have to do to get that kind of undivided attention?

You looked at Ahmed. "Tell me more about your brother. About Muhammad."

Ahmed gleamed with pride. "A beautiful boy of twelve. Black hair in long curls. He wants to cut it because the other boys tease him that he looks like a girl. But I say no. Don't cut. Silly, no?"

You grinned. "No. Not silly."

As we rolled through the city, Ahmed rambled on. "We play soccer together. Would you believe? He is already better than me, Madel...Madele...so sorry. Hard to say your name."

You gave him a smile I would have died for. "Call me Maddy."

Ahmed laughed. "Yes! Maddy. Is beautiful!"

Sickening. Rami and I rolled our eyes at each other.

High on his new-found friendship, Ahmed continued. "Do *you* have a brother, Maddy?"

Suddenly, all the joy went out of the car as you turned away and looked out the window. "Yes, but I can't help him the way you do with Muhammad. My brother is very sick. He needs a lot of money for his care, and I can't help him."

Ahmed touched your arm. "I'm so sorry. Your family cannot help?"

You shook your head. "They're the ones who *made* him sick."

Ahmed let a moment pass before he spoke again. "What is your brother's name?"

Your response came in a whisper. "John."

Ahmed leaned back in his seat. "In my religion his name is Yahya, and he was a great prophet. His name is sacred, like your brother. You will find a way to help him, Maddy."

You rubbed a tear away from the corner of your eye. "No. There's no way. Not now."

At last, I thought to myself. *An opportunity!*

Seeking a deeper kinship, you made a big mistake. One that I would use.

You asked Ahmed about the one thing he never spoke of. "What about *your* family, Ahmed?"

Rami and I exchanged quick glances. That subject frightened even him. Ahmed gripped the steering wheel and bit down on his lip. I wedged myself between his seat and yours, keeping my voice low.

"Life is cheap over here, Madeline," I said. Cheaper than your war in Afghanistan. At least you can properly bury your dead. Here they have no such luxury. Ahmed's parents were disappeared. No one knows where they are; he only knows that they're not coming back."

Quickly, you turned to Ahmed. "I'm so sorry...I didn't mean..."

Ahmed relaxed and looked at you. "It is all right, Maddy. You did not know."

Rami bowed his head in reverence. There *was* some semblance of a human being in him after all. I waited. Now you were vulnerable. I leaned in closer to you. "Maybe I can help you with your brother...with John."

The gleam of hope in your eyes came with affection that I could feel. A swarm of passion rushed through me. I wanted more of it.

We had to pass through the Old City to get to my apartment. Regrettably, that meant driving through the Souq el Hout marketplace on Al Rashid Street. A great place to go if you want to take your life into your hands.

Before we even got there, you stared at all the apartment houses in various degrees of destruction. I couldn't believe that some of them were still standing after all the bombing they'd been through. Row after row you saw their torn away walls exposing bathrooms with dangling plumbing, living rooms with scraps of broken furniture, terraces at any moment about to break free from their moorings.

Down on the street you gazed at one burnt out car after another. The ones that still had their paint were pierced with dozens of bullet holes. I could tell by the grim look on your face that you'd seen it all before in Afghanistan. Good. I'd need that toughness if I was going to make you my gun running partner.

But the worst was coming up fast. The gun markets. Now I'd need my best skills of rationalization if I was going to convince you that I was a legitimate gun trader among an army of gun pirates.

The gun market that day was the usual scene of pandemonium and insanity on full display. In the dozens of dirty stalls packed together, AK-47s, Turkish and Belgian handguns, many in their original packaging, were spread out on table after table.

Potential buyers thought nothing of testing the guns by firing them randomly into the air with no concern for the crowds surrounding them. People ducked their heads as the pop-pop-pop of expelled rounds continued. Serious injury from bullets falling back to earth was common in the area.

In a place where people use to sell crafts; leather goods, handmade jewelry, scarves and silk dresses, everything had changed. First came the fireworks, followed quickly by tasers and stun batons. Finally, we got handguns and pump-action shotguns.

Many of the sellers of today were kids who couldn't have been more than seventeen, wearing baseball caps turned sideways and Nike T-shirts. Others had strings of gold chains dangling from their necks. They all engaged in animated conversations as younger kids roared around the stalls on BMX scooters.

As we weaved our way through the crowded street, one of the adolescent sellers pointed a pistol to his head and stuck out his tongue at us. All his friends had a good laugh, but no one laughed as hard as Rami. He came forward and nudged Ahmed.

"Did you see that kid? He was funny!"

I glared at him. "You used to be part of that rabble before I tamed you." Then I looked at your reflection in the rearview mirror. "Our friend here was once demonstrating a weapon and accidentally shot an innocent bystander. Fortunately, the man received only a minor wound, but it took a lot of talking with my contacts to get Mr. Rami out of jail."

You looked back at me in the mirror. "Who *are* your contacts?"

Smart kid. You caught me off guard, but only momentarily. "People in the government that are trustworthy."

You turned around in your seat and faced me. "But if Rami did what you said, why is he working for you?"

Rami grabbed the back of your seat. "Because I'm not a deserter! Eh, Maddy? You ran away!"

Unmoved and unafraid, you stared back at him. You were going to be even better than I thought. Ahmed gave you a wink and a quick thumbs up. I spoke up again.

"He's good at keeping the crazies away from my warehouses even though he used to be one of them. Don't let what you see here bother you too much. Just don't ever come here. There was a journalist who was shot and killed here last week in a drive-by. It was his first day in the country. He hadn't reported on anything yet. Anyone can be mistaken for anybody else down here."

That didn't seem to bother you too much, which bothered *me*. It was meant to scare the hell out of you, but you were too preoccupied as you scanned all the stalls and their stacks of weapons.

You looked back at me. "So, all these guns came from Gaddafi's warehouses when he was overthrown, right? I saw it all on CNN when I was on base."

You might be a tougher case than I thought. "Oh yes, the ubiquitous network. Don't believe everything you see there, Madeline."

That didn't stop you. "And you took guns from the warehouses like everybody else?"

Sometimes you must tell the truth in order to find your way to a lie. "Yes, everybody did. It's the only way they have of protecting themselves from warlords, rebel militias, and other lunatics in this part of Tripoli."

You continued your cross examination. "But you sell guns to other parts of the world. You told me as much in Afghanistan."

Time to get creative. "I sell them to people trying to stay alive in all the power collapses in this part of the world. If you watched CNN, you know about the Arab Spring...the revolutions against oppressive regimes."

That slowed you up a bit. As we finally drove out of the market, you stared out the window. I could tell you were trying to process everything I'd said. Now I had to try to close the deal. I had a deception ready if I needed it. Always good to have one at hand.

I leaned in and put my hand on your arm. "I sell guns through the government contacts I have here. They move them on through middlemen. It's all done with the proper End User Certificates."

You gave me a quick look. "What are those?"

Good. You didn't know about EUCs. That was going to come in handy later. "Those are meant to assure that all the guns that are sold are not coming from a country under UN embargo."

You were quick to come back at me. "But isn't Libya under embargo after everything that's happened over here?"

I was expecting that. "Yes, it is. But my sources move them to countries which are not."

You pulled away from me. "Sounds like a roundabout way to get around the law."

I nodded. "That's right, but how else can desperate people fight back at dictators? The United States wants to stop the Taliban from turning Afghanistan into authoritarian rule, correct?"

That hit home. You looked away. Up until now, Ahmed and Rami weren't paying any attention to our conversation. Rami's only concern was in getting paid and Ahmed only wanted to take care of his brother.

But then Rami had to forget himself. I think he wanted to get even for the way you stood up to him. He sat up in his seat. "What do you care what Mira does?" he shouted at you. "You have no country!"

You reached back and grabbed him by the shirt. "Yes, I do!" You shoved him back into his seat. The look of shock on his face was priceless. He didn't know how tough a battle-hardened veteran was.

Ahmed tried to play peacekeeper. "Maddy, is all right. He doesn't know what he says."

Rami grumbled some obscenities in Arabic. I worried. I knew your kind of patriotism could sour a good business deal. But I still had your little brother for leverage. Thank God for that.

Another problem was coming up fast, though. In only a few minutes you'd see the *other* Tripoli. The one a universe away from what you'd just witnessed. Once you saw the high-end fashion stores, the elegant coffee houses and five-star hotels, you'd have more questions for me.

I'd managed to pass your cross examination back at the gun markets, but when we eventually got to my apartment and you saw the way *I* lived, your curiosity could turn to cruelty.

I wasn't worried. I had another advantage over you. One you were yet unaware of. I knew a broken human being when I saw one. I've seen thousands. You weren't just a fugitive from the army. You were a fugitive from life.

I knew it when we pulled you out of the ditch in Afghanistan. Anyone else would have been already dead from heat exhaustion, dehydration, or both. I've seen many die that way. I knew it when we were on the road, and you singlehandedly took on the Taliban while me and my crew stood back like helpless bystanders.

The fact that your beauty could still stun me even with your torn clothes and mud encrusted on your skin, was one thing. But your power to stay alive overwhelmed me. I wanted to be part of it. To hold you and absorb that strength. I was sick of all the sickness that surrounded me. I was sick of having only myself to hold onto. I wanted to be held by another.

The first thing you saw when we got to the shopping district were the high fashion women's stores. Their tall glass windows encased by shining chrome frames, displayed mannequins in all the latest western wear; bright, free flowing skirts, sleek black pants, six-inch heels and multi-colored sunglasses too large for anyone's eyes.

Then came the exquisite, not to mention highly expensive, jewelry stores. In their shadow box windows with polished walnut walls, necklaces and bracelets studded with gems and diamonds, languished on black velvet pillows. In another window, precision watches that had the price of a house, were mounted on white suede pedestals.

We drove past American brand blue jeans stores while other establishments offered the latest and loudest in athletic shoes. I watched your eyes. First there was wonder and then a look of disdain. That's what I'd hoped for.

"Shocked by the contrast, Madeline?"

Seemingly unimpressed, you looked back at me. "Not really. I grew up in a slum within walking distance of a rich neighborhood."

Just as I thought. "But no one was selling AK-47s on the street."

That got your attention. You looked down. "No, they weren't."

Your naivete made me smile. "This is what happens after the fall of a forty-five-year brutal regime. Reminds me of Lebanon when I was a kid."

I let that sink in. I had more for later. We passed out of the shopping district, the Corinthia hotel looming in front of us. Its twin towers, curved in concrete stood twenty-eight stories high. Businessmen and diplomats from everywhere enjoyed the five-star amenities of the hotel that overlooked the Mediterranean Sea.

Just before we got to my apartment, we drove past one of Tripoli's best coffee houses. There were hundreds in the city, but they didn't have the same clientele, nor the same ambiance. I told Ahmed to stop the car. I wanted you to see how the rich relaxed.

Out on the circular courtyard, surrounded by tall palms and large potted plants, half a dozen or more broad white umbrellas covered polished wood tables. Men in suits, women in elegant summer dresses, languished in woven wood chairs. Waiters in white jackets served them iced coffee and cold fruit drinks.

I looked back at you. "Wouldn't that be a nice way to spend an afternoon? They're not worried about a drive-by shooting or where their next meal is coming from. In Lebanon, it wasn't enough for me to *own* a gun, I had to be *in* the gun business if I wanted to survive."

Ahmed and Rami nodded in grim agreement.

"It was the same for these two men. What about you, Madeline?"

You stared at the lounging coffee drinkers with a look of disgust. "If only I'd had a gun. I would have shot my stepfather."

I let your words trail away. You didn't need to say anything more. I didn't know yet the womb from which you had sprung, only that it had to be as wounded as the one from which I had emerged.

Ahmed and Rami dropped us off at my apartment. You were quick to notice my Porsche SUV in the driveway. But it didn't command your attention for long. You were too struck by the modernist design of my two-story home.

Around the driveway and continuing to the front, you saw the three-foot wall of smooth white sandstone. Above, you gazed at the second story which seemed to emerge from the first, as though drifting in midair. You saw my balcony with its ferns overflowing the walnut railings. There was a similar apartment in the back, but it didn't have the view I had of the sea. I could already see the two of us out on the balcony at sunset, sharing a glass of wine. I was getting ahead of myself. I knew how *that* could lead to disappointment.

When we stepped up to my front door you seemed fascinated by its shadowed glass exterior. You saw its elegance without knowing its secret. From inside I could easily see whoever was at my door, but they couldn't see me.

Once inside, you looked around at the living room with its black leather couches facing each other. Between them was my long, beveled glass coffee table, books and dried flower arrangements strewn on its surface.

Your eyes gazed at the large abstract paintings on the walls, the thick brush strokes of yellow and blue swirling on canvas. You looked to the left and saw the dining room with my mahogany table and matching chairs. Off to the right you could just see enough of the kitchen to observe the appliances with brushed chrome exteriors.

You turned around to me. "I'd say the gun business has been awfully good to you."

I had to smile. Even in your haggard state, you knew how to come up with a sarcastic remark. "It is self-indulgent, isn't it, Madeline? That's what comes from having nothing for so long. You want to get even, right?"

By the hard look on your face I could tell I'd struck a nerve. I knew enough of you already to know that like all the world's damaged, you wanted retribution wherever you could find it.

I pointed to the staircase that led up to the bathroom and bedrooms. "Let's go upstairs so you can get cleaned up. I'll find some clothes for you. I think we're about the same size."

When we got upstairs you went into my bathroom with its marbled walls while I went into my bedroom with its wall-length closet. I found a white Chanel blouse with short sleeves that I knew would be perfect on you. I stroked its silk texture knowing soon it would be against your skin. There was a pair of black pleated trousers hanging nearby that would make a complete outfit.

From the closet floor I pulled out a pair of black espadrilles, hoping our shoe size was close enough. Then, from numerous bureau drawers, overstuffed with lingerie, I found some new underwear, trying not to imagine it on your body.

My desires were in check until I passed by the bathroom and saw your naked silhouette through the frosted shower doors. Attempting to make a quick retreat, I laid the clothes on the dressing table, but then you slid the shower door back and stepped out.

For a moment you were startled, not having heard my entrance over the sound of the shower. "Sorry, I didn't hear you come in."

I didn't gaze at your nakedness. I didn't need to. I could feel its power, its nearness. Time to play pretend. "My fault. I'm always popping in at the wrong time. I'll go down and get some food started for us. I bet you're hungry."

You laughed. "Starved!"

I went down to the kitchen and threw together some big salads. Then I got some fruit and yogurt, put it all in the blender, and made fruit shakes. I spied some chocolate in the back of the refrigerator, hoping you liked sweets as much as I did. I had a feeling you did.

Then, just as I was laying it all out on the dining room table, you came down the staircase. I couldn't believe how good you looked in the outfit I'd chosen. The silk blouse formed to your shoulders and fell to your waist like it was tailor made. The pleats of the black slacks slid down your legs as if they were a part of you.

A moment of desire mixed with envy overcame me. I could never look that good in those garments. Nobody could.

You gave me your first broad smile. "Do I look all right?"

I pointed to the full-length mirror next to the stairs. "See for yourself."

You went to the mirror and made a few turns, seemingly pleased. Then your look turned dark. "Not bad for a deserter."

I came behind you and put my hands on your shoulders. "None of that matters now. Come on, let's eat."

As you sat down at the table, I went to get a carafe of sparkling water and some glasses. When I came back, you'd already inhaled half your fruit shake and were working on the salad. I poured the water into a glass that you quickly grasped from my hand.

I felt that I was watching a kid who'd missed his lunch and was late for dinner. "Hey, slow down. You're going to get a case of indigestion, and I'll have to hold you over the toilet."

You laughed with food still in your mouth. "Sorry. My table manners aren't very good. Too much time in soldier's chow lines."

"It's OK. I like watching you enjoy yourself."

After we finished, I went back to the kitchen and made espresso. I put the little ceramic cups on a big silver serving tray, along with a carafe of white wine and glasses. I didn't forget the chocolate. I put that on a tiny tray of its own along with everything else.

When I came back to the dining room your eyes lit up at the sight of the chocolate. I knew it. You ate it up as if it were your last chance to have any kind of sweet at all.

When everything was gone, we were silent for a while. Through the louvered slats of my wooden blinds, I watched the sun going down. Out on the Mediterranean Sea, the never-ending waves rolled up onto shore, unaware and indifferent to the earth's endless suffering.

I saw you looking down at your wine glass, your fingers turning on its stem. "I never thanked you. Not properly."

I gripped my wine glass. "No need."

You leaned across the table. "I still don't know why you did it."

"Maybe because you reminded me of myself from a long time ago."

"Lebanon?"

This kid was too damn smart. I looked down at the scraps of vegetables left over from my salad. I would have killed for any one of them when I was a child on the streets. "Yes. Lebanon."

You moved your chair closer to mine. "What was it like?"

"Sure, you want to hear?"

You put your hand on my chair. "Yes. I do."

I looked back at the sea. The sun was gone. Now the waves were black, almost invisible. "All right, Maddy. May I call you that, or is that nickname reserved only for Ahmed?"

You grinned. "Of course, you can."

I put my hands on the table, palms down. Testimony must be given in a sober fashion. "When I was twelve all my family were either dead from bombings or disappeared, like Ahmed's. I had to rummage through garbage and beg on the streets. At night I covered myself in thrown away newspapers to stay warm. Then I turned to petty theft, selling whatever I stole on the black market. It was never enough though. I almost starved. Then something worse than hunger happened to me."

You sat back in your chair. "Worse than starving?"

I looked straight at you. "Them. I had to worry about *them*."

"Who do you mean?"

"Human traffickers, Madeline. Sellers of flesh. I'd escaped their notice before, but now that I was *blossoming*, I gained their interest. A *lot* of interest."

The look of shock on your face was priceless. Even war hadn't prepared you for the *real* world…the underbelly. Your innocence made me smile. "Shocked? Want me to stop? You said you wanted to know."

You sat up straight. "No, I do want to know."

I ran my hands over the table. "I was trafficked for about a year. The way I got through it was by detaching myself from my physical body. I made a new body, one that was safe, hovering over the one being used. Most of the time it worked, but not always."

I hate moments of self-revelation. The air around them is too thick to breathe. I fumbled with my wine glass, almost spilling it over. You straightened it by putting your hand over mine. I wished you'd left your hand there instead of letting it slide away.

"You never tried to get away?"

I had to suppress my laughter. "You don't run away, sweetie. They only find you. The first time I tried it; I didn't get more than three blocks away before Hassan––that was my handler's name––caught up to me. That earned me a good beating. Not having learned my lesson, I tried it again. That time I got a lot farther before another pimp got hold of me and sold me back to Hassan. Pimps love runaways. They're good for business. Unfortunately for me, the second beating I got was worse than the first."

You sank back in your chair, your eyes in dull disbelief. Oh God, now I knew what was coming...sympathy. The sentiment that weakens us all.

"Mira, I'm so sorry. That should never happen to anybody. How did you finally get away from him?"

I smiled to myself, relishing the memory I was about to express. "I guess you'd say I gave Hassan a rude awakening."

Your head turned to one side. "What do you mean?"

"While he was sleeping, I stabbed him to death with his own knife. Had to plunge it into him eight times before he gave it up."

You squeezed my arm. "Good. He deserved it!"

It felt so good to be held by you, even if it was only a single hand at arm's length. "Yes, his untimely death proved very advantageous. I took all his money and went into the gun business. There were plenty of arms left behind by the Israelis and Hezbollah, after all the invasions. I learned how to put a crew together. Men who were tough but could be controlled. Men must be controlled, you know?"

I looked for a sign of assent in your eyes. Something that would tell me you agreed. I saw only a pondering look. Not good.

I got up from my chair. "I think we need a drink, don't you? How about some brandy?"

You nodded. "Sounds good!"

I went out to the kitchen and got my best French brandy out of the cupboard. I found my crystal brandy snifters, the ones with the cut glass embroidery on their bowels.

When I brought it all into the dining room and set it down on the table, you looked dazzled. "Wow! This looks too good for me."

I poured some brandy into the snifters. "You deserve it after what you've been through."

You put your hand on the snifter, feeling its etched patterns. "Nothing, compared to what *you've* been through."

I sat down at the table. "You know, it's funny. I never told anybody my life story before. Who'd want to listen, anyway? Most of the people around me have got too many similar stories of their own."

Your fingertips dug into the cut glass. "It's that bad over here, isn't it?"

I took a sip of brandy. "You don't want to know. But enough of all that. Time for *you* to go to confession. Tell me how the world has slammed you. I bet it's an interesting story."

You took a slow sip of brandy and set down your glass. "You make me feel ashamed, Mira. Compared to you, my story is nothing."

I leaned over the table. "Go ahead and try me."

You put your elbows on the table and rested your chin on your folded hands. "I wish I'd had the courage to stab my stepfather Frank, the way you did your pimp. Frank had more than beatings to keep me terrified.

"My mother brought him home from one of her alcoholic benders one night, both drunk to exhaustion, but not too intoxicated to have sex on the floor, right in front of me and my brother. John was seven then and I was twelve, like you were when you were on the streets. I guess I have that much in common with your story."

I crossed my arms on the table. "I have a feeling you have a lot more. Keep going."

You ran your hand through your hair and down the back of your neck. "Frank took up residence in the only bedroom of our sleazy apartment. After that, John and I had to sleep on the couch. When Frank wasn't drunk, he was violent, nervously awaiting the next welfare check to feed the alcoholic addiction of himself and my mother.

"If the check was late or didn't come at all, he took it out on me, slapping me around and pushing me against the wall. I fought back with everything my little girl body had, kicking and biting him, cursing and spitting on him."

I loved your courage. "I knew you were tough!"

You gripped the arms of your chair. "Not tough enough. Frustrated with the way I could take it, Frank decided to pick on John, my shy, sensitive little brother. One night, Frank punched John so hard, blood flowed from John's mouth. When Frank saw me rush over to John, covering his body with my own and wiping away John's blood, he knew he finally had what he wanted.

"After that I was powerless. I had to spend all my time trying to keep John away from Frank. It was a full-time job, and I failed at it...many times. I know that the beatings Frank gave John, led to John's drug addiction later. It was all my fault."

I sat back and crossed my arms. "So *that's* your brother's problem."

You rubbed your fingertip in a drop of brandy that had spotted the table. "Yes."

I waited a moment. "How long has he been using?"

You looked up at me. "Off and on for the last few years. Lately, it's worse."

Your finger continued to rub the table, even after the brandy stain was gone. I placed my hand over yours. "And in Afghanistan, you weren't exactly in a position to help him."

Your finger finally relaxed. "Not for the kind of care he needs. Sacramento can't cope with the opioid crisis."

I moved my hand away. "Sacramento. That's in California, isn't it? That's the city you're from?"

You grinned. "The worst part of it." You stared at the brandy bottle on the table, watching its curved design catch light from my overhead candelabra lamp. "The question now is, where do I go from here?"

You got up and went into the living room. As I came up behind you, you did something terrible. You reached back and took my hand. The desire to embrace you was unbearable, but you were too vulnerable now. We both were.

You let go of my hand and looked at my books on the coffee table; Dostoyevsky, Faulkner, Hemingway, all of them with titles in English. "Is this where you learned to speak English so well?"

I sat down on one of the facing couches. "Not originally. The story of how I learned to speak the language is so ridiculous, I'm embarrassed to tell you."

You smiled as you sat down on the other couch. Strange how causing another to smile can return so much warmth. Dangerous. "Well now I *have* to know how you learned it."

"One of the girls I was trafficked with knew some English. She learned more by reading American romance novels. Don't ask me how she got a hold of them. She taught it all to me."

"But you went on to read all these. Why?"

I looked away at the abstract paintings on the wall, the ones I'd paid so much for. Wasn't it all like this, random strokes thrown together in chaos? I looked back at you. "I hoped that one of them could answer the question of why we're all here. All I got were more questions."

I got up and walked around the room. Your eyes followed me in a way that made me uncomfortable. "I had to learn English anyway, if I was going to make it in the gun business. English is the lingua franca, the 'common language' of the world. There are millions of native speakers, but more than a billion people around the globe speak it."

You fell silent for a moment. Then you hit me with a bullet. "Why do *you* think we're here?"

You were making yourself out to be a hard case. I stopped pacing and looked at you. "Women like you and I weren't meant to know."

You touched Hemingway's *Farewell To Arms.* "I read this one in high school, before I was expelled for truancy and fighting. The two lovers were so beautiful, but in the end, she dies."

I had to take your mind away from tragic stories. I sat down next to you. "What would you think if I taught *you* Arabic?"

That snapped you out of your romantic fantasies. "Why would I want to learn it?"

"So, you could come to work for me. You'd make more than enough money to get John the kind of care you want for him. You said you wanted to help him. This is your chance."

I thought I'd have to use my best negotiation skills to bring you around, but inside of twenty-four hours you agreed. The sound of your brother's name was more than enough to make you, my partner. If I had known then the agony you were about to cause me, I think I would have killed us both. There's no point in living without the person you love.

Freeport isn't exactly a quaint little village. Even driving out here at 3AM, the ramshackle farms at the foot of the levee look pathetic in the moonlight. The river on the other side is not bad, even though the waves are slapping up against broken up banks.

I got to the house I had found on the Internet, pulled my car to the side of the road and turned off my headlights. I left the engine running. I looked down at the dilapidated cottage at the end of a long earthen driveway.

Were you down there Madeline, you and lover boy? I thought if I came in the middle of the night, I'd catch you both at your most vulnerable. Were you fast asleep now with *his* arms around you?

I looked about, but didn't see any sign of the SUV you'd stolen from me. I gripped the 9mm pistol in the holster strapped to my side. I felt the diamond pattern of the pistol's grip in my palm.

I cut the engine and got out. I walked down the path and up to the front door. It was half opened. If the two of you were in there, you weren't too concerned about security. Who'd steal from you anyway? You both had nothing.

I took my pistol from its holster and flicked off the safety. I slipped through the front door and into the living room. I looked around at all the worn-out furniture. On one of the end tables there were two half empty cups of coffee. I felt them to see if they were still warm. Ice cold. Next to the coffee was a half-eaten piece of toast.

I went into the dining room and saw items strewn on the table; plates with food fragments, knives and forks scattered about, crumpled paper napkins. Someone was either very messy, or in a big hurry to get away.

From there I went to the kitchen. Dish towels were piled up on the kitchen table. Next to them was a notepad. I picked it up, fanned through the pages and stopped when I saw the scribbled names of several airlines.

I went up to the bedrooms. I had to use soft steps to climb the creaking staircase. When I got to the landing, I saw the bathroom at the end of the hall and two bedrooms in front of me. The door to the bedroom on my left was wide open, a well-made single bed in the center and posters of rock stars on the walls. Must have been Eliot's teenage sanctuary. How sweet.

The door on my right was closed. Gun in hand, I turned the knob and threw the door open. The bed was empty, but you were still there. The smell of you. The closed door had sealed your essence in its walls. I knew your scent so well by living so close to you. I never took it for granted.

You'd be doing something ordinary, passing me in our kitchen when a whiff of your long black hair would flow past me. It always smelled of jasmine, no matter how many of my expensive shampoos you used.

Your skin. I'd smell it in the clothes hanging in your closet. The dark, rich oils of your flesh, lingering in an enclosed space.

Of course, *his* smell lingered as well, the mixture of leather and dirt, but yours rose above it all in invisible clouds.

I looked down at a tragedy spread out before me. Did you have to leave in such a hurry that you couldn't have at least made the bed? As it was, the sheets and blankets were turned and twisted in human forms. I thought I could just make out the shape of *you* on the right side of the bed.

Like a fool, I stood there and addressed the leftover impression of your precious body. *Where did you go, Madeline? Where would you go?*

I wanted to lay down in the place where you'd been, caress what was left of you, but I knew if I did, I'd never get out of there. So, I stood there and wept.

CHAPTER 9

FLIGHT INTO FEAR

When Madeline and Eliot got to the airport, they scanned the departure screen for their flight to LAX, the first leg of their long journey. Next to their flight number they saw "delayed" in bright red letters.

Eliot went to the airline desk and came back a few minutes later. "She said they've got some kind of technical problem with one of the engines. They should have it fixed inside of an hour."

Madeline sat down on one of the long rows of black leather seats in the departure lounge. "That gives Mira another hour to find us."

Eliot sat down next to her. "She couldn't move that fast."

Madeline shook her head. "Eliot, by now she's been to the house."

"How can you be so sure?"

Madeline looked out on all the departing planes on the runway. One of them was revving its powerful jet engines while another took flight, off to somewhere where it was safe. "Because I worked for her. She made more deals and sold more guns because she was always one step ahead of her competition. Now, she's a step behind, but she'll make it up, believe me."

Eliot gripped her hand. "We've made it this far…gotten away from her twice."

Madeline watched a plane ascend and bank to the south, imagining the passengers inside, comfortable and assured of their destination. "Mira has probably already done business with the guy you sold the Range Rover to, buying it back at a quarter of its price. She knows how to intimidate."

Eliot felt Madeline's hand slide away from his. He had to find a way to bring her back to him. "Have you ever been kissed in an airport?"

She turned to him and smiled. "I think I would have remembered."

He touched her face. "Like to try it now?"

She took his hand again. "In front of all these civilians? They might get embarrassed."

He ran his fingertip over her upper lip as he stroked her lower lip with his thumb. She remembered how he had done that the first time they made love. As their lips met, an older couple passed by them and smiled.

Madeline blushed and pulled away. "See! Now you've embarrassed *us* in front of senior citizens. You should be ashamed of yourself!"

The affection didn't last. Madeline looked out on the runway again. "You know this is the easy part, right? After we get to Los Angeles, we'll have to pass through customs to get to Germany."

Eliot put his arm around her. "The passports have worked before. They'll work again."

Madeline pulled away from him. "Even after everything that happened in Sacramento with the ATF? Tom told you we were headline news. They've got to be watching the airports."

Eliot knew she was right. He had to try to allay her fears. "But They'll keep looking for us in Sacramento."

"I know someone who won't. She knows we can't stay in this country."

He had to get the thought of Mira out of her head. "If we can make it out of LA, it should be easier in Germany and Beirut. I'm sure it will!"

They had a three-hour layover at LAX. More than enough time for the memories of Mira to form in Madeline's mind, as she and Eliot nervously awaited their flight to Germany.

Everything had happened fast with Mira. She had known Madeline was desperate to get in touch with John and send him money to get into the best rehab center. So, Mira immediately had drawn a check for ten thousand dollars from one of her many anonymous accounts, funds that were invisible and untraceable. Per Madeline's instructions, the check had been sent to Sacramento General Delivery along with a letter from Madeline, telling John how to subscribe to an encrypted email service, as Mira had requested. Future payment for John's care would come from offshore accounts in the Cayman Islands, where no one cared who you were and what your business was.

Mira had told Madeline all these methods were necessary to protect Madeline from those who were looking for her. Madeline didn't know yet that subterfuge was a necessary part of everything Mira did in illegal gun sales.

Once Madeline and John were in contact with each other and John entered rehab, he was soon sending back glowing reports of his progress and telling Madeline how grateful he was.

No one was more grateful than Madeline. One afternoon, after getting a particularly hopeful email from John,

Madeline rushed down from her bedroom and threw her arms around Mira, whose hands were full of leftover breakfast plates. Shocked from Madeline's sudden embrace, Mira nearly dropped the plates to the table. "What did I do to deserve all this?"

Madeline held her closer. "It's John! He's doing even better than I hoped."

Mira pulled away long enough to set down the plates and then returned to Madeline's embrace. "That's great news, Maddy!"

Inwardly, Mira had congratulated herself. She'd done all the right things first. *Get them in touch with each other and then send the money.* Mira knew that gratitude would follow, which could all so easily evolve into a feeling of indebtedness. From Madeline's debt, vulnerability could be drawn.

Mira let her hands slide down the firm columns of Madeline's back. "I'm so happy John's doing well."

Madeline's eyes watered as she pulled away. "You brought him back to me."

Mira stroked Madeline's cheek. "OK. Ready to learn some Arabic?"

Madeline smiled and put her hands on her hips. "Will it be hard?"

Mira ran her finger along Madeline's jaw line. "Not for you. We'll make it fun!"

In the mornings Mira made a quick breakfast of fresh fruit and yogurt, wanting to get down to business as soon as possible.

"What about the coffee?" Madeline complained from the dining room.

"No coffee or anything else," Mira shouted from the kitchen. "You've got work to do young lady. If you do well, I'll make you a cappuccino this afternoon. Otherwise, nothing!"

Madeline sank back in her chair. "You make me feel like I'm back in the army."

Mira came into the dining room and flung open an Arabic primer on the table. "You are!"

After long language lessons in the morning, Mira made salads for the two of them. Although Madeline had trouble with some pronunciations, Mira couldn't help but be impressed at the speed of Madeline's learning.

Madeline was aware of her fast assimilation and wasted no time bragging about it. At the end of one excellent morning session, Madeline smiled and leaned back in her chair. "I think I deserve *two* cappuccinos today, don't you?"

Mira went to the kitchen and warmed up her imported espresso machine. "We'll keep it at one!"

"Oh c'mon, Mira! You don't think I'm doing well?"

Mira knew she couldn't let Madeline become too over-confident. One mispronounced word could foil a good arms deal and even lead to violence. "Not bad for a westerner. Although I learned English faster from your trashy romance novels than you're learning Arabic."

In the late afternoons, with Mira and Madeline's lessons winding down, Ahmed and Rami always came to the house. Mira had strictly informed them not to come before that.

Rami was always the first one through the door and Madeline was the first one he always spoke to. "So, American, do you see now how much better Arabic is than English? English so crude."

His remark only made Madeline smile. "And you speak it cruder than anyone!"

Before Rami could offer a comeback, Madeline had her arms around Ahmed. "How is your little brother Muhammad? Still beating you at soccer?"

Ahmed laughed as he held Madeline close. "Yes! And he eats all the food in the house. Three times I must go to market!"

Mira stood back; her arms folded. *All morning long with Maddy and not so much as a single touch.*

Ahmed took a step back. "How is John? Better now?"

Madeline turned and smiled at Mira. "Yes. Much better!"

At last! Mira thought to herself. *Some recognition.*

Mira began to ponder ways of using Ahmed as a bridge to Madeline. "All right, Maddy. If you do as well tomorrow as you did today, you and Ahmed can take a stroll by the sea."

Madeline and Ahmed gave each other another hug.

Rami grumbled. "Silliness. All silliness."

Madeline found it strange that Mira never talked business with Ahmed and Rami in the house, always leading them into the patio and speaking in hushed tones.

When Mira came back in the house, Madeline questioned her. "Why don't you talk business with them in front of me! I'm going to have to learn that, too."

Mira was quick to evade, seeking something she was far more interested in. "There'll be time enough for that. Don't I get one of those Ahmed hugs after putting up with you all day?"

"Of course, you do." As Madeline embraced Mira, she also found it strange that Mira seemed to linger in their embrace, as if seeking something more.

Now, as Madeline and Eliot stood in line to have their passports checked, she knew why, but she had far more fearful things to worry about.

The line Madeline and Eliot were in was long and slow moving. The other lines were moving much faster, passports easily scanned, passengers on their way to boarding.

"Should we move?" Madeline said.

Eliot shook his head. "We don't want do anything to arouse suspicion."

They looked ahead for the source of the delay in their line. The customs agent was running a particular passport again and again, each time becoming more frustrated. The agent was a broad-shouldered man with dark features. The passenger before him was a slim man with blonde hair, tapping his fingers on the counter, anxious to board.

The agent and the slim man began to exchange words that Madeline couldn't hear but could tell were not pleasant. She grasped Eliot's hand. "What if that happens to us?"

Eliot stroked his fingers over the back of her hand. "Just stay calm. Remember how you used to steel yourself before you went out on missions?"

Madeline looked back at the customs agent who had now called over a security guard. "Yeah, but that was war."

Eliot put his arm around her. "So is this."

Madeline heard someone behind her, speaking in German. She turned to see an older couple shaking their heads, obviously in a hurry to get to Frankfurt, or some town nearby in Germany.

Eliot saw the line getting longer as people muttered angry expressions to each other. "What's taking so damn long? Hell of a way to start a vacation!"

Madeline watched the security guard as he took the slim man's passport from the agent, pressed it flat on the scanner and gave it a slow slide. It checked. Everyone let out a sigh of relief.

When Madeline and Eliot's turn came, the agent's eyes narrowed on them. He opened a drawer beneath his desk and stared at something Madeline and Eliot couldn't see. The couple held their breath. *Was the agent looking at their service photos?"*

The agent closed the drawer and ran their passports. They didn't scan. The agent glared at Madeline and Eliot. He was in no mood for more trouble. He ran the passports again. They checked.

As the couple walked through the skybridge to their plane, Madeline wrapped her arm around Eliot's waist. "I'd love to kiss you right now. I don't care if it *is* an airport!"

Eliot put his arm around her shoulders. "Would you settle for a peck on the cheek?"

It was eleven hours to Frankfurt, with another long layover before they would finally fly out to Beirut. As they settled in for the long flight, Eliot pushed back the armrest between himself and Madeline and held her close. He felt a quiver go through her body and knew she was still affected by their close call with customs.

"You're not still nervous about that customs guy, are you? I told you our passports would be OK."

Madeline looked up at him. "Yeah, but I didn't like when he looked in that drawer."

Eliot gave her body a shake. "Probably looking at a porno magazine. He looked like the type."

They laughed as Madeline laid her cheek against Eliot's chest. They were silent for a moment and then he took her hand and held it out before him, staring at it, as if discovering it anew. In a slow motion he kissed her palm. She felt his lips brush over her skin, his warm breath. No one but Eliot had ever kissed her hand before, could move her the way he did.

Later, with the lights turned down in the cabin and all the passengers sleeping, Madeline stayed awake, watching

Eliot sleep. She'd done it many times before in Freeport, without ever telling him about it, of course. *He'd think I was weird, crazy, or both.*

She leaned back in her seat and remembered how Eliot's warmth and sense of humor reminded her so much of Ahmed, and she was back in Tripoli.

Madeline recalled the afternoon breaks, when Mira allowed her to stroll the seashore with Ahmed. On one particular day, pretending to be serious, Ahmed turned to Madeline. "I don't know what I do with Muhammad."

Madeline smiled. "Eating you out of house and home again?"

Ahmed stopped and put his hands on his hips. "Of course! But no matter how many soccer balls I buy him, they all disappear!"

Madeline leaned against the low sea wall. "So, what does he do with them all?"

Ahmed grinned and crossed his arms. "He give them all away. I know he does. He doesn't think I know, but I see him!"

Madeline gave Ahmed a playful shove. "That's a good thing…he's generous!"

Ahmed laughed with his deep, rich voice and gave Madeline one of his big bear hugs. "Yes, he will be a good man." Then he pulled away, holding Madeline's arms. "How is John now, still doing well?"

Madeline gripped Ahmed's arms. "Yes. They may even let him go into outpatient therapy, so he can live outside the center."

"That is wonderful, Maddy."

Madeline turned and put her hands on the sea wall. She looked down at all the multicolored umbrellas on the beach. Under their rainbow canopies, people talked and sipped cold drinks. She watched sunbathers sprawled out on beach towels as swimmers dove into the sea. "It's all due to Mira. I owe her so much."

Ahmed stood close to her, resting his arms on the wall. "Mira's business…it is dark sometimes, dangerous. I don't want to see you get hurt."

Madeline smiled and patted his arm. "I can take care of myself."

Ahmed's mood turned dark as he stepped back and spread his hands out on the wall. Farther out to sea he saw cargo ships pulling away from the harbor, knowing many carried contraband guns. "Maybe Mira likes you too much…I know her."

Madeline was surprised to see Ahmed's warm, dark eyes in deep thought. "It's because of everything she and I have been through," she said. We both need a friend. We've never really had one."

Ahmed fixed his eyes on her. "Beware of friends that ask too much. I will say no more. I must be careful myself."

The otherwise cheerful walk turned cool as Ahmed's words seeped into Madeline's thoughts. He was someone she trusted. She saw a freighter far out to sea and wondered if it was going as far as America. "I should get back, Ahmed."

Ahmed grasped her arm. "So soon?"

Madeline put her hand over his. "Yes, I've got a lot of learning to do."

When Madeline returned early from her walk, Mira was in the downstairs bedroom that she used as an office. Madeline had passed by it before, noticing only the large screen computer mounted prominently on Mira's imposing oak desk.

Now, Mira was typing fast on a laptop computer placed on the open center drawer of her desk. Deeply engrossed, Mira had not heard Madeline's entrance into the apartment.

Then Madeline appeared in the office. Startled, Mira was quick to close the laptop and shut the center drawer.

Madeline stepped back. "Oh, did I scare you? I'm sorry."

Mira got up from the desk, rushed over to Madeline and put her arm around her shoulders. "No, not really. Just doing some paperwork." Mira led the two of them out of the office and into the dining room. "You're back early. Don't tell me you and Ahmed ran out of little brother stories."

Madeline noticed how nervous Mira appeared to be. "No, just wanted to get back to learning."

After a long afternoon of Arabic lessons, Mira and Madeline stood out on the balcony, watching the sun go down into the sea. It was the time they treasured most, along with their most treasured treats, wine and chocolate.

Mira swirled the wine in her glass. "So how was your time with Ahmed, today?"

Even the mention of Ahmed's name made Madeline smile. "He talked a little about how well Muhammad is doing. I talked a *lot* about how well John is doing."

Mira looked down into the dark red wine in her glass, the depth that seemed to have no bottom. "Sometimes I wish *I* was John."

Madeline stared at her. "What do you mean?"

Mira set down her glass and ran her hand through Madeline's hair. "Even from seven thousand miles away, he has all your love."

Madeline touched Mira's arm. "But you know how grateful I am to you. How grateful John is."

Mira was about to embrace Madeline when the phone rang downstairs. "Dammit!" Mira cried. "I told people not to call at night."

Madeline sipped her wine. "Let it go to voicemail. You can always call them back."

Mira knew she couldn't. The deal she was working on was high risk and the client was nervous. "I'll take care of it and be right back. Stay right here."

After a wait, Madeline went downstairs and into the hallway that led to Mira's office. She could hear Mira's angry voice on the phone. From the Arabic Madeline had learned, she could hear Mira saying: "Stop being afraid!" and then something about "Syria".

Madeline peered into Mira's office and was surprised to see she was talking on a burner phone. The phones intended to be used once and then discarded or destroyed. Madeline had seen many of them used by Taliban fighters in Afghanistan. But the call had come from the landline. Madeline was familiar with its loud ring.

When Madeline approached the office door, Mira ended the call and threw the phone into an open desk drawer. Madeline noticed several burner phones in the drawer.

Feeling uneasy to enter, Madeline stood in the doorway. "What was that all about?"

Mira tried to compose herself, but Madeline could see she was shaken. She'd never seen her that way before. "Just a stupid client. You'll learn how to deal with them."

Madeline had also known Mira's angry voice before, but it was always under control. All this was different.

Madeline looked down at all the phones in the drawer. "Why do you have so many?"

"For my client's security. Let's get back to our wine."

A few days later, Mira announced she had to leave on business for a day or two. "It's that same stupid client I talked to the other day. I've got to meet with him to calm him down."

"OK, I hope it all works out."

As Mira left, she hugged Madeline and kissed her cheek. "Don't forget to work on your Arabic while I'm gone and don't spend too much time on those seaside strolls with Ahmed!"

Madeline thought of Ahmed's warning, still brewing in the back of Madeline's mind. She went into Mira's office and stood before her desk. She knew she had no right to open the center drawer. Minutes passed as she struggled with herself. She yanked on the drawer. Locked.

Madeline paced back and forth in the office, reminding herself of how much Mira had done for her and John. How could she betray Mira's trust now?

Madeline went to the kitchen and found an ice pick. The perfect instrument to pick a lock. She'd learned how to pick them when her stepfather Frank locked all the family's money in a strong box, using all the funds for alcohol and almost nothing for Madeline and John.

Madeline went back to the office and slid the ice pick into the center drawer's lock. She felt the tiny metal pieces in the interior turn and then give way. She pulled the drawer open and opened the laptop.

The webpage that emerged on the laptop's screen reminded her of something she had seen before. While on base, she and all the soldiers had access to the Internet, but were specifically told to never go to any page whose site name ended in dot onion, instead of dot com. The dot onion websites were part of the Deep Web, where your identity and location could not be known.

The Deep Web could also allow a user to eventually access the Dark Web, which allowed access into illicit websites. Madeline remembered that Mira had told her the laptop was for the security of her clients and perhaps it was, but the webpage Madeline stared at now brought back painful memories.

Madeline remembered a soldier on base who became addicted to conspiracy theories and roamed the Dark Web. She'd warned him about his actions, but he had only become belligerent. At the time she and the soldier were both privates and she had no authority over him. She could have reported him, but they'd been in combat missions together. Madeline knew that once that bond is formed, it's impossible to break.

Later, the soldier began to visit websites that sold guns illegally. The sites offered guns whose serial numbers had been erased and could be exported to any country at low prices. Madeline had pleaded with the soldier to stop, but he continued until he was found out and sent to a military prison.

The webpage Madeline was looking at now was identical to what she'd seen on the soldier's laptop. Then she noticed something else. Beneath Mira's desk, tucked away on a shelf of its own, sat an Internet server.

Madeline was aware of the server that occupied a space on a bookshelf in Mira's bedroom. It was the same server Madeline shared to stay in touch with John, on the laptop Mira had given her. This server was different.

Now, as Madeline and Eliot landed in Frankfurt and reclaimed their bags before flying out to Beirut, Madeline wished she had listened to Ahmed's warning about Mira... especially the last one.

CHAPTER 10

MIRA'S REMORSE

So where have the lovers flown to? Some country that doesn't have an extradition treaty with the United States? Russia, China, Africa? I don't think you'd try any of those. The first two probably wouldn't have you, and Africa is on fire with insurrection. I've sold more guns to Africa than any place else, except for the Middle East. You'd never go back there. Too many bad memories for both you and Eliot, dear Madeline.

I've got to get out of here myself. My leverage could run out at any time. When your country was stupid enough to trust an ally with an arms shipment abroad and the guns fell into the wrong hands, I knew all about it. That information was enough to get me out of your country's cozy little jail in Sacramento and into a lavish hotel. Thank God, they still don't know about the Syria deal, at least not yet, and I've got to leave before they do.

What they'd really like is for me to *completely* disappear. They're certainly not above murder if it suits their purposes. No government is.

Where are you, Madeline? Is Eliot holding you now? I can never be touched by another human being until I'm held by you. I want *no one* to touch me before that. You've turned me into a reluctant celibate, Maddy.

I remember the day I came back from my business deal with my nervous Tripoli official. I thought you'd be glad to see me, but I didn't like the tentative look in your eyes when I came through the door.

You gave me a hug so slight I barely felt it and when I tried to kiss your cheek, you were already sliding away.

You turned away from me. "So, how is the deal going with your client?"

At that point the deal was going well, but I was still nervous about the risk, and I think you saw it. My cover-up powers were beginning to fail me. Probably the result of falling in love. "Oh, fine. He's just the anxious type, know what I mean?"

You gave me no response. When we had dinner, you were unusually quiet. Later, when we were out on the balcony, you barely touched your wine. You looked out at the sea, lost in thought. Then you stared at me. "Are you sure this deal you're working on is legitimate?"

"What do you mean?"

You lifted your wine glass but then set it down. "I know you sometimes have to go the long way around to do your business, but how far is the long way?"

Too smart. Too damn smart. "Look Maddy, I made a lot of money for us today. For us and for John. If this deal goes through, we can retire. John could even come and live with us once he's out of rehab."

You took me into an embrace deeper than I had ever known. Your arms wrapped around my shoulders as if they were a lost precious possession, suddenly found. I felt your torso become one with mine, the breathes from your body passing through me.

The history of all my embraces fell before me. The loving embraces of my family, torn away. The men who had bought me, using embraces as a threat. The men I had used, taking their embraces in exchange for physical pleasure alone. All that was gone.

I think I could have taken you then, but that would only have been the passion of the body, pathetic in comparison to what you'd just given me. I had to pull away or I'd be lost.

"OK, Maddy, you've learned enough Arabic now. Time for you to start earning your keep around here."

The next day I took you to the back of my apartment house where I kept my beat up, but highly serviceable Toyota truck. You looked shocked at all its dents and chipped paint. "Where did you get this thing?"

"It may not look like much Maddy, but it's a real work horse. It's good for moving guns from the warehouse I use strictly for storage, to the one I actually use to sell and ship the guns. Rami and Ahmed have got a truck more beat up than this. You've only seen them in my Land Cruiser."

You got into the truck with me. "Why not use that or even your Porsche SUV?"

We buckled up and I started up the engine. "Because they would arouse too much suspicion, dear. We must worry about warlords, rebel militias and assorted crazies showing up at my warehouses."

"And where are they?"

I drove us out to the street. "About ten miles outside the city. You'll see. They're in an abandoned village."

We cleared the city limits and rumbled along the back roads, rocking in our seats over boulders, gravel and chunks of dirt. You put your hand on the roof to brace yourself. "I feel like I'm back in Afghanistan in a Humvee."

When we got to the village you stared at all the rundown huts, their roofs collapsed into their walls. You looked at the burnt-out cars without wheels and then turned to me. "I've seen this scene too often. Isn't it funny? The truck can be demolished, the engine useless, but they always take the tires."

"It's the same everywhere, Maddy. Anything that can transport them to somewhere where the bombs aren't falling." We looked at each other in a moment of shared experience. If I wasn't careful, you'd become too good a friend to make love to. "C'mon, let's go see what Ahmed and Rami are up to."

When we walked up to my warehouse with its earthen walls and mud and straw roof, you looked a little surprised. "*This* is your warehouse?"

"Don't let the exterior fool you. Except for the wide door in front, it only looks like a big hut. Like I said, we have to keep a low profile."

I opened the front door and as we went inside, you were shocked to see the walls with aluminum framing and the smooth concrete floor.

Ahmed saw you first. "Maddy!" He dropped the gun he was handling onto the broad worktable in the center of the room. "So long since I see you!"

You laughed and rushed over to him. "You saw me yesterday, you nut!"

He took you into one of his big bear hugs, your feet leaving the floor. "Never get enough of Maddy."

As the two of you separated your faces blushed. *Affection,* I mused to myself. *The dearest of all emotions and the hardest to achieve.*

Rami grumbled as he checked the action on a handgun. "I try to work here. No time for foolishness!"

Ahmed laughed. "Pay no attention to that one, Maddy. Hey! You want some coffee?"

"Sure! Why not?"

Ahmed went to the corner of the table where he kept his ancient stove top espresso maker on an even older hot plate. He was about to pour some espresso into a cup with well-worn stains and then stopped. "This one no good. Too dirty for my Maddy. I get another."

You smiled and put your hand over his. "That one's just fine."

He blushed again. When was all this blushing going to stop?

"OK, if you say so, Maddy."

I couldn't wait to see your reaction to Ahmed espresso. It could summon the deceased. When you took a sip, your eyes expanded as you put your hand to your heart. "Wow! That's good. Good and *strong*!"

"That's right, Maddy. Make a real woman of you!"

I stood back and folded my arms. "She already is a real woman. All right you guys, back to work. I've got to show Maddy around."

I decided to start with what you already knew before I got to the more exotic hardware. I took you over to the green wooden crates, stacked almost to the ceiling. I opened one that was on the floor. "As you already know, these are for AK-47s."

Before I could pull one out, you already had your hands on it, sliding the action back and forth and sighting it. You looked to the left and saw the boxes filled with clips of 373 AK-47 ammo. You inserted one into the gun and sighted it again.

Rami looked up from the gun he was working on. "Don't you point that thing at me, Maddy. I have gun of my own!"

You pulled out the clip and threw it back into the box. "I only point at things I intend to kill. So far, you're not one of them."

Angered, Rami got up from his chair. Ahmed put his hand on his shoulder. "She only tease you. Sit down."

Rami sat down, muttering Arabic obscenities. Thank God, you hadn't learned any of those yet.

I took the gun from you and put it back in the box. "You surprise me, Maddy. I thought US soldiers only used the M4 carbine."

You stared at the guns in their crates. "Some of us were trained to use them. If you lose your weapon in a fire fight and there's a dead Taliban fighter nearby with an AK-47, you use that." You put your hand on the gun. "One killer feeds from the death of another."

I couldn't let you get morbid on your first day of employment. "Let me show you something you *haven't* seen."

I took you to the other side of the warehouse. You saw different kinds of weapons, either handguns stacked on the floor in their original clear packets, or rifles suspended on rods with long strips of plastic in between them.

"The handguns you see are all hi-power. The rifles are used by snipers. All of them come from the FN Herstal company in Belgium."

You picked up one of the handguns. "So, these must be the ones Gaddafi imported."

"In the thousands, Madeline, by way of Turkey. There's more in the other warehouse, off in the woods."

You noticed Ahmed struggling with the slide of a 9mm pistol. "You're doing it too fast, Ahmed. It's only getting jammed. Here, let me show you." You took the gun from him and moved the slide in a slow, even motion. "See? That way the round can enter the chamber or be ejected with no hassle."

Ahmed smiled and gave you a slap on the back. "Yes, I see! Sorry, Maddy. I get too excited you being here."

I glared at him. "Yes, you do."

You saw Rami with a small hand grinder erasing the serial number from a rifle and turned to me. "Grinding out serial numbers? Is that really necessary?"

"It's for the security of my clients, so weapons don't get traced back to them."

I thought my simple ploy would be enough, but I didn't like the look on your face. Next, you saw Ahmed replacing the barrel of a Zoraki 906 blank firing pistol with a different barrel, converting it into a lethal weapon. I didn't think you'd ever witnessed that before and I knew I had to be careful to explain it.

"You've probably never seen one of those, Maddy. It fires blanks, but Ahmed is doing a live fire conversion. A lot of those guns were converted and used against demonstrators during the Arab Spring revolts."

"And you're doing the same thing."

Very quick and I knew I had to be faster. "But not for the same purpose. I ship those to rebels in Africa who want to overthrow tyrants." I didn't mention that I was selling them to both sides.

You looked around at my stockpile. "How often do your buyers come here?"

"Almost never. We prepare the shipment and the official I work with has them picked up. Sometimes we deal directly with a client that my government guy recommends. We've got one coming tonight. You should be here."

That night we all went back to the warehouse. It was supposed to be routine. You helped Ahmed carry the crates of AK-47s up to the front door. Rami didn't want your help as he lumbered with boxes of ammunition that weighed more than he did.

I waited outside for the buyers. At first, they looked more than legitimate, pulling up in a new Toyota Hilux pickup, complete with roll bar. There were two men in the cab and two in the truck bed.

I should have been suspicious when all of them got out, moving slow. Genuine buyers are in a hurry to get in and out. Beware of slow-moving men.

None of them was wearing a sidearm, as far as I could see. Another bad sign. Three of the men were big and dressed in black with close cropped hair and trimmed beards. The fourth man was slender, balding and wearing a suit. That was at least one good sign.

Instead of getting down to business, talking about how many guns they wanted to buy and at what prices, they made small talk, asking us how we were doing and how was the business. They never looked at the crates of AK-47s, one of which I had open, along with an open box of ammo, all for their inspection.

Ahmed and I gave each other a quick look. Rami saw it and looked nervous. You saw it all, sensing our collective tension. You knew enough Arabic by now to make your own small talk. You asked them how *they* were doing in the polite Arabic phrases I'd taught you. They were surprised by your use of the language and complimented you on your pronunciations. You smiled, thanked them and then gave me a knowing glance.

It all happened fast. One of the men in black grabbed an AK-47 in one hand and an ammo clip with the other. He snapped the clip in place, waved it at all of us and shouted at us to raise our hands.

We held up our hands and stayed calm, except for Rami. He shook with fear. If he kept that up, he'd get us all killed.

A second man seized our side arms. The third man pushed us up against the warehouse. The bald man grinned. This was an execution. Take the guns and leave no living witness.

The man with the AK-47 pressed it against your body. "So, American whore. You never see home again!"

With the barrel of the gun turned away, you grabbed it with one hand and punched him with the other. As he fell, you took the gun, turned it on the others and shouted: "Get back you bastards!"

One of the men reached for a pistol tucked in the back of his pants. You shot him in the foot. He fell to the ground in agony. You pointed the gun at the bald man's head. "Get out! Now!"

The other men hoisted their fallen comrade into the truck bed as he moaned in pain. When they drove away, you sprayed bullets on both sides of the truck. They accelerated.

Rami was still shaking as Ahmed threw his arms around you. "You save my life, Maddy. All I could think of was Muhammad, left without me. You save his life, too."

I put my arm around him. Dammit, he *was* a good man. "She saved us all, Ahmed." I turned to Rami. "Although there was one who didn't *deserve* saving."

Rami straightened himself. "I not afraid. One day I show you…especially you, Maddy!"

When we got back to my apartment, I knew I'd have to have a long, stern conversation the next day with my Tripoli official for recommending those goons to me. They probably plied him with lots of cash and like all corrupt politicians, his greed overcame his common sense.

But that was for later. Right now, I still felt the rush of

everything you'd done back at the warehouse. It frightened and thrilled me at the same time. I never knew I could be so sexually aroused.

Later, we went out to the balcony. You sipped your wine and then set down your glass. I rested my hand on yours. I wanted to feel that power within you…that courage. "You made us all look weak out there tonight. Ahmed and I thought it was over. Rami was going to pieces. You made it all look routine. Is that how you got through two tours in Afghanistan?"

You looked out at the sea. "Nothing is routine in war."

I stroked the sleeve of your silk Chanel blouse, the first garment I'd given you. "What were you thinking when they lined us all up?"

"I wasn't."

"You had to be thinking of something, Maddy."

"No. You have to react. You think, you're dead."

You looked down at the waves that crashed on the beach below us. Your eyes were lost in some dark memory I could never understand.

I was in a trance of my own as I let my hand slide down your torso. I continued to let my fingers move until they formed to your hip.

You looked at me as if you were only now aware of my presence. You glanced down at my hand. "I'm going to go down. I need some rest."

As you rushed away, I told you to sleep well, knowing full well that I wouldn't. I could still feel the warmth of your body on my hand.

The next day we acted as if nothing had happened. Over breakfast we made small talk. I brought up the fact that we had a new cache of arms to prepare for shipment. The only thing different was your lack of eye contact with me.

I knew bringing you to me would require stronger methods and I knew just the person to help me…John.

Two days later you came down into my office. "Is your Internet working? I can't bring up anything."

"Let me try." I clicked on the Internet icon. "No. I'm not getting anything either."

"Maybe we should try shutting down."

"Good idea. If that doesn't work, we can always try a power off."

You rushed upstairs. A few minutes later you called down to me. "My shutdown didn't work. Did yours?"

"No, it didn't. Let's go for the power down."

Five minutes later you ran into my office. "It's still not up!"

I shook my head. "Neither is mine."

"Mira, this is serious! I can't reach John, and today is the day for the money transfer!"

"Yes, I know. Let me make some calls."

"Please, do. If that doesn't work, get somebody out here!"

I got up from my desk and put my arm around you. "Of course, I will. It'll be all right."

You sank into me. I could feel your breasts against mine.

"I'm sorry, Mira. It's just that…".

"I know. We'll get it fixed."

That afternoon I got some tech guys out to the apartment. I knew they'd never find the way I'd disconnected the Internet. Savvy technology had yet to reach Tripoli, even in its finer neighborhoods.

I'd had to learn hardware *and* software the hard way. If you're not tech smart in the arms business you'll never be anything but small time, like those idiots on Al Rashad Street.

After the techies left, shaking their heads, you were frantic. "What are we going to do? If we don't get the money to John, they'll throw him out of the rehab center!"

I lead you up to the balcony, my arm comfortably around your waist. "They're not going to do that. They'll give him at least thirty days. In the meantime, we'll get everything fixed."

You gripped my arm. "Can't we use one of those Internet cafes in town?"

"A haven for identity thieves, Madeline. Besides, the way we transfer the money has to be covert to be safe for both you *and* him."

Although the way you stroked my arm seemed to be in an absent-minded way, I was keenly aware of it. "Couldn't I at least just email him?"

"And have your whereabouts found out?"

"I don't care if they find me. Let them send me to Leavenworth!"

"You won't be much help to John there."

You looked down at the sunbathers on the beach; couples under umbrellas, smiling and waving to their children playing in the sand, young couples diving into the water together, or walking hand in hand along the shoreline.

"If I could just *see* him. Even if it was only once."

I ran my hand through your hair. "You will, Maddy. You will."

That night I heard you weeping in your bedroom. Good. I wanted you to suffer the way I had, and I knew it was only a matter of time before your sorrow brought you to me. I didn't have to wait long.

You burst into my bedroom, threw yourself on the bed and wrapped your arms around me. Through your nightgown I could feel your naked body. The closest I'd ever come to it. Every muscle, every bone in you trembled and quaked. I clutched your torso as your sobs crested over me, one wave after another.

I'd used guile and treachery to gain it all, but none of that mattered. You were too wonderful in grief for me to feel regret. I didn't care what happened after this, whatever it was. In this moment, these seconds you were mine and I was happy to play the role of your dark protector.

"Hush," I whispered in your ear as I kissed your tears and stroked your hair.

Your weeping subsided. Your body came to rest on top of me. I felt as if I was a part of you, more than if we had actually made love.

I was supposed to be the one comforting you, but the warmth of your body erased all the cruel embraces of my past. Now I *was* lost.

When you pulled away from me and sat up on the bed, I felt more bereft than when I was twelve years old and alone on the streets.

You rubbed away your tears with the back of your hands, looking like a child. "I'm sorry, Mira. I didn't mean to get so…"

Then I forgot myself. "Sorry? After what you've just given me?"

You looked at me, incredulous. "What do you mean?"

I sat up in bed. "I just meant I want to be here for you, always."

I didn't deserve the smile you gave me, but I took it. "I'll get some better techs out here tomorrow and we'll get it fixed. I promise."

You held me.

Oh God, Maddy, not <u>again.</u> I can't take another one.

I didn't know then that you would try to take your life away from me in a way more violent than I could ever have expected.

CHAPTER II

AHMED'S WARNING

Madeline pretended to sleep on the eleven-hour flight to Germany, but Eliot knew better. He touched her hand. "You're not fooling anybody, you know."

She turned away from him. "Go to sleep. I'm all right."

He put his hand on her shoulder. "No, you're not. What is it? You're not still worried about Mira, are you? We're thirty thousand feet in the air!"

She turned back to him. "I wouldn't be surprised if she walked down that aisle right now and shot us both."

"If she did, our pressurized cabin would collapse, and we'd all fall into the Atlantic Ocean in a fiery ball."

"Stop kidding around, Eliot. She's got a big advantage now...revenge. That makes most people reckless. Mira gets smarter."

Eliot took her into his arms. "I don't care how smart you think she is; she'll never take you from me. Nothing will!"

Madeline looked at the inflight magazines tucked loosely in the back pockets of the seats in front of them. She stared at the well-worn pages and imagined the dozens of strangers that had browsed them as a means to kill time. *Time. Memory. Her worst enemies.*

Madeline turned away. "I'm going to sleep now."

She knew that was impossible as she remembered the day Mira brought new techs out to the apartment. They were the ones Mira had promised would finally fix the Internet problem, so that Madeline could finally reach John.

Madeline became impatient, pacing the floor as the techs worked. She knew what she really needed was to get away. Let them get on with it, and then she would come back to find everything working. But she also knew she could not do just that.

And then Ahmed showed up.

"Made*leen*!" he shouted, as he came through the door. "You, see? I finally learn how to say your name!"

Madeline laughed and hugged him. "You still don't have it right, but that's OK. I like Maddy, better. Especially when *you* say it."

Ahmed pulled away. "What, you not proud with me? After all hard work I do to say it right?" Ahmed put his hands over his chest and continued his teasing. "Oh, Maddy, you break my heart. How can you treat me like this? I thought we friends."

Madeline gave his shoulder a soft punch and hugged him again. "Quit fooling around you big nut! We'll always be friends."

Mira stood back in envy. *Better to get the two of them out of here than have to witness anymore of this.* "Why don't you and Ahmed take a walk," she said. "I'll keep an eye on the techs."

Madeline and Ahmed walked out to the seaside, pausing as they always did at the low sea wall.

"Is Muhammad still giving away all the soccer balls you give him?"

Ahmed smiled. "Yes, always it has been his way to give to others, even when he was little boy. Now, in a few years' time he will be a man, but I will never forget him as child."

Madeline placed her hands on the sea wall, rubbing her palms into the hardened rock. "I wish I could have memories like that about John. All I can see is the frightened kid I tried to protect and couldn't."

Ahmed put his hand over hers. "Mira said there is problem with Internet. You cannot reach John."

Madeline looked out on the sea, the relentless waves that reached out to an endless horizon, all of it implacable to human suffering. "If I don't reach him soon, they'll be nobody to help him."

Ahmed grasped her hand. "Then you must go to him."

"You know I can't. I'm wanted there."

"There is more trouble for you here, I think."

"What do you mean?"

Ahmed stepped back and folded his arms. "I know nothing of Internet, but I know the men Mira has at her apartment. They may be good with computers and such, but I do not trust them."

Madeline drew close to him. "Why not?"

"They do many things in the city besides Internet…bad things. And there is more, Maddy."

"What are you talking about?"

"The way Mira looks at you now. Never have I seen her look at a woman that way."

Madeline turned away as pieces of memory began to form in her mind. Mira's prolonged embraces, the hands that seemed to seek more intimacy. "I don't know how I'd get back to John. How I could help him."

Ahmed put his arm around her. "You are strong woman. You will find a way. You and John will survive, just as Muhammad and I have."

When Madeline got back to the apartment the techs were talking to Mira in Arabic. They were two young men in black slacks and well pressed white shirts. The taller one was saying that something had been done to the Internet connections that they couldn't understand.

As they left, Mira turned to Madeline. "They still can't seem to find anything. They said...".

"I know what they said, Mira."

"I'm sorry, Maddy. I don't know what to do."

Madeline glared at Mira. "Are you *sure* you don't?"

That night Madeline would have given anything for a single night's rest, but sleep was impossible. Staring up at the ceiling, she saw John at the rehab center, desperate and confused. She saw him being turned out of the center and knew he would rather die on the streets than go back to the county facility, which had never helped him.

She saw him wandering on the streets, alone and adrift. How long would it be before he started using again...days, hours, minutes?

She saw him cursing her, blaming her for everything and knew that he was right. How had she let herself get involved with a woman who in the end only wanted her body?

She should have seen through it all. There were so many signs that she had ignored, signs of the willful ignorance that would bring about John's destruction. Every arms deal that she had known about or done was illegitimate, and she had ignored all that for John's sake. This bitter irony sent tears rushing down her face. In the middle of the night, she finally fell asleep.

But the nightmare awaited her.

She felt it come alive like a sudden flame, bursting in her mind as she slept. It had followed her that night in Afghanistan as she ran away from what she had done. It had been with her when Mira had found her on the road and saved her from certain death.

It had been waiting as she had accepted Mira's help to help John. Waiting for an opportunity.

Go on, the nightmare whispered in her ear. *Let the crushed pieces of your life seem to fall in place as you aide your lost brother, I will wait for you. Make Ahmed your beloved friend. I am waiting. Tell all the lies you have told to yourself. I am still waiting. I am that nightmare! I am the ghosts of the unarmed woman and her unborn child that you murdered and I will wait no longer!*

Madeline sat up in bed. She went downstairs and into the kitchen. She grabbed a steak knife from the wooden block. She held the blade over her left wrist. *Yes,* the voice said to her. *First one wrist and then the other.* Madeline's hand trembled.

Go on now. Do it. You know you must. I won't stop until you do. Do it and you'll be free.

Madeline slashed her wrist. Blood gushed forward. She grabbed the knife with her left hand and slashed the other wrist. Blood flowed from the vein. She cried out and collapsed on the floor.

Mira heard the scream and rushed downstairs. "Jesus Christ! What have you done?"

Blood continued to spurt from Madeline's right wrist. Mira knew if she pinched the vein she might save Madeline's life. She knelt and held the vein tightly between her thumb and index finger. With her other hand she grabbed the landline phone on the kitchen counter and called for an ambulance.

As Madeline lost consciousness, the last thing she heard was Mira saying repeatedly, "Don't die. Don't die!"

Mira grabbed a dish towel from the counter and pressed it tightly on Madeline's other wrist. When the first responders arrived, they applied bandages, put Madeline on a gurney and slid her into the ambulance. Mira went with them.

As the ambulance sped through Tripoli, siren blasting, Mira put her hands on Madeline's body, strapped in place. For the first time, Mira saw her hands covered with Madeline's blood. She pulled away and saw the red imprint of her hands on Madeline's nightgown.

I did this, she said to herself. *I caused it. The only person precious to me, the only one left to me, and I have thrown her at death!*

When they got to the hospital Madeline was given a transfusion. Her wounds were stitched and bandaged. She had to stay in the hospital for two days. On the first day Mira came to visit her.

When Mira came through the door, Madeline was sitting up, pillows propped up behind her. Mira had brought a bouquet of flowers in a vase and set it on the table next to Madeline's bed. "How are you feeling?"

Madeline looked down at her bandaged wrists. "Like a fool."

Mira was glad to see the color in Madeline's cheeks, but her eyes were vacant, her long, black hair hanging limp around her neck. Mira stroked Madeline's cheek and brushed back her hair. "You're not the first one to try it. Believe me, I know."

Madeline put her arms under the sheets. "They told me how you pinched the vein. They said that saved my life. How did you learn how to do that?"

Mira sat down on the chair next to Madeline's bed. "From the trafficked girls I worked with. One of them showed me how to do it. Some of the girls couldn't take it anymore and just wanted to check out. I saved two of them that way, but neither of them meant more to me than you."

Madeline slid one of her arms from under the sheet and stared at her bandaged wrist. "Maybe you shouldn't have learned that."

Mira got up from her chair and touched Madeline's arm. "Don't talk like that. "You're alive!"

"Am I?"

A day later Mira brought Madeline back to the apartment. As Madeline sank into the couch, Mira was animated. "I'll make you some of your favorite things...fruit shake, cappuccino, and I just might have some chocolate!"

Madeline acted as if she hadn't heard her. "The stitches have to come out in a week. They said they could come out here to do that... I'll have scars, of course."

Mira stopped what she was doing. "We all have scars, Maddy."

Madeline got up from the couch. "I'm going to go upstairs for a while and rest."

"Don't you want to hear my good news first?"

"Good news?"

"Yes. We got the Internet back!"

For the first time in days, Mira saw Madeline's eyes light up. The thick, black eyes that moments before drifted through clouds, were now alive. "When was this?"

"Just today! Before I picked you up."

Madeline went to the kitchen. "I'm going to need your help, Mira. I can't do any typing for at least a week. We've got to get an email to John and send the money."

"We can do it right now! You can dictate the email to me, and I'll transfer the money."

They went to Mira's office. As Mira sat down and opened her laptop, Madeline pulled up a chair next to her. Mira brought up the Internet and typed in John's email address.

Madeline got up and hovered over Mira. "Tell him the money is on the way. No, tell him first why I couldn't reach him. Why I couldn't…"

Mira put her hand on Madeline's shoulder. "OK, Maddy. OK. Let's go slow."

Madeline sat down and dictated the email to Mira. When Mira was done, she turned to Madeline. "Does that look about right?"

Madeline sat back. "Yes, I think so."

"I guess you don't want to tell him what happened to you, what…"

"No. No, I don't. Now send the money."

Mira made the transfer and the two of them went out to the kitchen. Madeline tried to drink the fruit shake Mira had prepared for her, but her hands were still too weak, the glass trembling between her fingers.

Mira steadied the glass. "Do you want me to help you?"

Madeline set the glass down on the counter. "No, I just need to go slow. Can you check to see if John has replied yet?"

"Maddy, let's give him a chance, OK? You need to eat. Let's sit down at the table."

They sat down and Madeline took slow sips of the fruit shake. Mira looked at Madeline's bandaged wrists. *She's alive. That's all that matters.*

There was a soft tapping at the door. Mira got up and opened it. "Oh, you two."

Ahmed stood on the threshold; his head bowed. Rami was behind him, looking sheepish.

Ahmed looked up at Mira. "So sorry, Mira. I thought maybe Maddy sleeping. I don't want to disturb."

Mira pulled back the door. "She's right here. I should have never told you what happened."

"Maddy!" Ahmed cried out. He rushed over to Madeline, about to embrace her, and then saw her wrists. "Oh no, I should not hug you."

Madeline got up and embraced him. "It's all right. I always have a hug for you, Ahmed."

Rami shook his head. "Why you do this to yourself, Maddy? Makes you look like fool."

Ahmed pulled away from Madeline. "Quiet you! *You* are the fool."

Mira looked at Rami. "Yes, he is. Go back to the car, Rami. Maddy, I'll go check to see if John has replied yet."

Rami left, and Madeline and Ahmed sat down at the table. "Maddy, you are feeling better now?"

"Yes, I'll be all right."

Ahmed looked away. "Maybe it is my fault. I talk too much...frighten you."

Madeline looked at Ahmed's soft eyes, the eyes of a boy in a man's face. "No. Never. It was something that happened a long time ago, in the war."

"Nothing is a long time ago in war. I know too the wounds that will not heal. The ones that no one can see."

Mira came back into the dining room. "Just got a reply from John. Come and see."

Ahmed got up from his chair. "You will want to see what your brother has to say. I will leave now, but I will pray for you."

Maddy kissed his cheek and rushed into Mira's office. She sat down at the desk and read John's reply. Mira stood at a respectful distance.

Dear Maddy,
I didn't know what was going on. Thank God, I got your email! I was afraid you were in trouble and there was nothing

I could do to help you. Are you, all right? You've helped me in so many ways that I'll never be able to repay. I'm sorry I'm such a useless brother, caused you so much pain.

I knew that somehow though you'd reach me. You've never given up on me, always there to protect me, no matter what happened. I don't deserve a sister like you, but I'll never let you go, no matter where you are.

The center was getting nervous about payment, even saying I might have to leave. The money you sent came at just the right time. Write to me again, soon.
I love you,
John

Madeline reached back and took Mira's hand.

That evening, Madeline stood out on the balcony, staring out at the setting sun as its colors faded first to orange and then blood red, before it died into the sea. *How could I have been so selfish? What would have happened to John if I had died?*

Mira came up with a glass of wine in her hand and stood next to Madeline. "The doctor said you should get some counseling."

Madeline watched as the waves of the sea rushed forward and relieved their burdens on the shore. "I don't need any of that. Not after the email with John today."

Mira sipped her wine. "I thought you'd feel that way, but there are other things we've got to do for you."

"Such as?"

"Such as healthy foods, exercise and *no* stimulants."

Madeline smiled. "I wondered why you only brought one glass of wine."

Mira put her arm around Madeline's waist. "There will be time for that."

In the days that followed Madeline stuck to the regime Mira set for her. Breakfast was the same fruit shake but mixed with green vegetables. No cappuccino and no coffee. Lunch was a big salad with almost no dressing. Dinner was fresh fish. No wine.

For exercise they started with short walks and worked up to longer ones. In a few days Madeline was jogging on her own. A few days later a nurse came out to the apartment and removed Madeline's bandages and stitches.

Sitting at the dining room table, Madeline stroked the scars on her wrists. "I came so close...so close."

Mira came out of the kitchen. "I've got something that'll help you forget that."

Mira went up to her bedroom and came back with a pair of woven bracelets. She sat down next to Madeline and slid the bracelets onto her wrist. "This is the finest threaded silk you'll ever see. I've been wanting to give them to you for a long time. I thought the lapis blue strands would remind you of the sea you love so much. The yellow ones are for your afternoon walks with Ahmed."

Madeline smiled and ran her fingers over the bracelets. "What are the green ones for?"

Mira laughed. "Maybe for all the vegetables I've forced down you!"

Madeline formed the bracelets to her wrist. "They're so beautiful. Where did you get them?"

"They're the last thing I stole before I left Beirut. I wanted at least *one* beautiful memory of that place before I left it for good."

"But this is all you have left of your home."

Mira looked out at passersby on the street, carrying bags from designer stores. "I watched people in Beirut load up treasured belongings onto carts, only to see them hit by bombs a few miles later. A few minutes later. Even in their homes. Nothing lasts."

Madeline rubbed the multicolored strands. "I'll take good care of them. I'd love to wear them when I jog, but my sweat would probably ruin them."

"Not at all. You can rinse them out and they'll be fine. Like I said, the finest silk."

The next day, Madeline came in from a run, breathless, but smiling. "Have I earned a cappuccino yet?"

Mira grinned and went to the espresso machine. "Maybe...a little one."

As Mira made the cappuccino, Madeline sat down at the table and took off her warmup jacket. Mira stared at Madeline's torso covered only by a tank top. She saw the perspiration that glistened on Madeline's skin, the streams of sweat that created darkened stains on Madeline's thin garment. *Look away,* Mira said to herself. *Look away.*

When Mira placed the cappuccino on the table and sat down, Madeline grabbed the cup and took a long drink.

Mira put her hand on Madeline's arm. "Hey, slow down. You're not Wonder Woman yet!"

Madeline put down the cup and smiled. "I feel like it. It's been tough, but you brought me through it!" Madeline hugged Mira.

Mira stroked Madeline's back. *Maybe, Maddy...maybe there is yet...*

Madeline pulled away and took another sip of cappuccino, slower this time. "You know what I really miss, though?"

"What's that?"

"Ahmed."

Mira sat back. "I was afraid you'd say that. He called earlier and asked if he could see you."

"Really? Did you tell him to come by?"

"Yes, unfortunately. He should be here in a few minutes."

Madeline sprang up from her chair. "Great! I'll go up and take a shower before he gets here."

Mira watched Madeline run up the staircase. *Like she was going out on a damn date.*

Ahmed arrived and he and Madeline went out for a walk, arm in arm. "I can't believe how strong you look now, Maddy...how beautiful!"

Madeline clasped his arm. "But I can't be more beautiful than Muhammad, right?"

Ahmed blushed. "I see the beautiful things inside of him. Things only I can see."

They stopped at their usual place by the sea wall. Ahmed looked out at the waves. Madeline looked down at the sand below, the millions of granules that would outlast them all. "I wish I could see John right now."

Ahmed put his arm around her. "You will, Maddy. You will."

Madeline looked up at him. "I hope it hasn't been hard on you and Muhammad that Mira couldn't do her business...the Internet being down."

Ahmed stepped away. "I don't know...maybe I should not say."

"Say what?"

Ahmed rubbed his beard. "While you were in hospital I came to Mira's apartment one day. I hear Mira on the phone in her office, angry. More angry than I ever hear her. At first, I think I should go, but maybe I can help. I walk quiet to her office, stay away from door, but I can see her inside, her back to me. She is saying something about Syria. I saw on her desk, computer is open. Internet is on."

Madeline stood back in horror as jagged pieces of her memory created a dark mosaic. Mira had said the Internet only returned the day Madeline came back from the hospital. Madeline remembered all the techs that had come to the apartment, unable to do anything. She especially remembered the last two, whom Ahmed had warned her about.

Then the darkest memory came to Madeline as she recalled the day, she had forced opened Mira's desk and seen a second server underneath. The Internet––*Mira's* internet— had to have been working the whole time.

Ahmed couldn't help but see the angry look on Madeline's face. "Maddy, I am sorry. I should not have said anything. I don't understand about these things...I"

For Ahmed's sake, Madeline composed herself. "It's all right, Ahmed. So, what did you do after everything you saw that day?"

"I went away. I did not know what to believe. Now I think I have done something wrong."

"You didn't do anything wrong. Not you."

CHAPTER 12

RECKONING

It was 1am when Madeline and Eliot landed in Frankfurt. They had an eleven-hour layover before they flew out to Beirut and decided to go to a nearby hotel until then.

They checked in and went to a fourth-floor room which had a balcony that looked out on the airport runways. As Eliot set down their bags, Madeline pulled back the balcony's sliding glass door and stepped out, where Eliot joined her.

Together they watched jets taxi on the runways, lining up behind each other, one after another, each going to some faraway land.

Eliot pointed to one of the planes. "Where do you suppose that one is going?"

Madeline watched as the plane took flight. "Doesn't really matter. The world is such a small place anyway. Nobody knows that better than us. However far away we go, it'll never be far enough."

Eliot put his arm around her. "It's all right, Maddy. We'll be safe where we're going."

"I hope so. You know what I'd really like to do right now?"

"I assume, sleep!"

Madeline rested her head on Eliot's chest. "No, make love. "But I'm too exhausted."

"Don't tell me you're making that kind of an excuse already. That's only supposed to happen when we're an old married couple!"

"Is that your idea of a marriage proposal?"

Eliot laughed and held her closer. He watched as another plane took to the sky, off to another country. "It doesn't matter that we can't make love, as long as I can hold you."

They went inside, lay down on the bed and continued to hold each other. Her cheek against his chest, she felt his breath slowing down, fainter, softer, until her own breath seemed to merge with his and she could not discern the difference between the two. The life forces of their bodies, the thing that *gave* them life, moment to moment, now seemed stronger than any time they had made love.

They drifted off to sleep, but as dawn arose a few hours later, Madeline woke up. The warmth of Eliot's body was still there to comfort her, deeper, even stronger than before. His breath was almost imperceptible now. The only thing certain was the slow, even beating of his heart.

Careful not to wake him, she slid out of his embrace. His arm drifted onto the sheet, unaware of her absence. She got up from bed and watched him sleep, the way she had so many times in Freeport, without his ever knowing about it.

The repose of his body was perfect, free of tension. Seeing him this way she felt that he was under her protection, safe as long as she watched over him.

But it was an illusion. She thought that maybe one day she would confess to him how that had been so. She saw him smiling as she told him of all the times, she had allowed herself the fantasy that even with the world after them, *she* could keep him from harm.

She saw herself blushing as she gave up her cherished memory to him. She saw him smiling and laughing as he held her. She even heard him talking.

"Why didn't you ever tell me about that before, Maddy? It's beautiful!"

Because, Eliot. Because.

She wondered if other lovers allowed themselves similar illusions. She'd never *been* a lover until Eliot. She'd come to him out of the hands of men who'd only wanted to use her, and she had used them, taking the physical as a pathetic substitute for tenderness.

She went to the balcony and watched the sun emerge from the horizon as if it were an embryo, finding the world for the first time and giving it yet another chance at rebirth.

She only had to look down at the planes taking off to realize that this was just another day, one more chance to be squandered as people moved about the world, seeking new ways to destroy each other.

She looked back at Eliot. He had turned on his side now, away from her. Would he turn away from her forever if he knew what she'd done to Ahmed? Eliot said he would forgive her anything, but could even Eliot's love sustain that?

That dark thought brought back blackened memories of Mira. *Go on,* the voice of death told her once again. *You know they'll always be there. Why try to escape them? It's useless.*

Madeline recalled the day Ahmed had told her he suspected Mira had been using the Internet, while acting is if it were down. That guise had awakened a fury in Madeline's blood, but she couldn't show that to Ahmed, and she wouldn't show it to Mira.

Instead, Madeline had walked back to the apartment with her "combat face" on. She would deal with her enemy in a stone-cold fashion, the only way to defeat them.

Madeline entered the apartment without making a sound. She heard Mira's raised voice in her office. As Madeline eased her way down the hall she could see Mira on the phone, shouting into the receiver.

"This deal is done! You can't stop it now. Quit obsessing over it. None of the other deals ever bothered you. This is the one that's going to get me out of this damn business!"

Madeline thought Mira was talking to the client who had given her so much trouble, but then she heard something more. Something much worse.

Mira paused for a moment before continuing her rant. "What? So, what if women and children are in the crowds? It's the rebel's own fault for letting them be there! The Syrian government must do *something* to stop the demonstrations."

Mira slammed down the phone as Madeline entered the office, startled by Madeline's sudden presence. "I didn't hear you come in. How was your walk with Ahmed?"

Madeline glared at her. "Enlightening."

Sensing Madeline's mood, Mira attempted nonchalance. "Really? How so?"

Madeline stood in front of Mira's desk. "He let me in on a little secret of yours, although he didn't mean to. He said he'd seen you on the Internet while I was still in the hospital. *You* told me we didn't get it back until the day I came home."

Mira shuffled some papers on her desk. "He doesn't know what he's talking about. When did he see me on the Internet?"

Madeline spread her arms and gripped the desk. "He came to the apartment one day when you were railing on the phone, too angry to notice his presence. He saw your open laptop with the Internet on. As furious as you were, he didn't want to stick around."

Mira closed her laptop and pushed in the drawer. "He's got his days mixed up. He always was the slow one. I should have never let him come to work for me. He's too much like you, always gushing over little brother."

Madeline leaned across the desk. "You had the Internet up the whole time. *The whole time!* And now you're sending guns to Syria to kill innocent civilians! I heard you on the phone."

Now, Mira gripped the desk and leaned in, the two women face to face. "What, you think I'm the only one doing this? I'm nothing compared to *your* country. Last year they exported forty-six billion dollars in weapons. You don't think some of those weapons fell into the wrong hands? I know of at least one deal where they did. You don't think there are others? Impossible."

"They don't send them to kill unarmed people."

Mira crossed her arms. "Oh, really? Tell it to the people of Lebanon…all the weapons I saw scattered on the streets between invasions with US markings on them. All the corpses piled up, women and children included. They're the first to die. Don't tell me you weren't ever involved where some of them weren't killed."

Madeline turned away as tears came to her eyes. "I never did it on purpose…I didn't mean…".

"Oh, so now we hear the truth. What little atrocities have *you* committed?"

Madeline came around the desk and shoved Mira against the wall. "I never hurt anybody the way *you* do! How could you do that to all those people? How could you do that to me and to John? Why *him*?

Madeline was shocked to see tears flow down Mira's face.

"It was the only way I had to bring you to me. I'd do it all again if it would make you love me."

Madeline stormed out of the office and went up to her bedroom. Mira remained against the wall, weeping.

Now, Madeline turned to see Eliot rising from bed. "How long have you been up? Didn't you get any sleep?"

"Some. Enough."

Eliot put on his jeans and T-shirt and came out to the balcony. "Are you sure about that?" He took Madeline's shoulders and looked into her eyes. "I don't like those red lines I see."

Madeline turned away. "Just jet lagged. I'm all right."

Eliot held her. "Everything's going to be fine now. Just four hours to Beirut and we're safe."

Safe. What did that word mean? She'd given up that word when she went to war. That's how she kept fighting. Live every day as if it were your last. That was the deal, the contract. The only way to keep fear at bay, get home and be safe. But the memories after war—*her* war, contained far more terror.

"You'd better get dressed, Maddy. We want to go down and have breakfast before our flight."

When their plane took off, Madeline looked back on the city, dozing in the early morning as sunlight glistened on the plane's silver wings. She took Eliot's hand. *Maybe we really will be free this time.*

They flew over Austria, Bulgaria, Turkey. Madeline looked down through the clouds at the cities below. "I wish we could stay up here and just look down on it all."

Eliot put his arm around her. "We've got a life to live, Maddy. There's a space down there for us."

She wished he were right, but as they sat back, she felt the dark thread of memory take hold of her. She knew it had the power to reach her and weave itself into her mind *wherever* she was. Time and space meant nothing to dark recollections. She recalled the confrontation with Mira.

Madeline paced in her bedroom, knowing she had to act fast. She couldn't spend another day under Mira's roof. She had to get away and back to John.

But she would need money to do that…a lot of it. Money for an airline ticket, money to help John, and most of all, money for a passport. The only way to get that was on the Black Market and that meant Al Rashad Street with all its dangers. There was no other way.

She heard Mira leaving the house. Madeline went to the window and saw her driving away in her Porsche SUV. This was her chance. Although Madeline knew most of Mira's money was in offshore accounts, she remembered seeing bundles of hundred-dollar bills in Mira's desk.

Madeline made a quick change into a pair of blue jeans and a T-shirt, hoping it would allow her to blend in on Al Rashad Street. She took only a shoulder bag with a few essentials, not wanting to show any sign of a hasty exit.

Then she saw her wrists. She stared at the colorful silk bands that Mira had given her with such thoughtfulness, wondering to herself how anyone who had saved her life twice, could be so indifferent to the lives of so many innocents.

There was no time for that. She yanked off the bracelets and threw them under the bed. She went down to Mira's office, pulled open the desk drawer and shoved the money into her bag.

But she would need transport. It was too far to Al Rashad Street. Too much distance in which Mira could find her. She went to the back of the apartment house and got into Mira's beat-up truck. Thank God, the keys were in the ignition! She fired up the engine and drove out to the street. As she raced down the road, even faster thoughts rushed through her mind. How would she go about this? Who would she talk to? Wouldn't asking for something like this make her a target? Of course, it would.

She knew that with her black hair and dark features she might pass for a local, but she would have to speak perfect Arabic...street Arabic. She'd learned enough jargon spending so much time with Ahmed, but could she really fool anyone? *Oh, Ahmed, where are you now that I need you so much?*

She got to Al Rashad Street, parked the truck and got out. Nothing had changed since the day she'd driven through there with Mira. If anything, it was worse. Now, almost all the gun sellers looked like teenagers. From their grimy stalls they handed over 9mm pistols and AK-47s, accepting money and talking on their cell phones at the same time.

Madeline looked at one seller who couldn't be more than fourteen. *Back home he'd be working at a fast-food restaurant, selling nothing more harmless than a hamburger. Home. John.*

Some passersby gazed askance at her, but most were too busy buying weapons to be concerned with one more woman.

Move, Madeline. Move. Make something happen.

Going through the throng of gun buyers, Madeline noticed a vendor off to one side, oddly out of place. His stall was clean and well kept. He had no guns for sale, no pistols or rifles, only long strands of silver necklaces hanging in front of him.

Madeline realized he had to be a throwback to the time when the market was solely inhabited by craftsmen. The time Mira had mused about as they cruised through the market on their way to her apartment.

The necklace seller was a middle-aged man with a well-worn but neatly pressed white shirt. The fact that he was

balding only made his soft black eyes appear more ingenu-
ous. No one was paying any attention to him, but Madeline
felt she knew him. He was somebody's husband, somebody's
father, doing what little he could with what little he had.

She knew she had to start off by being polite. She
stepped up to his stall and placed her hand to her heart.
"As-Salaam Alaikum." Peace be unto you.

He touched his heart and gave the response. "Wa-
Alaikum Salaam." And unto you, peace.

For a while they exchanged other courteous phrases
until he politely interrupted. "You are American?"

She knew she had to come up with a story—fast. One
that would touch the heart of what appeared to be a tender-hearted man. "Canadian."

"May I ask what brings you to Libya?"

Madeline bowed her head. "I don't wish to burden you
with my troubles. That would be unkind."

The man looked into her eyes. "We all have them, but
Allah is merciful."

"I must depend on Him now, since there is no one else
to help me and my husband."

The man leaned over the counter. "What has befallen
you?"

"My husband is from here. We met in Canada and were
married. I converted to Islam. He is suspected of being a
terrorist, but with Allah as my witness, I swear my husband
is innocent."

Madeline hated invoking a deity to lie to someone who
appeared so dear, but there was no other way.

The man paused before speaking again. "My name is
Salem. What may I call you?"

"Madeline. My husband and I had to flee Canada and
come here. A man who said he would help us stole our

passports. Now we must leave again but have no way of doing so."

Salem's eyes were even softer when worried. "What is your husband's name?"

Madeline thought of the kindest name she knew. "Ahmed. He would be with me today, but he must remain in hiding. Forgive me for asking this, I know I am a stranger to you, but do you know of anyone who could provide us with passports? We are desperate."

Salem rubbed his chin as he looked about at all the gun dealers. He leaned in closer to Madeline and spoke in a whisper. "I do not know about these things, but it is said that Mr. Khan on Shawgy Street deals in such business."

Madeline reached into her bag and grasped two one hundred-dollar bills. She placed them into Salem's hand and put her hand over his. "I know I may offend you by doing this, but it is all I have to give for your kindness."

Salem pressed the money back into Madeline's hand. "Your troubles are great. I cannot accept."

"Take it for your family, then."

"Allah watches over them. May He watch over you and your husband."

Shawgy Street was nearby. Madeline asked a woman in the neighborhood for the home of Mr. Khan. The woman pointed to an upstairs apartment in the next building.

Madeline entered a dusty hallway with a decaying staircase. The warped boards beneath her feet threatened to give way as she went to the second floor. She saw a tall door that had once been grand, with carefully carved panels, now crusted and dirty. She noticed the doorknob with its intricate engravings, the silver patina rusted away. She knocked softly on the door. No response. She was about to knock again when she heard a deep voice from inside.

"Who is there?"

"A client."

Moments passed with no further word from the baritone voice. Madeline wondered if she had been heard and was about to speak again when from inside, she heard a low murmur.

"Enter."

Madeline opened the door to see a man sitting erect in a leather wing back chair. Although the chair showed signs of age, its deep creases cracking here and there, his slender figure made it appear elegant, as his long arms rested in a languid pose on the chair's armrests. In front of him stood an oak desk with scrolled wooden designs, chipped on the corners, but well-polished.

He was a man in his fifties with a full head of black hair, streaked with silver. He wore a black sport coat and white shirt. The fingers of his right hand tapped on the chair's armrest as he eyed Madeline. "Ah, American."

Madeline grinned. "You knew that fast?"

"You don't know how obvious you are?"

Madeline attempted to exchange polite Arabic phrases.

Mr. Khan waved his hand. "You don't need to do all that. I speak English. Why are you here?"

Madeline sat down on a chair in front of the desk. "I was told you might be able to help me with a passport."

Mr. Khan leaned back in his chair, his eyes intent on Madeline, as he slid his index finger over his upper lip. "Who told you this?"

"A vendor on Al Rashad Street."

"Which one? Describe him."

"He's an older man with thinning hair. He sells necklaces."

Mr. Khan put his arms on the desk. "Oh, yes, Salem. Poor man."

"You know him well?"

"Not really, but one must know something about everyone in this city of one is to stay alive. You appear as though *your* life may be in some jeopardy."

Madeline looked away. "I need a passport to get back to America."

Mr. Khan narrowed his eyes on her. "What happened to the one you used to get here? Lost? Stolen? Why not go to your consulate?"

Madeline knew it was useless to lie. "I can't. I was in the war in Afghanistan. I…"

Mr. Khan waved his hand again. "Allegiances mean nothing here. They change by the hour. Money is the only constant. How much can you pay?"

"Five hundred."

With a long sigh Mr. Khan sat back and gripped the arms of his chair. "I will forgive the insult since you are obviously new at this business."

Madeline fidgeted in her chair. "Seven hundred then?"

"Why do you insist on insulting me with such a paltry sum? A thousand. No less."

Madeline knew that would barely leave her enough for an airline ticket. "My resources are limited. Could we settle on eight hundred?"

Mr. Khan glared at her. "To say that you try my patience would be an understatement. A moment longer and I will ask you to leave."

"All right, then. A thousand."

Madeline reached into her bag, counted out ten one hundred-dollar bills and laid them on the desk.

Mr. Khan shook his head. "No. Five hundred now and the rest later. Amateurs! You are the misery of my life."

Madeline took back five of the bills as Mr. Khan rose and took a camera out of his desk. "Stand over there against the wall."

Madeline went to a white backdrop. Mr. Khan snapped her picture. "Come back tonight. It will be ready."

Madeline left and descended the ancient staircase. *Tonight. I've got an afternoon to kill. By now, Mira knows I'm gone.*

When Mira came home, she went to Madeline's bedroom. Something wasn't right. The bed had been made in a hurry, covers shoved up under pillows. She went to the closet. Everything seemed to be there. She paced the room, searching for anything that appeared out of order.

She stood next to the bed, staring down at the wrinkled bedspread. *All I ever wanted was to lie next to you.* Then she felt something under her foot. She bent down and saw Madeline's bracelets crumpled beneath.

She grabbed the cellphone from her purse and called Ahmed. "Have you seen Madeline today?"

"No, I have not. I thought I would come by later. She is not home?"

"Not right now. Probably out for a walk."

Ahmed sensed Mira's nervousness. "Is something wrong? Should I come by now?"

"No. Stay where you are."

Mira clicked off and called Rami. "Madeline's gone. I've got to find her."

"Gone? Where would she go?"

"I don't know, but I've got a good idea."

"I'll get Ahmed."

"No! Not him. Get Tareq. He'll know what to do. Come over here after you talk to him."

As Mira hung up, Rami was worried. Mira hadn't used Tareq for a long time. Only when violence was necessary.

Rami called Tareq. "A friend of Mira's is missing who must be found."

A stern voice answered. "How much will she pay?"

"You know she always pays more. She will pay double for this one, I think."

"Double? Come now."

Rami turned off his phone and went to Mira's apartment. As they drove away fast in Mira's SUV, Ahmed saw them from the street.

Tareq's apartment was near Al Rashad Street. He was standing out front. He was a big man in his thirties with a shaved head and a tattooed face.

He climbed into the car. "Who is this friend you are looking for, Mira? Rami said you would pay more."

"It's a woman. American."

From the back seat, Tareq bellowed with laughter. "Woman? American? It will be easy."

Mira looked back at him. "Not so easy. She's desperate to get out of here and she's a combat veteran."

Tareq smirked. "So was I. So, what?"

"I've seen her take out bigger men than you."

"If she American woman, will be no problem."

Rami looked at Mira. "Where do you think Maddy will go?"

"Al Rashad Street. The Black Market is the only place she can get a passport." Mira looked back at Tareq. "Who's good with passports over there?"

"Khan. He is the best."

"Show us where he lives."

As they got to Khan's apartment and went up the stairs, Mr. Khan was locking the door to his office, about to leave.

"Excuse me sir," Mira said to Khan. "Have you had any visitors today, an American woman perhaps, young, with dark hair?"

In a slow fashion, Mr. Khan put his keys into his pocket and eyed all three of them, paying special attention to Tareq. He also noticed both men were wearing sidearms. "No one of that description has been here today."

Mira narrowed her eyes on him. "And you're sure?"

Khan jostled the keys in his pocket. "Quite sure."

Mira folded her arms. "We're willing to pay a large sum for information on her whereabouts."

Khan's hand shook as he felt for a knife in his pocket. "As I said, I've seen no such person."

Tareq pushed Rami aside, grabbed Khan and shoved him against the wall. "You are lying! Now tell us where she is!"

Shocked by Tareq's sudden assault, Khan let go of his knife and held up his hands. "I have done you no harm. Please leave me in peace!"

Tareq slapped him. "I will show you the meaning of harm!"

"That's enough!" Mira shouted. "We'll find her on our own."

Tareq released Khan, who was shaking from the attack. As Mira led her men down the staircase, Khan pushed back his hair, straightened his jacket and touched the cheek Tareq had slapped. *Thugs! Henchmen! Why did I ever leave Jordan?*

Down on the street, Mira turned to Tareq. "What were you thinking up there? We may need that man again!"

Tareq shrugged. "You said you want to find woman."

"Not that way! All right, you two. We've got to split up. If one of you finds her, call me on my cell. Otherwise, meet me on Al Rashad Street in a few hours, and Tareq…bring her back unharmed, understood?"

Tareq grumbled and nodded his head.

CHAPTER 13

BEIRUT

Madeline and Eliot landed in Beirut at 11AM. They cleared customs with no difficulty.

"See?" Eliot said, as they walked out of the airport. "I told you we wouldn't have any trouble."

Madeline looked about at all the taxis weaving in between each other as they pulled up to the airport entrance. She saw Lebanese looking jet-lagged, but relieved to be home. Mixed in with them were smiling tourists, anxious to go out on adventures in an exotic land.

But her recollection of the day she had had to hide out from Mira on Al Rashad Street, still haunted her. "Will we really be safe here, Eliot?"

Eliot saw the troubled look on Madeline's face. "Of course, we will. What is it, Maddy?"

"Nothing."

Eliot put his arm around her. "Don't give me that. What's wrong?"

"Never mind. We need to get out of here."

Eliot flagged down a taxi. As they got into the cab, the driver looked back at them and smiled. "Oh, American. Very nice."

Madeline looked at Eliot. "Wherever we go, they make us in a minute."

The cab pulled away and the driver looked at them in the rearview mirror. "So, where we go, Americans?"

Eliot leaned forward. "Can you recommend a good hotel?"

The driver scratched his chin. "There is nice one on Abdel Baki Street, but..." He rubbed his thumb over his index and middle fingers.

"That sounds good," Eliot said. "Take us there."

Madeline put her hand on Eliot's shoulder. "We should be careful with money."

"We've got more than enough. Besides, don't you think we've earned a vacation?"

Their driver took them past Tripoli's elegant Corniche, the broad esplanade that looks out on the Mediterranean Sea. Tall palm trees lined one side of the promenade. Across the street, new high-rise apartment buildings and condominiums enjoyed magnificent views from their terraces.

Couples strolled along the seaside walkway, holding hands and talking on their cell phones. All were dressed in the latest fashion, women in colorful tailored slacks and form-fitting tops. The men wore designer jeans and silk shirts.

Even the joggers that drifted in and out among the pedestrians had warmup suits with prestigious name brands emblazoned on their jackets and pants.

Madeline looked at their driver. "Does everyone here dress like this?"

The cabbie smiled and adjusted his weather-beaten baseball cap. "Oh yes, even when exercise. Must be your first time here, eh? You will get used to all."

Eliot looked out on the rock formations that jutted up against the promenade. "This has got to be our first stop after we check in to the hotel."

Madeline saw a woman pass by in a shimmering white dress that she could have worn to an opera. "No, our *first* stop should be to a clothing store!"

"I thought you said we had to watch the money!"

As they got close to the hotel their driver had recommended, the traffic was jammed. Horns blared in an uneven throng of vehicles, twisting and turning within inches of each other, trying to get the upper hand. Matters were made worse by foolhardy pedestrians, seeking pathways between the swarm of cars.

Madeline clutched Eliot's arm. "This is crazy. One of those walkers is going to get hurt!"

The cabbie looked back at Madeline. "Yes, always it is like this, but nobody—"

As one driver saw an opening and accelerated, a man stepped off the curb, about to be hit. The driver slammed on his brakes.

Madeline lurched forward and cried out. "No! Stop!"

The car stopped without hitting the pedestrian, but the man lost his balance and fell to the street. The driver got out and helped him to his feet. Madeline sank back and covered her face with her hands.

Eliot held her. "He's not hurt. He's safe."

Madeline's hands fell to her lap as a dreaded memory flashed behind her closed eyes. The sight of a stricken man, falling on Al Rashad Street.

When they got to their hotel and paid the driver, they stepped out to see a seven-story building made of smooth sandstone. Black awnings bearing the hotel's emblem, curved downward to the wide hotel doors, made of darkened glass.

As they entered the lobby, a tall man with slicked-back hair and an elegant pinstriped suit, stood behind a long counter made of polished cedar wood, native to Lebanon. The man spread out his arms on the counter, looking a little dubious at Madeline and Eliot's worn jeans, faded T-shirts and outdated luggage. His voice was imperious. "May I help you?"

"We need a room for a few days," Eliot said. "Possibly a week, until we get settled."

The man raised one eyebrow. "I see. What did you have in mind, a standard room on a lower floor?"

"Oh no, something with a view of the sea."

The man flipped through a catalogue of available rooms. "They are our most expensive. Can you provide a deposit?"

Eliot took a few one-hundred-dollar bills from his wallet. The man was quick to notice that Eliot possessed others. "Would this be enough, or do you need more?"

All signs of the man's previous haughtiness disappeared as he smiled and accepted the money. "That would be more than sufficient. Thank you, sir."

Madeline leaned across the counter. "Are there clothing stores nearby...you know, the best ones?"

"Of course, young lady! You must go to the Beirut Souks. All the designer stores are there. I can easily obtain a taxi for you."

Eliot wrapped his arm around Madeline's waist. "Let's get settled into our room first, then we can go shopping."

Their room was on the top floor with a broad view of the sea. As Eliot stood out on the balcony and inhaled the salt air, Madeline took in the bathroom with its walk-in glass shower and marble countertop. In the living area, she found an overstuffed couch with matching chair and ottoman. Behind a partition she saw the kitchenette, complete with wet bar. Lastly, she went to the bedroom with its king size bed, covered with an ample white comforter. She imagined herself and Eliot lying there. At last, they would have time to make love.

But that was for later. Right now, she *had* to go shopping. She saw Eliot leaning over the balcony railing, his face into the wind. *Doesn't that guy ever get enough of the view?*

They took a cab to the Beirut Souks. When they emerged from their taxi, they thought their driver had deposited them at the wrong place. All they could see was an ancient brick archway, capped with a dome.

Madeline looked in at the cabbie. "Are you sure this is the right place?"

The driver leaned over to her. "Oh yes, Miss. What you see is old Souks from long time ago. This is all that is left after the civil war, but inside you will see all new shops. Enjoy!"

When they stood back from the archway, they realized now that it had been integrated into a series of modern buildings, more than a block long. Going through the arch, they felt as if they were passing through time, until it opened onto a broad pedestrian walkway, lined with shade trees. On both sides of the interior boulevard they saw modern high-rise buildings, their ground floors lined with one designer shop after another. They smiled as they looked back at the archway and understood the architect's design. Blend the classical with the new in a perfect match.

They entered one wing of the shopping mall to see its long corridor and high, cathedral style roof. One after another, luxury stores presented all the latest fashions in wide, well-lit windows. Mannequins wore everything from designer jeans and jogging suits to dazzling evening wear.

"And just think, Eliot. The other side has even more!"

"I was afraid you were going to bring that up."

Madeline stopped in front of a men's store. "Know what we should do?"

"Go back to the hotel?"

"No, silly. Buy some nice things for you and then I'll decide on some clothes for myself."

Eliot folded his arms. "Oh, I get it. Make *him* happy and then go hog wild for yourself!"

She put her arm around him. "Something like that."

He kissed her cheek. *A kid at Christmas,* he thought. *I'd love her with nothing more than what she's wearing. But God, it's good to see her this happy.*

Madeline had to drag Eliot into the men's store.

"I don't need all this stuff, Maddy."

"Yes, you do! Look at all these people, the way they're dressed." From inside the store, they saw shoppers passing by wearing the latest fashions and carrying bags from up-scale stores. "Don't worry. I'll do the shopping for you. All you have to do is try them on and make sure they fit."

Eliot plopped down on a soft leather couch as Madeline selected jeans, slacks, dress shirts and shoes. Reluctantly, he went to the dressing room and changed.

Afterwards, they paid for the clothes and went back to the mall. Madeline rubbed her hands together. "OK, now my turn." She looked in the window of several stores before deciding on one which featured casual clothing. "This is what I'm looking for. Sophisticated but fun!"

As they entered the store they were greeted by a slender young woman in tailored trousers and a tuxedo style blouse. "How may I serve you today?"

"I love what you're wearing," Madeline said. "Is it available in the store?"

"Of course! I'm sure we have your size."

Madeline disappeared with the salesgirl as Eliot settled in on a white lounge chair. Another salesgirl approached him. "Would you like some coffee sir, while you wait?"

"I'd love some. I could be here for a while."

The girl left and returned with coffee in a demitasse cup, along with biscotti cookies on a small plate. As Eliot sipped the Turkish coffee, he saw a white, silk blouse laid out on a display table. *That would be perfect on Maddy.*

With the help of her salesgirl, Madeline chose tailored jeans, pleated slacks, long-sleeved blouses and fitted T-shirts. She finished her outfits with espadrille sandals in three different colors. She found a jogging suit that shimmered in lapis blue.

Madeline came out wearing charcoal gray slacks with a black silk T-shirt.

Eliot sat up in his chair. "Are you sure you're the same girl I came in with?

Madeline turned to admire herself in a three-way mirror. "I don't know about that, but I guess I'm not so bad after all!"

Even the salesgirls stood back in awe. "You make our clothes look so glamorous. You should be a model!"

As Madeline took another look at herself in the three-way mirror, Eliot got up and put his hands on her shoulders, smiling into her reflection. "Are you pleased with yourself, Miss Madeline?"

She leaned against his chest. "Yes. Yes, I *am*."

"You know what would be perfect, though?"

She turned and faced him. "What's that?"

"This blouse I saw while you were changing. It would be perfect on you!"

"Great! Where is it?"

Eliot went to the display table and lifted the blouse he had seen. "Isn't this beautiful?"

Madeline turned pale. The blouse was identical to another she knew. The first garment Mira had given her, now became a grim reminder of a final confrontation on Al Rashad Street, and all the bloodshed that followed.

"What is it, Maddy? You look like you've seen a ghost."

"I don't want that thing, Eliot. Put it back."

"You don't want at least to try it on?"

"No!"

Madeline went back to the dressing room, gathered up the clothes and laid them on the counter. As the sales-girls bagged the items, they gave each other puzzled looks. Madeline walked out of the store as if Eliot wasn't there.

One of the salesgirls turned to Eliot. "What happened to her, sir? She seemed so pleased before."

"It's all right. Where's a good place for coffee around here?"

"There are dozens for you to choose from. One, only a few stores away."

Eliot caught up to Madeline, walking fast down the mall. "Hey, slow down," he said, as he turned her around. "You trying to get rid of me or something?"

Madeline pulled away and investigated a jewelry store window. She stared at wedding rings in tiny velvet boxes laid out on a satin scarf. *Could these precious things really hold two people together?*

Eliot put his arm around her. "What happened back there? I know it wasn't about a blouse."

"Nothing. I'm sorry."

Eliot stroked her cheek. "Come on, let's get some coffee. They said in the store there's a place close by."

They found the coffee house and entered to see black, wooden chairs and tables on a bleached hardwood floor. From above, gray, hooded lamps hung down, creating per-fect indirect lighting. The glass display cases showed salads, sandwiches and desserts.

Eliot spied waffles, topped with strawberries. "I've *got* to have that. I don't care if it is afternoon!"

Madeline saw a large salad with Greek olives and sund-ried tomatoes. "That looks like a healthier choice to me."

"OK, but don't try to steal any of my waffles!"

They went to the long, white countertop and ordered the food from a friendly, bearded barista. "Ah, faraway visitors! *Ahlan wa sahlan.* Welcome!"

As they sat down and enjoyed their meal, numerous pa-trons engrossed in Backgammon, still found time to nod and smile in Madeline and Eliot's direction.

Adjoining the coffee house was a boutique bookstore. Well-dressed customers carefully selected titles from the rows of books, mounted in cedar wood racks.

"I can't believe it," Madeline said, as she finished her salad. "These people aren't only cultured, they're friendly!"

Eliot reached across the table and squeezed her hand. "I told you we'd be safe. Hey, how about some of that Turkish coffee, like I had back at the store?"

"*I'm* up for a cappuccino!"

After they finished their drinks, they got a taxi back to the hotel. Riding along the seafront, Madeline noticed more high-rise buildings under construction.

Madeline leaned forward to talk to their driver, another friendly Beiruti, wearing a beret, formed to a rakish angle. "There's still so much going on in your city. Hasn't there been some trouble from the Syrian war?"

"Oh yes, Miss. Last year war came to us, Sunni Muslims and Alawites fighting, but always we build back up. It is our way!"

Madeline leaned back and looked at Eliot. "Not only friendly and cosmopolitan, but *resilient*!"

When they got back to the hotel, they asked the concierge about the best restaurants for dinner. Seeing the designer bags Madeline and Eliot were carrying, stuffed with new clothes, the concierge knew exactly where to send them. "Oh, you must go to the Ashrafieh district. It has the best. All the young people go there."

They went up to their room, showered and changed into the new clothes. Madeline admired herself in the full-length mirror. Eliot came up behind and held her close. "Do you think we can pass as sophisticates among all the in-crowds?"

"We'll knock them dead!"

They took a cab to the Ashrafieh district and saw many restaurants to choose from, but one stood out from the rest. Not only the busiest, but the most beautiful.

Outdoor diners lounged in a terraced garden surrounded by cedar trees. Beneath the tree limbs, brightly colored umbrellas stood over the polished wood tables as diners ate, socialized and played more Backgammon.

Their waiter was a young Beiruti, wearing a dinner jacket and a broad smile. "How may I serve you tonight?"

Eliot spoke first. "We're new here. What do you recommend?"

"Traditional Lebanese cuisine, or something more western?"

Madeline and Eliot spoke at the same time. "Traditional!"

Their waiter laughed. "Then we should start with hummus."

Madeline looked puzzled. "Isn't that kind of bland?"

"Not the way we do it."

Minutes later, their water returned with two earthen bowels of hummus, mixed with tahini, a creamy paste with a nutty flavor, topped off with chickpeas, garlic and a drizzle of citrus. Fried chips were included for dipping.

After Madeline and Eliot consumed the delicious mixture, their waiter came back to their table. "Now, you must have kibbeh. It, is our national dish."

The waiter disappeared as Madeline wiped her lips with her napkin. "I can't wait to try it!"

Eliot sat up in his chair. "If it's half as good as the hummus, I'll eat it all."

A while later the waiter set a large bowel on their table. It appeared to be filled with nothing more than fried meatballs.

Madeline looked at the waiter. "*This* is your national dish?"

The waiter smiled. "Wait until you taste it."

Madeline and Eliot bit into the crusty exteriors and tasted the spices mixed with sautéed peanuts, toasted pine nuts and simmered mincemeat.

They devoured them until there was only one left in the bottom of the bowel.

"I won't fight you for it, Maddy. I'm afraid I'd lose."

"You would!"

"How about we settle it with the random elevation of a semi-precious metal?"

"What?"

"A coin toss."

"Now *that* I might lose. You take the last one."

"Oh, if you *insist*!"

When their waited came back, he smiled at the barren bowel. "So, you were obviously not disappointed. Are you ready for dessert?"

Eliot sat back, his hands on his stomach. "If only I had room."

Madeline laid her napkin on the table. "Me too, but I'm too full. We need to go for a walk."

"I'm not sure I can move!"

Madeline tugged on his arm. "Come on, we'll feel better afterwards."

They paid for their dinner and decided to take their walk on the promenade. The sun was going down as they strolled along. Out to sea they saw Pigeon Rock, one of Beirut's most famous landmarks. The rock formation stood like a sentinel, two hundred feet high and nearly eighty feet wide.

They stopped to watch. The last rays of sunlight fell over the rock, and the waves beneath it seemed to slow down, as if in preparation for nightfall.

They saw other young couples standing near them, gazing at the rock and holding each other close, its most romantic moment not to be missed. Eliot wrapped his arm around Madeline's waist. "I wonder how many times these kids come out here to see all this."

Madeline put her arms around him. "I wish *we* could do this every night."

Eliot kissed her cheek. "We *can*, Maddy...as much as you want."

They kissed each other again. But as they came out of their embrace, Madeline saw that everything had changed. The waves around the rock, only moments ago appearing so comforting, now crashed and sprayed against the limestone. The rock had turned black, its shape reminding her of a corpse.

The other couples were gone. Eliot took her hand. "I guess the show's over, but we can see it again tomorrow."

"I don't want to come back here again."

"But I thought you liked it so much."

"Don't ask me about it, Eliot. Let's go."

Eliot put his arm around her shoulders and kissed her cheek. "It's all right. We can come back some other time... when you're ready."

Madeline looked back at the rock. *Ready. How can I ever be ready to tell him what I did on Al Rashad Street?*

CHAPTER 14

KHAN'S WARNING

The next morning Madeline and Eliot went to the lobby and asked about apartments for rent.

The concierge smiled as he saw their new clothes. "I assume you seek the most fashionable ones?"

Eliot grinned at Madeline. "As long as it has a balcony with a view!"

Madeline gave him a shove. "You and your view. I want to be close to the stores!"

The concierge reached for a business card on the counter and handed it to Eliot. "There are many such places to satisfy *all* your needs, but one in particular that I think will please you. It's on Hamra Street, only a few blocks from here. Tell Mr. Dahir that I recommended you."

They walked to what was Beirut's most desirable district. New apartment buildings stretched along the boulevard on both sides of the street, the flat facades containing luxurious design hints of what was inside each building. The buildings at the corners had curved facades, a sophisticated softening of the architecture.

Madeline grabbed Eliot's arm. "We've *got* to get one of those corner apartments. Can you imagine standing out on one of those balconies?"

"I thought you didn't care about the view!"

"I don't. But out there I'd feel like royalty…and safe"

As they walked to the address on the business card, they saw many sidewalk cafes with people sitting on high stools, sipping coffee and engaged in animated conversation.

Farther down were clothing stores and banks. Dealerships displayed the latest in sports cars and SUVS.

On the side of one office building, a three-story high advertisement for a coffee house was spread out on the wall. The giant photo in high resolution depicted coffee cups, filled to the brim with dark espresso.

Eliot gazed at the rich representation. "I can taste that coffee from here. We've got to find that place!"

"Let's find the apartment before you lose your mind over coffee."

Madeline pulled him away and they found the apartment house they were looking for. The front of the building was a series of eight-foot-high glass panels. The entrance doors had long, clear handles, capped with silver plating.

In the lobby, a stout, middle-aged man lounged on a long, leather couch, puffing on a cigar.

When they entered, the man sat up, brushed away a few errant ashes from his double-breasted blazer and walked up to them with a smile. "Good afternoon! How may I help such a lovely young couple?"

Madeline did the talking. "We're looking for an apartment. Are you Mr. Dahir? The concierge at our hotel recommended you to us."

Mr. Dahir buttoned his blazer and straightened his tie. "Yes, I am. We have several apartments available. Allow me to show you."

"We're interested in one of the corner units."

"High up and with a view," Eliot interjected.

"I'm sure we can accommodate you. I have one on the seventh floor, in fact. Let us take the elevator."

As they went up in the smooth-moving elevator with walnut paneling, Madeline and Eliot introduced themselves. When they got to the seventh floor and Mr. Dahir unlocked the apartment, he was about to describe the luxurious appointments of the living room. But the couple were far too interested in the balcony, and brushed past the agent, sliding open the curved balcony doors and stepping out.

Eliot looked out to sea. Madeline looked down on the busy streets below, crowded with shoppers and businessmen.

Mr. Dahir politely cleared his throat. "Will you permit me to show you the rest of the apartment's amenities?"

"Of course," Madeline said, turning away from her view. "Please do."

The agent led them back to the living room with its white, U-Shape sectional sofa, resting on a blue Persian rug. In the center of the couch complex a broad coffee table lacquered in black held vases with fresh flowers, fashion magazines and the remote for the wide screen TV, which was mounted on the wall. Next to that was a Mediterranean style table with a large desktop computer.

Mr. Dahir took them to the adjacent dining room with its long, oval shaped table and slender wood chairs, all the ensembles made of dark oak. Above, a candelabra style lamp created a soft light over the entire setting.

Next, they were shown the kitchen area. All the appliances were finished in brushed chrome. The surrounding cabinets shined in a light-colored teakwood. On the ceramic countertop, a marble cutting board was laid out next to an espresso machine. Eliot put his arm around it. "I could have my first cup before we ever went to a café!"

Madeline opened the stove. "I don't think we'll need to order out much. I'd love to cook in here!"

Mr. Dahir rubbed his hands together. "Lovely, lovely. Now we should see the bathroom. I think you'll be impressed."

He directed them down the hall to the bathroom. They saw the alabaster sink with a gilded mirror above it. An old fashioned clawfoot bathtub stood nearby, made modern with ornate brass fixtures.

Mr. Dahir stood next to the bathtub. "Isn't it beautiful? Perfect for one to lounge in."

Next, the agent led them back to the hallway. "Let us finish with the bedroom. It's charmingly done."

Madeline and Eliot entered the bedroom and immediately saw its broad picture window with sheer white curtains. Nearby, abstract paintings hung on the walls while elegant lamps stood on either side of the bed.

Madeline grasped Eliot's arm. "It's perfect. Let's take it."

That night the couple decided to eat in. They got some food from a local store, including a bottle of wine. After dinner, they sipped on the wine until the bottle was empty.

Eliot put down his glass and gave Madeline a sly grin. "You thinking what I'm thinking?"

She smiled. "Absolutely."

They went back to the bedroom and slid the covers off the bed, looking down at the clean, white sheets and pillows, and then back to each other.

"It's been a long time, Maddy."

"Too long."

He smiled. "I don't know if I remember how."

They undressed, laid down on the bed and wrapped their arms around each other, fully enfolded.

Their movement together came in slow, deliberate motions, each entrance and withdrawal recalling and reliving precious moments from the past.

But there was more. Everything had been made dearer by absence, and now Madeline felt certain they had created an embrace so unbreakable that nothing could ever harm them again. She wanted to keep Eliot like this, sheltered within her. But in time he slid away, holding her hand until he fell asleep.

Sleep. That was her enemy now. She knew that it was at times like this that brought on her worst nightmares. They always came whenever she experienced ecstasy, jealous of its power over her, as they were anxious to take her into dark waters and to erase any bliss.

She fought to stay awake as long as she could, but the death voice was stronger. *You know you belong to me. I'll be here after all your others are long gone. You are mine and always will be.*

The nightmare unfolded in slow motion. She saw herself standing on the street outside Mr. Khan's office, wondering how she could hide herself until nightfall and return for the forged passport.

Afghanistan had been easier. There she had been armed with a rifle, a helmet with night vision goggles, and comrades who knew how to conceal themselves among trees and brush.

But now, in this dream, she was unarmed in a broad afternoon sunlight and well knew that Mira was more dangerous and desperate than any Taliban fighter.

Madeline also knew that Mr. Khan's slow-moving neighborhood was no place for a hideout. There was only one place she might make herself unseen, using throngs of people as human camouflage—Al Rashad Street.

The dream went on. Madeline walked to the arms bazaar, which was very active on this quiet sunny afternoon. She mixed in with the crowds, slowly scanning the multitude for any sign of Mira's face.

Buyers and sellers haggled over prices, exchanging heated words. Boom boxes blasted as people shouted into cell phones to make themselves heard.

Then a shot rang out. Madeline rushed for cover behind one of the stalls. The stall owner and his assistant laughed at her, prone on the ground. It was only a buyer testing a weapon. Routine.

The afternoon wore away to shadow. Madeline couldn't wait any longer. She went to Mr. Khan's office, a few blocks away. Going up the staircase, she was surprised to see him pacing back and forth in the hallway. He stopped at the sight of her. "Ah, at last you are here! Another minute and I might have been gone."

Madeline rushed up to the landing. "What are you talking about? I came early, hoping you might be finished."

"Finished with your passport, but not my *fear*!"

"What happened? Are you in trouble?"

Mr. Khan tried to collect himself. "Trouble for both of us, unfortunately. I had some visitors this afternoon claiming they know you."

"Who? What did they look like?"

Mr. Khan straightened his collar. "A striking woman with a distinct Lebanese accent and quite determined to know of your whereabouts."

"Who did she have with her?"

"Two men. One who appeared innocuous enough, even weak, if one can appear so while wearing a sidearm."

"What about the second one?"

Mr. Khan touched his cheek, still sore from Tareq's slap. "Quite violent. He didn't *need* a sidearm."

Madeline knew the first man was probably Rami, but the second one couldn't be Ahmed. Mira had hired a thug to do her dirty business. "Did you tell them I'd been here?"

"No, but if the big one had struck me again, I fear I might have. Let us finish our deal so we can both be gone."

As Mr. Khan handed her the passport and Madeline gave him the money, she held his hand for a moment. "Thank you, for *all* your help".

He looked down at her hand. "I don't ordinarily ask client's names, nor do I ever defend them in any way, but at this point it might be appropriate for me to know yours."

"It's Madeline."

In this moment in the dream, Mr. Khan offered Madeline the only kindness it contained. "Good luck, Miss Madeline. Allah be with you."

As she descended the staircase, she was warmed by the thought than even among the nefarious, there was sometimes protection.

But when she opened the front door to leave, someone put a hand on her shoulder. She made a fist, turned to strike and stopped. It was Ahmed.

"Maddy, what are you doing here?"

"Oh, thank God, Ahmed. I almost hit you!"

"What has happened? Why did you leave?"

Madeline grabbed his arm. "I'll tell you about it outside. Come on, let's get out of here."

Out on the street, Madeline pulled them into a sunken doorway. "How did you find me?"

"Mira called me and said you were gone. I said I would come by, but she said no. I did not like the sound of her voice...so nervous, not like her. I walked to Mira's house, and I see her and Rami driving away...fast. So, then I went to my truck and followed them."

"Did you catch up to them?"

"Only long enough to see them pick up a man named Tareq. He is evil man. Does many bad things. Then they drive away quick."

"Were you able to keep up? Where did they go?"

"I followed them to Al Rashad Street, but then I lost them. I saw *you* there, but then you disappeared. I walk around the neighborhood, looking for you. I saw you going into apartment house, far down the street. When I go inside, I see you coming down the stairs. Maddy, what is going on?"

"Listen Ahmed, Mira has been deceiving me all along and now she's sent guns to Syria, to kill innocent people. I can't stay here. I must get back to America...to John."

Ahmed put his arms around her. "I will help you. I will not let *any* man harm you!"

Madeline sank into his arms. "You don't know how badly I needed one of your hugs right now."

They came out of their embrace, but he continued to hold her shoulders. "How can I help you to escape?"

"I bought a passport from a man in that apartment building, where you found me. All I need now is a ride to the airport."

"I will get you there. I promise!"

They rushed to Ahmed's truck, but as they got to the corner, there were people waiting for them....

Madeline's nightmare had become too terrible, and she forced herself awake. She looked over at Eliot, who was sleeping peacefully. How could she ever tell him about the last time she had seen Ahmed?

An hour later the sun rose. Eliot rolled over to Madeline and held her close. "That was wonderful last night, Maddy."

Madeline was amazed at the power of the nightmare. It had wiped away all the joy of their lovemaking.

Eliot got up and quickly dressed. "Right after breakfast, we should go for a jog."

Madeline turned on her side. "*You* go for a jog. All I want is some sleep."

Eliot tugged on her shoulder. "Come on, don't you want to stay in shape?"

Madeline snapped back at him. "In shape for what? What's the point?"

Eliot stepped back, pausing a moment before speaking again. "How about some breakfast, then? What would you like?"

"Just coffee. Anything strong."

"Cream and sugar?"

She sat up and ran her hand through her hair. "Black."

Breakfast was in silence. Eliot made eggs that Madeline didn't touch. He picked up the coffee pot. "Another cup?"

She rubbed her face. "Yes."

"You want to tell me about it?"

"About what?"

"What's hurting you."

"It's not hurting *you*!"

He reached across the table and took her hand. "Anything that hurts you, hurts me."

She grasped his hand. "Let's just go for a walk."

They went out to the Corniche. In the early morning there were only a few people walking the esplanade, and Madeline felt as if she and Eliot had it all to themselves.

She looked out on Pigeon Rock. It didn't seem so foreboding now as the sun slowly rose above it, the natural edifice glorious in the sea. *Maybe I can make love without fear.*

But as they reached the end of the walkway, a dark premonition enveloped her. The doctors on the base had called this "precognition." She insisted to them that she had such moments, and even though the physicians knew they existed, they would only say that such feelings could not be medically substantiated.

But *Madeline* knew. She'd had them before when she went out on missions in Afghanistan, and especially on the night she murdered the innocents.

"Let's go back, Eliot. I don't want to see anymore."

"You sure? It's a beautiful day."

"I know, but I've had enough…too much."

When they got back to the apartment, Eliot took two bottled waters from the refrigerator and handed one to her. "You ready to talk?"

She did her best to put up a front with a broad smile. *Dammit! He knows me too well.* "I'm OK…fine."

"You want to go to that bar down the street and get a beer? Best thing to cheer you up."

She couldn't maintain her coverup and lost control. "I don't need cheering up!"

"Maybe I should leave you alone for a while. Mind if I go to the bar on my own?"

She was about to agree when the dark premonition came over her, stronger this time. It billowed up in her mind as black smoke. *If only I could see it! If only I could know it before it hurts us both!*

She only knew that it was out there, waiting to strike.

Eliot stood up. "I'm going to take off. I'll just have one beer and be right back."

Madeline sat up from the couch, an abrupt movement startling to Eliot. "No! Don't go there!"

He took her shoulders. "Why not? What do you mean?"

"I don't know. I just have a bad feeling."

"I think all you need is some rest. Go in and lie down. I'll be back soon."

"Oh, Eliot." Madeline looked away. "Please! Don't be gone long."

As Eliot left, Madeline went to the bedroom and lay down. She didn't understand what was going on, but she knew that, when Eliot returned, she had to tell him about Ahmed.

Eliot went down to the street, but as he walked to the bar, two men followed him. Men from his past.

CHAPTER 15

REVENGE

When Eliot sat down at the bar, he thought of Madeline, alone at the apartment. He knew what she'd been through. He also knew there were limits to the comfort he could give her. *Let her be alone for a while to work things out for herself, then I'll give her all the love I can, if it's enough.*

The bartender asked him what he would like. Eliot scanned the rows of beer bottles behind the bar. The one on the end made him smile.

"I'll have a Guinness."

Will's favorite. The one they always shared together whenever they were on leave. *Will. What is he doing right now? What are they doing to him? Will I ever see him again?*

Lost in reverie, Eliot did not see the two men at the end of the bar, staring at him. The last time they had been this close to Eliot, they were chasing him in the wilderness of Afghanistan, along with an entire band of other mercenaries. At this moment, suddenly, they saw a chance for revenge.

The thin Australian with the long red beard grinned at his friend, the stocky Englishman with the clean-shaven face. "What do you think of this, James? There *is* justice after all."

The Australian went over to Eliot, sat down next to him and slapped him on the back. "Well, if it ain't our old friend, Mr. Eliot! You remember me, don't you, your old fighting comrade, Nick? Over yonder is James. Me and him was having a little R&R over here and who should we see but the man himself. The one that left us with not so much as a fare thee well. Come on over and let us buy you a pint."

Eliot glared at him. "I'm fine where I'm at."

"What? You don't want to talk over old times? *We do.*"

Eliot gripped his beer bottle. "I've got nothing to do with either one of you. Get away from me!"

Nick motioned to James, who came over and sat on Eliot's other side. "Hello, Eliot. It's been quite some time. You're looking well."

Nick pushed his shoulder into Eliot. "Yeah, since he turned tail and ran like a scared jack rabbit!"

James pressed himself into Eliot's other shoulder, the two men holding him in a vice. "It might interest you to know that we've been shadowing you for days and you were apparently unaware of it. Thought a fighter of your caliber would have noticed that."

Nick laughed. "Ah, but our boy here has decided to fall in love in the meantime, and ain't she a beauty, James?"

"Quite fetching, I must say."

"Yeah, wouldn't mind some of that myself! Be a shame if something happened to her."

Eliot knew that as long as Nick and James had him trapped between them, there was nothing he could do. But there was a way out: make a scene. He took hold of his beer and pushed it over the bar. It fell back to the bar floor, pouring out its contents.

The bartender rushed over. "What is this gentleman? What happened here?"

Nick saw Eliot's ploy. "Our friend here got a little nervous, barman. Sorry about the mess."

"I did it on purpose!" Eliot shouted at the bartender. "That beer was flat! What kind of lousy joint are you running here?"

The bartender glared at Eliot. "If you do not like it here, go elsewhere! Get out of here now, all of you, or I call police!"

Nick grabbed the bartender by the lapel of his jacket. "You're not calling anybody! Get back where you belong!"

Customers from tables close by got up from their chairs, staring at the commotion.

James came around to Nick. "Calm down! Don't make it worse."

Nick pushed the bartender back. He smashed into the bottles of alcohol displayed on glass shelves behind him. Bottles of whiskey and wine crashed to the floor.

"Just what you wanted, eh?" Nick yelled at Eliot. "Got yourself a good diversion. We'll see about that!"

James saw the bartender on the phone and put his arm around Nick. "Give it up, mate! He's calling the cops! There'll be another time."

Nick tried to pull away from James. "No! Now!"

Eliot knew he had an advantage. There were two of them, but one was enraged. Rage. The killer of reason. He would use that to even up the odds.

Eliot looked at Nick and James. "You hired soldiers never know how to control yourselves. You're no better than punks!"

Eliot's insult stung both men. James released Nick and they both came at Eliot. Out of control, Nick swung a wild punch at Eliot. Eliot dodged the blow, pushed his shoulder into Nick's midsection and slammed him against a wall. James came behind Eliot and wrapped his arm around his neck in a choke hold. Eliot shoved his elbow into James's ribs. Nick was about to throw another punch, but Eliot smashed his fist into his face. James hit Eliot with a kidney punch. Eliot winced from the pain, but quickly turned and head-butted James. He fell to the floor.

Two policemen came through the door. Eliot rushed past them and ran down the street. He had to get to Madeline.

Where is he! Madeline thought, as she paced the living room, running her hands up and down her crossed arms. *"How long does it take to have a damn beer?*

She looked at the clock in the dining room and realized he had been gone for just twenty minutes. She thought she had rested longer, but her premonition gave her no respite. Now, in her panic, it joined forces with the nightmare she had left unfinished, and once again the death voice found its perfect opportunity to speak to her.

Did you think you could escape me in waking hours? Never. I can come to you whenever I want. Go on now. Finish your terror. Remember the rest.

To take herself away from dark memory, Madeline went to the balcony and looked down at the street below. She scanned the many faces. Was that him…there? The one in the blue shirt? No. He didn't have Eliot's Walk, which was head up, proud and strong.

But the strong could be destroyed in a second. She had seen it a hundred times in Afghanistan.

She thought if she stood watch long enough, stared at enough faces, he would magically appear among them. *Stupid, Madeline! Wishing won't bring him back.*

Her feeling of dread increased as she returned to the living room and sank down on the couch. She covered her face with her hands, as if to deny the past's rising up and taking hold of her. But the light seeping through her fingers brought inescapable memories.

She could see it all now.

That day Ahmed had found her and had promised he would get her to the airport. The airport... and then she would be back to John. But they had barely reached the corner, before they saw Mira with Rami and Tareq.

Mira had walked up to Madeline. "Did you *really* think it would be this easy? I thought you knew me better. I'm not done with you yet, Madeline Crowne!"

Tareq pointed at Madeline and turned to Rami. "*This* is woman you so scared of? She is nothing! I will show you."

Before Tareq could grab Madeline, Ahmed got between them. "Go away you! We want nothing to do with your kind!"

Tareq shoved Ahmed aside and gripped Madeline's arm. She kneed him in the groin, and he fell to the pavement in agony. Rami reached for his gun. But Ahmed yanked it away from him. "No one will harm Maddy! I swear by Allah!"

As Tareq got to his feet, Mira took his sidearm, came behind Madeline and pointed the gun at her head. "You want to see her dead? Drop the gun, Ahmed!"

Ahmed let the gun slide out of his hand and fall to the sidewalk. "Maddy, I am sorry."

Madeline kicked her foot into Mira's leg. Mira dropped her gun and fell back against a wall. But as Madeline retrieved Mira's gun, Tareq picked up Ahmed's pistol, about to shoot.

Madeline turned to fire. Ahmed got in between. "Maddy, no!"

But the round had already fired, ejecting its metal jacket as the bullet spun from the rifled muzzle and struck Ahmed's chest. Madeline stared in horror at Ahmed on the ground.

Tareq turned to shoot Madeline. Mira jumped to her feet and seized his arm. "No! Not her!"

Tareq shoved Mira away. "You wanted this woman! I give her to you…dead!"

Mira grabbed Tareq's wrist, pointing the gun upward. The gun fired several times into the air. People flung open their windows, shocked at what was happening below.

Madeline dropped her gun and ran, quickly disappearing into the oncoming crowd of people, anxious to see what had happened. In the distance, sirens rang out. She didn't see any of the others' faces. She saw only Ahmed's as he lay on the ground. The face of so many she had seen in war…the muscles limp, the gray pallor of the skin.

A block away she saw a policeman rushing towards the scene. She slowed down and took a few deep breaths. But as the policeman drew near, her face gave her away. Her skin was still flushed from everything that had happened and worse, there were tears in her eyes. Tears that she had not realized had formed, as she had thought of Ahmed.

The police officer was a veteran and knew shock when he saw it. He also suspected Madeline could be a witness or a suspect herself. He stopped before her. "Did you see what happened down there? Were you involved?"

Madeline quickly wiped away her tears and looked away. "I didn't see anything. I don't know what happened…I".

He knew she was lying. The terror on her face meant she had to have seen something or been involved herself. He took her by the arm. "Come with me."

Madeline pushed the officer against a wall. Before he could raise his nightstick, she yanked it away from him. She struck the back of his knee, sending him to the ground. As he got to his feet, she grabbed the nightstick with both hands and shoved it hard into his side. He fell again, this time in agony.

On the couch, recalling this, Madeline dropped her hands from her face and fell back. She still could not figure how she had escaped that day and made her way to the airport. It didn't matter. Nothing mattered.

She went back to the balcony and gripped the concrete wall that surrounded it. She looked down at the street, several stories below. It would be so easy. Fly out and it would all be over.

Go on, the voice told her. *Do it. It's the only way you'll be free.*

Then Eliot was behind her, holding her in a close embrace. "Maddy, there's something I've got to tell you!"

She turned around and saw the fear in his eyes. She felt his breathing against her. "What happened? Are you, all right?"

He sat down on the couch, rubbing his hands over his face. "Just when I thought nothing else could happen to us. Just when I thought…".

She sat down next to him, putting her arm around his shoulder. "What are you talking about?"

He got up and paced the room, his body still shaking. "Down at the bar…I ran into some guys I worked with when I was in that rogue mercenary band. They want to get even with me for deserting them. They've been watching us. They've seen us together…the way we are."

She got up and held him. "Don't worry. Together, we can take care of them."

He pulled away. "No! You can't be involved!"

"Why not?"

"Because they'd go straight for you! They told me as much today. I took them out, but they'll be back. I'm sure they know where we live."

She crossed her arms. "Then we'll let them come to us."

He grasped her shoulders. "You don't understand. I don't care what they do to me, but I can't let them hurt *you*!"

"No, you don't understand. I'd rather be dead than lose you."

That night they sat down at the dining room table. As Eliot was about to begin the meal, Madeline put her hand over his. "Wait. Now there's something I've got to tell *you*. We can take care of whatever is ahead of us, but I've got to tell you now about everything from my past…all of it."

He put down his fork. "I thought I knew everything about you."

"Not this."

She told him the entire story of what had happened that horrible day, she was amazed that some of its terror seemed to drain away, knowing that she was confessing to someone who loved her.

He did not need to utter a word. His eyes said everything. Understanding. Compassion.

When she finished, he held her close. "I knew there was something you were holding back. I didn't want to press you, though. Thank God, you've told me now. None of that was your fault. We both know that anything can happen when guns are drawn."

The death voice was gone. She felt it disappear… invisibly. "Eliot, you've freed me."

"No, you just freed yourself."

The next morning, they were going for coffee when Eliot took Madeline by the arm.

"Maddy, that's them…right on the corner."

Nick and James stood directly across the street. Both their faces were heavily bruised.

Madeline took a hard look. "You sure did a job on them. I'm surprised they're back."

"Yeah, but even from here you can see the anger in their eyes."

Madeline put her arm around Eliot's waist. "Good. Angry people make stupid mistakes, and we've got another advantage."

"What's that?"

"They don't know I'm a combat veteran."

Eliot and Madeline knew that, in daylight, they were safe. Nick and James would not do anything that could be easily witnessed. They would wait until the couple went out at night and then follow them back in the darkness.

The next night Madeline and Eliot made it easy for their pursuers. They deliberately went out late to an outdoor restaurant. As they walked back to their apartment and neared an alley, they heard footsteps behind them.

The steps moved faster as the couple ducked down the alley, which led out to a broad street.

Eliot turned to Madeline. "It's working."

They heard the sound of two snaps, followed by two clicks. Madeline looked at Eliot. "They've got tactical knives."

Eliot knew. These were combat weapons, sharp enough to shave with.

They turned and saw Nick and James brandishing the knives. The stainless-steel blades glistened in the darkness.

Nick grinned. "Well now, what do we have here? The two lovers together after a fancy dinner. Hope you enjoyed it. Could be your last!"

Madeline surveyed Nick and James. "You two look like you been hit by a truck, and it only took one man to do that."

Eliot stepped forward. "And he can do it again."

James gripped his knife. "Ah, but now you've got a pretty lady to protect. Won't be so easy."

James lunged at Madeline. She stepped aside, grabbed his wrist and punched his face. Nick raised his knife to stab Eliot, and Eliot, ducking, grabbed him and slammed him into a wall. James pulled Madeline to the ground. His knife fell from his hand and they both struggled to retrieve it.

Nick slashed Eliot's shirt, cutting his skin. But Eliot was able to kick Nick's leg from under him. As Nick fell, Eliot grabbed the knife and held it to Nick's throat. "Move and I'll kill you!"

Madeline got hold of James's knife and twisted his arm into a hammer lock, striking his head with the butt of the knife. "Try anything else and I'll use the other end!"

"All right!" James shouted. "All right!"

Madeline and Eliot released them. As both men rose, their faces showed new wounds on top of the old. They stumbled out of the alley, muttering obscenities.

Eliot laid the knife on the ground, carefully, soundlessly. "They won't try anything else. And even if they do, we'll be gone. Back. The U.S. You know we have to. It's the only way. Give ourselves up."

In the morning, they went out for breakfast, near the Corniche. Both were silent for a long time, knowing the inevitable had come to pass. There were only so many ghosts they could run from.

Madeline looked out at Pigeon Rock. It was, as always, impervious to pain. It had been there unmoved for centuries and would continue to stand its long watch long after she and Eliot were gone.

Eliot watched the couples walking the esplanade, smiling and holding hands. There was nothing keeping those pairs from being parted.

Eliot reached across the table and took Madeline's hand. "At least I might be able to see Will again, if he's still alive."

Madeline ran her hand over his fingers. "John could be gone too, or back on the street, using again."

Eliot leaned forward, rubbing his hands together. "Even if they are still with us, we won't be much help to them when we're in Leavenworth."

Madeline stood up and took Eliot's arm. "Come on, let's go for a walk. May be one of our last chances."

He smiled and took her hand. They crossed the street and strolled the broad walkway. Eliot looked out to sea. "I'll miss all this."

"Me, too. Sometimes it made me feel that time didn't exist."

He held her. "It doesn't, Maddy. Not for us. They can put all the time between us they want, but we'll always be inside each other."

They walked for the rest of the morning, but as they turned to go back and cross the street, the traffic had increased in their absence.

Eliot shook his head. "Damn cars! That's one thing I won't miss."

Madeline stepped back from the curb. "How are we ever going to get across this?"

"Wait for an opening. It'll come."

Some of the cars slowed to a halt, giving up. Others changed lanes, seeking an opening as horns blasted. A police officer on the other side of the street saw Madeline and Eliot, stranded on the sidewalk. He stepped out into the street, held up his hand to stop traffic, and waved at them to cross.

"Come on, Maddy! He's waving us through."

But Madeline could not move. There it was again. That foreboding feeling. The voice had gone, expelled by Eliot's love. But her premonitions had not.

The police officer waved again, impatient with Madeline's reluctance.

Eliot tugged her hand. "What's wrong? We've got to go!"

Then, as Madeline forced herself to cross, from out of the pack of cars, a vehicle roared forward, heading in their direction. Eliot pulled Madeline to the other side as the car hit the curb and sped away.

"Son of a bitch!" Eliot shouted. "What the hell did he think he was doing?"

As the car disappeared from sight, Madeline saw that it was a beat-up Mercedes, with darkened windows.

"Got everything packed?" Eliot said the next morning as he closed his suitcase.

"I think so. Whatever we forget won't matter. Not where we're going."

"Maddy, we'll still have a chance to talk at our trials. Chance to explain everything."

"What good will that do?"

Eliot put his arm around her. "Sometimes the truth can be stronger than you think."

Madeline smiled and embraced him. "The wishful thinker."

He kissed her cheek. "One last cappuccino?"

"Sure. Why not?"

They went to a sidewalk café that overlooked the sea. Sitting under a colorful umbrella, they sipped their drinks, each lost in their own thoughts.

How long will they keep her from me?
Will I ever see him again?

Eliot left a tip on the table and stood up. "All we have to do now is book the flight."

Madeline couldn't stand to see him looking this sad. "Think the military will have a welcoming committee for us when we land back home?"

They laughed as she got up and embraced him. Then, she saw a car slow down and pull to the curb not far from them. The driver lowered the window. The face within looked older, tired, but the eyes were alive with anger.

Madeline pulled away from him. "That's her!"

Eliot turned around. "Where?"

"Right there, in the Mercedes. Mira. She's looking right at us."

But before Eliot could get a better look, Mira sped away.

"Are you sure that was her?"

"Positive. It was her in traffic yesterday. The car that raced through."

"If that was her, why did she take off like that?"

"She's sending me a message. Wherever you are Madeline, I'll find you."

Eliot led her away. "Let's get back to the apartment. Don't worry, we'll be gone before she can do anything."

Madeline stopped. "No! We're not leaving before this is settled between her and me."

"Maddy, just let it go! It doesn't matter now, anyway."

Madeline's voice grew strident. "It *does* matter! Can't you see that?"

"I can only see her hurting you again," Eliot said. He too spoke more loudly. "And I won't let that happen!"

Passersby looked askance at this couple having a pitched argument on a public street.

Embarrassed, Madeline took his arm. "We'll talk about it in private."

Back at the apartment, their argument continued.

Eliot grabbed the phone. "I don't care what you say, I'm booking that flight right now!"

Madeline took the phone away from him. "That won't do any good. The only way is for me to go to her!"

"Not without me you're not!"

Madeline set the phone down on the table. "Eliot. We've never talked to each other this way."

Eliot looked away. "I know. I'm sorry. I'm already making it worse for you."

They sat down together on the couch. "Eliot, try to understand. This is something that has to be settled between women. I know a better way to deal with her without violence."

"You're sure?"

"Yes. I'm sure she knows where we live. All I have to do is go for a walk."

That afternoon Madeline went out to the street as Eliot watched her from the balcony above, gripping the railing.

She didn't have to walk far before she saw Mira standing on a corner. Madeline was immediately struck by her disheveled appearance. Her usual uniform of black turtleneck and slacks was rumpled, worn. The long, black hair was still arranged in a bun. But errant strands hung down loosely about her neck.

Mira looked Madeline up and down. "You're looking wonderful. Remember who taught you how to dress that way?"

"Looks like you've fallen on hard times. What a pity."

Mira smirked. "Yes, well, we don't *all* have the luxury of going about with a well-dressed lover, having a gay old time.

I can only imagine what goes on between the two of you at night, up there in your sumptuous apartment."

"Imagine as much as you want, Mira. What he and I have together is something you'll never have."

"Such words! And from one on the run. The two of you can't go on forever, you know. There'll be an accounting."

"Not before I'm finished with you."

Mira laughed. "Always quick with a quip. Come on up to my place. I've got some good news for you."

Madeline crossed her arms. "What good news could you possibly have for me?"

"A chance at redemption, Madeline. Let's go."

They walked for three blocks, then turned down an alleyway. Staircases in disrepair led up to three story apartments. As they ascended the steps, gripping the fragile railings, Mira looked back at Madeline. "I apologize for the absence of an elevator. I trust you can make it to the top, unaided."

"I don't need any help from you."

Mira opened the door to her apartment, and they stepped in. Madeline looked around at the wreckage of frail furniture, peeling wallpaper and dirty floors. "Quite a comedown from your place in Tripoli."

Mira tossed her keys onto a crumbling nightstand. "At the moment, my resources are strained."

"I thought you said you'd never come back to Lebanon."

"Precisely what I thought you'd think. But chasing after you has caused my past to catch up to me."

"Syrian deal fell through?"

Mira lit a cigarette and tossed the match into a broken ashtray. "Worse than that. Proud of yourself?"

"Yes…yes, I am."

Mira inhaled from her cigarette, dabbed a piece of loose tobacco from her tongue and flicked it away. "I bet you are. But enough of all that. I'm here to deliver glad tidings. You'll be interested to know that your precious Ahmed survived what you did to him."

Madeline felt the breath go out of her body as she collapsed on a couch. "Ahmed is alive!"

"No thanks to you. Does this make us friends again?"

Madeline stood up. "Never! We never were. That was all a deception. *Your* deception!"

Mira let her cigarette drop to the floor. She rubbed it out with her shoe as tears formed in her eyes. "Would one kiss have been so terrible, Maddy? One?"

Madeline looked at the crushed cigarette on the floor, its embers slowly dying out. "I'd pity you, but you don't deserve it."

"Hate, then? I'll take that if it's all I can get. At least that's something of you."

"You don't deserve that, either. The only thing you deserve is indifference. That's what I came to give to you today. Time will take care of the rest for me."

As Madeline left, Mira sat down on the fragmented couch and wept.

CHAPTER 16

SURRENDER

Walking back to the apartment, Madeline wondered why she did not feel triumphant. She had overcome Mira without a single physical blow, but the wound she had inflicted on her— was more devastating than any aggression that could have transpired.

But then there was Mira's pathetic plea, asking even for hate, rather than to be abandoned—and alone.

I should be proud of myself, Madeline thought. *I've rid the world of another gun dealer without a conscience. She won't have the fortitude to evade her pursuers. Not now. Not after what I've done to her.* She lowered her head and felt even more remorse. *Why do I feel so hollow inside?*

She knew why. The spontaneous attraction Mira had felt for her, so intense, so heartfelt, could happen to anyone. Turn a corner one day and behold a human who appeared more precious than all the others. The same thing had happened with Madeline and Eliot.

What would *she* have done if she had suddenly found herself alone in a war-torn city, the way Mira had. Would she sell her body? Would she kill, the way Mira had murdered her pimp to gain freedom? Would she descend into the Black Market to survive?

Madeline knew she would have done it all if it meant keeping John alive. But she still had him, and Mira had no one.

Eliot jumped to his feet when Madeline entered the apartment. "What happened? Are you, all right?"

Madeline slowly slid her handbag off her shoulder, letting it fall to the couch. "I'm OK. She won't bother us anymore."

"So, what did you do? What did she say?"

She sat down and looked up at him. "What would you do to survive?"

He sat down next to her. "What are you talking about?"

"Would you do terrible things if you had to?"

He sat back. "I feel like I already have, the way I left Will in Afghanistan. Then working with those mercenaries."

"I know all that. But what if we couldn't be together? What if I didn't love you?"

He got to his feet. "Now, you're scaring me. What went on between her and you?"

"Nothing...you wouldn't understand."

"It must be *something*...talking about not loving me!"

She stood up and embraced him. "I'll always love you. Nothing can change that."

They booked a flight to the United States. Despite their numerous connections to Sacramento, neither talked about what they were both thinking as their plane landed there. Eliot turned to Madeline. "I've got to try to see Will. Could be my last chance."

Madeline held his hand. "They spotted you at the VA Hospital before, remember? You barely got away."

"Yeah, but we've been gone for so long that they might have stopped looking. They do that sometimes with deserters."

"Not with us. We've gotten too much attention. Besides, I've heard about deserters in the United States. Get pulled over for a traffic ticket. Apply for a job, and your name pops up in the FBI database. They don't have to keep looking. They keep you on the run, always hiding out. What kind of life would that be for us?"

Madeline watched the passengers filing out of the plane, on their way to the ordinary…reunions with loved ones, returning to jobs.

Eliot sank back in his seat. "Maybe turning ourselves in could get us a lighter sentence."

"Not likely. You know what the penalty is for desertion in time of war. Life."

The cabin emptied out. Madeline turned to look out her passenger window. Through the small oval, she saw another plane about to ascend into the sky. She tried to discern a face in the windows of the nearby plane, anyone that was free to go wherever they wanted, live their lives however they wanted. But there was nothing. It was too far away.

Eliot looked across the aisle and through the window, he saw Sacramento International Airport. Nothing had changed since they had left. Everything had held itself in place as he and Madeline had run from one terror to another around the world.

The flight attendants and crew looked curiously at the couple still seated. One of the attendants approached them. "Is anything wrong, folks?"

"No…nothing," Madeline said.

As they claimed their bags, Eliot took out his cell phone. "I've got to call the VA Hospital and see if they'll tell me anything about Will."

Madeline took her phone out of her purse. "I'll call John's facility. I know he can't be there, after I couldn't send the money anymore, but maybe they'll know if he went to county rehab."

Eliot turned away and dialed his number. "Hello, I'm calling about a patient...William Madsen."

"I'll have to look up the file," the receptionist said. "Can I put you on hold?"

"Sure."

Seconds ticked away into minutes. *How long can it take to look up a damn file!* Eliot thought to himself. He knew it could simply mean the receptionist was busy, but then again, he knew the hospital may still be on the lookout for the army fugitive who had tried to see his friend and beat up two guards in the process.

Finally, the receptionist came back on the line. "William Madsen is no longer a patient here, Sir."

"Did they send him to another facility? Some other hospital?"

"I'm sorry. We're not allowed to say."

Eliot clicked off.

Meanwhile, Madeline called John's rehab center. "Hi, can you tell me if John Crowne is still registered with you?"

"One moment, please," the receptionist said. "I'll have to check."

Madeline heard the sound of typing. Typing that took far too long.

Maybe he found a way, Madeline thought. *Maybe they kept him on somehow!*

The receptionist returned. "Mr. Crowne checked out some time ago."

"Can you tell me when that was?"

"I'm afraid I can't."

Madeline gripped her phone. "Do you know if he went to another facility...the county rehab center, perhaps?"

"I can't tell you anything more, Miss. We're bound by the rules of patient confidentiality."

Madeline turned to Eliot. "Any luck?"

He shook his head. "No. You?"

"Nothing."

Eliot dialed another number. "I'm going to try Will's parents. They might be able to tell me something."

Madeline spotted a coffee concession. "I'll get us something to drink."

When Mrs. Madsen answered Eliot's call, he was surprised at how feeble her voice sounded, tired, barely audible. "Hello...who is this?"

"Hi, I'm trying to get in touch with Will."

Silence. Then a low, moaning sound, almost inhuman. Weeping. The sound of an old woman's weeping trembled and cracked.

Mr. Madsen came on the line. "Whose calling, please?"

"Old friend of Will's."

"Our son died three days ago."

As Eliot slowly put his phone away, Madeline returned with coffee. When she saw the tears in his eyes, she set the coffee down on a bench. "What happened?

"He's gone. Died a few days ago."

She put her arms around him. "Oh, Eliot. I'm so sorry."

They sat down on the bench. Eliot leaned forward and rubbed his hands together. "If I could have just *seen* him one more time. Even if he didn't know me anymore!"

She wrapped her arm around his waist. "Maybe it's better this way. His kind of PTSD..."

He sat back and looked at the coffee next to them. "A few days ago, we were having coffee on the Corniche, taking in the view and he…"

"It doesn't matter now. You couldn't possibly have known what was happening to him."

Eliot watched the travelers passing by them, taking their existence for granted. "Will is dead. I'll never see him again."

She kissed his cheek. "He's alive as long as you love him."

He stood up. "So, the rehab center wouldn't tell you anything?"

She looked down. "No. I can check with county rehab, but they probably won't tell me anything, either."

"At least they can tell you if he's been there or not."

Madeline stood up and saw a trash can stuffed with litter. Used coffee cups, half eaten food, magazines, all the things people casually abandoned before moving on with their lives. "We can try it. But John told me so many times he'd never go back there. He'd rather be dead, than go to county."

They took a taxi to the county facility. Even though Eliot insisted on going in with her, she made him stay outside. When she emerged from the facility doors a few minutes later, the look on her face frightened him.

He took her aside. "Did they tell you anything?"

She shook her head. "He was here, but only for a few days before checking himself out. He's probably back on South Side, trying to score opioids again."

"Then we'll go to South Side."

They took a bus to the worst of Sacramento's neighborhoods. The lumbering vehicle was so crowded they had to stand in the aisle, holding onto the looped handgrips as fellow passengers jostled against them.

Madeline looked out at the decay. Once grand Victorians turned into dirty tenements. Burnt out cars parked on dried out lawns. If anything, it was worse than it had been. Now, there were even more homeless, wandering the streets, speaking to themselves in unintelligible sentences.

Some things hadn't changed, however. There were still prostitutes on the stroll, along with their pimps. And on corners, here and there, drug dealers still dealt in death. She recognized their body language from the time she had last been here. They leaned against stop signs, glancing occasionally at their watches, appearing to be waiting for a friend. Others held up newspapers, as their eyes scanned the neighborhood. Madeline wondered which one of them was slowly killing her brother.

They got off at a stop in front of Our Lady of Guadalupe Catholic Church. By day, it held services, as children played in the park across the street—or swam in the city pool.

But at night, the church locked its doors. Anyone fool enough to enter the park in darkness, faced muggers concealed in groves of bushes.

Eliot pointed to a rental sign in front of an apartment building. "Right there. Let's get that one."

Madeline looked at the two-story structure. Cracks snaked through its plaster exterior. Rust stains framed the windows, some intact, others broken. "Why not? It won't get any better."

They rented an apartment on the second floor, facing the park. Going down the hallway, the frayed carpet beneath their feet carried the distinct smell of urine. From the other rooms they heard harsh coughing and loud radios.

Inside their apartment, they threw their bags down on a sagging double bed. Eliot surveyed the bathroom, its sink and tub with water stains etched into the aging porcelain.

Madeline went to the kitchen and saw a small refrigerator with a missing door handle. Dirty handprints were smeared into the absent space. The kitchen faucet made a steady drip. On the countertop, the ragged power cord of a hot plate was plugged into an exposed outlet.

They joined each other in front of the apartment building's one saving grace, a single picture window that overlooked the park. They looked down as preschoolers on swings, smiled and strained to take themselves higher. Others thrust down the slide, laughing as they landed in a sand pit.

Eliot grinned at the scene below. "Look at them. They're not afraid of anything."

Madeline looked down at the window's rust stains. "They're loved."

Nearby mothers carried on conversations, watching their children at the same time. One of the mothers rushed over to the slide, scooping up her child as he slid to the bottom and into her arms. Another mother called out admonishments as her daughter carelessly bumped into another child.

Eliot put his hand on the window. "How would *we* have raised kids?"

Madeline brushed away some dust from the windowsill. "Better than we were."

He turned away. "When do you want to start looking for John?"

"Tonight. I'm glad we got this place. There are bound to be dealers working in the park, along with other criminals."

They waited until after midnight before entering the park. At first, they saw only a few homeless people, passed out on benches. Further on, two men in tattered clothes huddled together, sharing a cigarette and a cheap bottle of wine.

Madeline looked at Eliot. "We should split up. I'll go over this way. You go the other."

As they parted, Madeline saw nothing. But then, from a cluster of trees, a man in a torn overcoat walked fast in her direction, gripping something in his pocket. As he neared, she saw the flash of a knife in the darkness.

Then Eliot was beside her. The would-be mugger quickly disappeared.

"OK, Maddy, that's it. No more splitting up!"

"I could have handled him."

"I know, but that's enough for tonight."

Madeline saw a public restroom, near the end of the park. Its peeling paint and crumbling tile roof were made somewhat visible by a light at the entrance. To one side, two men stood closely together. In the half-light, she could barely make out the man facing her. His collar was turned up and he had black hair. But the man with his back to her had blonde hair, combed back and to the side, just like John's.

She grabbed Eliot's arm. "Right there! I think that's him!"

She walked fast towards the restroom. Eliot clasped her hand. "Slow down! We'll scare them off."

But she couldn't. She pulled away from him. The dark man saw her coming and motioned to the other. The blonde man turned. She saw a piece of his profile in the splintered light. *It could be. It could be!*

Both men ran away. Eliot caught up to her. "Was it him? Could you see?"

Madeline looked down. "I don't know. I don't think so."

In the day, they went to the corners on which Madeline had seen drug dealers, but saw only strung-out addicts, making quick exchanges of money and drugs, one palm pressed into another.

When they returned to their apartment, Madeline went to the window. "It's no use."

Eliot put his arms around her. "We could try a while longer."

"No. It's time to turn ourselves in."

That night they made love for the last time, cherishing every second. Holding each other close, they silently felt their own thoughts.

I'll remember all this, the way she feels right now.

I'll never forget the way he holds me…safe.

The next morning, they took a taxi to the local FBI field office. As they neared their destination, Madeline turned to him. "There's one thing that might help us."

"What's that?"

"Since we were both deployed to Afghanistan from Fort Hood, they might try us both there. We probably couldn't have physical contact, but I think we might be able to write letters to each other."

He grasped her hand. "Oh God, I hope so. It would make things so much easier. I know they'll appoint free attorneys for us. One of the guys at the Bagram base was tried there and acquitted. He said they gave him a good lawyer."

"I hope we're as lucky. OK, the first thing we have to do is ask our lawyers if we can stay in contact in *any* way!"

When they got out of the cab at the field office, Eliot paused at the entrance. "We'd better say good-bye now. We won't get another chance."

She stared into the green eyes she had loved for so long. "I wish there was something I could say, something I could give you…".

He took her hand and pressed it to his chest. "All I need is to hold your hand, one last time."

They went inside and identified themselves. The agents had no trouble finding their names in the National Criminal Database. Madeline and Eliot's cases had made headlines, and they were still being sought after.

They were taken into custody and later handed over to military authority. But Madeline had been right. They would both stand trial at Fort Hood, Texas.

Upon their arrivals at the fort, they were transported twenty miles to the Belton County Jail, which functioned as the fort's stockade.

There, they were separated. The impact of being parted was greater than either of them could have imagined.

How can I make it without her?

How can I get through this if he's not near me?

The commanding officer of the base ordered their General court-martials, reserved by the military for the most serious crimes. A jury of five was empaneled along with a military judge.

The Judge Advocate General office appointed free attorneys for Madeline and Eliot. Madeline received Captain Marion Evans, a seasoned professional. Eliot was given Lieutenant Thomas Styles, new to the office.

When Captain Evans came to meet with her client, they had barely introduced themselves, when Madeline spoke up. "Can I write letters to another inmate?"

The diminutive attorney with short, dark hair, slowly set her briefcase on the floor and sat down on the cell's single chair. "It's nice to meet you, Sergeant First Class Crowne. In answer to your question, yes, pre-trial detainees are allowed to write letters, receive phone calls and have visitors. I know you have an association with Staff Sergeant Lange."

"Are he and I that well known?"

The captain crossed her arms and leaned forward. "His case and yours have received a lot of media attention, but we need to discuss *your* situation now. Won't you sit down?"

Madeline sat down on her bunk. The captain took a folder from her briefcase and turned through the pages of a file. When she looked up again, she saw tears in Madeline's eyes. "Sergeant, are you, all right?"

"You're going to ask me about what happened, aren't you...that night in the village?"

Marion placed her hand over Madeline's. "Let's take this one step at a time. Remember, I'm here to help you. I know what your file says. Tell me your side. There's always another side."

Madeline told her story. In the beginning, she was able to relay all the events of that night, but as she came to the moment when she had killed an unarmed pregnant woman, she began to break down. "I *did* try to help that woman! I put pressure on her wound, but it was too late. She died beneath my hands." Tears flowed down Madeline's face.

The captain offered her a tissue. "I can see this is difficult for you. Would you like to stop for a while?"

It struck Madeline that telling it all to a sympathetic stranger, seemed to relieve some of her pain. "No, I'm all right. You've probably never heard anything this horrible."

"I've heard many things, but if what you're telling me is the truth, your story is the saddest."

"It's the truth."

Marion drew closer. "Sergeant, the fact that you tried to give aide to the injured woman could be helpful to us. Did anyone see you do that?"

Madeline shook her head. "I don't know, Captain. Maybe Jim Clay. PFC James Clay."

Marion turned another page in Madeline's file. "You can call me Marion. We've been trying to reach James Clay. He made a statement saying that he too thought the woman was an enemy and was about to take aim himself. His statement didn't say anything about you giving the woman help.

"Two other soldiers who were further away stated they saw you take clear aim and fire. PFC Clay's testimony could be instrumental to us, but we've been unable to find him. After being honorably discharged from the military, he was recently arrested on a domestic violence charge and jumped bail."

Madeline looked away. "I remember Jim. He was a good soldier and a good man. I wonder what happened."

"Don't worry, Madeline. I'll continue to stay in touch with law enforcement in Galveston, the place of his initial arrest, to see if he's apprehended. He could be a big help."

"If he's on the run, I don't see how he can be. Then there's the fact that I panicked and ran away myself that night. Makes me look guilty, doesn't it?"

Marion closed the file. "It does, but we still have a case. I want to talk about the things in our favor. Would you like some coffee first?"

"I could use some."

The captain had some coffee brought to the cell and waited a while before continuing. "First of all, you're a veteran of two tours in Afghanistan. You rose through the ranks and led soldiers in combat engagements. You were awarded a Silver Star."

Madeline set down her coffee. "And I killed an innocent woman and child."

"I know. But we have to focus on our argument."

"Do we have one?"

Marion took a sip of coffee. "Yes. It's called 'the fog of war'. You may have heard of it. The army understands that civilians die in every war because of accidents and split-second judgement calls. That's what happened in your case. You thought you saw an armed enemy coming at you and you fired."

Madeline looked at the bars on her cell door. "Yes, but without a witness, is that argument any good?"

"It might be. The court is aware of your service record, and under the Uniform Code of Military Justice, they've decided to charge you under Article 119, Involuntary Manslaughter."

"What's the maximum penalty?"

"Ten years. But I'm going to work hard on your case. We might be able to get the charges reduced."

Madeline looked down at her hands and thought of the last time Eliot had held them. "Do you think I've got any kind of chance, Marion?"

Marion put her hand on Madeline's shoulder. "I'll see you again in a few days. Don't give up hope on me, Madeline."

Marion took writing materials from her briefcase and handed them to Madeline. "These are acceptable for letter writing. As I said, you're also allowed visitors. Do you think you'll have any?"

Madeline thought of John. "The only visitor I could have is my brother John, but that's impossible."

"Too far for him to travel?"

Madeline looked away. "No, he's addicted to opioids. I was able to help him for a while, but now he's back on the streets...somewhere. He may not even be alive."

"I'm sorry, Madeline. Addiction is a horrible thing, especially when it's family."

As Marion left, Madeline sat down on the chair and the small table next to it.

Dear Eliot,

I know you're not far away, but it feels like a million miles. I'd give anything to hold you. I wish we'd done more of that before we parted, but I know now it would have only made things harder for both of us. You were right to make it quick.

I think of all the times you held me, tried to remember every embrace. Sometimes just having you near me, close to me all the time, was all I needed. But then, at night, feeling your breath against my body as we fell asleep, feels like the dearest memory of all. I wish I hadn't taken it all for granted, that you'd always be there, especially now. At least we have this.

I hope they're treating you all right. My condition is good. They've given me a good attorney, a woman, who in spite of everything, makes me think I've got some kind of chance. I hope you get a lawyer as good.

I'd better get a letter soon from you, Eliot Lange! Miss you more than I can say.

I love you,

Maddy

When Madeline re-read her letter, its optimism surprised her. Marion's counsel had given her courage, but she knew the voices of a military court would not be as sympathetic.

CHAPTER 17

TRIAL

Eliot didn't like the look of his attorney. The law books with which he was fumbling as he entered the cell, seemed bigger than he was. He could not have been more than five feet tall. He was bushy haired with horn-rimmed glasses and wearing a uniform a size too big for him.

He put his books down on the cell table, set his briefcase on the floor and extended his hand to Eliot. "Good afternoon, Staff Sergeant Lange. I'm Lieutenant Thomas Styles. I'll be representing you."

The two men shook hands. Eliot sat down on his bunk. The lieutenant sat down on the chair adjoining the table, but before he could pull a file from his briefcase, Eliot was already talking.

"Excuse me, Lieutenant, but before we get started, I've got to ask you if I can write to another military inmate here."

The lieutenant removed his glasses and set them on the table. Eliot noticed how kind his eyes appeared. "I assume you're referring to Sergeant First Class Madeline Crowne. You and she…"

"Yes. We know each other."

The lieutenant sat back. "So-the media says. It's a shame the way they exaggerate things without knowing all the facts. Of course, you can write to her."

Lieutenant Styles became taller in Eliot's eyes. "Thank you, Sir. It'll mean a lot to both of us."

The lieutenant picked up his glasses, tapping one of the temple tips to his mouth. "Her case is particularly difficult, more so than yours, I'm afraid."

Eliot looked down. "I know." When Eliot looked up again, he saw a slight smile on the lieutenant's face.

"But she has an excellent attorney...one of the best."

"That's good to hear. Thank you for telling me that." Eliot paused before asking his next question. He didn't want to offend his attorney, understanding as he appeared to be, but he had to know how experienced he was. "Have you been a military attorney for long? I don't mean to pry, it's just...".

"A legitimate question," the lieutenant quickly responded as he put his glasses on. "I'm somewhat new at this. I was a civil attorney for about a year, but after 9/11, I volunteered for the army and was eventually assigned to the Judge Advocate General's Corps. From the outset, I knew I wanted to help combat soldiers who were in trouble. I know how anything can happen in war, and I didn't want to see any serviceman go to prison for something he didn't do. Things are bad enough as they are... all the soldiers we've lost."

Eliot leaned forward, rubbing his hands together. "Too many."

"Exactly," the lieutenant said, as he stood up and began pacing the cell, his hands clasped behind his back. "I witnessed cases where it was clear a soldier had committed a crime and was sentenced. That's justice. But I've seen other trials where I felt there was room for doubt. I think your case leaves room for *considerable* doubt."

Any fears Eliot had about his attorney's experience were quickly dispelled. He knew he had the right man. "What makes you think that, Lieutenant?"

The attorney stopped pacing and leaned against the cell door. "First of all, it doesn't make sense. On the surface, it appears you and PFC William Madsen were deserting. As you went 'outside the wire' the alarm was sounded, and soldiers came after you. In their pursuit, they heard shots ring out. When they caught up to you, they saw PFC Madsen running away. You were kneeling next to an Afghan villager, seriously wounded. Next to you was a rifle. You then got up and fled the scene. Sadly, the villager later died from his wound.

"But if you were deserting, why would you kill a civilian? Did he, or any of the other villagers that were awakened by gunfire that night pose a threat to either of you in your escape?"

Eliot leaned back against the cell wall. "No. But none of it happened that way."

The attorney sat down, looking carefully at Eliot. "Tell me what happened. All of it."

"First of all, Will had PTSD...bad. They should have sent him home sooner. God, if only they had. I tried to help him, but it didn't do any good."

The lieutenant saw tears beginning to form in Eliot's eyes. "And you and he were very close, were you not? Your commanding officer said you were."

"Yes, since we were boys. Best friends...always. On that night, I woke up and saw him take his rifle and run out of the barracks. I chased after him. When he got close to the village, he started yelling crazy things and shooting wildly into the air...out of his mind. I tried to take the gun away from him, but he wouldn't let go.

"Some of the villagers came out of their houses. They all ducked for cover, but one of them stayed behind. When I finally got the gun away from Will, it fired a round and struck the villager that hadn't taken shelter.

"Will ran away. I still had the rifle in my hands when I ran over to the man who had been hit. I dropped the gun, got down next to him and put pressure on his wound. It was bad…really bad. I knew if he didn't get help soon, he'd bleed out. Then the other soldiers caught up to me and…".

The lieutenant leaned in. "And then what happened?"

Eliot wiped tears away. "I don't know. I lost my head… got up and ran."

"And I understand William Madsen has recently passed away."

Eliot ran his hand over his face. "Yes, not long ago."

"I'm sorry. It's hard to lose a best friend."

"More than you know. If only I'd stayed and tried to explain. If only I hadn't abandoned him like that…"

The lieutenant got up and went to the cell door. "No one knows what they'll do in a situation like that, but we have to talk about your defense now. On that night, did any of the villagers see that the bullet from the rifle was an accidental discharge?"

Eliot shook his head. "I don't know. I couldn't say."

"How many villagers would you saw were present? Roughly."

"Maybe half a dozen, something like that."

The lieutenant stroked his chin. "The army did question the villagers, but only much later. The inhabitants stated that though they were shocked by what they saw, none of them tried to attack either you or PFC Madsen. Apparently, there were a few others who were closer to the scene that night but had recently moved away. They might have been helpful to us."

"Even after what happened?"

"Yes, but there's another question to be answered. One that leaves room for doubt, on our side. Why would you shoot someone, intend to injure or kill them, and then go to the wounded party? Again, it doesn't make sense."

Eliot looked down. "Neither did my running away… only made me look guilty."

The lieutenant straightened his uniform. "Yes, there is that, but let me tell you what we're really up against. In our favor, we have your service record, which is excellent. You're a decorated veteran of two tours."

Eliot looked away. "And I'm also a deserter. There's no mistake about that."

"No, there isn't. But there's more. The army is particularly concerned now about any Afghan civilian killed by US forces, or any soldiers contracted by our government to fight in the war. You may have heard about a recent case in which private military contractors murdered innocent civilians. Now, there's politics involved. Politics and press."

Eliot got up, hands on his hips. "And that only makes matters worse."

"Not necessarily. Since we know that none of the villagers posed a threat to either you or William, the only danger you were facing were the soldiers advancing on you, and you didn't fire at any of them. It's not reasonable to believe that you would shoot an unarmed man, simply because he failed to take cover. It was an accident you didn't mean to make happen."

Eliot rubbed the back of his neck. "But that would be on my word alone."

"Precisely. We're going to continue to find the villagers who moved away, but it's not easy. Although the Afghans are clannish, they're also nomadic and their borders are extremely porous. They're also afraid to make any statement that would make a US serviceman appear innocent, in the death of one of their own. The Taliban have been known to severely punish any such action…even making an example of an entire village."

Eliot sat down on his bunk. "It doesn't look good. Exactly what charges am I facing?"

The lieutenant took a file from his briefcase. "Under the Punitive Articles of the Universal Code of Military Justice, you fall under Article 118, intent to kill or inflict great bodily harm, and of course, desertion." The Lieutenant replaced the file and handed Eliot writing materials. "You can use these for letter writing. I'll be back in a few days, hopefully, with better news. Stay with me, Staff Sergeant. We may yet find a way."

They stood up and shook hands. "Thanks for taking my case, Lieutenant. You make me feel like I might have a chance, in spite of everything."

The lieutenant turned to leave but then turned back. "Oh, you're also allowed visitors. Do you think you'll have any…family, friends?"

Eliot looked down. "No. They're all dead."

That night, Eliot sat down to write a letter to the only person left in his life, the one who meant more to him than anything.

Dear Maddy,

It's only been a few days since we said goodbye, but it feels like an eternity. Now, I wish I hadn't made us separate so quickly. I thought it was the right thing to do at the time, but I'm aching to hold you, if only for a moment.

The only thing that keeps me going is the memory of you, the scent of your hair, the feel of your skin, the way you always held me. I shouldn't go on like this. I know it only makes it harder for both of us, but Maddy, it's all that I have. We can write letters to each other, thank God, and I can't wait for a letter from you. Make it quick, OK? I need it. Bad.

My attorney is a good guy, on my side, all the way. He told me you've got one of the best lawyers. That was great to hear. My lawyer is trying to run down any villager who might have seen that it was an accident when I shot and killed that Afghan man, but he's having a hard time finding one. Things don't look good without a good witness.

Here I am going on and on about me. I'm sorry. I'm more concerned about your case than my own. Has your attorney been able to find any soldier in your unit who witnessed what you did that night? Seen that it was not your fault? That you didn't mean to do it? That could mean so much to us.

Of course, we still have desertion against us. I don't see how we can beat that, but oh, Maddy, if I had the power right now, I'd rather see you go free than myself. Just knowing you were free in the world would give me enough strength to face anything. And maybe, in time, you could find someone more deserving of your love than me.

I love you,
Eliot

That night, alone in their cells, Madeline and Eliot tried to concentrate on each other, but it was no use.

Of all the civilians I could have mistakenly killed, why did it have to be a woman bearing a child? A child who never had a chance to live because of me. What would that child have been like? What would its life have been like? Who would they have loved? Who would have received that love?

Eliot was lost in his own desolate monologue.

Whatever they do to me, it can't be as bad as the thought of killing an innocent man and abandoning my best friend. My friend who needed me so much. Why didn't I stay and try to explain?

The next morning Eliot received Madeline's letter. Clasping it in his hands, reading it repeatedly, he felt as if she were with him. A day later, Madeline received Eliot's letter.

His words brought tears to her eyes, until she reached the last paragraph, and her sweet sorrow turned to instant anger. *How could he ever suggest, even though it's impossible, that I should go free if he weren't with me? And worse, how could he ever even hint that I would love someone else?*

Madeline's responding letter was immediate.

Damn you, Eliot Lange! Don't you ever again say anything about me going free without you! And never say I could love someone else! I can only love you, you big idiot!

OK, I said all that and you better remember it. The rest of your letter was beautiful. But that's the only nice thing you're going to get out of me today. And I'm waiting for a letter back from you along with a big apology.

I love you,
Maddy

Eliot got Madeline's letter a day later and despite its ire, it made him smile. Take everything else away from her, but she still had that spunk. Maybe it *was* a good idea that he wrote what he did.

He sat down and wrote his response, trying to make it as groveling as possible.

Dearest Maddy,

I beg you to forgive me for my thoughtlessness. I don't know what I was thinking. I thought I was being unselfish, but I realize now I was being self-indulgent. Can you ever forgive me? I hope so.

Of course, neither one of us could ever really be free if the other was without freedom. The only thing in my life that's perfect, is your love for me.

I pray that you will forgive me for offending you the way I did.

I love you,
Eliot

Eliot's letter had the desired effect. A day later it was Madeline's turn to smile as she read his romantic and penitent words. They would be the kindest words she would hear for a while.

Their trials were staggered. Madeline's proceedings began a few days before Eliot's. Before the trial, captain Marion Evans visited Madeline again, going over their line of defense, how they would proceed and the customs of the court. How Madeline would need to present herself. But beyond all that, Madeline felt Marion's comfort, her warm manner, her confidence in their case.

On the first day of the trial and before being transferred from the Belton County Jail to the courtroom at Fort Hood, Marion came to Madeline's cell, carrying a sergeant-first-class's uniform. "You'll need to wear this. How are you holding up today?"

Madeline stared at the uniform she had once worn so proudly. Seeing it now brought back painful thoughts. She knew she had to overcome them if she was going to make it through the day. "All right, I guess. The letter writing has helped a lot."

Marion smiled. "Good. We're going to need you to show a brave face today. I know you can do it."

As Madeline changed into the uniform, she turned to Marion. "Have you had any luck finding Jim Clay?"

"Not yet, but we're still working with local law enforcement in Galveston. Don't give up hope."

When they arrived at the courtroom, Madeline looked around at the court's trappings. Beyond the tables reserved for the prosecution and defense, a long wooden table, deeply varnished, was mounted at a higher level. Six leather chairs stood in a row behind it. Seated in the center was the military judge, a man in his forties with short, cropped hair. On either side of him was the five-member panel of other officers, three men and two women. Behind them stood the United States flag, along with the flags of all the military branches.

As Marion and Madeline took their seats at the defense table, Madeline looked across the aisle at the prosecution table. Captain David Harris, in his early thirties, stared straight ahead, his square jaw firmly set. Madeline couldn't help but notice that he had a full head of blonde hair, just like John's.

What was John doing right now? Was he even alive? *Dammit, Maddy!* She cursed herself. *Concentrate!*

The charges against Madeline were announced and the court heard the opening statement from the prosecution. Captain Harris rose and presented his argument. "This is a clear case of a soldier who lost control under fire. Our fighting forces depend on leaders who can maintain discipline, especially over themselves in combat situations. Sergeant

First Class Crowne failed in her duty, not only taking the life of an unarmed woman, but of that of her unborn child. What is more, the fact that she panicked and deserted the soldiers she was meant to lead, made them even more vulnerable to enemy fire."

As Captain Harris continued his statements, Madeline felt her heart crushing within her. She knew this would be hard, but to hear it all stated in a room of strangers, *official strangers,* struck her harder than she could have ever imagined.

Seeing her client sinking back into her chair, Captain Evans turned and looked at Madeline. Marion's expression said it all. *Keep it together. Sit up straight.* Madeline sat up and squared her shoulders, even as she was fighting back tears.

After Captain Harris finished his opening remarks, Marion stood to address the court. Harris narrowed his eyes on her. He knew she was an excellent attorney and though her case lacked the essential witness she very much needed; he also knew she had never lost a case.

"This case is not as transparent as the prosecution would believe," Marion began. "To begin with, the accused before you today, is a veteran of two tours in Afghanistan. Her leadership and courage are proved by the fact that she was awarded a Silver Star, an honor not lightly given.

"Although we know that some of our soldiers, very few, have willfully committed heinous acts in combat, it is unlikely to assume that anyone with a service record like First Class Sergeant Crowne's, would do so.

"What *is* logical, however, is that in the 'fog of war', mistakes, based on split-second decisions while under fire, can and do happen. There are many such instances. None of us want to see an unarmed, innocent civilian killed, but in combat, especially as it occurs in a war such as Afghanistan, where civilians often unwittingly find themselves caught in crossfires, this kind of tragedy can occur."

Captain Evans went on to say that although it was clear her client had indeed deserted, given the vulnerability of the Afghan woman who was killed, Sergeant Crowne was overcome by feelings of guilt and remorse. Even the most hardened fighter would be.

The captain concluded her argument by saying that the defense was trying to locate PFC James Clay, who had been present on the night in question and later given a statement that he too, had thought the Afghan woman was a combatant.

When Marion took her seat, she thought she saw signs of sympathy from two court members, but she knew she would need two more if she were going to win her case, and that would not be easy.

Captain Harris saw the same reactions, but he was happy to see the Judge maintaining a stoic look. Harris also knew he had a bigger advantage. His witnesses were on hand, ready to testify. Evans's witness could be anywhere.

On the second day of the trial, the prosecution called PFC Joseph Winslow to testify. He was a slender young man with light brown hair. His pale green eyes appeared nervous as he looked around the courtroom and took the witness stand. Then he saw Madeline. His eyes softened at the sight of her. She gave him the same look.

Marion put her hand on Madeline's arm and whispered to her. "You can look at him, but not that way."

Madeline looked straight ahead as Captain Harris rose and approached the witness stand. After asking Private Winslow several preliminary questions, establishing dates, time and location, the captain got down to the heart of the matter. "PFC Winslow, how would you describe the scene on the night of the engagement in question?"

Private Winslow looked down, rubbing his hands together. "It was crazy…chaotic, I mean. There were a lot of Taliban coming at us, more than we thought there'd be. More than we were told. We were trying to hold on to our position, but we kept losing ground. I didn't think we were going to make it. We'd already lost several of our guys and others wounded." He looked at Madeline. "Sergeant Crowne was trying to keep us together, keep us going…".

Harris interrupted. "Please confine your comments to the actual scene."

Captain Evans objected. "Your honor, any credible comment on the situation that attests to my client's character, should be admissible."

The judge nodded. "Sustained. I'll allow it."

Harris glared at Evans. "Let's move on to what happened next. During the intense firefight, did you see Sergeant Crowne shoot an unarmed civilian?"

Winslow looked away. "There was a lot of smoke in the area, but Ray, Private Raymond Marks and I, were on a small embankment and could see below where Sergeant Crowne and some others were. What looked like a woman carrying a staff, came running out of the village in Sergeant Crowne's direction."

"And then what happened?"

The private covered his face with his hand. "I saw Sergeant Crowne aim and fire. The woman fell to the ground. Private Marks and I couldn't believe what we were seeing. I think it hit me harder than him. A few minutes later we saw Sergeant Crowne drop her weapon and run away."

Harris returned to his table and turned to Captain Evans. "No further questions. Your witness."

Marion rose slowly from her chair. She went to the witness stand and stood close to Private Winslow. "You stated that there was a lot of smoke in the area that night. How smoky was it where Sergeant Crowne was?"

"More. Quite a bit more."

"Do you think she had as clear a view of the scene as you and Private Marks had?"

"Not as good as him and me."

"So, it's possible, is it not, that under the circumstances she could have mistaken the Afghan woman as a combatant?"

Captain Harris rose from his chair. "Objection! Calls for a conclusion on the part of the witness. We have no way of knowing precisely what Sergeant Crowne could, or could not see from her vantage point, even if there was a large amount of smoke."

The judge agreed. "Sustained."

Marion continued her cross examination. "Private Winslow, before Sergeant Crowne fled the scene, did you see her do anything else? Give any aide to the injured woman?"

Winslow looked away. "No...no I didn't."

Marion stepped back from the witness stand. "Private, how many engagements were you in with First Class Sergeant Crowne as your leader? Approximately."

"A lot. At least six, maybe more."

"And how would you say she conducted herself as a leader in those combat situations?"

Private Winslow looked at Madeline. "She was the best. However bad things got, she was always better. She saved a lot of us."

Despite her attorney's advice, Madeline felt tears begin to form in her eyes.

Marion took a chance. She knew it would lead to an objection, but she had to try to establish doubt in any way she could. "Private Winslow, do you think Sergeant Crowne would willfully shoot an unarmed civilian?"

Captain Harris slammed his hand on the table. "Your Honor, I must object! Once again, Captain Evans is calling for a conclusion from the witness. I think we've heard enough about Sergeant Crowne's sterling service record. That doesn't conclude that she couldn't lose control and commit an illegal act."

The Judge sustained the objection and looked at Captain Evans. "Do you have any further questions for this witness?"

Marion took her seat. "None, Your Honor."

The Judge dismissed Private Winslow and turned to Captain Harris. "Call your next witness."

PFC Raymond Marks was called to the stand. He was a stocky man with dark features. Harris had saved him for last. When he'd interviewed both Winslow and Marks, he'd seen dangerous indications of sympathy for Madeline on Winslow's part, but he knew he would need both witnesses if he was going to prove his case and Marks was another story.

In interview, Marks talked dispassionately about the incident that night. Yes, initially, he had been shocked by what he had seen, but he was certain that Madeline had taken deliberate aim at the Afghan woman.

As Harris walked Marks through the same questions he had given Winslow, he was pleased to see Marks maintaining his stoic composure. When Harris got to his final question, he felt certain he had the upper hand.

"So, Private Marks, was there any doubt in your mind that Sergeant Crowne's actions that night were deliberate?"

"Yes, I believe they were."

A palpable silence fell over the court. Then Madeline broke down. Hearing the events of that night described in such grave terms, the tears flowing down her face were not enough to contain her grief. Sobs shook her body, coming one after another.

As Marion consoled her client, the court gave the opportunity for cross-examination. Her arm still around Madeline, Marion looked up at the judge. "I have no questions for this witness, Your Honor."

Despite her warnings to Madeline, Marion knew that such a show of emotion might be helpful to her case. Even military juries could be moved.

Marion was given the opportunity to present witnesses. "Your Honor, we ask for the court's indulgence. There was another soldier who was present on the night in question, PFC James Clay, who later gave a statement saying Sergeant Crowne's actions were justifiable.

"Unfortunately, we've been unable to locate Private Clay. His last known whereabouts were in Galveston. We have an investigator trying to find him, but Private Clay's circumstances present difficulties."

The Judge narrowed his eyes on Captain Evans. "What are you referring to?"

Marion took a breath. She knew what she was about to say was not going to help her case, but she had no choice. "Private Clay was recently arrested on a domestic violence charge. He was allowed to post bail but failed to appear in court as scheduled."

The two jurors who had previously seemed sympathetic to Madeline, now appeared skeptical. The judge leaned back in his chair. "I'll give you two days to produce your witness."

Captain Harris was pleased. *Even if she does find him, what good is the testimony of a bail jumper?*

Court was adjourned for the day. Captain Evans and Madeline went back to the Belton County Jail. Madeline sat down on her bunk. "It doesn't look good...none of it."

Marion sat down next to her. "You can't look it at that way. We've managed to establish some doubt. That's a good thing. If we can..."

"Just find Jim Clay," Madeline interrupted. "But he's in so much trouble. I still don't understand it. I can't imagine Jim mixed up in domestic violence. He was such a gentle guy by nature, always passing out candy to Afghan kids. Once, I saw him *save* a kid who was in the line of fire."

Marion put her arm on Madeline's shoulder. "We don't fully know his situation, but if what you're saying is true, there might be some explanation for his actions. My investigator has been working closely with the Galveston Police Department to locate him. He's told them that Jim is needed to testify as a defense witness in a military trial and they're willing to cooperate."

Madeline looked away. "Yeah, but we both know the court won't like it...the way Jim jumped bail. And we've only got two days to find him!"

Marion's cell phone rang. She looked at the caller's number. "It's my investigator." Marion listened intently to the caller's voice. "All right. Good. Call me back as soon as you know for sure."

Marion clicked off and looked at Madeline. "Our guy thinks he may have spotted Clay!"

Madeline sat up. "Where? Is he sure it's Jim?"

"Not positively, but he's following him now."

Madeline shifted in her chair. "How good is your investigator? Can you trust him?"

"Absolutely. He's never failed to bring in a witness for me."

"Even when he's on the run like this? Marion, I know what it's like to be pursued. For people like Jim and me our combat training kicks in. Even though I know Jim as a gentle guy, he's desperate now. Desperate to get away!"

Marion stood up. "Investigator Gomez knows how to deal with all kinds. Maddy, we have to believe in him! If he can bring in Clay, you could be cleared of the manslaughter charge!"

"Don't get my hopes up, Marion. It hurts too much to hope."

Marion resumed her seat next to Madeline. "All right, let's get back to what we were working on…the testimonies so far."

Madeline rubbed her forehead. "How are we supposed to do that while we wait for your phone to ring?"

Marion gave Madeline a stern look. "Madeline… concentrate."

But even as Marion tried to appear calm, she was as anxious as her client to hear the vibration of her cell phone on the table next to her.

Two hours later, it rang. In a panic, Madeline reached for the phone. Marion grabbed it first. She listened carefully to her caller, a smile beginning to form on her face. She put her hand over the phone and turned to Madeline. "He's made a positive ID. It's Clay!" But as quickly as the smile had come, it soon disappeared, replaced by a grim look. "OK, yeah. No, it's all right Joe. Just stay on it."

Madeline got to her feet. "What is it? What happened?"

Marion clicked off her phone. "He found him all right…but he got away. Dammit! I never knew Joe to lose someone."

Madeline sat down on her bunk. "I told you…desperate." She looked out at the calendar hanging on the cell block wall and pointed to it. "See that, Marion? It's the 31st of August. When my guard rips that month away tomorrow, the clock starts ticking and it won't stop. Two days in September can go by awfully fast."

CHAPTER 18

DEFENSE

The next morning Eliot's trial began. Lieutenant Styles had met with him in the preceding days and gone over their defense strategy. When they arrived in court, Eliot maintained his composure, the way his attorney had instructed. He knew that would be the easy part. Even as he heard the charges read against him, he looked straight ahead.

But Eliot also knew what was coming. In the hours that would follow, arguments would be presented, legal maneuvers would be employed and worst, the dreadful events of that night would be on full display in front of a room full of people he did not know, and never would have known, had he not abandoned his friend.

The prosecution attorney was Captain Phillip Hoffman, a middle-aged man with dark hair, going gray at the temples. In his opening statement, he went over the known facts of the case. Then he went on to attack the defense strategy.

"The defense will state that on that night, PFC William Madsen was having a psychotic event, brought on by PTSD. The prosecution will not argue that Private Madsen possessed that anxiety disorder. That was later established.

"The defense will also argue that in a fit of aberration, Private Madsen was firing an M4 carbine in the vicinity of the Afghan village. If that were the case, why was Staff Sergeant Lange seen in possession of the weapon when the soldiers pursuing the deserters, came upon him and Private Madsen?

"It will be argued that Sergeant Lange was in pursuit of Private Madsen that night, trying to prevent him from harming himself or others. If that were true, why would Sergeant Lange then later flee the scene? Why would he not surrender to his pursuers and attempt to explain what had happened?"

Captain Hoffman turned and looked at Eliot. "But no, he deserted the army and the country he was sworn to protect, leaving behind a dead Afghan civilian and the man he *says* was his friend."

Eliot held back his tears. He had promised himself he would not weep. That, he would do in private. Will was dead, but the memory of how Eliot had abandoned him, lived on in an agony even more painful than the loss of Will's life.

The defense was allowed their opening statement. Lieutenant Styles rose and addressed the court. "Why would a man who rose to the rank of Staff Sergeant, serving two tours in Afghanistan, leading men in combat and later being awarded a bronze star, suddenly desert his post? What possible motivation could he have to do that?

"We know from Staff Sergeant Lange's commanding officer, as well as other soldiers in his unit, that PFC Madsen and he were the closest of friends. The bond between them was made stronger by the fact that their friendship reached back to boyhood. After 9/11, they even entered the military together, fighting side by side in Afghanistan.

"On the night in question, Sergeant Lange awoke to see Private Madsen arming himself with a rifle and running 'outside the wire.' Private Madsen was spotted by guards on duty and the alarm was sounded. With no thought for himself, Sergeant Lange pursued his friend, even after soldiers chased after the two men.

"When Sergeant Lange caught up to Private Madsen, he was firing his rifle wildly into the air, possessed by PTSD. Sergeant Lange attempted to take the weapon from Private Madsen but was unable to do so.

"During their struggle, Sergeant Lange was finally able to wrest the gun away from Private Madsen, but in the process the gun accidentally went off and struck an Afghan villager. Sadly, the villager later died from the wound.

"Private Madsen then ran away. Sergeant Lange went to the man who had been shot and tried putting pressure on the man's injury. Meanwhile, the soldiers that had been pursuing Private Madsen and Sergeant Lange then came upon the scene. They saw Sergeant Lange, a rifle next to him, and beneath him, the injured man. Realizing he would be seen as guilty, and suddenly possessed by panic, Sergeant Lange then fled. His sudden desertion left no doubt in the soldier's minds that Sergeant Lange was guilty.

"But this begs a question. Why would a man who had shot another, then go to the injured party? To shoot him again? He could easily do that from where he was. To think that Sergeant Lange would go to the villager after shooting him, is a challenge to credulity.

"We are not arguing Sergeant Lange's desertion. That is apparent. We *are* saying there were extenuating circumstances.

"Several days after the events, Private Madsen was found in a comatose state. His PTSD was diagnosed, and he was sent home for treatment, but much too late. His disorder *should* have been recognized and dealt with long before. Tragically, he has since passed away. Another one of our soldiers, lost to the horror of war…needlessly."

When Lieutenant Styles finished his opening argument, the court adjourned for lunch. Later, the prosecution presented two witnesses who were part of the five-man unit attempting to capture Eliot and Will on that night.

The testimony of both soldiers matched and was conclusive. They had seen Eliot with a rifle near him and not far away, the wounded Afghan. Captain Hoffman knew he needed no further witnesses.

Lieutenant Styles declined cross-examination. When given the opportunity to present witnesses of his own, he offered accounts by three villagers who were present on the night of the incident.

"Your Honor, we have sworn statements from several Afghans on the incident in question. Although they were shocked by what they saw, they clearly attest that they made no attempt to intervene, and that Sergeant Lange did not discharge his weapon in their direction, or in any way threaten them.

"They go on to say that there were two Afghans immediately on the scene before them and could provide a more accurate account. One later moved away and our investigators have been unable to locate him. The second, however, is believed to have immigrated to the United States. We've been looking through immigration records and hope to know his location soon."

As in Madeline's trial, the court gave lieutenant Styles forty-eight hours to find his witness and adjourned for the day.

Back at the county jail, Eliot sat down on his bunk and looked up at the lieutenant. "Do you think you've got a chance at finding this guy?"

Styles dug his hand into his pocket. "I sure hope so. We don't have much to go on. One source told us he *thought* he immigrated to the United Sates. We've got that and a last name—Kohdr. That's it."

Eliot leaned against the cell wall. "Not much to work with."

Styles jiggled the keys in his pocket. "No, it's not, and you wouldn't believe how many people immigrated from the region at that time."

Eliot smirked. "Needle in a haystack."

"You can't look at it that way, Eliot. I've still got more records to go through."

Eliot rubbed the back of his neck. "Yeah, but even if you do find him, we have to hope he saw that it was an accident."

The lieutenant put his hand in his other pocket, shaking his loose change. "I know, but at least we've got a paper trail we can follow. That's *something*."

Eliot pointed to the lieutenant's pockets. "Sir, would you mind not doing that? I've nervous enough."

The lieutenant withdrew his hands and crossed his arms. "Sorry, me too. It's just that we're so close and still so damn far!"

Eliot smiled. "First time I heard you curse."

"I don't, normally. But we've got some doubt going now. All we need is our eyewitness. Mr. Kohdr."

That night, in Las Cruces, New Mexico, Abdul Karzai was going through the torment of his life. Sleep was impossible. The slender young man sat on the edge of his bed, running his hands through his thick, black hair.

He knew he would have to make a choice, the most difficult of his life, and worst of all, he had to make it now. Time was running out. Even if he got on a plane to Fort Hood tonight, he might be too late. The news report he had seen an hour earlier on CNN, had said the trial of staff sergeant

Eliot Lange was not going well. He was expected to be found guilty. But Abdul knew that he was not.

Abdul fell back on his bed, staring up at the ceiling. This was more dangerous than all the combat engagements he had gone out on with US soldiers in Afghanistan, working as their interpreter, or "terps" as the soldiers liked to call them.

But then he had had only himself to worry about. Now, he knew that if he stepped forward for Eliot Lange, Abdul's family, thousands of miles away in Afghanistan, could be facing torture and death, and there would be nothing he could do about it.

Turning on his side, covering his face with his hands, he remembered all the things he had done as an interpreter for the United States. Later, when he had quickly picked up technical skills, he was moved into Intelligence, time and time again picking up encrypted Taliban messages and foiling their plans.

He had done his job so well he was allowed to emigrate to America, working remotely now as a special government analyst, picking up Taliban "chatter" on the Dark Internet.

His supervisor was so impressed with Abdul's performance, he said he would help him bring his parents and young brother to the United States, a dream Abdul had often wished for.

Now, Abdul felt that dream being crushed into his chest, and in its place the worst horror of all—Taliban reprisals. He knew the wide arm of CNN encircled the world, and terrorist networks would be quick to see a story involving an Afghan man coming to the defense of a US soldier. Especially a soldier accused of killing an unarmed villager.

Abdul also knew that the media would waste no time in reporting that he had been responsible for gaining information that led to the failure of Taliban raids. And even as the news would be regaling him as a hero, the Taliban would be pinpointing anyone related to a traitor.

Abdul had witnessed the horror of Taliban reprisals. In their aftermath, he had seen the women who had been raped, the men beheaded. Even children had not been spared. He felt a knife piercing his heart as he thought of his brother, only ten years old now.

And Abdul knew that even though he was continents away, the tentacles of terror could reach out and kill him. He got up from his bed, pacing the room as he talked aloud to himself.

I can't die! How can my family survive without me? They need all the money I send home. They can't cultivate barren earth, torn up by explosions!

Agonized by questions that could not be answered, he sat down in a chair and recalled the night it had all begun with Eliot Lange.

It had been Abdul's job that night to care for a sick goat. He had been chosen among all the young men in his village for the all-night vigil because of his love for animals, knowing instinctively how to care for them.

As he had rocked the animal in his arms, making soothing sounds as the goat trembled, he suddenly saw a soldier shooting his gun at the trees and shouting words that made no sense.

Abdul could not believe what he was seeing. How was it possible? The American soldiers had always protected his village. He had become friends with some of them. They liked the shy kid with the sweet smile. Abdul had learned a lot of English from them, hoping one day to become an interpreter for the army. He wanted to repay them for keeping his family safe.

But now, Abdul saw a US soldier shooting in every direction. Then villagers were coming out of their houses, stunned by what they saw. All of them dove for cover, but one. He had been too shocked to move. Then another soldier emerged from the darkness. He tried to take the rifle away from the soldier that was firing, but the man would not let go.

At last, the second soldier seized the rifle, but then it went off in his hands, a bullet striking the villager that had stayed behind.

As the crazed soldier ran away, Abdul saw the second one going to the injured man. He saw the soldier kneel and put pressure on the villager's wound.

From out of the woods soldiers with flashlights came on the scene. In the bright light they saw the soldier next to the wounded villager, a rifle nearby. The soldier stood up and ran away. The other soldiers shouted at him to halt, but he continued to run, disappearing into the forest.

In the time since that night, Abdul had often wondered what had happened to the soldier who had only wanted to stop violence and had accidentally killed an innocent man. Abdul knew then that even if the soldiers were not able to capture the man, he would be lost, alone in a country with no one to help him.

Now, Abdul knew that man's name—Eliot Lange. And from the news report Abdul had seen, he knew Eliot's face. The same frightened face Abdul had seen so long ago.

Now, rubbing his hands together, Abdul had the power to help Eliot Lange. But that help would come at a cost too terrifying to think of.

After that horrible night, Abdul had wanted to tell the army what he had seen, but his father had been too afraid to allow it. His father had told the family the Americans could no longer protect them, and they left for another village.

Protection, Abdul now thought to himself, as he continued to wring his hands. *What protection could my family have now? Wouldn't I be betraying what my father had done to protect us all? What good would it do to protect a man I don't even know? What kind of man is he that I should put my family in danger that way?*

The answer came to him in a bitter irony. *The kind of man who had only tried to stop violence and suffering.*

That same night, all the pressure was on Joe Gomez. Even though he had only spoken to Captain Marion Evans on the phone, he could feel the tension in her voice. As a federal investigator with ten years' experience, the stocky, middle-aged man with a black crewcut, was trained to sense fear. And Marion Evans was afraid. He had never known her to be that way.

He had also never known her to want a suspect so badly. This James Clay must be something special. Gomez had never failed to bring in a suspect for Evans, but Clay was another story.

Gomez had spotted him earlier in the evening, and had been amazed at how quickly Clay had disappeared, almost as if he were a ghost.

Maybe it's not so surprising, Gomez had reasoned to himself. *The guy is a woman beater and a bail jumper. Coward… the worst kind.*

Joe Gomez may never have caught up to James Clay, had he not suddenly been haunted by the image of his battered ex-girlfriend, and stopped under a streetlamp.

For days, as James had run from one hiding place to another, his torment was intensified by the thought of what was happening to his ex-girlfriend. Was her new boyfriend beating her up again? What is he doing to her right now?

He leaned against the streetlamp; the terror of his thoughts too burdensome to bear. *I told Cheryl that guy was no good, but she was too blind to see it. She should have trusted me. Christ, we stayed friends, even after we broke up. Dammit, Cheryl!*

Impulsively, he had jumped bail in a vain attempt to go to Cheryl's aide. *Stupid!* He now thought to himself. *How could I have gone to her house? That's the first place the cops would look for me. They've probably got a guard posted there right now.*

Lost in guilt and remorse, James failed to see the man who had followed him earlier, the one he had been able to get away from. That man had not looked like Galveston police, not even their plainclothes officers. That man seemed more like the Military Police; James had known in Afghanistan. It didn't matter. That man was now rushing towards him.

James bolted away from the streetlamp and ran down a darkened street. He heard the man running fast behind him. Up ahead, James saw a bar that was so busy, the noise spilled out onto the street.

James burst into the bar, crowded with so many people, there was only room to stand. Hoping to conceal himself until he could find the back door, James bumped into one patron after another. But with his height well over six feet and his sandy blonde hair, Joe Gomez had already spotted him and was now sifting himself through the crowd.

Looking back over his shoulder at Gomez, James collided with a customer. The customer's beer crashed to the floor. Angered, the customer threw a punch at James. James ducked the punch just as Gomez was now face to face with him. James pushed the customer into Gomez. Both men fell to the floor.

James saw the back door straight ahead of him. He threw his shoulder into it and ran down the street. But Gomez was right behind him.

Before James could confront his pursuer, Gomez already had James's arm twisted into a hammerlock, shouting at him.

"I'm not Galveston PD! I'm federal!"

Angry and in pain, James shouted back. "So, what do you want *me* for?"

"You're needed to testify in a Military Trial… for Madeline Crowne!"

With his free arm, James rammed his elbow into Gomez's mid-section. As Gomez pulled back in pain, James ran away.

Many blocks later, realizing he had escaped, James slowed down, a bitter reality overtaking him. *Oh God, Maddy! How could she be on trial? She saved my life once!*

Joe Gomez knew he had at least one cracked rib. As he touched his side and winced from the pain, he knew the feeling. He had had two ribs cracked when he had served in Iraq, in Operation Desert Storm, and now, James Clay had brought back bad memories.

Gomez went to a local hospital to get bandaged up. He felt too battered to call Captain Evans with bad news. He would call her in the morning.

The next day, Captain Evans and Madeline tried to sit down to serious work in Madeline's cell, but their thoughts were too distracted.

"Marion, why didn't your investigator call last night, even if it was to say he didn't have anything?"

Marion put her hand over Madeline's. "He'll call as soon as he catches up to Clay." Marion had no sooner said those words, when her phone rang. She looked at the caller ID and turned to Madeline. "It's Joe!"

Madeline leaned in, desperate to hear good news, but she did not like the look on Marion's face. "No, it's all right, Joe. Just try to stay with him."

As Marion clicked off, Madeline sank back on her bunk. "Jim got away, didn't he? I knew it."

Marion stood up and went to the cell door, turning away from Madeline. Madeline's fear increased. Marion had never turned her back on her.

Marion crossed her arms. "I didn't realize how hard it would be to bring him in."

A sardonic smile crept onto Madeline's lips. "You didn't? Do you know how hard the US Army taught us to evade, to escape…especially from capture? Don't you think it's funny that that skill is being used against me now?" Madeline broke into laughter, even as tears came to her eyes. "I think that's funny! Don't you?"

Marion had been worried about Madeline's mental state before, and now was terrified, even as she felt her own stability shaken. She had to do something…fast. She spun around and seized Madeline's shoulders.

"Look at me, Sergeant First Class Madeline Crowne. You are the woman awarded a Silver Star for bravery! We need that courage now! Do you understand me?"

Tears rolled down Madeline's face as she rose and put her arms around Marion. "Oh God, Marion. How could I make it without you?"

A few minutes later, Marion received another call, this time from the Judge Advocate General's office, reminding her that she had less than twenty-four hours to produce her witness.

Although Abdul Karzai had had no sleep, his mind was clear. He called Fort Hood and asked to be connected to the attorney representing Staff Sergeant Eliot Lange. When the phone rang in Styles office, he let it go to voicemail. He had no time for another annoying call. He was too busy combing through immigration records, trying once again to find the name of Kohdr. Then he heard the caller leaving a message.

"Hello, my name is Abdul Karzai. I saw the report of Sergeant Lange's trial on CNN. I was present on the night Sergeant Lange is accused…"

Styles snatched the phone into his hand. "Hello…hello! Whose calling?"

"Abdul Karzai, sir. You're the attorney defending Sergeant Lange, correct?"

Styles sat up straight in his chair as a lump formed in his throat. "Yes…yes, I am. I'm Lieutenant Thomas Styles. You have information for my client?"

Abdul's voice softened. "I do. I know Sergeant Lange stands accused of willfully killing an unarmed Afghan villager, but that's not true. Your client is innocent, if there is such a thing in war."

Styles gripped the arm of his chair. What kind of witness was this? "I see. And you were there that night?"

Abdul's voice was so low, Styles had to strain to hear him. "I was. I saw the rifle go off in Sergeant Lange's hands as he took it away from the other soldier, who appeared to be out of his mind."

Styles waited a moment before asking his next question. "Did you see Sergeant Lange do anything after that?"

As Styles sat on the edge of his chair, Abdul seemed to hesitate. "Yes. He went to the wounded man and put pressure on his wound. Then other soldiers appeared, and Sergeant Lange ran off into the forest."

Styles could not believe his good fortune, but something was wrong with this witness. He seemed detached, as if he was reporting something someone else had seen.

"Well, this is wonderful news, Mr. Karzai. I can't tell you how grateful I am that you called; how grateful Sergeant Lange will be when I tell him you've come forward. But I'm a little confused. I've been looking for an eyewitness with the name of Kohdr."

"Someone has given you the wrong information, Lieutenant. Kohdr is my mother's tribal name. My father's is Karzai. That's the name I had to use to immigrate to the United States."

Styles mind was reeling as he tried to put the puzzle together. "Where are you now? And more importantly, how soon can you be here? We're running out of time."

Abdul now spoke in a clear voice. "I'm in Las Cruces, New Mexico. I work remotely as an Intelligence Specialist for the US government."

Styles was dumbfounded. *How strange can all this get?* "I see. Let me put you on hold for a minute so I can book you a flight out here."

When lieutenant Styles turned to another phone on his desk and quickly called the Las Cruces airport, he got nothing but bad news. There were no flights going out to Killeen airport in Fort Hood, until tomorrow morning.

Dammit! Styles cursed to himself. *If only he'd called sooner! Tomorrow I'll have less than a day left.*

Styles booked the earliest flight and switched back to Karzai. "Mr. Karzai, I just reserved a flight for you tomorrow morning at 10AM. I'll meet you at the airport. Mr. Karzai...are you still there?" The line seemed to be dead. A moment later, Styles barely heard Abdul's breathing. "Did you hear what I said Mr. Karzai?"

"Yes... I heard you, Lieutenant."

Styles breathed in relief. "This is a courageous thing you're doing, Sir. I'll see you in the morning."

Courageous? Abdul thought, as he tossed his phone aside. *"What's so courageous about betraying your family?*

Styles jumped up from his desk, went out to his car and drove fast to the Belton County Jail. He got to Eliot's cell and grabbed him by the shoulders.

"You're not going to believe this! From out of nowhere, an Afghan, Abdul Karzai, just called me and said he saw the whole thing that night. He saw the rifle go off accidentally in your hands and shoot the villager. He even saw you trying to help the man who had been shot!"

Amazed, Eliot looked at Styles. "It can't believe it! But I thought you were looking through immigration for the name of Kohdr."

"It was a crazy mix-up, but I've got him on a flight out here tomorrow, and none too soon. Talk about the nick of time! The only thing that concerns me now is his attitude."

Eliot took a step back. "What do you mean?"

Styles stroked his chin. "Can't really put my finger on it. Don't get me wrong. He's a bright guy. He went on to become an interpreter for the army. When he immigrated, he went to work for the government in the Intelligence Service. Talk about credentials.

"But while I was talking to him, he seemed so detached from the whole thing, almost cynical."

"Should I be worried, Tom?

"I hope not."

Meanwhile, Abdul went to his apartment window, looking out on a street scene. The day before he had barely noticed the people going by, going about their ordinary business. What was his family doing right now? Probably something as common as the people below him, completely unaware of the danger they were in.

I can still get out of this…tell Styles I'm sick…run away, anything!

Abdul fell on his bed and wept. He cried until he realized what he had to do.

CHAPTER 19

RECKONING

An hour later, captain Marion Evans was shaking Madeline's shoulder. "Maddy! Maddy... wake up! I've got good news!"

Madeline thought she was dreaming. She had been in and out of nightmares all night long. She shook her head, trying to gain consciousness. "Marion? What's going on?"

"Jim Clay just turned himself in!"

Madeline sat up. "No! When?"

"An hour ago. He called Galveston PD. He said he'd come in voluntarily, but only under one condition."

Madeline grabbed Marion's arm. "Which was?"

"That he'd be able to testify for Madeline Crowne. Even though he and Joe got into a fight, Joe was able to tell him you needed his testimony."

Madeline ran her hands over her face. "God, I don't believe it."

Marion smiled. "Neither did I. And I've got more good news."

"How could there be anything else? That was all I needed."

Marion crossed her arms. "You'll need this. You've got a visitor. Your brother, John."

"Johnny!" Madeline trembled as tears ran down her face. "He's alive! She looked around herself, searching, confused. "Have you seen him yet? Does he look all right? Does he…".

"He's fine, Madeline. The approval process for visitors usually takes a while, but I've managed to speed up the process. He's waiting for you in the visitor's room."

When Madeline was led to the visiting area, she couldn't believe her eyes. Sitting with his hands neatly clasped on a visitor table, she saw the John from before.

Now, his blue eyes were clear, alert. Now, his blonde hair was full again and neatly parted. Now, he was smiling at her.

She sat down opposite him and tried to hold back tears as words poured out of her mouth. "John! What happened to you? Eliot and I looked for you everywhere on South Side. I didn't even know if you were alive! I was afraid…"

John grasped her hand. "Maddy, slow down. You always were in such a hurry. I'll tell you everything."

Madeline sat back in her chair. "Please do, and don't leave anything out."

John smiled. "OK, first of all, I'm clean. I've been that way for six months, twenty-two days, and this morning. You know how I beat it? It wasn't the fear of overdosing. At one point, I didn't care anymore. I just wanted out.

"One morning I ducked into a coffee shop to get in out of the rain. There I was, soaked, filthy from living on the streets and broke. I sat in the back, trying not to be noticed, but the shop owner kept staring at me. I thought he was going to throw me out when he walked over to my table, but instead he brought me a cup of coffee.

"It turns out he's a recovering addict himself and he knew a strung-out junkie when he saw one. His name is

Mark Lafores, and he helped me get clean. He gave me a job in his shop, kept a close eye on me and coached me every day."

Madeline wiped away tears. "That's wonderful, Johnny. But how did you know I was here?"

"From the newspapers. When I told Mark about it, he gave me the bus fare out here. But how's it going with your trial now?"

"It's better. *Much* better. We've got a witness who can say I didn't mean to shoot that woman."

"That's great, Maddy. Just what I wanted to hear!"

Then a guard walked over and told them their time was up. Slowly, they stood and faced each other.

"I wish I could see you again Maddy, but I've got to get back. I can't be away from my coach for too long. Mark is my lifeline...know what I mean?"

Madeline smiled. "And you're mine."

They clasped hands as tears formed in their eyes.

"We're going to make it, Maddy. Both of us. No matter what's happened, we're going to make it. I know we will."

That morning, lieutenant Styles went to pick up Abdul Karzai at the airport. In the back of his mind, Styles was still concerned about his conversation with Abdul. He had seemed so unemotional, so removed from something that was so crucial.

Styles suddenly realized he was doing 45 in a 25-mile zone and took his foot off the accelerator. *Slow down, Tom. This is no time for an accident!*

The lieutenant arrived at the airport and quickly found the departure gate for Abdul's flight. Standing directly in front of the skybridge, Styles closely examined each passenger as they came down the extended tube. He knew at least that he was looking for a young, middle eastern man.

But none of the faces that passed by him fit that description. They were all locals of varying ages, parents with children, older couples carrying souvenirs. Where was he?

Styles felt a thrill go through him when he sighted a man with dark features, but no, he was older, with thinning hair. The skybridge emptied out. Desperate, Styles headed down the tube.

When he got to the cabin, a flight attendant gave him a curious look. "Did you forget something, sir?"

Styles wiped sweat from his forehead. "No...I wasn't on the flight. I'm looking for a passenger I was supposed to meet."

The flight attendant took a step back. "They've all disembarked. You can see for yourself."

Styles felt his heart sinking as he looked out on row after row of empty seats. *My God, what am I going to tell Eliot?*

Then, from the very rear of the plane, Styles saw a small, dark man, slowly rising from his seat.

"That's him!" Styles shouted. "It has to be...right back there!"

A second flight attendant came out of the cockpit and turned to the first. "How did you miss him?"

The attendant shrugged. "I thought I checked all the seats."

Styles rushed down the aisle. "Mr. Karzai? You *are* Abdul Karzai, aren't you?"

"Yes," Abdul said, in a softened voice. "Lieutenant Styles?"

Styles shook Abdul's hand. He noticed how limp it felt. "I've got a car waiting for us. I'm so glad to see you!"

On their drive to the fort, Abdul's silence made Styles nervous. He tried to make light of the situation. "You had me scared there for a minute, Mr. Karzai. Wasn't sure if you were really on the plane or not."

Karzai looked out the window. "You can call me Abdul."

"Abdul, thank you. We'll need to go over the case once we get to my office. Go over your testimony."

Abdul shook his head. "I know what to say. We don't have to go over all that."

Styles grew increasingly nervous. "Is something wrong, Abdul? You seem so...distracted."

Abdul looked out at the cars passing by. "I have other things on my mind."

"Could I ask you to share them?"

For the first time, Abdul looked directly at Styles. "Do you know what a Taliban reprisal is? Do you have any idea?"

Styles shifted in his seat. "I've heard of them...not much more."

Abdul looked down. "Not much more. Yes, that's what most Americans think. I've *seen* them. You would not believe what one human can do to another."

Styles had no idea where this was leading. He only knew that it frightened him. "It must have been horrible for you. To witness something like that."

Abdul glared at Styles. "Yes, witness. And now I am *your* witness. And soon the whole world will know it, especially the Taliban."

Styles pulled over to the side of the road. "I don't understand. What are you getting at?"

Abdul grabbed Styles arm. "My family! In Afghanistan! You don't think the Taliban will know that I helped an American soldier?"

Styles bowed his head. "I had no idea. And I can't imagine how hard it must have been for you to call me."

Abdul looked out the windshield. For the moment, the road seemed to lead nowhere. "I could be assassinated myself, not that my life matters."

Time hung in mid-air as both men looked out on the barren landscape, implacable to human suffering.

Styles turned to Abdul. "What made you decide to finally come forward?"

Abdul rubbed his forehead. "I almost didn't. But then I thought of something. It wasn't all the things the United States has done for me, making me an interpreter, allowing me to immigrate, have a good job and send money home. None of those things."

"What was it then?"

Abdul looked at Styles. "I couldn't keep living, knowing that a man was being prosecuted for something he didn't do."

It was exactly what Styles wanted to hear, but it was all overshadowed by the possible threats to Abdul and his family. As Styles drove them back on to the road, his mind was lost in an internal monologue.

Can I really put this man on the stand, knowing the risk he's taking? In his frame of mind will he really be a good witness? Will he break down in cross-examination?

Styles looked over at Abdul, his eyes hooded, staring down at the floor of the car.

Would I do what he's doing if I knew my loved ones may be in danger? I don't know, but a man is being tried for a killing he did not commit. That's all I know.

Styles looked out on the road ahead of him. A road that led to a fort and a courtroom. A bitter irony simmered in the back of his mind.

At last, we found the witness we've being looking for, the man who saw everything, the man who can save my client from years of imprisonment, but how much can you ask of a man?

They arrived at the fort and went to the lieutenant's office. "Before we go over your testimony Abdul, I want to say it took a lot of courage for you to come in. More courage than I've ever seen."

Abdul looked around at the lieutenant's office, the law degrees framed and mounted on the walls. "Courage can be a hollow word, Lieutenant. But I'll do the best I can for you."

Styles called the Judge Advocate General's office and informed them that he had his eyewitness and was ready to proceed. Captain Hoffman was also made aware of Abdul's presence and though he was surprised by the sudden turn of events, he immediately went to work on a new strategy.

Styles also knew he would have to inform Eliot that even though they now had their key witness, that same witness may still be grappling with terrible fears. Although Abdul had seemed to calm down once they got back to the fort, Styles knew that Hoffman was a highly experienced attorney and would quickly pick up on any tension he could sense in someone's testimony.

Once on the witness stand, Abdul would be firmly in Hoffman's grasp and there would be little Styles could do about it.

Styles arranged a room for Abdul and had a car pick him up. Then he drove slowly to the Belton County Jail. He felt his heart sinking, knowing that the elation he and Eliot had shared once Abdul had come forward, would now be darkened by fears neither he nor Eliot could fully comprehend.

"So, how did it go with Karzai? Does he seem all right now?" Eliot said, quickly getting up from his bunk.

Styles slowly sat down on the cell's single chair. "His testimony is fine, just like I told you, but we've got another problem."

Eliot did not like the look on Styles face. "What's going on?"

"Sit down, Eliot. Let me try to explain it to you. It's not easy. Your case is headline news…world news. Abdul is afraid for his family, back in Afghanistan, possible retaliation from the Taliban."

Eliot leaned forward. "Oh, Jesus. I didn't think of that."

"Neither did I, but we've got to work with it."

Eliot stood up and went to the cell door. "God, I don't think I'd want him to testify under those circumstances. I don't care what it would mean to me."

Styles rose and placed his hand on Eliot's shoulder. "You're an innocent man Eliot Lange, and you deserve justice. Sometimes justice is painful."

"Yeah, but Lieutenant…"

"Look. Hoffman will sense Abdul's uneasiness and try to use it, but Abdul is highly intelligent. I think he can stand up to it."

Eliot gripped one of the cell bars. "I hope you're right."

When court was called to order the next day, Abdul took the stand. Styles was careful to point out Abdul's background, as well as his impressive life since his time as a shepherd in a small village.

The lieutenant then took Abdul through everything that had happened that night, focusing particularly on the facts that not only was the shooting unintentional, but that Eliot had even gone to the aide of the wounded Afghan. Abdul's responses were clear and concise, answering every question without hesitation.

Eliot stared at the man on the witness stand, a man whose existence he was totally unaware of only twenty-four hours before, and now, this stranger was giving testimony that could mean the difference between a few years for desertion, and a decade or more of Eliot's life. *Ten years with Maddy. Ten years of loving her, having her close to me. But how can she be free? It's impossible. None of it would be worth living without her.*

Lieutenant Styles saw Eliot rubbing his temples and gave him a stern look. Eliot sat up straight in his chair.

Although it seemed to Lieutenant Styles as well as the court, that captain Hoffman had little to work with in cross-examination, the experienced attorney knew that he had more.

"So, Mr. Karzai, you say that you were not only sure that Sergeant Lange's shooting of the villager was accidental, but that he later attempted to help the villager that was fatally wounded. Are those true and correct statements?"

Abdul looked directly at captain Hoffman. "Yes, they are."

Hoffman turned away. "And even in the darkness of that night, you saw all this transpire?"

"Yes. I was close by."

Hoffman turned back to Abdul. "Do you know what the penalty for perjury is Mr. Karzai?"

Abdul narrowed his eyes on Hoffman. "I know that it's a serious crime."

Hoffman got close to the witness stand. "Yes, it is. And you have testified, under oath, that Sergeant Lange tried to help the man he had unintentionally wounded. Correct?"

Abdul straightened himself. "Yes, that's correct."

Hoffman took a step back. "Yes, but what did Sergeant Lange do *after* the soldiers pursuing him arrived on the scene?"

In a voice barely audible, Abdul replied. "He ran away."

Hoffman gripped the witness stand. "What was that you said, Mr. Karzai? I didn't hear you."

Abdul glared at Hoffman. "He ran away!"

Hoffman slammed his hand on the witness stand. "He ran away! Even though he could have asked the other soldiers to help him with the wounded man, he ran away!"

Abdul came face to face with Hoffman. "He tried to help that man! It's what I saw!"

Lieutenant Styles got to his feet. "Objection! The prosecuting attorney is trying to intimidate the witness."

The judge disagreed. "Overruled. I'll allow it."

Hoffman stepped away from the witness stand, allowing the dust to settle before he spoke again, this time in a softened voice. "And so, Mr. Karzai, you are testifying to this court that Sergeant Lange's sudden heroism, instantly turned to cowardice once he feared for his own self-preservation. No further questions, Your Honor."

Court adjourned and the lieutenant and Eliot went back to his cell. Styles sat down on Eliot's bunk, rubbing his hands together. "That was rougher than I thought it would be. Abdul stood up to it, but Hoffman was still able to drive his point home."

Eliot sat down next to him. "I didn't like the looks on the juror's faces...especially the judge."

Styles leaned back against the cell wall. "Hoffman is a good attorney. Experienced in military law...unlike me."

Eliot put his hand on Styles shoulder. "Don't say that, Lieutenant. You've done everything you can to help me... more."

Styles smiled. "I think at this juncture you can start calling me Tom. We're alone in the same lifeboat."

They laughed, but only momentarily. Eliot stood up and crossed his arms. "So, how bad did he hurt us? Tell me straight."

"I always have been Eliot, and I always will be. But now I'm worried. Hoffman has made you look worse than a deserter."

Two Galveston police officers brought James Clay to the interview room where captain Evans was waiting for him. One of the officers took off Clay's handcuffs and stood behind him as Clay sat down at a table, opposite captain Evans. The other officer stood outside.

"I'm Captain Marion Evans, Mr. Clay. I'm representing Sergeant First Class Madeline Crowne in her trial. To begin with, I want to thank you for…"

Clay quickly interrupted, reaching over the table. "I'd do anything for Maddy. She saved my life once!"

The Galveston police officer placed a firm hand on Clay's shoulder and put him back into his chair. "Take it easy, Clay. It's not your trial."

Immediately, Marion was concerned about Clay's frame of mind. "I was about to say that Madeline and I are very grateful for you voluntarily surrendering to Galveston law enforcement, so you could appear here today on her behalf."

Clay looked down, shaking his head. "I'm sorry, Captain. It's just that when it comes to Maddy…"

As his voice trailed away, Marion thought she saw a tear form in one eye. *Not good,* she thought to herself. *In an instant, he went from excitation to near tearfulness. A bad mixture for a military trial.*

"Mr. Clay, I'm also aware of the domestic violence charge against you. We could be helpful with that."

Clay looked up. "What do you mean?"

"Your cooperation could mean a possible reduction in your sentencing."

Clay leaned back in his chair. "It was a stupid thing I did. I wanted to save my old girlfriend from being beaten up by her new guy. The cops thought I was the one abusing her. Then, like an idiot, I jumped bail, thinking I could help her. I only made matters worse for both of us. Anyone as stupid as me deserves to be locked up."

Marion pitied the man before her, but his emotionality concerned her far more. "After the trial Mr. Clay, whatever the outcome, I'll be certain to advise the Galveston Court of your cooperation."

Clay looked down. "I don't know if it would be worth it if what I say doesn't get her off. I'm looking at six months, maybe a year. She's facing a lot more."

Marion smiled. "Mr. Clay, we'll notify them in any case."

"Yeah, but what's it going to look like when I show up at Maddy's trial in handcuffs with two cops?"

Marion sat back. "My guess is the prosecuting attorney won't say much. Not at first. He'll let that speak for itself and carefully bring it up in his summation."

James rubbed his chin. "I guess I can't tell them the reason I jumped bail."

"No, you can't. That's a civil matter and it has nothing directly to do with Madeline's trial. This is a military court." Marion opened a manila folder and brought out a stapled document. "But we still have your statement from the night you, Madeline and other soldiers were engaged with Taliban forces. Let's go over that."

She turned the first page back and ran a finger down the left margin of the next. "You stated that on that night, you saw a figure emerge from the smoke of battle, and thought it was an enemy fighter holding up a weapon. You were about to fire, but Madeline fired first. When you both saw that it was an unarmed civilian, a pregnant woman, holding up a staff, and you realized what had happened."

James rubbed his forehead. "I can still see the look on Maddy's face, the horror in her eyes. There was nothing

I could do, but I *knew* it was a mistake. It happens over there sometimes. But why did it have to be *that* civilian? *That* woman?"

Marion looked at the man who was trying to hold back tears. "It's bound to happen, especially when so many villagers are mixed in with the Taliban. So, after that, Madeline dropped her rifle and ran away, correct?"

Suddenly, Clay sat up in his chair. "Yeah.... No! Wait! She tried to help that woman, now I remember! She put pressure on the woman's wound. Tried to stop the bleeding. I saw it!"

As much as Marion was pleased to hear what Clay was saying, it also came as a big disappointment. Nothing like that had appeared in the statement he had made after the incident.

Marion leaned across the table. "James. May I call you that?"

"Sure, but make it Jim."

"All right. Jim, what you just told me could be of great value to Madeline's case, but I didn't see any mention of that in your original statement. Can you explain that?"

Clay rubbed the wrists that still bore the mark of his handcuffs. "I got confused. They wanted us to make statements so fast. There was a lot of pressure on us from the big brass. They were getting pressured by the media, you know?"

Marion tapped her hands on the arms of her chair. "Yes, I know. But if we use what you just told me in court, the prosecuting attorney will be certain to point out that that information did not appear in your statement. Madeline told me that she had attempted to give aide to the wounded woman, but she didn't think anyone saw her do that."

Clay got up from his chair. "I did. I know I did!"

The police officer pushed him back into his chair. "Dammit, Clay! You do that again and you're going back to jail."

Clay slumped in his chair. "I'm sorry, officer. I won't do it again."

Marion put her hands on the table. "Jim, you have to understand. Captain Harris, the prosecuting attorney, will be hard on you if we try to use what you just told me. Can you stand up to that?"

Clay let out a deep breath. "Yes, for Maddy I can. I swear I will."

"Good. We'll be counting on you."

The interview over, Marion knew what she had to do, as much as she dreaded it. Driving over to the Belton County Jail, she felt a pang in her chest. She knew she would have to tell Madeline that their star witness, the one who had finally come forward after so much conflict, the one who could save Madeline from years of imprisonment, was a deeply emotional man.

Worse, Marion knew if she used what Clay had just told her, it would come at a big risk. It could be enormously helpful to develop sympathy on the part of the court, but that could backfire.

Harris could easily object that Clay's sudden remembrance was 'firsthand hearsay' coming long after Clay's original statement, and therefore not admissible. That objection could certainly be sustained and that would be the end of it—seemingly.

But as Marion got closer to the jail, she realized if she could get Clay's new information stated just long enough to arouse sufficient empathy from the court members, it might work.

Still, there was the question of Clay's state of mind. Harris would sense that and use it to discredit Clay completely and the case would be lost.

Marion parked her car at the jail and went to Madeline's cell. She knew she would need her client's approval before embarking upon so great a gamble.

Before the guard could even unlock the door to Madeline's cell, she had her hands on the bars. "Marion! God, I thought you'd never show up."

Marion entered and sat down on the cell chair. "I'm sorry. It took longer than I thought."

Madeline noticed that Marion was looking downward. "Hey, you're not looking at me. What's going on?"

Marion looked directly at Madeline. "You want the bad news first?"

Madeline sat down on her bunk. "Yes. Absolutely."

Marion leaned forward. "PFC James Clay has just given me some astonishing news."

"Nothing bad, I hope."

Marion stood up and sat next to Madeline on the bunk. "Yes and no. Remember how you told me you tried to help the wounded woman...put pressure on her wound?"

"Yes, I remember."

"And you didn't think anybody saw you do that, right?"

Madeline shifted on the bunk. "No, I didn't."

"Well, Jim Clay did."

Madeline grasped Marion's arm. "He did? God, that's great!"

Marion put her hand on Madeline's shoulder. "Not so great. Under pressure by the military to give an immediate statement, James failed to include that fact."

"But couldn't he include it now when he testifies?"

Marion clasped her hands together. "Let me give you a quick lesson in the law, Maddy. A long time ago, James Clay made a statement. A statement he had to swear to. That's hard evidence. If he now amends that statement in your favor, that would been seen as hearsay and not admissible."

"But it's the truth, Marion. Jim wouldn't lie about something like that!"

Marion returned to her chair. "You're forgetting that he's appearing on your behalf. That presupposes the possibility of bias. However, if you choose, and remember, I'm saying if *you* choose, we could go ahead and use it. Even if Harris objects, which I'm sure he will, it would still be heard by the court members. They can go along with procedure all they want, but they're also human beings, capable of compassion."

Madeline sat up straight. "Then let's go with it."

"You're sure?"

"Yes."

"OK, Madeline Crowne, but meanwhile, we've got another problem."

Madeline shook her head. "How could there be more?"

"There is, Maddy. When you were serving with James, did you know him to be an emotional person?"

Madeline looked out her cell window, the clouds floating by like so many distant memories. "Yes, he was that way, especially with the kids, giving them candy and things, like I told you before. It hurt him to see children caught up in war. You could see it on his face."

Marion crossed her arms. "Well, he's even more emotional now. Probably the result of being on the run and his intense desire to save you. He said *you* saved his life on one occasion."

Madeline turned away from the window. "Yes, but I bet he didn't tell you that he once did the same for me."

"No, he didn't Maddy, but if his sensitivity is as obvious as you say, and I've seen it myself, firsthand, Harris will be all over it. If Jim caves under the pressure, his entire testimony could be completely discredited. Are you still sure about your decision?"

"Yes. I trust Jim and most of all I trust you."

After Marion left, Madeline returned to the cell window. Now, she saw only a sky of steel gray, and the window's black bars.

CHAPTER 20

VERDICT

Eliot and Madeline had wanted to write letters to each other sooner, but events had been moving too fast for them to do so. Now, they could.

Dear Maddy,

I hope your trial is going well. Write to me as soon as you can and let me know. My trial has just had a big breakthrough, but it may have come at a terrible cost.

We finally found a witness who saw that I accidentally shot the Afghan villager that night. Lieutenant Styles had been told by a source in Afghanistan that this man, Abdul Karzai is his name, may have witnessed what happened. The source also said they thought he had immigrated to the United States.

My attorney had looked hard for his name in immigration records, but with no luck. Then, from out of the blue, Mr. Karzai called Lieutenant Styles and said he would be willing to testify for me. Karzai had seen the news of my trial on CNN.

I know this all sounds too good to be true, but it comes with a lot of pain. Abdul was frightened that by giving testimony, his family back in Afghanistan, might be threatened by the Taliban. Lieutenant Styles and I felt horrible about it.

I told Styles I wasn't sure I wanted Abdul to testify, knowing the threat his loved ones might be under, but the Lieutenant and I decided to go through with it. Do you think I did the right thing, Maddy? God, I hope so. I hope I haven't made you ashamed of me. That's the last thing I'd want.

Although Abdul gave brilliant testimony, the prosecuting attorney went on the attack when it was his turn to cross examine, and he did everything he could to break Abdul down. Abdul took it all, but the prosecutor still made me look like the worst kind of coward, because I ran away from everything.

I'm worried, and not just for myself. What if Abdul has gone through all this only to have it all wasted? Then he and I both lose. It's a crazy world darling, full of heroes and cowards! I hope I won't have to spend ten years or more feeling like the world's worst deserter.

All right, enough of my self-pity. I'm still more concerned about your case than mine. I could do all the time they could throw it me, but if I knew you were cleared, at least of the big charge against you, I'd be all right. Even from a distance, I can still love you.

With all my heart,
Eliot

Later that day, Madeline wrote back.

Dear Eliot,
First, you could never make me ashamed of you. Everything you've done while we've been together was out of love.

I know how hard it must have been for you to accept Abdul's testimony, but it was still the right thing to do, and even if it turns out badly, the truth is what counts, whatever the cost.

As far as what's happening with me right now, I've got good and bad news. Let me give you the good first. I know, you and I always wanted to face whatever bad things life was giving us right away, but my good news is too wonderful to hold back.

John is alive! He came and visited me. Can you believe it? What's more, he's off drugs and he's got a job! He's doing extremely well, almost as if his dark days had never happened. Just seeing him for a few minutes is something that will always warm me, something I'll never forget.

But that brings me to the bad news. Just like you, we now have an eyewitness who saw that I didn't mean to kill that woman and her unborn child. A soldier who fought alongside me, Jim Clay was there that night and saw it all. We had a hard time locating him and an even harder time bringing him in.

It turns out Jim was recently charged with domestic violence and jumped bail. But when he found out I was in trouble, he turned himself in. This sounds great, I know, but it won't look good when Jim is brought to the trial in handcuffs, accompanied by two police officers.

Then there's other things we've got to worry about. Although Jim even saw me try to help the woman I'd shot, he didn't include that in the statement he made after the incident. He was under pressure to make a statement and only remembered he'd seen that after my attorney interviewed him. That's bad news for my case.

Marion told me that that information can't be included now, but she's going to try to find a way to bring it up in court to get help from the jury. We need all the help we can get.

But we've got another problem. Jim is a great guy, tender-hearted, but he gets easily excited, emotional. Marion is afraid the prosecuting attorney will see that and try to break him down.

Like you said, it's a crazy world, but whatever happens, nothing can stop us from loving each other, no matter how much space or time they put between us.

I'll write to you as soon as my verdict comes down.

I love you so much,
Maddy

The next day Eliot's trial resumed. There was nothing left now but summations. Captain Hoffman rose to present his closing argument. "We've been asked by the defense to believe in this case that Staff Sergeant Lange, on the night in question, awoke to see PFC William Madsen, arming himself with a rifle and deserting the base they were both assigned to.

"Believing Madsen was in the throes of a psychotic event that might cause harm to himself or others, Sergeant Lange then also deserted and chased after Private Madsen. A seemingly noble act on the part of a friend.

"We will not refute the testimony of Mr. Karzai as to what later transpired. It's clear now that the Afghan villager was killed by a bullet accidentally discharged by Sergeant Lange. However, how are we to believe that Sergeant Lange was so brave, so loyal to his friend, that he would later run away from the soldiers pursuing the pair?

"Why would Sergeant Lange not explain to the soldiers what had happened and ask for their help in capturing Private Madsen, who could *still* be a threat to himself or others? The answer is cowardice. Cowardice to his friend and to his country. I ask for the maximum penalty for desertion…five years."

Eliot was concerned when the court allowed lieutenant Styles to present his summation. The lieutenant stared straight ahead, as if he had not heard the judge. Eliot looked at the short, bushy haired man with horn rimmed glasses, still looking like someone's kid brother. Seconds ticked away as Styles seemed to be lost, staring at something visible only to him.

The judge grew impatient. "Lieutenant Styles…summation? The court is waiting."

Suddenly alert, Styles looked up at the judge. "Yes, of course, Your Honor. My apologies."

The lieutenant stood and walked slowly in the direction of the jury, hands held behind his back, his head slightly bowed. He then turned and looked out on the back of the courtroom.

"No one knows what they will do once arms are fired, and bullets are expelled into the air. Arms are without conscience. Bullets seek whatever target they can find, indifferent to injury. In combat situations, the bravest of men may breakdown. The weakest may suddenly summon courage from a place they didn't know existed and perform heroic acts.

"Staff Sergeant Lange was in numerous engagements and proved himself more than worthy, more than courageous. But how far can courage be tested before it fails?"

Lieutenant Styles turned and faced the judge and jury. "Who, even among the bravest, could say without hesitation how they would perform in any given situation? Some would say they would perform their duties, whatever the cost. Others would say it would depend on the circumstances. The wisest would simply say they could not know."

The lieutenant looked directly at Eliot.

"Even friendship can be pushed to the brink. One man may defend a friend with his own life. Another may be forced to carry on in battle, even as his friend lay wounded. Even a lifelong friendship can fail when the mind becomes paralyzed, unable to comprehend the horror surrounding it."

The lieutenant looked back at the jury.

"Yes, Staff Sergeant Lange deserted his duty, but worse of all, he deserted his best friend. The sentence for that has no reprieve. We ask then for a sentence of one year for desertion only."

The lieutenant had delivered his closing argument more as a soliloquy than a summation and the judge and jury were clearly moved. One juror placed a hand over her face. Another stared at Eliot with a look of sympathy. The judge momentarily lost his upright posture, remained still for a moment as though contemplating what he had just heard, and then quickly turned through some papers before him.

As the judge and jury deliberated over Eliot's trial, Marion was back at the Belton County jail, busy going over her courtroom strategy with Madeline.

"All right, this is how it'll go, Maddy. After I'm finished with Jim on the witness stand, I'll ask him if there's anything else he wants to add to his testimony. At that point, he'll bring up the fact that you went to the Afghan woman and put pressure on her wound, trying to stop the bleeding.

"If Jim can make that statement before Harris can object, it could make a big difference for us. But remember, Harris will have gone over Jim's original statement as much as I have, probably more. I'm sure Harris has been looking for anything he can use against us."

Marion shook her head, looking at the floor.

"And added to this, we still have to worry about Jim himself. I'll go over everything with him as soon as I leave here. They've got him in another cell in the jail."

Madeline crossed her arms. "And we've got to pray Jim can keep it together."

Marion lifted her eyes to Maddy's. "Exactly. Jim swore to me he would, but even before I end my examination of him, my feeling is, Harris will already sense that Jim is on edge and try to break him down. It's a risk, Maddy. It could pay off, or it could blow up in our faces. Are you still sure you want to go ahead with it?"

Madeline looked straight ahead. "Yes. Whatever happens, at least the truth will be out there."

Marion left and went to Clay's cell. Before the guard could unlock the cell door, Clay was on his feet. "Did you talk to Maddy? Is she all right?"

Marion entered and sat down on the cell chair. "She's fine, Jim. She's holding up very well, but I want to know how *you're* doing now."

Clay sat down on his bunk, running his hands through his hair. "I'm OK. It's just that I'm still worried about my ex-girlfriend, Cheryl. I'm afraid her new guy may be beating her up again. I'm sorry, Captain. I know I shouldn't be thinking about that now. Maddy's in a lot deeper trouble."

Marion sat back in her chair, already deeply worried. "Yes, she is. And I can certainly understand your concern over your old girlfriend. There's not much you can do to protect her now, but you *can* help Madeline."

Clay sat up, suddenly alert. "And I will!" He seemed to gather himself. "I promise I will!"

But by degrees, Marion's anxiety increased. "That's fine, Jim. But we need you to remain calm during your testimony. We plan on taking a risk with that and your presence of mind is crucial."

She leaned forward, to make sure his eyes were on hers, and that he understood what she was saying.

"Let me lay it out for you. After you've finished testifying that what Madeline did was unintentional, I'll ask you if there's anything else you would like to add to your testimony. That's when you'll state that you also saw Madeline go to the wounded woman and put pressure on her wound to try and stop the bleeding."

Marion's lips tightened a moment, and she took a breath.

"We need to get that out there, Jim. It's essential. So, make it as simple and straightforward as possible, because I can tell you that a second later, Captain Harris, the prosecuting attorney, will be on his feet, objecting that what you said did not appear in your original statement and is therefore hearsay and totally inadmissible."

Clay looked down, trying to digest everything Marion had just said. She gave him a moment before speaking again.

"Are you all right with this, Jim? Do you understand?"

Clay sat up, suddenly calm. "Yes. Yes, I do, Captain."

"But can you do it and still keep your composure?"

Clay looked directly at Marion. "For Maddy, I will."

The next day Madeline's trial resumed. James Clay was brought into the courtroom by the two Galveston police officers. As they removed his handcuffs, he and Madeline looked at each other in mutual sympathy.

Marion was quick to lean close to Madeline. She spoke in a guarded whisper. "You can look at him, but not that way."

Madeline turned back and looked straight ahead. She struggled to control her emotions, and felt that, despite the terror of this event, she could do so. As one of the police officers led Clay to the witness stand, the judge and jury looked suspiciously at Clay. Clay was then sworn in.

Captain Evans got to her feet. "Your Honor, at last, we have an eyewitness that can testify to my client's innocence. PFC

James Clay was present on the night in question. His current situation is obvious. He is being held on a civil charge that has nothing to do with this case. Therefore, we will not speak to that. We will say, however, that when Mr. Clay was informed of my client's trial, he voluntarily surrendered to Galveston law enforcement so that he could appear here today."

The judge was silent for a moment, tapping the end of his pencil on court documents. "Go ahead with your witness, Captain."

Marion went on, to establish with Clay the circumstances of the engagement in which he and Madeline were involved in that night. "And you say that on that night Mr. Clay, there was a great deal of smoke in the area from the ongoing battle. Is that correct?"

Jim appeared in command of himself. He leaned forward to speak, and when he did, the calm in his voice gave his response measure…even a kind of authority. "Yes, a lot. At times, I could barely see my hand in front of my face."

"And then what happened, Mr. Clay?"

"I saw someone coming out of the smoke. It looked like someone holding up a rifle. I was about to fire, but Madeline…uh, Sergeant Crowne… fired first. The person we thought was an enemy turned out to be an unarmed villager. A pregnant woman."

Marion was pleased to see Clay remaining calm, even as he stated the incident's final tragedy. "So, in the smoke and confusion," she said, "you could easily have shot the woman yourself. Is it fair to say that?"

Clay glanced at Madeline, and then, gathering himself, turned back to Marion. "Yes. A second before, it could have been me."

A profound silence fell over the room. Two of the jurors shaded their eyes. The judge himself appeared moved, slowly removing his glasses. Madeline braced herself. She worried that the tears she had been holding back would now appear. She sighed and successfully calmed the tears.

Captain Harris didn't like it.

As Clay's testimony had unfolded, Harris had more than once shifted in his seat, knowing that this kind of real drama could severely damage his case. He had to do something. An opportunity was about to present itself.

Marion came close to the witness stand. "Is there anything else you would like to add to your testimony, Mr. Clay?"

Jim looked at Madeline. "Yes. I want to say that after shooting the woman, Sergeant Crowne realized what had happened and went to the woman, putting pressure on her wound to try and stop the bleeding."

As soon as Clay's words breathed air, Harris was on his feet. "Objection! *Nothing* like that appears in Mr. Clay's statement after the incident. This is pure hearsay!"

The judge struck his gavel. "Sustained."

Not satisfied with that, Harris went further, pointing at Marion. "You have deliberately led this witness into an illegal maneuver. The most unethical one I have ever seen!"

Marion got to her feet. "Your objection has been sustained! How dare you now impugn my character?"

Harris turned towards her. "Because you have broken the law!"

The Judge slammed his gavel. "I warn both counsels to restrain themselves."

Harris shook his head. "My apologies, Your Honor, but the defense counsel had brought to this courtroom a witness she has manipulated. A witness brought to this court in handcuffs…"

Marion fired back. "His legal situation has nothing…"

Clay jumped up from his chair, pointing at Harris. "You can't talk to her like that! She's trying to help an innocent woman!"

The police officer pushed Clay back into his chair as the judge hammered his gavel. "Order! I will not warn counsels again. And another outburst like that Mr. Clay, and I will hold you in contempt."

Silence slowly settled across the courtroom. The jurors looked on with stern faces. Madeline leaned close to Marion. "It's all falling apart," she whispered.

Marion put her hand on Madeline's arm and leaned close. She lifted the hand to her lips, to hide them. "Wait." She, too, whispered. "We still got it out there."

The judge gripped his gavel as he looked at Captain Harris. "Your witness, counsel."

Harris rose and straightened his uniform, collecting himself before he went to the witness stand. "And so, Mr. Clay, can you tell us what Sergeant Crowne did after she had killed the Afghan woman and her unborn child?" Harris looked back at Marion. "*That* does appear in the statement you made after the incident."

Clay looked from side to side, gripping the arms of his chair.

Harris got close to the witness stand. "Did you understand my question, Mr. Clay? What did Sergeant Crowne do?"

Clay looked down, muttering to himself. The judge pointed his gavel at him. "The witness will answer the question."

Harris put his hand on the witness stand. "Did you hear the Judge, Mr. Clay? Answer the question!"

Tears in his eyes, Clay looked at Madeline. "She ran away."

Harris turned away and looked at the judge and jurors. "She ran away. A deserter and a coward!"

Clay shot up from the witness stand. "She's no coward! She's the bravest woman I ever knew!"

The police officer again shoved Clay into his chair. The judge pounded his gavel. "I will not warn you again, Mr. Clay!"

Harris crossed his arms. "I have no further questions for this witness, Your Honor."

The judge tossed his gavel to the desk. "Very well. We'll hear closing statements tomorrow."

James Clay was led away in handcuffs. As he passed by Madeline, he stared at her. "Maddy, I'm sorry…I—"

The police officer led him away.

Once Madeline and Marion had returned to the county jail, Marion sat down on the cell chair as Madeline paced back and forth. "I don't know who I feel sorrier for, Marion," Madeline said. "Jim or me. I know he meant well, but he couldn't control himself."

Marion took Madeline's arm. "Sit down, Maddy. It's not the end of the world."

Madeline sat down on her bunk. "Are you sure? You saw the way Harris took Jim apart…got him to blow up."

"I know, but did you see the court's reactions when Jim said it could have been he who shot the woman? That admission struck a nerve."

Madeline rubbed her forehead. "I hope you're right. It's just that *hearing* it all again, everything that happened that horrible night, over and over again. I wanted to scream!"

Marion took Madeline's hand. "It's all right, Maddy. You held yourself together beautifully. I'm proud of you."

The next day, the court informed lieutenant Styles that they had reached a verdict. He immediately went to Eliot's cell. "They're ready for us. We've got a verdict."

Eliot stood and straightened himself. "That was pretty fast. Is that a good or bad sign?"

"You never know with a jury, Eliot. Could be either way."

"Whatever way it is Tom; I want to thank you for all you've done for me."

The lieutenant smiled. "We've been on a long journey together. I hope I've done enough."

When they arrived in the courtroom and seated themselves, lieutenant Styles turned to Eliot. "Don't look at the jury or anybody else but the judge. Understood?"

Eliot looked straight ahead. "Got it."

Lieutenant Styles looked across at captain Hoffman. The two exchanged a polite nod. With the jury already seated, the judge entered and took his chair. He looked directly at lieutenant Styles and at Eliot. "Counsel and the defendant will rise to hear the verdict of the court."

The lieutenant and Eliot stood at attention. The judge read from the court's decision. "We find the defendant, Staff Sergeant Eliot Lange, not guilty under Article 118, intent to kill or inflict great bodily harm."

Eliot maintained his composure, even as he held his breath, waiting to hear the next verdict. The judge continued. "Under the charge of desertion, we find the defendant guilty. We will now proceed to sentencing. It is the judgement of the court that under the circumstances of this case, the defendant shall serve one year of confinement at the U.S. Army Disciplinary Barracks at Fort Leavenworth, Kansas."

For the first time in court, the lieutenant and Eliot were able to smile at each other. Captain Hoffman came across the aisle. "Congratulations, Lieutenant. I have a feeling I'll be addressing you as Captain very soon."

Lieutenant Styles shook Hoffman's hand. "Thank you, Sir."

Hoffman smiled and shook his head. "I have a feeling it was your summation. Much as I hate to admit it, that was one of the best I ever heard."

"You did a fine job yourself, Captain."

"Even if I *did* lose?"

Styles gripped Hoffman's arm. "Justice won. That's all that counts."

Eliot wanted to get back to his cell as fast as he could and write a letter to Madeline, but he knew that he could not. There was something else more urgent.

He turned to lieutenant Styles. "What about Abdul? Has he spoken to his family? Are they, all right?"

Styles put his hand on Eliot's shoulder. "I talked to him this morning, just before he left. He's been calling home every day and everyone is fine. His supervisor had already been trying to help with getting his family over here. Now, *I* can help. I know a good immigration attorney; I guy I went to law school with. Between all that and everything Abdul has done for our government, I'm sure we'll get them out."

Eliot gripped the lieutenant's arm. "Thanks, Tom. That's a big load off my mind."

The following day, before going to court for summations, captain Evans met with Madeline in her cell. The captain saw the nervous look on Madeline's face, her eyes looking from side to side. "Maddy, you've got to keep it together now. I know you're worried about Jim's outbursts in court. I also know that having to once again relive that tragic incident had to have been painful for you, but the judge and jury will want to see you steadfast."

Madeline smiled. "Well, I couldn't do any of this if—"

"You have to, Maddy."

"—if I had any other attorney than you."

Marion put her arm around Madeline. "All right, then. Are you ready?"

Madeline stood at attention. "Yes, Captain."

The mood in the court was somber as Marion and Madeline arrived. Captain Evans tried to read the expressions of the jury but saw only blank faces. The judge called the court to order. He motioned to the prosecuting attorney. "Captain Harris, you may present your closing argument."

Harris rose and stood in front of the jury. "This case is not as complicated as the defense would have you believe. It comes down to a single act."

He paused, allowing the silence to take on weight.

"The death of a mother and her unborn child is beyond tragedy. No two victims could be more innocent."

Again, silence.

"We all know that mistakes happen in war. That goes without saying."

He turned toward Madeline and pointed at her directly.

"But why, after realizing what she had done, did Sergeant Crowne not resolve to state the actual circumstances of the event, once the engagement was over? After all, she had PFC James Clay as an immediate witness, dubious as his testimony may be. We have *two* witnesses who stated Sergeant Crowne's act was deliberate. And so, we come back to the *single event* I referred to earlier. The tragedy of two innocent victims is horrible enough, but the fact that Sergeant Crowne deserted stands as evidence to her guilt. And since that desertion occurred in time of war, her sentence should exceed the maximum of five years. The prosecution rests, Your Honor."

The judge turned to captain Evans. "You may present your summation, Captain."

Captain Evans rose from her chair. "Your Honor and members of the jury, in the fog of war, even a veteran like

First Class Sergeant Crowne, can become paralyzed by the sight of something more horrible than she had ever seen. Something she never thought she would *ever* have seen. In that situation, who would not? Who could even imagine it? True, our soldiers are trained to face all circumstances, and, yes, there are rules of engagement in place. But can those same rules account for everything, however dreadful? How far can they be stretched before they burst, and prove everything within them of no avail?"

Now Evans allowed a moment of silence. It was a moment that was longer than either of those from her opponent. Indeed, before she spoke again, she could sense the beginnings of discomfiture on the part of the judge and jury. She spoke before the judge could intervene.

"In response to the prosecution's attempt to make my client appear cowardly, I would refer to Sergeant Crowne's outstanding record as a soldier.

"Also, the prosecution has tried to discredit the testimony of James Clay. True, Mr. Clay is an emotional man, but comrades in arms are often that way when it comes to defending each other. The bond between them, fighting side by side, facing death every day, is timeless and forever. That same union is what we all depend upon to keep our country safe. We go about our daily lives, unaware of the horror that our fighting men and women must endure."

Evans turned away from the jury and gestured toward Madeline.

"Yes, Sergeant Crowne deserted her post." She turned back toward the jury, this time with a look of actual rectitude, the sense that she was certain her words held the truth. "But she is not guilty of deliberate murder. Therefore, the defense believes she deserves no more than the minimum sentence for desertion."

Although Captain Harris's arguments had been convincing, Captain Evan's summation contained a heartfelt emotion that could be seen on the faces of the judge and jury. One female member of the jury looked at Marion in awe. The other stared at Madeline in sympathy.

Captain Evans and Madeline had barely returned to her cell when they were told a verdict had come down.

Madeline looked at Marion in shock. "That was fast! What does it mean?"

Marion put her hand on Madeline's shoulder. "It could mean anything. Stay with me, Maddy. I think we're going to be all right."

They returned to the courtroom and stood to hear the verdict. The judge looked at Madeline. "The court has found that Sergeant First Class Madeline Crowne, is not guilty under Article 119, of the Universal Code of Military Justice, Involuntary Manslaughter."

Madeline gripped Marion's hand but continued to look straight ahead. There was still one more charge to hear.

The judge put down the verdict and took off his glasses. He looked directly at Madeline. "Our military courts are allowed a certain amount of discretion, especially in cases involving extenuating circumstances. We believe, Sergeant Crowne, that your case qualifies under those conditions, and therefore, find you also not guilty of desertion."

Madeline looked at Marion and was surprised to see her eyes glistened with tears. Marion was careful to hold them in place.

Back at the Belton County Jail, Madeline was dumbfounded. "I still can't believe it. I don't know how you did it, Marion."

"I had a big advantage, Maddy."

"What do you mean?"

"I had you. People believe you. They saw your remorse for what you had done and felt that was punishment enough. I hope, in time, you'll fully forgive yourself."

Madeline smiled, even as tears began to form. "Is it permissible to hug one's defense counsel?"

Marion embraced her. "I think we'll make an exception in your case."

Madeline slowly came out of their embrace. "Forgive me, Marion, but I've got to..."

"Write a letter to Sergeant Lange?"

Madeline laughed. "Yes! Right away."

As Marion left, Madeline sat down to write to Eliot, trying not to write too fast.

Dear Eliot,

My verdict just came in they've found me not guilty of manslaughter _and_ desertion! I still can't believe it. None of it would have been possible if I hadn't had Marion as my attorney. I'll never forget her.

I'm overjoyed of course, but it's all overshadowed by what happens in your trial. Please write me as soon as you can. No matter what happens, I'll always be with you.

I love you,
Maddy

The guards at the Belton County Jail thought Eliot was celebrating his own 'not guilty' verdict as he jumped up and down in his cell with a big smile on his face.

Then, when Eliot suddenly sat down and quickly scribbled out a letter with tears in his eyes, they thought he was completely crazy.

Maddy!

I can't believe it. I'm so happy for you, but there's more. My attorney worked so hard for me and with the help of that eyewitness, they found me not guilty of the major charge. The only bad news is I'll still have to serve a year for desertion. But it'll go fast, darling. Think of it. In a year we'll be together again!

I asked Lieutenant Styles if he could do one more favor for me, although he's already done so much. I asked if you and I could see each other before I go to Leavenworth. He said he'd see what he could do. Pray for us, Maddy. Seeing you again would mean so much.

I love you,
Eliot

Captain Marion Evans was way ahead of Eliot. She'd already spoken with lieutenant Styles, and they arranged for Madeline and Eliot to see each other before he had to leave for Kansas. The attorneys had even made it possible for Madeline and Eliot to have physical contact…embraces only.

A room was prepared for the visit. Eliot got there first, accompanied by a guard. As much as Eliot wanted to pace the room as he nervously awaited Madeline's arrival, he knew his guard would not like it, so he sat at the table in the center of the room, clasping his hands together.

When Madeline entered, Eliot stood up. His body was trembling. Madeline hesitated at the door's threshold, unable to believe it was really him.

They drew close to each other. As they were about to embrace, Eliot turned to his guard. "They said we could hold each other, right?"

The guard crossed his arms. He offered a slight but commiserative, smile. "Just don't get too cozy." He looked to the side.

They held each other in a strong embrace. Madeline pressed her cheek into his chest. "It feels like a million years."

Eliot ran his hand over her back. "Feels like yesterday."

Madeline took a step back. "I'll never be far away from you. I'm going to move to Kansas, and I'll visit you every day that they'll let me."

Eliot stroked her arm. "Oh, Maddy, that'll make the time go so much faster."

Madeline touched his hair. "Have you thought about what you want to do when the year is over?"

Eliot laughed. "You mean…besides holding you?"

"Yes. Besides that!"

Serious now, Eliot sat down at the table. Madeline sat across from him. "I want to help vets with PTSD. Get the training for that. It's the best way I can think of to honor Will. What about you?"

Madeline leaned back in her chair. "It's a toss-up. I could become a military attorney like Marion and help other vets who've been wrongly accused. It would be a good way to honor *her*."

Eliot turned his head to one side. "So, what's the other choice?"

Madeline rubbed her hands together. "Help women who are victims of sex trafficking. I saw what it did to Mira. One cruelty creates another. It has to stop somewhere."

Eliot's guard stood back in amazement. For years, he had escorted soldiers back and forth from their jail cells and in and out of courtrooms. He had seen it all. Guilt and innocence, denial and betrayal had all passed his way. But now, as he overheard Madeline and Eliot's plans to come to the aid of others, he realized he had never witnessed nobility. Now, he had.

www.ingramcontent.com/pod-product-compliance
Lightning Source LLC
Chambersburg PA
CBHW020555120726
47903CB00001B/261